Praise for *Every Thug Needs a Lady*

"Rise and take your seat beside me on the throne. After reading this—it's official, you have now been crowned The Queen of Thug Love Fiction."

—The Queen of Hip Hop Fiction, *Essence* and *Black Issues*
#1 best-selling author Nikki Turner

"Wahida puts it down for the females, letting it be known that dudes don't stand alone in the streets; there are real women that stand with them."

—Eyone Williams, author of the "hard" novel *Fast Lane*

"*Every Thug Needs a Lady* was a perfect sequel. An exciting page turner. I can't wait to see what Snake has in store in Part Three! Wahida is developing. I felt her growth. *Every Thug* is phenomenal!"

—Chi Ali (Griffith)
Elmira Correctional Facility

"You nasty as Hell!"—Monique, Queen of Comedy

"Your concept is HOT. Everyone I passed it to enjoyed it."

—Shyne Po'

EVERY THUG NEEDS A LADY

WAHIDA CLARK

Dafina
Books

KENSINGTON PUBLISHING CORP.
http://www.kensingtonbooks.com

DAFINA BOOKS are published by

Kensington Publishing Corp.
850 Third Avenue
New York, NY 10022

ISBN 0-7582-1288-7

First Kensington Trade Paperback Printing: October 2006
10 9 8 7 6

Printed in the United States of America

Special Note to My Beloved Fans

You are the Greatest. Thank you for your dedication and support.

What you have in your hands is the raw, uncut, revised and improved edition of *Every Thug Needs a Lady*.

Yes, still raw and uncut with even more sex scenes. So spread the word that everyone will want to read this again. It's fire and smoother.

Lil Yolanda Carter, thank you for your editorial assistance and for burning the midnight oil with me. I really appreciate it. Peaches (Adriene H.), thank you so much for your help as well. You are on point. Sylvia R. Webster, your legal mind is awesome. Angela Ahladis, thanks for helping with the discussion questions.

Hang tight for the next one: *Thug Matrimony*.

Stay Up!

Wahida

wahidaclark@hotmail.com
wahidaclarkpresents.com

Acknowledgments

To my eyes, ears, and right hand: Kisha, you da man, homie! I am so blessed to have you on my team. You be holdin' it down. Thank you for your perseverance and uncountable sacrifices. You know I got nothin' but love for you even though I push you to the limit. But it's only because I like for you to use your full potential. Hijrah, thank you for allowing me to blow up your phone bill and for all the photocopies and packages you mailed me. Nadia Benders, thanks for the copies and packages you mailed me as well. Birdie Evans, thanks for being there.

To all of my fans and readers: I love y'all and truly appreciate the support and all of the feedback. To all of my peeps on lockdown, especially the Brothas and Sistas in New York, y'all and the rest of the East Coast been holdin' it down like troopers for this Sista. To my Brothas and Sistas on lock in the Dirty South, y'all next in line. To my West Coast peeps on lock, where y'all at? Y'all need to make some more noise fo' me. I got much love for y'all as well.

To get specific, Doggy Mac, That Philly Cat, you hooked a Sista up with *The Thugz We Love*. Y'all look out for this Brotha's poetry. He got mad talent. Steven "Triggaman" Walker, doing time in AR DOC: Thanks for going above and beyond the call of duty and assisting your Sista in whatever she asks of you.

To everybody else who has been promoting like mad, copying and passing out flyers, sending me names to build my mailing list, at bookstores or on the street saying, "Buy this book!"—It's so many of y'all: Belinda Marshall, Meeka Short, Woo Cooley, Randy Wilson, Kelle H., Trev Carson, Kris Stevenson, Rhonda Fitch, KK Wall, Bree, Shan, April, Fred & KK Hatcher, Harry Johnson, Jerry Thompson, Raquel T., Tiffany Edwards, Vernetta

Banks, Mo Thompson, Annie Ford, B. Maxie, Kaywan, Michael W., Najee Hijr, and Teesa.

The Women of FCDC—Kim, Alicia, Rissa, Tink, Mariah, Kiesha, Tasha and Monique. Thanks to Richards: I got love for you and you know who you be. Melvin Johnson, you know whatz up! Thanks!

To my real street team: Jamil, Omar, Hasan, Jabar, Husein, Hakim, Aziz, Samad, Razzaq, and Najm, I know y'all got me covered if no one else does.

Project Pat, Chi-Ali: The Ghost, Styles P, thanks for the blurbs. Nikki Turner, The Hustler's Wife, thanks for holding it down while on tour for a Sista on lock, who can't. 'Preciate it. To Shannon Holmes—"B-More Careful"—and Roy Glenn—"Is It a Crime"—thanks for keeping it real and keeping in touch.

To all the poets and authors on lock tryin'a make it happen: Doggy Mac aka Corey Maxey, Jamel Bakari, Dakim Forster, Dontez Mack, Deon Earnest, Melvin Johnson, Lil Wil Berry, Anthony "Bang Wayne" Malone, Alfred Lamar Scott, Edward Julian, Julius Vann, Sherri Cooper, Don Wood, Leevon Young, Louis Bailey, Parish "Pee" Sherman, Jamaica Charleton, Desi Sykes, Gary "Freeze" Adams. Do you! You got what it takes; the world is ours. Let's do the damn thang!! But where my Sistas at?

Thanks to all the Black bookstores and street vendors especially my New Yorkers. Thanks! I get mad reports about y'all holdin' it down for a Sista. Holla at me. Let me hear from y'all!

Doug Banks and DeDe Maguire, Tom Joyner, Wendy Williams, Steve Harvey, Don Diva, Feds, Felon, XXL, Source, and Vibe, where is my interview? I can't get no love.☺

To y'all moviemakers: Spike Lee, Ice Cube, and Damon Dash, holla at your girl! Whatz up? Speaking of Damon Dash and making a movie, write me and let me know who you think should play Angel, Kyra, Jaz, Roz, Snake, Marvin, Faheem, Trae, Nikayah, and Kaylin. Real quick let me tell you who I got in mind: Snake—LL Cool J or Laurence Fishburne; Marvin—Allen Payne,

Ice Cube, Shemar Moore, LL Cool J; Faheem—Morris Chestnut, DMX, Chris Webber; Trae—DMX, Method Man, Treach; Ty— Usher, Sticky Fingaz; Kaylin—Tyson Beckford, Allen Payne, Cameron; Angel—Sanaa Lathan, LisaRaye; Kyra—Nia Long, Sanaa Lathan; Jaz—Terrel Hicks, Jada Pinkett-Smith, Lil' Kim; Roz—Lark Vorhees, Stacy Dash; Nikayah—Jaheim. Holla back!

Carl Weber: One love! Thanks for staying on board until we got this done.

Last but not least, thanks for all of my fan mail, especially during my stint in the hole from New Year's Eve '02 until August '03. However, it's all to the "G" because I went in a caterpillar and emerged a butterfly! Watch out for my third street novel *Payback Is a Mutha.*

You know tha drill! Holla at ya girl!

Wahida Clark
c/o Upshaw
P.O. Box 8520
Newark, NJ 07108
wahidaclark@hotmail.com

Chapter 1

Kyra showed the last of her baby shower guests to the door and thanked them again for the gifts. She closed the door and yelled, "Where my dawgs at?" She was hollering for Jaz, Angel and Roz. The three of them had already flopped down on Kyra's Italian leather furniture.

"Where on earth are you going to put all of this stuff?" Roz asked Kyra. "The baby's bedroom already seems too crowded."

"Who are you telling? I don't think I have to buy anything," Kyra said, looking around at all of the gifts.

"That's what baby showers are for, to get *everything!*" Angel said. "And when are you allowing us to throw yours?" She pointed at Jaz.

Jaz yawned. "I'm not sure yet. Y'all the ones giving it. Just let me know when y'all ready. Even though I'd rather wait until after I have it."

"It was supposed to be a surprise," Roz said sarcastically. "And what do you mean 'after you have it'?"

"I don't like surprises. And I haven't been in a festive mood." She turned toward the kitchen where Kyra was and yelled, "Can I have another piece of cake?"

When Kyra came out of the kitchen she was carrying a tray with a bottle of Dom, a bottle of sparkling grape juice, slices of cake, champagne glasses, and a bag of weed. "Roz, I know you got some paper," she said as she set the tray down.

"I sure do," Roz answered, rolling over and grabbing her Chanel bag from under the coffee table.

Kyra plopped down on the couch and poured two glasses of champagne and two glasses of the non-alcoholic bubbly for the pregnant sisters. "I'd like to say a few things to y'all," she announced. "For starters, I can't thank y'all enough for the beautiful baby shower. Y'all really went all out; the gifts are all of that. I don't know where everything is gonna go, but we'll figure something out. Second, I love y'all. Y'all are the sisters I never had. And for real, if it wasn't for everyone's support—not to mention your competitiveness—I wouldn't have finished school. I wouldn't be where I am right now." She stopped and smiled at them. "Of course, y'all didn't have anything to do with this big belly."

"I would hope not!" interrupted Roz. They all laughed.

"Anywho," continued Kyra, "even though I left y'all for a couple of years and got off track, you all still let me back in, accepted me with open arms, encouraged me, and pushed me to reach my goals. We did it, y'all! We stayed on track in spite of all the obstacles. Angel, all you have to do is pass the state bar and we'll have our own corporate lawyer to handle our business. Jaz, all you have to do is walk across the stage and get that first piece of paper before going on to medical school. Roz, you tackled two majors and are now prepared to take two state exams, one for physical therapy and the other for respiratory therapy. I gotta walk across that stage and get my piece of paper on my way to graduate school to study and become a doctor of psychology. Soon we'll be four sisters with bachelor's degrees or better, straight from the hood. None of us are drug addicts or carry ourselves as hos. We're happy for the most part. Two of us are engaged to good, strong brothas, and, hopefully, the other two won't be too far behind." They all agreed with Kyra. They were proud of their success and accomplishments.

"Roz, did you roll the weed?" Angel blurted. Roz dumped the joints on the table.

"Oh yeah," Jaz said. "I'd like to make an official toast." They all took a glass and raised it in the air for Jaz's toast. "A toast to life, love, peace, and happiness. Congrats to Angel, our own corporate and entertainment attorney. Congrats to Roz, who doubled up in physical therapy and respiratory therapy! Good luck in opening your own practice and healing all of those fine, rich-ass ball players. Congrats to me. I am now a fuckin' scientist with offers from five graduate schools. And congrats to Kyra, a future head doctor, a.k.a. psychologist. And she got accepted at six graduate schools. My sisters, I think we all did pretty damn good. Even though we are all fine and beautiful we didn't get a man to depend on for food, clothing, and shelter. We handled our shit." They put the glasses to their lips and drank continuing to congratulate themselves.

"We put us first," Kyra continued. "We can hold it down on our own if we have to. But, for real, having a good man—another half—sure makes things a lot smoother. This toast goes to us. I love y'all, my sisters forever!" They touched glasses again and finished their drinks. "Um, can you fire it up, my sister?" Angel pleaded, looking at Roz, who passed everybody a joint except for Jaz.

"Where's mine?" Jaz whined.

"I ain't messin' with you and that crazy-ass Faheem. If he found out that I gave you and his unborn child some weed I'd never hear the last of it."

"Give me the bag then. I'll roll my own."

"Nope!" Roz said, lighting her joint.

"Kyra got one and she's pregnant," Jaz whined.

"Marvin ain't gonna trip as bad as Faheem would," Roz explained.

"C'mon Roz," Jaz begged.

"Here. We'll split this one." Kyra passed Jaz her joint. "If you get busted, you on ya own!" They all started laughing.

"Thank you Kyra." She looked at Roz and stuck her tongue out at her. She took a drag. "I want to get my party on, too."

"Turn on some music," Angel ordered. Kyra picked up the remote and pointed at the stereo.

"Oooh! Turn that up! That's the shit!" Roz was bobbing her head. *"How did you get here? Nobody 'sposed to be here. I tried that love thing for the last time. My heart says no, no. Nobody 'sposed to be here, but you came along and changed my mind."* Roz was singing along with Debra Cox.

"What's up Roz? Who is he?" Angel probed. All eyes were now on Roz.

"What?"

"You heard what I said."

"I'm too embarrassed to tell y'all," Roz answered.

"Who is he?" Angel probed again.

"His name is Trae."

"Trae! Oooh!" Jaz emphasized his name.

"You are scandalous," Kyra added.

"Who is Trae?" Angel was puzzled.

"This big-ass baller from New York," Jaz told her.

"You are scandalous!" Kyra repeated. "First of all, you know how fine Tyson Beckford is, right? Well Trae is finer than him. He has big, pretty eyes, thick eyelashes, thick, dark, eyebrows and thick, pretty lips. Second of all—this is the kicker—he's Nikayah's partna. His boy. I repeat, his boy. That is downright scandalous Roz. What is up with you? Tell me you're joking!"

"So that means he's paid then, right?" Angel was looking back and forth at Kyra and Jaz for an answer.

"Can I talk?" Roz said.

"He got a coupl'a whips," Kyra said, ignoring Roz. "He mostly be in that fly-ass black Lincoln Navigator with the chrome. He always has his hair in braids. Dayum! I'm getting excited just talkin' about him. If I didn't have Marvin I would be trying to hit that my damn self!" They all laughed.

"Kyra! Can you stop lusting and shut up? Can I talk, please?" Roz asked, relighting her joint.

"The floor is yours," Kyra said. "I gots to hear this. Inquiring minds do want to know. Go ahead."

"Shut up Kyra!" Jaz said. "Let the girl talk."

"Jaz I don't know why you frontin'. You know I'm not lying," said Kyra, refusing to give up.

"She ain't lyin', y'all. The bitch ain't never lied!" Everybody burst out laughing. "If I wasn't crazy about Faheem, I'd be wanting to hit that myself. And yes, like Jaheim said, *'it would be because of the ice I see.'*" They all laughed again. "Naw, I'm playing. And for the record I said *if* I wasn't in love with Faheem."

"Can I talk now?" Roz made eye contact with everybody, and no one said a word. "Thank you! First of all, he's not just a baller."

"Bullshit!" Jaz interrupted. "Faheem only associates with ballers. I ain't bragging or nothing, but y'all know Faheem ain't nothing nice. He thinks he's the president of the ballers club. He knows he's the shit, and that's how he carries himself. Plus, I saw that nigga at Faheem's apartment around the time my sister fucked up her life." Jaz noticed Roz staring at her. "I'm sorry. Go ahead, Roz. I didn't mean to interrupt."

"Yes you did!" everybody yelled in unison.

"Anyway," Roz continued, "the brotha got a bachelor's degree from Long Island University. So he's not just a straight thug. And yes, the nigga is straight-up fine. I do have to give him that. His braids? I've been keeping his hair up for him. As a matter of fact, I've been doing that for the last couple of months. Did he hit it yet? Nope. Why? I know he wants to, but it's a couple of things making me hesitant. One, he's Nikayah's boy. Two, no more thugs for me. I lose too many peeps to that lifestyle. They either go six feet under or get locked down. I'm running from that shit. You want to know if I'm feeling him? Unfortunately, hell fuckin' yes! When he's around, the hair on my skin stands straight up. And he calls me by my middle name, Tash. He doesn't say Tasha. He calls me Tash."

"Dayum. It's like that?" Jaz asked.

"Yeah, baby, it's like that. He got my head spinning and it's scaring me. He got a small diamond on the tip of his tongue and I want to feel it, if you know what I mean!" She didn't mention kissing him at the club a few weeks ago.

"How much time did Nikayah get?" Angel asked.

"Twelve years. His appeal is about to get heard. At least that's what he told me."

"Dayum," everybody chimed in. They all liked Nikayah.

"So what's up with y'all? How you gonna just dog our boy out like that?" Angel asked.

"Puhleeze! Let me tell y'all about little, innocent-ass Nikayah. Y'all know we've been kickin' it for almost five years now. And for the last two of them I've been going down to that fucking prison faithfully, every weekend unless I have a semester where I have to take a Saturday class. Well, your boy apparently had my schedule screwed up. I pop up for a visit on a Saturday because I didn't have a class. I was all happy and shit at the opportunity to see him two days in a row. I go bouncing my happy ass up in there, and he's all hugged up and kissing on this other female."

"What?" yelled Kyra.

"That ain't all," added Roz, obviously choking up. "He was rubbin' her stomach. The bitch is pregnant!"

"You lyin'!" said Angel, hands covering her mouth.

"That's fucked up, dawg. I'm sorry to hear that shit," said Jaz. "So what happened?"

"First of all, it was so fucking embarrassing, mainly because everybody—the guards, the regular visitors, the inmates—know me up in there. I was wondering why it got so quiet and folks was whispering while I was walking by. I was trying to be cool and front like it wasn't no big deal. I grabbed a chair and sat right in front of them. I turned on my physical therapist voice and acted like I was interviewing a client. I got right up on her and said, 'Hello, I'm Rosalyn, and you are?' I think she said 'Simone' or something like that. Then I asked, 'Did Nikayah tell you that he has a woman, me, Roz, who has been his woman for the last five years and that I've been coming to see him in this rat hole ever since he's been here? That would be two years. I'm driving a 2000 Beamer that this nigga bought, and he pays my mortgage every month. I guess that's why he feels justified in thinking that he can act like a playa. You been kissing him, right?' She looks at me all crazy. 'Well, y'all was kissing when I walked in the door. You see that corner over there?' I pointed to where we usually get busy. 'Last Sunday he ate my pussy right over there.' The yellow bitch was turning red by now.

"Then I faced Nikayah and asked, 'Am I the other fuckin' woman, or is she? How long has she been coming down here, Nikayah?' He wouldn't answer so I pushed him. He said, 'Roz, what difference do it make? Why you trippin'? You my woman. I take care of you and she know that.' I said, 'Fuck that shit, Nikayah. Answer the fuckin' two-million-dollar question. How long you been playin' me?' So he says, 'Ain't nobody playin' no-body, Roz. She been comin' down here for a minute.'

"I screamed, 'For a minute? The bitch looks six months pregnant!' Then he says, 'Let me talk to you in private,' and grabs my arm. I fuckin' punched him in the head screaming, 'Fuck you, Nikayah. I'm outta here.' Then I punched him in the face. Then I told her, 'You can have his sorry ass and all the visits.' I looked at him one more time and told him, 'I'm glad I didn't keep your babies!' as I headed for the door. That last comment slipped out. That nigga came running behind me, and I got scared and started walking faster until the guard told him to go sit down. He kept screaming, 'You got an abortion.' And that's the last time I seen or talked to him."

"Dayum," Jaz said. "When did all of this happen?"

"It's been three months."

"Why didn't you tell anyone?"

"Too fuckin' hurt to talk about it. Plus I'd rather tell all of y'all at once instead of repeating it over and over. I'm trying to put him behind me."

"What's the matter with three-way?" Kyra asked. "We use it all the time."

"Kyra. Y'all just don't know. I didn't feel like talking about it until now—since all of us are here. I was hurt. Well, I'm still hurt but not as much. He fucked me up. I still can't get over the fact that he played me like that. I could see if I was fucking around on him, but he knew I wasn't. He got too many eyes and ears out here. Plus, he would have sensed something when he saw me. Niggas ain't stupid. So now it's fuck him! It's over. I don't accept his collect calls. I don't answer his mail. And if I didn't have so many peeps on lockdown I would have put a block on my phone. But most of them gonna have to go through so much drama if I changed the number. So I just decided to leave it."

"So tell us again how did Trae get in the picture?" Kyra wanted to know.

"Nikayah had Trae for a while bringing me money and checking on me to make sure I was okay."

"That was dumb," Jaz said.

"Obviously. But Trae is his boy—or supposed to be. So one day he stopped by to check on me and his hair was in a big-ass 'fro. He asked me if I could braid. I told him, 'yeah.' Then I hooked him up. Ever since then he's been makin' sure that I keep it up for him, using that as an excuse to come over. Of course we talk while I'm braiding. That's how I found out about his bachelor's in marketing and public relations. I like him . . . but why does he have to be Nikayah's boy? And why does he have to be so deep in the drug game? I chose to get away from that lifestyle. I got caught up before. I lost my pops to it, my mom, friends, relatives, and my man of five fucking years. Now this nigga is trying to invade my space . . . and it's fucked up because I like him . . . a lot."

"What do you mean, you got caught up before?" Angel quizzed.

"That's a whole 'nother story."

"We got time," Kyra added.

"I'll tell y'all, but first let me throw this out there."

"Oh, gosh. Now she's gettin' ready to get all philosophical and shit," Jaz joked.

"No, check this out," Roz said, puffing on her joint. "What's up with this picture? We are all intelligent sisters, right?"

"Right," they all agreed.

"We all are fine, right?"

"Right," they all said again.

"We all got college degrees, right?"

"Right."

"So why do we attract the niggas that's out there pimpin', slangin', bangin' and ballin'? You know what I mean? Why not the niggas who are professionals: doctors; lawyers; investment bankers, and niggas like that? Y'all feel me?"

Everyone was silent. They were replaying in their minds what Roz had just said. Angel puffed on her joint and looked around at everybody, "I think it's because we're young, we're fine, and the ballers . . . well, that's what they chase. But I am with Roz, I am through with that lifestyle."

"You got a point," Kyra said. "But we're attracted to them just as much as they're attracted to us. Y'all know them hustlin', thuggish niggas turn us on. So don't front."

"Yeah, that's true. But at the same time if we hung out around the professional brothers, we would be attracted to them. If they hung out around us they would be attracted to us. It depends on what and who you want. It seems like most women look for the thug in every brother. Baller, hustla, slanger or professional, thug me out, baby!" Jaz drooled. "Take charge, baby!"

"Right! Right! That's what I like about Trae. He likes to run shit. Take over. I don't know about the next ho, but that shit turns me on," laughed Roz. "I know I don't want no weak-ass, pushover nigga."

"Turns you on? Look at me. I was sprung over a pimp. I was crazy about him. He was always runnin' shit. And now Bilal has been trying to push up on me, but I've been duckin' him out big time. I'm scared of that nigga. I won't even tell him where I live. Plus I'm a lawyer now, I can't be fucking with them criminal niggas anymore," Angel said.

"Yeah, he came over here a couple of times to see Marvin. He's a fine black brotha. I heard he's a ho with your baby momma drama, so you better keep ducking him out if you don't wanna get caught up. At least we attract all the fine niggas, even if they're thugs," Kyra said, bursting with laughter.

"Take the weed from her," Roz snarled. "Ain't shit funny. This is serious."

"It's funny to me!" she said and kept on laughing. Then they all started laughing. Roz crawled over to Kyra and took the joint then went over to Jaz and took hers.

"Y'all not supposed to be smoking anyway," Roz snapped.

"Come on, *Tash*," Jaz joked, "this is the first time I got high since I've been pregnant."

"Don't call me Tash. Only one person is allowed to call me that."

"Well, excuse me, *Tash*, but since you're so serious, tell us about you getting caught up out there. How come you never told us that story?"

"The same reason you didn't tell us about you cooking meth for the last year or so. You feel me?"

"I feel you," Jaz whispered.

"What's up with your case anyway? I still can't believe you did that shit," said Angel, getting into lawyer mode.

"I was sentenced to seventeen years," Jaz answered. "Faheem paid a sentencing lawyer to make sure that I don't start my sentence until after I have the baby. Then I have to self-surrender." She leaned back into the recliner. "Then he paid a lawyer to handle my appeal to make sure that I can remain out on bond pending the outcome of the appeal. Just getting the damn thing heard can take anywhere from six months to two years." She took a gulp of her grape juice.

"Seventeen years? You didn't want to sign the fuckin' plea bargain?" Roz wanted to know.

"Girl, fuckin' with Faheem, his motto is 'death before dishonor.' He said to trust him and do it his way or take the highway. So here I be."

"I have to give it to you. You sure are handling it well," Roz told her. "Putting your life in a nigga's hands."

"Shit! I wasn't at first. I was stressing like crazy until Faheem threatened my ass. He told me that if something happens to his baby because of me stressing it wasn't going to be nice. So I said 'Fuck it. I'ma chill the fuck out. You want to run thangs? Then go right ahead my brotha.' That's why I've been chillin'. If things don't turn out right, I'ma fuck him up and go to prison for some real shit!"

"Girl, you silly!" Roz told her.

"Silly? I am dead serious."

"Now see," Roz said, sitting up, "you and Kyra, y'all's shit is rare. Like some storybook shit. Dude gets in the game. Dude gets legal. Dude gets out of game. Dude gets girl. Dude marries girl. They have kids and live happily ever fuckin' after. Wait! Let me back up. Dude is a good man. Dude loves girl. Dude don't fuck around on girl, causing a whole lot of drama. That shit is one-in-a-million odds, like hitting the fuckin' lottery!"

"Wait!" Angel said, holding up both hands. "Don't leave out, dude can fuck! Dude can keep a hard-on until girl comes. And comes. And comes again." They all started laughing. "I ain't mad at y'all. Because I know I'ma get mines one of these days."

"Me neither. I ain't mad at y'all. I got a feeling that Trae is all of that," Roz said.

"Why is that Tash?" Jaz asked jokingly.

"None of your business! But one thing for sho': If he ain't all of that, I'ma clown his ass big time. And stop calling me Tash!"

"Oh, so you do plan on allowing him to hit it?" Kyra asked. "Bitch you need to slow your roll!"

"Chill out. I'm still investigating. Basically I'm just waiting until I'm ready. Plus I want to see how bad he wants me, how patient he'll be. Shit I don't know what the fuck I'm planning."

"Oh, so you got it like that?" Angel asked. "You need to make up your mind. You just said you were done with that lifestyle, but at the same time you're plotting and scheming. What do you think you can have your cake and eat it too?"

"Yes, I do. So when are y'all getting married?" Roz asked, putting her foot on Kyra's knee, trying to change the subject, because she really had mixed emotions on the situation.

Kyra pushed her foot down. "I'm not sure when I want to do it. Marvin told me to let him know when I'm ready. What about you?" Kyra looked at Jaz.

"We're waiting until Faheem's dad comes home next May. He'll have done nine years."

"Dayum," said Roz. "Everybody is trying to get their hustle on and they're just locking us away and throwing away the keys. And that's another thing. See . . ."

They cut Roz off. "Oh, gosh! Here she goes again," everybody sang at once.

"Naw, for real, y'all, listen. See, everybody is trying to survive. Them. Us. We go after the ballers because they're obviously trying to surviving. Nobody wants to be all poor and shit, suffering. Folks are chasing that American dream that's on TV. Now, I'ma be quiet."

"Yeah, right! You said that two hours ago," Kyra said. "What about our graduation party? Y'all wanna have it here?"

"Of course, I thought that was already decided." Jaz responded.

"It was," Angel said. "Just don't invite the whole city. And Kyra don't have that baby until afterwards."

"I'll do my best," Kyra answered sarcastically.

"Okay Tasha. We're giving you the floor again. Tell us this big secret that you keep trying to keep to yourself." Jaz leaned back and waited.

Everybody turned towards Roz. She fell back onto the floor and stretched her long legs onto the arm of the chair. "This shit better not leave this room," she warned. She put both her hands under her head. She knew her girls wouldn't tell this to anyone.

"Remember when I moved here from Chicago with my grandma because I told y'all my mom was sick?" She went on, not waiting on a response. "Well, Human Services came and took me, my brother and my sister from my parents. They were strung out on crack. Me, I was ten years old when I had started selling. By the time I turned twelve I was hangin' out with my fast-ass cousin, Miranda, who was fifteen. We started smoking it and got strung out. I lost interest in selling and focused on smoking. Miranda was sucking dicks to get high, and so I started sucking them too. She was my hero. I was trying to be like her.

"Then I started laying on my back. I was a twelve-year-old crack ho. Shit, when I was selling, my pops made sure me and my brother had a whole block to ourselves at age eleven, I knew how to buy, cook, cut, weigh, and bag. I could run my own shit. That's why when a lot of niggas step to me I don't give them the time of day. That shit don't impress me. I can get my own. I can talk to a nigga for three minutes and know if he's really a hustler or not. My moms and pops were hustlers. But then they started smoking. I don't know how that shit happened. It was downhill from there. You can't sell and smoke the shit too. And once I started smoking it was downhill for me. My peeps didn't even try to stop me. I was twelve but looked fifteen or sixteen. Y'all see how tall I am and how big my breasts are. I was twelve and fuckin' grown-ass men for a rock. To this day, I never found out who called Human Services on us, but I think it was my Uncle Tommy, my mom's brother. But whoever it was, they didn't call until after my nine-year-old brother got murdered."

"Murdered?" they all screamed.

"Yes, murdered. His name was Antoine. He was holding some dope somewhere in the house for this dealer named Turner. My mom found the dope and smoked it all up. Antoine thought he lost it, and so that's what he told Turner. Turner blew his brains out with a 9, and he was only nine."

"Goddamn!" yelled Kyra.

"That sounds like some shit you read in ghetto fiction," shrieked Jaz.

Angel was silent, wiping tears off her face, Roz continued. "So about two days later they came and locked up my pops and my mom. They took me, Kevin and Trina and put us in a foster home. I stayed with them for about a month. Then they came and took me to a group home for teenage substance abusers and the abused. I was getting counseling seven days a week. About three months later, my grandma came and got us, and that's how we ended up here in Jersey."

"Dayum! Did that dude Turner go to jail?" Angel wanted to know.

"Nah, Kev smoked him. Kev was selling, too. Trina was the only one who didn't get caught up at that time. But now I'm worried about both of them. Kevin, if he don't slow down, will be goin' to jail or six feet under. He loves hustlin'. That's the difference between the young hustlers and the ones who been out there for a few. The older ones are trying to get the fuck out. The young ones, they like to floss and fuck everything with two legs, and most of them have no agenda or a stash. I don't know what's going to happen to him. All Trina's doing is fuckin' one hustler after another, just like them girls in *Coldest Winter Ever.* Did y'all read that yet?" Everybody answered no. "Y'all are so sorry," Roz told them in disgust.

"Fuck you Roz. You know the semester just ended—finals and shit," Kyra snapped.

"Hell, yeah. I'm studying for the bar," Angel said.

"Why are you always recommending shit for us to read anyway? What you getting? A percentage from the books we buy?" Jaz asked. They all laughed.

"Go to hell," Roz said. "Y'all should be glad I read shit first and let y'all know if it's worth your time or not. I should be charging for my services. When I used to go see Nikayah I used to have to sit for hours before they let me inside the visiting room. So I used that time to leisurely read.

"But, as I was saying, add to your list *Uncle Yah Yah* by Al Dickens and *Until Tomorrow* by Iyanla Vanzant. But my sister Trina reminds me of the character Winter and the girls in her crew. She thinks her looks and the fact that she can suck a dick is going to allow her to live in luxury for the rest of her life. She has no skills and no foundation. I keep telling her that it don't work like that. She's stupid enough to start carrying dope for them. Then when something goes down she's gonna be left holding the bag. Next thing you know, she's locked down and calling me collect, asking me to send her some commissary money because them same niggas won't even accept her collect calls. So there, y'all." She stood up to stretch before lying down again. "I've just shared all of my baggage with y'all. I feel like today was a therapy session." Roz stretched her arms and put them back under her head.

"I can't believe you never told us that shit," Angel was dumbfounded.

"I can't believe she went through all of that and came out like she did," Kyra added.

"I'm just fuckin' speechless," Jaz said.

"If it wasn't for prayers to the Creator and for my grandma, I'd be messed up," Roz said. "A'ight, let's change the subject. This shit better not leave this room."

"A'ight. It's my turn. I need to tell y'all something," Angel said, sitting on the floor.

"I hope you are going to tell us that you are ready to move on with your life," Kyra interrupted. "You've been through a lot. And, please, no more pimps. Have you been tested for AIDS?" she asked with a worried look.

"Yes, twice in the last year. And, like I told you, Keenan didn't fuck them hos," Angel said, rolling her eyes. "Now, as I was saying, at the office where I'm doing my internship, one of the partners, a fine older brother, Najee Roberts, has been checking me out. He asked me out to lunch a couple of times, but I've been declining. I'm like Tash. If he really wants me, he'll be patient." Roz high-fived her. "But I am investigating as well. I'm inviting Najee to lunch with me and my cousin, Morrie."

"The undercover bisexual." Kyra confirmed. He was her cousin too.

"Yep," said Angel. "Our DL cousin."

"Eww! Morrie's gay?" shouted Roz.

"Yep! But you would never know it. Thugged-out, big-buffed brotha. He can spot another brother who's down," said Angel.

"You're a mess," Jaz teased. "I thought you had some real grime to tell us."

"Just being cautious. I am not allowing a dirty dick all up in my pussy!" They all burst into laughter.

"Seriously though, that's fucked up that you don't know what's up with Snake. What did you see in him other than his good looks?" Kyra asked, though she still hated him.

"Girl, you just can't let it go, can you? I loved that nigga almost more than life itself. I didn't give a fuck what nobody said. One thing I can say about him is he never lied to me. He was always straight-up about everything. I was either with it or not. That nigga never lied. I loved him just for that. But what happened to him I don't know. No body ever turned up. No one seems to know shit. So, you know what, I've slowly moved on with my life.

"Like I was saying, after I pass the bar, they say I have a job. If I take it—which I most likely will—I'm moving to New York," Angel grinned. "This little birdie will be leaving the nest. Looks like we all are ready to leave the nest."

"I believe you're right. Marvin is talking about moving to Cali," Kyra said, rubbing her belly. "You know that's where his family is."

"I'm not sure what I'm going to do yet. I know I won't be living in New Jersey. I'm still doing research. I'm going where there are plenty of athletes and injured folks. I need clients. My cousin

Stephon who lives in Cali said to let him know if I want to come out there. So, wherever the clients are, that's where I'm going," Roz said. Everybody turned to look at Jaz, who was scrolling through a message on her pager.

"Faheem is on his way to pick me up," Jaz announced.

"Where is your car?" Kyra asked.

"Getting detailed."

"Call him and tell him you got a ride home. I'll take you," Kyra assured her.

"He hasn't seen me in two days. He wants to come," Jaz said with a smile.

"I ain't mad at him," Angel said. "Tell us your plans."

"Well, if I win my appeal, we're going to the ATL, Texas or Cali. I got school offers from each place, so I told Faheem we'll do whatever he wants to do. So yes, it does look like everybody will be moving on. I can't believe that shit. Can y'all?"

"Not really. Seems like yesterday y'all were in the 8th grade and I was in the 9th," Angel reminisced.

"I know that's right," Kyra beamed.

"Let's not think about us going our separate ways just yet. We still got a graduation party and Jaz's baby shower," Roz said. "And we still got to graduate." Everybody laughed. "And let's clean up this weed before Faheem gets here."

"Oh God," Jaz said, popping the recliner straight up, "I gotta go brush my teeth and gargle and wash up a little." She got up and went toward the bathroom. "Gotta hide the evidence."

"Give me a hug, y'all. I'm getting ready to bounce," Roz said, grabbing Angel. "Love you." Then she grabbed Kyra and said, "Love you. Let me go find Jaz. Peace out!"

After saying goodbye to Jaz, she left. Angel then wrapped up some cake for her mom and sister and she too left.

Just as Jaz plopped back down in the Laz-E-Boy, Faheem was knocking at the door. Kyra let him in. He kissed her on the cheek and headed for the living room.

"What up, ma?" He grabbed a chair and placed it right next to the recliner. He lifted Jaz's blouse and stared at her stomach—a new habit he acquired and began rubbing it. Just then the baby started moving. He leaned over and kissed wherever he saw movement.

"How's my baby?" Jaz asked him, brushing hair off his neck. She could see that he just came from the barbershop. He pulled her shirt over her stomach and gave her a kiss, pulling on her bottom lip.

"I'm tired as hell. You feel like driving home?" he asked, kissing her again and rubbing her belly.

"I don't mind driving. You could have went straight home. I had a ride," she said, caressing his back up and down.

"Times when I'm feeling like this," he paused and looked at her, "when I go home and get in the bed, I want my wife laying next to me."

Kyra came back into the living room and kissed Faheem on the forehead. "Thanks for the crib that turns into a bed. It's nice, Faheem."

"It's all about you, Ky. Where are you gonna put all this stuff?" he asked, looking around in amazement.

"I have no clue."

"You better think of something. You ready, baby?" he asked, turning to Jaz.

"Yup we're ready." He lifted her up out of the Laz-E-Boy. Jaz went over and hugged Kyra goodbye.

"Tell your man I'll holla at him in a day or two," Faheem said, taking Jaz's hand and heading out the door.

Chapter 2

Roz reached over and turned off the ringer on the phone before she picked it up. She didn't plan on taking any more calls until she got up.

"Who is this?" she asked, half asleep.

"This is Trae."

"Trae. What time is it?"

"It's almost 8:30."

"What is so important that you have to call me so early?"

"I need you to braid my hair. I'm on my way over."

"Trae, I'm still in the bed. I'm tired. It's too early. Call me later," she yawned.

"C'mon Tash. I'm already on my way over."

"Why do you insist on calling me Tash?"

"Your middle name is Tasha, right?"

"Yeah, but I prefer Roz. How do you know my middle name?"

"Well, I prefer Tash. It's sexy; you are sexy. Plus it starts with the letter T. Roz don't fit you. Anyway I got tickets to go see Musiq and Jill Scott tomorrow. After you braid my hair can we go to New York to shop? I want you to kick it with me today and tomorrow. I'm on my way over. Tash! You heard what I said, right?"

"Trae, why can't you call me a little later?"

"C'mon Tash! All you gotta do is braid my hair and the rest is on me. You might as well get up 'cause I'll be knockin' on your door in about fifteen minutes." He hung up.

"Aaargh!" she gritted her teeth. She hung up the phone and sat up in the bed. "This nigga is crazy and arrogant," she mumbled. She stumbled out of bed and went to turn the shower on.

After she jumped out of the shower and brushed her teeth she pulled her hair into a ponytail and threw on a pair of sweatpants and a T-shirt. She turned the ringer on the phone back on because she remembered she was expecting a call regarding the hottest cities for athletes. After she made up her bed she heard knocking at her door. She opened the door, stepping aside so that Trae could get past her. But instead he stood right in front of her.

"How did you get up here?" she asked.

"The front door was open. The lady was sweeping the steps." He looked at her face, saw the attitude, and gave her a lazy grin. She looked for the diamond near the tip of his tongue and thought about how it would feel, then immediately disregarded the thought. "I know you ain't mad. Look, I brought you some coffee and donuts."

"I'm not a cop, Trae. Plus, I don't even drink coffee." She stubbornly remained at the door.

"What is it that you would have preferred me to bring?" He kissed her on the cheek and noticed that her nipples were hard. "You might as well close the door because I'm not leaving."

Trae had been patiently waiting for her to cool off from her relationship with Nikayah. Nikayah was his boy and that nigga, but he wanted Tasha real bad and could see that she was someone worth waiting for. He liked the fact that she held it down for a nigga even when he got locked down. He knew Nikayah was playing her, and so it would be just a matter of time before she found out. And she did.

For real, Nikayah had fucked up by sending Trae over to check on her. He had been wanting to get with her since the first time he saw her. He couldn't help it. He had been looking for a square to settle down with and Tasha was perfect. She was fine, smart, sexy and loyal, and she understood what it was like for a nigga to be out there hustlin'. He had given her three months to get over Nikayah and was now determined to stake his claim. She was either feeling him or she wasn't. That night when she was out at the club with Shanna he could tell that it was on even though she was hesitant. He was planning on finding out today what was up.

She slammed the door and looked at his big-ass Afro. "Trae, I just did your hair."

"I know. But we going out tomorrow night so I need it done over," he said, looking her up and down. "Damn, girl! You look good even in sweats and a T-shirt. How tall are you?"

"Why? What does that have to do with anything? Come sit over here so that I can hurry up and get rid of you," she hissed, grabbing a chair and motioning for him to sit down. *This nigga is too fine*, she said to herself. He had on a black Sean Jean jean vest with no shirt and some baggy jeans to match, with black Timbs. Straight-up thuggish. His muscles were flexing, and his chocolate, dark brown skin was nice and smooth. *Those eyes. Those lips.*

"How tall are you?" he asked again.

"How tall are you?"

"I'm six feet."

"Well I'm five-nine," she answered, fingering his hair. "Did you wash it?"

"I got it washed last night."

"Why didn't you get whoever washed it to braid it?"

"Because I wanted you to braid it. Damn, girl, you cranky as hell. I guess you aren't really a morning person. What? You gotta problem with braiding it for me?"

"Yes, I do. You come over unannounced 8:39 in the morning, and get me out of my nice warm bed."

"It's 8:50 and I told you I'll make it worth your while. But before we get started, pop in your Love Jones CD for me."

"Who told you I had Love Jones?"

"I saw it."

"Why are you looking all in my stuff?"

"It's only CDs."

She got up, grabbed the African Pride hair grease, a pick and a comb. Then she flipped through the CDs until she found Love Jones and popped it in. "How do you want it?"

"Hook a nigga up. I gotta show Allen Iverson how this is done. I'm wearing a suit tomorrow."

"Why are you here so early, Trae?"

He started laughing. "Damn Tash, you really trippin' about this 8:30 action. I just wanted to catch you before you went to see your man." He figured he'd just throw that out.

"So what . . . your intentions were to stop me from going?"

"Yeah."

"That's cold, Trae. He's supposed to be your boy."

"He's a business partner. You haven't been going to see him anyway. What's up with that?"

"That's the past. I don't even want to talk about it."

"Oh, it's like that, huh?"

"Yup. It's like that." That made Trae's heart smile. "Now will you please hold your head still?" His cell phone rang. "Don't you dare answer it until I'm finished."

He turned the cell phone off, but left his pager on. "You still got feelings for Nikayah?"

"What?"

"You heard me. Answer my question."

"Why is it so important to you that I answer that question?"

"Why are you giving me such a hard time? You know I'm feeling you Tash, and I'm trying hard not to step on you and Nikayah's shit. Now if it was somebody other than Nikayah, I'd just say 'fuck him.' I would have stepped all over him whether you still had feelings or not. That's why I'm asking."

"What if Nikayah still has feelings for me?"

"Fuck him. I'm tryin'a find out what's up with you even though

I can see that you fuckin' with me, playin' mind games and tryin' to be all hard."

She pretended as if she didn't hear that last comment because he sure was right. She wasn't giving in too easy.

"What if the situation was reversed? You were locked down and I was your woman, and he was out here?"

"If I was locked down you still would be my woman. I wouldn't do no shit that would make you cut me off. You been with that nigga for how long?"

"You are nosy, aren't you? You know the answer to that question."

"What's it been? Three, four years?"

"Almost five."

"Damn! You hold it down for a nigga, don't you?"

"What are we playing fifty questions? Besides I said I didn't want to talk about him."

He ignored her. "So what's up? Am I stepping on my man's toes or what?"

"What do you think?"

"You don't want to know what I think."

"I know what you think," she said.

"Good. So you know what's up and that I think we'll discuss this later. But right now I'm taking you shopping in New York, and tomorrow night I'm taking you out."

"I know what you think," she pressed.

"A'ight then. Since you want me to ask, tell me. What do I think?"

"You don't give a fuck whether I still have feelings for him or not. You're just going to push your way into my space regardless. Rather pushy, wouldn't you say?"

"You like for a nigga to be pushy, don't you? What? So I guess that means you just ain't gonna give me the pussy. I'ma have to take it, right?"

"Whatever turns you on."

"You know you turn me on, but I bet before it's all over, you're gonna be begging for me to hit it. I won't have to take it."

No, that nigga didn't go there.

"You wish. I see you got jokes or you smoking something. I know you're used to having your way, but you ain't hittin' this."

"Aight. We'll see," he smirked.

It took her a little over an hour to finish. Afterwards she greased his scalp and then stood in front of him to check out her handiwork.

Damn, this cocky-ass nigga is fine, she kept thinking to herself.

"Am I straight?" he asked.

"You straight. Tell Iverson's stylist to holla at this playa for some lessons."

Before she could back away, he put both hands on her waist and guided her to straddle his lap. "Come here."

"What do you think you're doing, Trae?" she said, not resisting.

Without taking his eyes off hers he said, "I just want to talk to you." He grabbed her butt with both hands and pulled her right up on his dick and began rotating her hips in a slow and subtle manner.

She watched the muscles in his biceps flex while fighting the desire to wrap her legs around his waist. "Trae, why are you holding me so tight?"

"Because when I make you my woman, I'm never letting you go." She slid her hands down on top of his to see if she could pry them loose, but he was holding on tight and still rotating her hips to grind on his dick.

Damn, this feels so good, she said to herself.

"Trae, I thought you wanted to talk," she whispered while trying again to pry his hands loose.

"I do," he said, looking into her eyes.

"So talk, because your dick is getting very hard. And it is feeling so good."

"I'm a'ight. We both got on clothes."

I'm not a'ight, her pussy screamed. She was trying to be cool, but the shit was feeling better and better. He was guiding her hips to apply the right amount of pressure. *This nigga really is bold. Heaven help me.*

"Tell me how you like it, Tash. What do I have to do to make you climb the walls?"

She slid her hands down once again to see if she could loosen his grip. "Trae, let me go." Her voice was now trembling.

He held on even tighter, leaned up, and began biting her nipples through her T-shirt. She arched her back and closed her eyes. He wasn't biting hard and he wasn't being gentle. It was just right. She was covered with goose bumps. The palms of her hands and her top lip were sweating.

BEEP! BEEP! BEEP! BRRNG! BRRNG! As if on cue, his pager went off and the house phone rang as he started sucking on her neck.

"Trae, I need to get that." He reluctantly loosened his grip allowing her to slide off him and go pick up the wall phone in the kitchen. She grabbed a pen and a sheet of paper. It was the market research rep giving her the demographics on areas that had clusters of athletes.

Trae followed her into the kitchen and stood behind her, wrapping his arms around her waist. She was trying to concentrate on the phone call but Trae's hard dick was feeling good as he pressed up against her butt. He slid his hand down inside her panties and ran his middle finger up and down her pussy and then circled her clit.

"Can you hold on, please?" she said into the phone, covering the mouthpiece with her hand. Trae was playing with her pussy and she was trying not to scream.

"Come for me, Tash," he whispered in her ear, loving her wet and juicy pussy. She was squeezing the phone tighter. Her mouth wanted to say "stop," but her pussy was saying "work those fingers a little faster."

"C'mon, ma, why you trying to hold back?" he whispered,

while kissing her neck and sliding his hand under her T-shirt to play with her nipples.

"No, Trae. Wait," she moaned as he put passion marks on her neck and massaged her clit a little faster. When her legs began shaking uncontrollably, she dropped the phone.

"Trae, wait," she moaned as she started cummimg and shaking. When she stopped shaking, he slid his hand out of her panties.

"That's what I'm talkin' 'bout," he bragged. She grabbed a dish towel and threw it at him. Trae's pager was blowing up and he left out the kitchen to get it. She picked the phone up off the floor and, too embarrassed to see if the woman was still holding on, hung up.

While Trae made some calls on his phone, she jumped in the shower. She couldn't believe she let him corner her up like that. It was as if he knew what buttons to push. That orgasm put her knees out of commission. If he wasn't holding her up, she would have collapsed to the floor. He was definitely smooth. *He didn't even undress me*, she thought.

She jumped out of the shower, oiled down and threw on a white, sleeveless blouse and some jeans. She put her hair into a bun and slipped into a pair of blue Gucci loafers on her way to the living room. "Trae, you didn't have my permission to decorate my neck like this."

"I couldn't help it, Tash. Some necks are very sensuous," he said, lighting his blunt. "You ready to bounce?"

"I did have other plans for today, Trae."

"Your plans are to roll with me," he said, looking her up and down. "Damn. You ain't got on no makeup and you still fine as hell. Look at your skin. It's so pretty. Are those real?"

"Is what real?"

"Your breasts."

She started laughing. "You was biting and feeling all over them. You couldn't tell?"

"Shit. I didn't handle them the way I really wanted to. They look so perfect. I wanted to be sure, so I'm asking."

"Of course they're real." She went to take out the Love Jones CD and turned off the CD player.

"Yeah, bring that and Marvin Gaye's *I Want You*," he said, putting out the blunt. "You ready?"

"Do I have a choice?"

"I'm afraid not."

The ride to New York was cool, thanks to the Navigator. Tasha fell in love with it. She felt so empowered and secure just being a passenger. Now she wanted to drive it. They talked a little about each other's backgrounds and goals. Tasha didn't go too deep into hers.

His parents owned B-Boy Snack Cakes, and he had plans for his own marketing and public relations firm. The *I Want You* CD played over and over in the background.

"A thug rockin' Marvin Gaye," she grinned at him.

"That's the shit Tash. A thug needs and wants that one special woman. Somebody who belongs only to him, who got his back and is willing to go the distance with him. That one who he could be all open for."

"A woman needs and wants that too Trae."

"I didn't say she didn't."

"Just making sure." She turned toward him. "You got a bachelor's degree. Why are you still out here putting your life and freedom on the line like this? I know you got enough money."

"Got caught up Tash. Gotta chase that paper a little while longer." He looked at her. "Take your hair down." She didn't move. "What, did I stutter? Take your hair down for me please." She kept looking at him as she slowly unraveled her bun, letting her hair fall. He reached over and ran his fingers through it. "Damn, it's soft and pretty. I didn't think it was yours." She felt her nipples tingle.

"First it was my breasts. Now it's my hair. Is there anything else you're curious about?"

"Your tongue ring, is it platinum?"

"Yup. What about your tongue ring? You don't wear it all the time, do you?"

"Nah. Just when I want to use it and just enough to keep it from closing up."

"Just when you want to use it. Okay then," she mumbled, smiling to herself.

He looked at her. "Can I kiss you?"

"Nope."

"Why?"

"Trae you're supposed to be driving. How are you gonna kiss and drive at the same time?"

"I'ma pull the fuck over."

She smiled. "Nah Trae. Keep driving dawg."

He laughed at her.

Once in New York, Trae handled his whip just like a New Yorker. He knew his way around. "Here we go," he said, squeezing into a parking spot.

After helping her out of the Navigator, they went to Bergdorf Goodman, where he made her try on a beaded silk chiffon dress by Geri Gerard. It was tight, showed plenty of cleavage, and had a long slit up the left thigh, revealing her long, smooth, caramel-colored legs. It cost $2900. He also bought her some Gucci shoes and handbag, with jewelry to match. Her outfit came to almost five thousand dollars.

They walked down the street, stopping at a jewelry store along the way. He replaced her platinum tongue ring with a diamond. His tailor was on the same block. As soon as he stepped inside, two salesmen approached him.

"Good afternoon, Mr. Macklin," the tall one with the long ponytail said.

"What's up, Anthony?"

"What can we do for you today?"

He gave him Tasha's dress. "I want to match her."

"No problem, Mr. Macklin. Right this way."

He ended up letting Tasha choose some dark brown, silk and sharkskin material. The salespeople were pleased with her choice. He dropped four G's for his suit, shirt and tie, and another fifteen hundred for some gators. They went to a cafe on the same block and ate lunch while his clothes were being made.

Once they had their outfits they put the bags in the back of the Navigator and headed for his apartment.

"How do you like living on Park Avenue?"

"It's a'ight, when I'm there. I ain't never had no problems."

They pulled into the underground parking lot, got his bags out of the trunk, and headed for the building. He stopped at his mailbox before they stepped into the elevator.

"Trae, your apartment is nice for a male," Tasha said, walking through the three-bedroom apartment.

"What was you expecting, Tash?"

"I don't know," she said, fiddling with the exercise equipment. "So this explains why you're so cut up and defined," she teased.

"I'm hardly here. I usually sleep here three or four times a week. I mostly drop in, shower, change, and I'm out."

"Who keeps it clean?" she asked, looking in the refrigerator.

"The building has maid service."

When she came out the kitchen he was taking his bags to the bedroom. The phone rang.

"Tash! Pick that up for me."

"Sure." Surprise evident in her voice.

"Hello," Tasha said. "Hello," she said again.

"Is Trae there? This is Monique."

"Hold on."

"Trae, telephone," Tasha hollered.

"Who is it?"

"Monique."

"Take a message."

She pretended she didn't hear him. "This is Tasha. He said he'll be right here." She wanted to see what was up.

"Trae telephone!" she hollered.

"I asked you to take a message Tash."

"She said she needed to speak to you."

"That's bullshit Tash, and you know it." He picked up the

phone. "What is it?" he snapped. He saw that Tasha was leaving the living room. "Tash come here! You ain't gotta leave out. She ain't nobody. Come here." When she walked back over to him he pressed the speakerphone button. He grabbed her and pulled her close. "It's all about you. Well, I'm trying like hell to make it all about you if you'd let me," he said, kissing her neck. "Monique what is it you want?" he hollered at the speakerphone. He kissed Tasha again.

"You could at least return my pages Trae." Then realizing the obvious she screeched, "I know you don't have me on no damn speakerphone!"

"Monique you got thirty seconds to tell me why you calling my house."

"I was calling to see if you was going to see Jill Scott and Musiq. I want to go," she whined.

"Monique I ain't fuckin' you. You ain't got it like that no more."

He turned his attention back to Tash. "Spend the night with me."

"I don't think so Trae."

"Why not?"

"I need to go home."

"Trae!" Monique hollered.

"Your thirty seconds are up."

"Fuck you Trae!" she spat, slamming the phone down.

He turned the speakerphone off. "I know that was a setup, telling me to come to the phone."

"What?"

"Don't play dumb," he said, caressing her butt. "C'mon Tash. Spend the night," he pleaded. He wanted to hit it in the worst way. She was extremely sexy to him.

"I think you're moving a little too fast."

"If you knew how long I've been waiting to get this close to you, you would understand."

"Maybe another time Trae. I need to get home," she pleaded.

"No, you don't. Let's go clubbin'. I'm taking the day off and I want to keep you with me."

"What am I going to wear? I know you don't expect me to wear this," she said, pointing to her jeans.

"Come on ma. You know we can go buy something to wear."

"Okay. Let's go." She was glad for an excuse to get out of his apartment before things got too heated too fast.

They went to Saks Fifth Avenue. She chose a short Chanel skirt, blouse, shoes, underwear and perfume. Trae bought himself a shirt that Tasha picked out. They then went back to Trae's apartment to eat, shower and change. Tasha fried some chicken, baked a couple of potatoes and made a salad.

Later that evening they hit the reggae clubs on Jamaica Avenue in Queens. It wasn't until 2:30 that they headed back to New Jersey.

Tasha reclined her seat all the way back and stretched out. "Trae I hate to admit it, but I enjoyed my day. I'm gonna sleep so good. You woke me up at 8:30. In another five hours we would have been up for twenty-four."

"We did have fun, didn't we?"

"Let me hear WBLS."

Trae turned the radio to WBLS and reached for his cell phone and two-way pager to turn them on. Two minutes later, they were both going off. Tash sat up in her seat when she heard Snoop's beat pumpin'. "Turn that up, Trae!" They both started bouncing and rapping like they had an audience. *"For the haters who be talkin' loud, runnin' his lips, trying to dis. He better lay low! For the girl who was saying I just broke her off then left, now she pissed! She better lay low. For the buster who be claimin' my hood but really ain't from my gang, better lay low! I hope you don't be thinking I be just talkin', runnin' my lips and won't do a thang. Really hope so!"* They both burst out laughing.

"Dayum, let me find out I got a gangsta broad," Trae joked.

"You ain't know?" she laughed. "I can't help it when Snoop come on. All of his shit be bangin'—him and Nate Dogg."

Trae just looked at her and smiled. "Looks like you're gonna be full of surprises."

"Listen who's talking! You're the one full of surprises. That stunt you pulled in my kitchen!"

"Did it surprise you?"

"Pretty much, yeah!"

"I got two extra tickets to the show. You know somebody who might want them?" Trae asked her.

Tasha thought about it. "Faheem and Jaz might want them." She looked at the clock. "It's Friday. Jaz is up, I'm sure. Let me call her." She grabbed her Gucci bag and pulled out her cell.

"When you get her, let me holla at Faheem," Trae told her.

Tasha's mouth dropped open. "How do you know what Jaz I'm calling? And you know Faheem like that to want to talk to him?" She knew the hustlers all traveled in the same circles basically. *But damn!* This was a little too close to home.

"Ma, go 'head with that. You know who I am." Just then Faheem came on the line. "Faheem? This is Roz."

"You sayin' my name as if some other nigga could be answering this phone. And I know your voice. Do you know what time it is?" Faheem scolded.

"Why you gotta get slick out the mouth? I'm just surprised you're home. I thought Jaz would be the one answering the phone."

"Girl, it is four in the morning and Ma is asleep, where you should be, where are you?"

"You're being a little too nosy Faheem," she teased.

"Girl you better stop playing and tell me why your ass in the street at four in the morning!"

"Okay *daddy*, calm down. I'm with Trae." She held her breath anticipating his response. She figured that she might as well tell him herself before someone else told him. He was quiet. Since he wasn't responding she needed to feel him out. "Trae has two extra tickets to see Musiq and Jill Scott tomorrow night. You want them?"

"Put that nigga on the phone," he commanded.

"Yeah he wants to speak to you." She tried to play it off then handed Trae the phone.

"Heem, what up nigga?"

"Shit, I can't call it." Faheem humbly stated.

"Shit nigga! I can't tell. You got the best hand. I'm trying to get where you at. As a matter of fact, I'm working overtime trying to be like you. Get the fuck out before it's too late."

"Yeah man, that's what's up. And that shit is real serious. So where you at?"

"Almost there. I can taste it."

"That's a good thing."

"Word on the streets is, you even turned in your playa's card!"

"Let a nigga find out you hatin'!" Faheem joked.

"Nah. Never that. Because that shit do get old after a while."

"Yeah. Especially if you got a baby on the way. From there it's all about family."

"A baby? Damn dawg if I had it like you I'd be home, chillin' and making babies too. I plan on being not too far behind you."

"Yo, so what's up? I hear that you and Kay are the people to see. You sure you ready to give all that up?" Faheem quizzed.

"On my life."

"What's up with Nikayah?"

"That nigga said it look like he's gonna win his appeal. But until then it's business as usual."

"I see. So what's up with my lil sister?"

"It's all love Faheem. I got her."

"A'ight nigga. That's family right there. How you treat her is how you treat me. Treat her right or don't even fuck with her."

"I hear you nigga. I got her."

"A'ight then."

Trae handed Tasha the phone. He listened as she let out a few laughs before hanging up.

"You want them to ride with us?" he asked.

"Do you?"

"Not really," Trae said.

"They'll probably go by limo anyway."

"How do you want to go? Limo? Helicopter? What?"

Tasha started laughing. "Thanks Trae but I'd rather push the Nav. I'm ready to drive it. It's making my Beamer feel like a Volkswagen."

"You can drive it," he said, staring at her.

"Why are you staring?"

"Tell me why you've been shutting me out for the last couple of months. I've been feeling you and I know you've been feeling me. So what's up?"

"I knew this conversation was coming."

"I'm sure you did. So what's up?"

"It's only been a few months since I've stopped fuckin' your partna, remember? I'm having a big problem walking away from five years and then going straight to boning his partna the next day. That shit don't seem right to me. I mean, damn, let the fucking sheets cool off. Plus, I can't do any more jail visits, and I definitely don't want to go to any funerals. Getting involved with a hustler, I'm staring all of that in the face. So that's what really has me putting on my brakes with you. It's not personal."

"Sounds personal to me. But check it Tasha, it's been, what, four months since you've been with Nikayah. Shit, the sheets got ice on them. Second of all, I ain't gonna be out here much longer. I'm wrappin' this shit up. And me and Nikayah, it's just business. So now what?"

She sat in silence for a while before asking, "What do you mean 'now what'? What do you want from me?"

"I want you—all of you. I don't want to just kick it. I don't want just a piece of you. I don't just want to fuck. I want all of you."

Tasha sighed while pulling at her hair. Emotions a melting pot. Fear. Skepticism. Lust. Desire. Finally she said "been there, done that, and never again. I already gave up all of me."

"With the wrong nigga Tash."

"How do I know you're the right one?"

"Give me a chance Tash, and you'll find out."

"A chance? I don't want to take *a chance* on you, Trae. What? You want me to roll the dice and maybe I'll be happy or maybe I'll get hurt? I don't think so."

"Oh, okay. Now we gettin' somewhere. So let me make sure I'm hearin' you right. It ain't Nikayah. You can tolerate me hustling. But you're worryin' about me hurtin' you?"

She turned her head and looked out the window in silence for the rest of the ride home. Trae threw on Marvin Gaye's *I Want You* CD and lit a blunt with a smirk pinned to his face.

After an hour they pulled up in front of Tash's three-family house. She lived on the 3rd floor. Trae got out and went around to the passenger's side to help her out the car then hugged her. "Tash believe me. I would never hurt you or leave you. Don't be scared of me. I just want to love you and make you happy. Give me a chance. You know this feels right. Why do I have to beg?" he whispered in her ear.

"You don't have to beg Trae. For real. I'm scared. Real scared. I've vowed to myself to never put my heart in the position for another nigga to stomp on it."

"Give me a chance and trust me a'ight? Tasha I swear to you, I got you." He told her that before turning her loose and taking the bags upstairs. "Where do you want me to set these?"

"Give me the dress. You can set everything else next to the sofa." She grabbed the garment bag that held the dress. "Thank you. This dress is so me."

"You make that dress look real good." He pulled out a knot and peeled off five hundred dollars, placing the bills on the coffee table. "This is for your hair and whatever else you need to do to drive a nigga crazy. I'll pick you up at 6:30."

"I have money to do all of those things."

"Keep the money Tash. Just be ready." His phone rang. He flipped it open. "I'm on my way, man," he said, then flipped it shut.

"I'll be ready. You just be on time," she instructed.

"When do you sleep?"

"When I can. Oh and you don't have to worry about me being on time," he said, leaning up against the door. "I can't wait to see you in that dress. I hope you don't plan on wearing any make-up. You don't need it. You're fine as hell without it."

"Are you leaving now?"

"Why are you rushing me out? I'm not gonna do anything to you."

"Right. That's what you said this morning when you had me sitting on your lap."

"You were in my house, in my shower, and I didn't bother you."

"Yeah, I'll give you that."

"Can I have one kiss and one hug?"

"Goodbye Trae. It is 4:30 in the morning."

"Come here, girl," he said' grabbing her and putting her back up against the door. He slid her arms around his neck and grabbed her skirt. Then he eased it up over her waist and held her close.

"Trae you said one kiss and one hug."

"I'm just making it one good kiss and one good hug."

She could feel him harden, so she kissed him on the lips. "There, you got your kiss and your hug."

"That don't count. You kissed me. I didn't kiss you." He was caressing her ass cheeks, pulling her even closer on his hard dick. "You drivin' me crazy Tash. You know that, right?"

"I wish I could say the same about you. You scaring the shit outta me. Look at me. I'm standing here with my skirt above my waist, hugged up with my ex's boy, who I've been kickin' it with all night long. What's wrong with this picture?"

"Business partna. And there is nothing wrong with this picture. Do you still have feelings for him?"

"No."

"Well then, let that shit go," he said, kissing her neck. "Time to move on . . . with me."

"How do you know it's time to move on?"

"Because just like you said I got you standing here with your skirt above your waist, your nipples are hard, and your pussy is wet." He lifted one of her legs and put it around his waist. "Damn, you feel good," he moaned, moving her up and down on his dick. "I can't wait to make you cum again."

"That won't be any time soon," she told him.

"How much money you want to put on that?"

"You talk a lot of shit."

"I can back it up. How much money you want to put on it?"

"What's the time frame?" she asked.

"The next twenty-four hours."

"Shit. You ain't hittin' this in the next twenty-four hours. How much we talking?"

"Oh, now you talkin' shit! I said the bet is I'll make you cum within the next twenty-four hours."

"A'ight. We on! How much?"

"If I win, you give me a chance with you. Take a chance with me," he said. "If you win, I'll buy you a car."

"It's on! Now let me go." She slid her leg down from around his waist, but he pulled it back up.

"Don't get scared. I ain't got my hands on your pussy. I still want my kiss." He kissed her for about five minutes. "When you came, your legs was shakin' like crazy. I can't wait to feel that shit again. That shit sent electric currents all through my body."

"Well, partna, you might as well order my Benz because you won't be feeling that electricity no time soon." He let her leg down, pulling her skirt back over her butt.

"I'll catch you later. Lock the door." He turned around, "Benz, huh?"

"You heard me. Benz. B-E-N-Z."

"A'ight, we'll see!" Then he pulled the door shut behind him.

Chapter 3

Roz's phone rang at 9 A.M. "Roz, I'm on my way over. You up?" Jaz sounded alert and chipper.

"No, I'm not up. Don't you have your keys?"

"Uh huh."

"Then wake me up when you come in."

"Girl, it's nine o'clock!"

"I didn't get in until 4:30."

"Oh, I gots to hear this. See you soon."

Jaz let herself in. She sat her purse on the sofa and headed for the refrigerator. She sliced off a piece of cantaloupe, poured a glass of apple juice before going into Roz's bedroom.

"Wake up, *Tasha*," she teased. "It's 9:30." Roz rolled over to the other side of the bed and Jaz sat down.

"I'm awake," Roz said, stretching. "I'm so tired."

"Faheem mentioned that you was out with Trae at three in the morning. What's up with that?"

"Jaz, it's too early."

"Come on. Tell me how that happened," Jaz said, slapping her leg.

Roz sucked her teeth and finally opened her eyes. "He came over about 8:30 yesterday morning for me to braid his hair. We ended up kickin' it all day and night. He took me shopping up top. We ate. I went to his house. We went clubbin', and we're going out tonight. That's it. That's all."

"Damn. You let him hit it already?" Jaz asked, disappointment evident in her tone.

"Nope!"

"Then why are all those hickeys on your neck?"

"You don't miss nothing, do you? FYI, he put them there. But, no, he didn't hit it."

"Faheem said he told Trae that he better treat his baby sis' good or else leave you the fuck alone."

"My big brotha said that?" She started laughing.

"Yup! He likes Trae. He said he's wild, but he's good peeps. FYI, Trae really blew up when Nikayah got locked up, taking shit to a whole other level. The nigga is paid and really is intending to retire. Faheem said he can't believe he took over Nikayah's business and his woman. How much did he spend on you?"

"You don't want to know."

"Yes, I do."

"About eight or nine G's. Then he left me five hundred to get my hair and shit done."

"Dayum! He ain't cheap, is he?"

"Not at all."

"He must want to hit it real bad. So what you gonna do?"

Roz sat up in the bed. "Girl, his timing is so off. And I'm so fucking scared I don't know what to do. He knows it, too. Nikayah really fucked it up for the next nigga. He probably did that shit on purpose. Gosh, I hate him! I refuse to visit another nigga in jail, and I'm not burying a dead body. I swear my gut instinct is screaming 'no drug dealers!' Yes, and Trae is wild. I overheard him talking on the phone. He ain't nothing nice. If he keeps doing what he doing, I believe he'll get merked before he gets locked up. I just wish like hell that I wasn't feelin' him. What should I do?" Roz pleaded.

"Damn, Roz. That is some scary shit. Remember when I

wouldn't even fuck with Faheem until he cleaned up his shit? I was like, fuck that life. I can do without all the drama. Even though I fucked up. So who am I to judge?"

"I'm feelin' you. Oh, but Jaz we had so much fun just kickin' it. He is all of that. So, I'm really caught between a rock and a hard place!" Roz rubbed her face with both hands. "Gosh, I am so tired," she yawned. "Get the tickets off my dresser. Does Faheem like Jill Scott or Musiq?"

"He likes 'em both, especially Jill Scott. Tell Trae we said thanks."

"Listen to you talking about we, sounding all married and shit."

"Don't be a hater," Jaz grinned.

"What time are you going to get your hair done? I gotta call and get myself an appointment. You want me to make you one, too?"

"Please? Call me and let me know what time. I'm on my way to the cleaners and the grocery store. I'll catch you later," Jaz said, taking the tickets off the dresser as she left.

By the time Roz got back from getting a manicure, pedicure and her hair done, it was almost 4:30. She opened the CD player and noticed that Trae still had two of her CDs. "Dang!" she said out loud.

She was always chillin' to those two CDs. She flipped through her stack and pulled out Carl Thomas, Jagged Edge, Case, Sade and Maxwell. She popped them into the five-disc CD player and pumped it up.

She made her a tub full of Calgon, lit a joint, wrapped her hair and eased into the hot tub water. She soaked a while before scrubbing down. She shaved and rinsed off before stepping out of the water to air dry. After flossing and brushing, she moisturized her skin and looked at the clock. It was 6:02. She flower-scented her entire body and took her time getting dressed. The dress did fit her perfectly. She needed no bra or stockings. She slipped her manicured feet into the Gucci high-heeled sandals and brushed her hair, letting it hang down her back.

When she heard a knock, she popped a peppermint into her mouth and reached for her Gucci bag and keys. She opened the door and was at a loss for words. Trae was fine, but this was really ridiculous. His tailored, dark brown suit fit him to a T. His silk shirt, open halfway down his chest, matched the dark beige in her dress. With the big-ass rock in his left ear and his braids, he looked like he belonged on the cover of *GQ*.

"Oh, you can't speak now?" he said, smiling.

"You belong on the cover of *GQ*, my brotha."

"I'm checking you out. Stand back. Let me see what you working with," he said, walking around her slowly. "Fuckin' fine! Perfectly fuckin' fine!" He even marveled at her beautifully designed toes.

She remained standing still while he circled her again, this time stopping behind her. She could feel his breath on her neck. He pulled her close, smelling her hair and neck. "You smell so good . . . so fresh and so clean. Do I make you nervous?" he teased.

"Wouldn't you like to know?"

"I know I do," he whispered, lips touching her ear.

"Are you done giving me the twice over?" she asked.

"Not really," he said, still holding her close and now kissing her neck. She closed her eyes.

"I'm kind of surprised that you're on time," she finally spoke.

"Why would I be late, knowing what I had waiting on me?" he asked, running his hand up her thigh.

"Are we ready to go Trae?"

"Aren't you going to turn the stereo off?"

"As soon as you turn me loose."

"It feels so good holding you. I don't really want to let you go. Your thighs are so soft and smooth." He was still rubbing her thigh up and down.

"Trae!" she snapped out of her reverie. "My pussy is starting to juice up."

He slowly turned her loose, and she went and turned off the stereo. Just then she saw him grab his dick and squeeze it. "Are you okay?" she asked, knowing otherwise.

"Hell, fuckin' no! I can't even think straight. I believe all my blood rushed from my brain down to my dick."

She smiled. "Let's go Trae. I'm ready to glide in the Nav!"

When they got outside to the car, he handed her the keys and took off his jacket.

"Oh, I got it like this?" she asked.

"You can drive, can't you?"

"Most definitely!" She grinned.

He walked her around to the driver's side and helped her up into the seat. He got in on the other side, hung his jacket up in the back, and watched her adjust the controls.

"You want me to take the Turnpike?" she asked, pulling out.

"If you want to."

"I do."

"Then let's roll!" Trae lit a blunt. "Do you want to eat before or after the show?"

"Afterwards. You straight?"

"I'm straight," he said, admiring her.

"Are you gonna stare at me the whole trip?"

"Pretty much."

She smiled and shook her head. "Don't let me forget my CDs this time. I went to listen to them, and they were gone. Why aren't you playing some music?"

"Why are you so nervous? I'ma ask you to relax."

"You're making me nervous staring at me."

"You shouldn't be. You're so fine. I'm glad you didn't wear makeup. You definitely don't need it."

"Thanks for the compliment. You know you are pretty fine yourself. But I'm sure you have a lot of women telling you that all the time. What, are you trying to get me in where you can fit me in?"

"Now why you gotta go there? I'm trying to give you the opportunity to run this right now. Once you do ain't no room for nobody else. It's all about you, Tash. You ain't know?"

"Of course I know. It's always about me. I'm just checking to see if you know what's up." She smiled at him. "I'm just messing with you Trae. I really shouldn't have gone there. This Nav don't drive, it flies," she said, trying to change the subject as she slowed down to enter the Turnpike.

"You don't have on a bra, do you?"

"No. You don't have to wear one with this dress," she answered with a puzzled look.

He leaned over and put his hand on her thigh. "Keep your eyes on the road and lift up."

"Lift up?"

"Did I stutter Tash? Keep your eye on the road." He lifted her butt and went to sliding her silk thong off.

"Trae!" she yelled as she tried to wiggle away from him.

"You gonna get us killed if you don't watch the road. Lift your foot off the gas," he warned.

She lifted her foot off the gas quickly, and he snatched her skimpy piece of cloth clean off.

"Trae are you fuckin' crazy? I don't believe you just did that!" she pouted.

He put them in the glove compartment.

"I had a feeling you were crazy. Now you just confirmed my suspicions," she mumbled, looking at him as if he was definitely insane.

"Keep your eye on the road and calm down. It's the dress. I couldn't help it. Damn, I got good taste! I was imagining how you looked under that dress. You don't have on a bra, but you had on panties. That was messing up my little fantasy, so the thong had to go. What's crazy about that?"

"So now I have to walk around naked because of your little fantasy?"

"You're not naked," he said, placing The Life Soundtrack into the CD and advancing to *Fortunate* before cranking it up.

When they pulled up in front of the club they had to wait behind the other cars for valet parking. Roz picked up her Gucci bag and pulled out her strawberry Victoria's Secret lip gloss and a compact mirror.

"Why are you putting on lipstick?"

"This isn't lipstick; it's lip gloss," she said, holding it up for him to see. "It's just a sweet, high-priced, shiny, designer Chapstick. Is that okay with you?" She waited for his approval before sensually applying it.

"It's flavored?" he asked.

"Taste like strawberry."

"Can I taste it?"

She looked at him then leaned over and pressed her lips against his. He licked her lips saying, "It does taste like strawberry."

"Told ya!" she said, applying a little more.

"Let me taste it again."

This time he ran his tongue over and around her lips then slipped it inside her mouth. "Mmm, you taste even better." Just then the valet opened her door. "Let me come over there and help you out," Trae said. He stepped out of the Nav, went around to the other side, and lifted her out, inhaling her perfume. "Um, you smell so good. Do I have to let you go?" he asked, squeezing her.

"Unfortunately you do, because you're holding up traffic," she reminded him. "Other people want to see the show as well."

As he kissed her lightly on the lips, he became aroused. "You feel that?" he asked.

"Um hmm," she moaned. Horns started honking "You breaking me down Trae."

"I'm tryin', but you damn sure ain't making it easy. C'mon," he said, taking her by the hand and grabbing the ticket from the attendant. "Don't go joyridin' in my shit, dawg," he told him, handing him a bill.

"I got chu, man!" the attendant said, pocketing the cash and giving him a pound.

Trae and Tash walked past the long line of people trying to get inside and went to another door. He knocked on it. When it opened, a gold-mouthed, bald-headed brother peeped out.

"Yo! What up, Trae?" he said, opening the door.

"You got it, Donny!" Trae handed him a hundred-dollar bill.

"Let me show you to your booth. And enjoy the show."

As they walked through the lobby a brotha with a camera hollered, "Yo! My man, you want a picture with the beautiful lady?" Trae stopped and looked Tasha up and down.

"Yeah, man. Why not?" He led Tasha over to the backdrop of the New York skyline. He moved next to Donny and left Tasha standing there.

"I know you're going to take one with me," she warned, her hand on her hip.

He smiled. "Can I please have one of you by yourself? You look good, ma."

"You ready?" asked the photographer. Then he looked at Trae. "How you want this, dawg?"

"Give me a full body and a close up." The photographer nodded and took both pictures.

"C'mon Trae." She held out her hand, motioning for him to come over. He bent all the way down, resting against her leg in the first picture. For the second one he sat in a chair while she sat in his lap.

"I know you want one standing up," the photographer predicted, trying to sell some more shots.

"Yeah, give me two more," Trae said, moving the chair aside. He grabbed her hand and pulled her close. "One like this up close and one full body." He then wrapped both arms around her waist.

"Yo, chief, give me a minute. I need to load up a new pack of film."

"Let me taste the strawberry lip gloss again." As she pressed her lips against his she felt his dick stiffen. He again ran his tongue over her lips and then inside her mouth. While their tongues danced inside each other's mouths, he was getting harder and she was getting wetter.

"I'm ready," the photographer interjected.

Their lips remained locked for another minute. Finally Tasha came up for air. "We're ready," she said, smiling for the pictures. After wiping lip gloss from Trae's lips.

After the photo session, Donny led them up front to their booth in the corner, leaving out the same way he came in. A bucket of ice and two bottles of Dom were on their candlelit table, which was covered with a crisp, white linen tablecloth. Trae let Roz slide in the booth, taking off his jacket and sitting next to her.

"You a'ight?" He smiled at Tash who was bouncing to Sunshine Anderson singing "Heard It All Before."

"I'm a'ight. You?"

"I'm good. You want something to drink?"

"A bottle of spring water would be nice." Just then, a waitress was heading toward them.

"What can I get you tonight?" she asked, never taking her eyes off Trae.

"Can you get my woman some bottled water and a club soda for me?" She quickly lost her grin, nodded and slipped away.

"Did I just hear you claim me?" she asked.

"Tash you're gonna be the one to have my babies."

She laughed, "I'ma take that as a joke because I see you're full of them."

"A'ight. We'll see. You sure you don't want none of this?" he asked, pointing at the ice bucket holding the two bottles.

"I'm sure. I gotta have a clear head when dealing with you. I don't know what to expect or what you'll do next. You already got me walking around without panties."

"I don't know why you trippin'. That shit is sexy, and it's only between you and me," he said, rubbing his hand up and down her thigh. He saw the waitress coming and pulled out his money clip. He paid her then motioned for her to keep the change.

"This club is tight. I like the atmosphere," she said, looking around. "And the booths add a nice touch."

"Yeah, you can enjoy the show without being all up on people," Trae said. He looked at his Rolex. "We have a half hour to kill if they start on time. What do you want to do?"

"Do you know where Jaz and Faheem is sitting?" she asked.

He shook his head. Couples were out on the dance floor, the deejay having slowed it down. The club was dimly lit other than the stage area which had a booming sound system. Trae grabbed her hand. "C'mon Tash. This is your song!"

Jaheim was singing, *Could it be the ice you see?*

"Oh, you wrong for that Trae. It ain't even like that."

He laughed. "Oh it ain't like that?"

"You should know. You the one who doin' all the chasing. Tash got her own ice, her own Beamer, her own house, and a job. *I* should be asking you, 'Could it be?' " They both started laughing. "Nah, but I am feeling you."

He pulled her close as they swayed to the smooth sounds of Jaheim. "How long you plan on playing hard to get?"

"Hard to get? I'm really trying not to fuck with you."

"Why not?"

"Because . . . I already told you." Their bodies were moving in sync to the music.

"Tell me again," he said, rubbing his nose lightly over on her neck and ear.

"Can't we just kick it from time to time just like we doing now?" She melted into him.

"Like we doing now? Ma, we on the verge of fuckin'."

"No, we're not."

"Yes, we are." He smiled and pulled her closer.

"What's so funny?"

"You're gonna have my last name and you don't even see it."

"Oh, am I?"

"Fo' sho'. Just watch."

"You're taking your personal pursuits a little too far, don't you think?" She tried not to laugh.

"A'ight, we gonna see who has the last laugh."

They were now swaying to the sounds of Eryka Badu singing, *"What you gonna do when they come for you? Work ain't honest, but it pays the bills."*

"This song means so much," said Tasha.

"I'm not gonna leave you hanging Tash. Believe that." The only thing he got from Tasha was a sigh.

He led her back to their booth after that song. As soon as they sat down Trae leaned over and kissed her, sliding one hand up her thigh and, with the other, moving her up to the edge of the cushioned bench.

"See what I mean? I never know what to expect next. What are you up to now Trae?"

He kissed her again and then inserted two fingers inside of her.

"Trae people can see us," she whispered, trying to keep her composure. Trae was actually trying to take her there.

"Nobody can see what I'm doing. My back is blocking you, and this long tablecloth is covering everything else. Plus it's dark. Just relax Tash," he whispered. He was moving his fingers in and out and all around at a slow pace. She was very wet. That told him it was all good. She was now biting her lip and breathing heavily.

"Trae baby, don't do this here," she pleaded, sliding her hand on top of his. "Please don't make me cum. I'll mess up my dress." She tried to grab his hand, but he kept on going. "Damn you Trae. Are you listening to me?" Her voice was now trembling.

"Relax ma. I got a big handkerchief. You won't mess up your dress."

"Damn this feels good," she muttered, her eyes closed. He picked up the pace a little, then pulled his fingers out and started pressing firmly on her clit with circular motions, just like he did to her in the kitchen. "Oh shit!"

When he felt the first contraction, he used his other hand to grab the big linen napkin off the table. As she started cumming her legs started shaking. He then kissed her to stifle her moaning. She rested her head on his shoulder, still breathing heavily and trying to get herself together as he wiped her off.

"Trae I can't believe you did that! I can't believe I let you do that! I am so fucking embarrassed," she said, looking around to see if anyone saw what had happened. He put his arm around her and tried not to laugh. "Let me go to the ladies' room. I see that smirk on your face."

He slid out of the booth and stood up. She slid over, and he helped her up. "Is anything on my dress?" she asked as she was turning around to see her butt.

"It's dark, baby. You cool. Go ahead to the restroom. I'll meet you back here," he said, cleaning up the mess before going to the men's room.

Tasha walked into the bathroom and didn't even notice Jaz washing her hands and watching her through the mirror.

"Miss *Tasha*, I was looking for you. Where are y'all sitting? And why are your cheeks so flushed?"

"You don't want to know why. Where are y'all sitting? Here, hold my bag."

"I just asked you that same question. Damn, what's Trae out there doing to you?" Jaz asked, trying to figure out what was up with her girl. She had grabbed a whole wad of paper towels and was soaking them in hot water.

"We're sitting up front in the corner," she said, disappearing into the bathroom stall. Where are y'all sitting?"

"Up front. We got good seats, but I keep having to walk a mile to come pee. You look like you're having a good time," Jaz said, trying to be nosy. But she knew what was up.

"So far I am."

"You wearing that dress, girl."

"That's all I'm wearing," Tasha said as she came out of the stall. She washed her hands, opened up her purse, and pulled out a toothbrush and toothpaste. Jaz was watching her brush her teeth. Then she put on more perfume and lip gloss.

Jaz was standing there laughing and rubbing her stomach. "Looks like you're getting into Trae."

"Is it that obvious?"

"Yup! What is he doing to you?"

"Talking shit and trying to have me all open."

"I see. Are you through yet? Sounds like the show is getting ready to start. Did you tell Trae we said thanks?" She was holding the door open for Tasha, who was brushing her hair.

"I told him. I'll call you tomorrow. Love you."

Jaz smiled as Tash gave her a hug and zoomed out the bathroom.

"I thought I was going to have to come and get you." Trae stood up as she slid into the booth.

"I ran into Jaz," she said.

"They straight?"

"Yeah, she told me to tell you thanks for the tickets." She snuggled up under him, resting her head on his shoulder.

"You know I won our bet, right?"

"What was that?"

"You heard me. Make you come within twenty-four hours. Remember that? It's done, Tash." She didn't say anything. "I'm just asking for a chance. Can't you at least give me that?" he asked, staring at her.

"A deal's a deal," she said, cutting her eyes at the stage. The show was about to start. The comedian Adele Givens was just finishing her routine. She had everybody laughing till it hurt except for Tasha and Trae. They were trying to connect.

Musiq Soulchild was up next. Trae lit a blunt, took a few drags then put it out. He noticed how quiet Tasha was. He looked at her and said, "I don't know why you're scared. Faheem done already threatened me. He said that if I don't put you on top of the world he was going to put a cap in my ass. I told him that's exactly what I was planning on doing. You heard me?"

"I heard you," she said.

Musiq laid it down. The entire club was really feeling him. Everybody was all hugged up. The crowd gave him a standing ovation and was calling for an encore. Tash asked to be excused and headed for the ladies' room again. The club was now well lit as the stage was being set up for Jill Scott.

As she headed back toward the booth, she noticed three females standing in front of Trae. She had no idea what this was all about. When she came up on them, she looked at them and at Trae, who proceeded to grab her by the waist, pulling her onto his lap.

"This is Monique and her crew. You know, the caller you refused to deliver my message to," he reminded her.

Monique and Tasha looked each other up and down. Then Monique said to her friends, "C'mon y'all, that bitch ain't nobody. She's just the flavor of the month."

"Bitch!" Tasha yelled.

"Who you callin' a bitch? Ho!"

"Ah, shit," Trae mumbled. Tash went to jump up, but Trae locked his arm around her waist. "Tash!" Trae hollered. "Fuck her! She ain't nobody."

Monique turned around and said, "Yeah I said it, bitch. You just the flavor of the month. You ain't nobody."

Tasha tried to get up again, but Trae wouldn't let her.

"Bitch, you're the fuckin' nobody!" Tasha yelled. "You was the one calling and begging for him to take you to this show. Bitch, you wish you was me. It's me who he brought to the show. It's me who is sitting right here on his dick. I'm the bitch who answered the phone in his crib when you called and he put your dumb ass on speakerphone. So obviously you're the nobody. If you was somebody you would have hung up on his ass."

"Tasha!" Trae yelled. She ignored him.

"While you was sitting there on the damn speakerphone, who was he begging to spend the night? Me, ho! I'm Tasha, the same bitch that's sitting right here on his dick, wearing a three-thousand-dollar dress and a fuckin' diamond on my tongue that he bought. My shoes cost more than all of y'all outfits put together. Who am I? Tasha, the bitch that you say is the flavor of the month. You need to take lessons from this ho, bitch, because it's all about me. You better recognize. And on a final note—I didn't even give up no pussy."

On that note, Trae spit out a mouthful of water he had just drunk. He loosened his grip, and Tasha jumped up. She tried to lunge at Monique, but Trae got behind her. He grabbed her by the waist, lifted her up into the air, and took her back to the booth.

"Let me go Trae !" she yelled, trying to break free.

"Yeah, let her go Trae," screamed Monique.

"Get the fuck away from here!" he yelled at Monique.

Spectators were standing around enjoying the action.

"Trae let me go!" Tasha said through clenched teeth.

"Tash!" he said, putting his hand under her dress, "Did you forget that you ain't got nothing on under this short-ass dress? It ain't that serious, ma. Why you wildin'?"

"Why was she over here in your face Trae?"

"Trying to start some shit. Fuck her Tasha. She ain't nobody. You sure is pissed the fuck off for somebody who ain't feelin' a nigga."

"Take me home Trae. I'm ready to go." Without letting her

go, he reached over, grabbing her purse and his jacket. By this time security had already come over, just walking around and combing the area.

They walked to the front in silence. He gave the valet his ticket and waited for them to bring the Nav around. He lifted Tasha into the passenger seat before getting in on the driver's side. She was looking out the window while Trae made calls on his cell phone. As soon as he set it down it rang again.

"What up?" he answered. "No shit! I'm on my way to the crib to change. Give me a couple of hours." Then after a bit of silence he said, "I don't give a fuck if it's five in the morning. Have that nigga there when I get there!" Trae hung up the phone, then turned it off.

They hadn't exchanged words during the entire ride to Trae's apartment. As he drove around looking for a parking space, he told her he needed to change clothes before taking her home. He found a spot in the rear of the lot and got out to help her out of the car. When he opened the door, she just sat there.

"Are you getting out or what?" She didn't answer. He reached over and turned her around to face him. He grabbed both of her legs and, wrapping them around his waist, put both of his hands on her butt and pulled her up close to him.

"I don't know why you let that bullshit get you all worked up like this. Like you said, it's all about you. So act like it," he commanded while caressing her butt and squeezing it.

She remained with her arms folded across her chest and wasn't saying anything. He started kissing her chin and took the kisses all the way down to her breasts. Not wanting to let her butt go, he used his teeth to slide the cut of the dress over her breasts to expose them. He felt her wrap her legs tighter around his back as he used his tongue ring to play with her nipples. When she began to breathe heavily, he laid her back across the seat, grabbed her legs and put her feet up on the seat. He leaned over and began sucking and kissing on the inside of her thighs. That made her skin tingle. She was now sighing and moaning as he ran his tongue ring up and down the inside of her inner lips. Then he started licking and sucking on her clit.

Tash was going crazy, but he stopped stimulating her clit as he went back to teasing all up and down her inner thighs. "Don't stop Trae!" she begged, grabbing his head and pulling it back up toward her clit. He then slid his tongue ring over her clit, circling it over and over, then up and down the middle of the opening of her pussy.

"Oh, God!" she kept hollering. He zoned back in on her clit and she grabbed his head tighter, rotating her hips. He went back to kissing and sucking on her thighs.

"Trae!" she yelled, trying to pull his head up toward her pussy, "don't stop. I was getting ready to cum." She was trembling and biting down on her lip as Trae kept teasing her to make the orgasm very intense. She was breathing hard and still had both hands on his head, even though she was trying to sit up.

"Trae baby, why'd you stop? Make me cum Trae," she said, trying to push his head back down. He resisted and went back to using his tongue ring on her nipples, "Trae are you listening to me?"

He grabbed her butt and pulled her up close to him. She raked her nails lightly up and down his back while kissing him and playing with his lips and tongue. He was playing around in her wetness with his fingers. He pressed on her clit, making fast, circular motions. She was gyrating her hips, and was on the verge of exploding when he removed his hand and went back to sucking her nipples. She dug her nails deep into his back.

"Ahhh, damn, Tash," he complained, "the nails, baby."

"Then finish what you started. Make me cum." She was moaning and shaking, but didn't lift up the nails. He sunk his teeth in the flesh right above her breast. She shivered and let go of his back.

"Mmmm. You like it rough, huh?" Trae whispered in her ear.

"Fuck me Trae," she groaned. "Let's fuck."

"Ma, do I hear you begging?" He smiled and grabbed one of

her legs, putting one leg up in the seat and the other around his waist as Tasha squeezed his dick, stroking it with both hands.

"That feels good ma," he said, kissing on her neck. She leaned back so that he could put it in. In one stroke, he rammed it all the way in until it could go no further, pressing deep and just holding it in. They both remained still, just holding each other, savoring their first encounter.

"Trae baby, this feels so good. Promise me you'll never leave me," she said, holding him tighter.

"Baby, I'll never leave you. I promise. I've waited a long time for you." His knees were getting weak as he tried to avoid cumming. "Damn, Tash, you feel so good," he moaned. He held it in deep while she gyrated her hips, riding his dick until her legs went to shaking. She was calling his name over and over as she collapsed on the seat.

Just then a car came around. Trae waited for it to pass by before pulling Tash up. He told her how good she felt and sucked on her lips and tongue until she became excited again.

"Turn around," he told her. "I ain't through." He leaned her over and entered her from the back, lifting her up with each stroke. Tash's legs were so weak he had to hold her up. Her entire body was trembling. He reached around to play with her clit while grinding even harder. Her legs went to shaking extra hard as she came. Then when Trae started cumming hard and long he collapsed on top of her.

"God, that felt so good," Tasha moaned.

"I can't wait to be able to wake up every morning and hit this," he whispered into her ear.

"Is that your plan?"

"Yes, it is," he said, easing up off of her and fixing his clothes. He helped Tash up and out of the car, straightening her dress for her.

"We really did mess the dress up this time, baby," he said as he opened the back door, got his jacket and put it on her. She smiled as she wiped around his mouth, telling him how good he handled his business. He closed both doors and headed for the building. They kissed during the entire elevator ride.

As soon as they got into his apartment, Tash kicked off her shoes. "Trae baby, I gotta take this dress off. I need something to throw on and I need to take a quick shower."

He hollered from the pantry, "Look in the tall dresser and get a pair of sweats or shorts and a T-shirt."

When he came in the bedroom to see if she found something to put on, she was pulling her dress over her head, revealing that beautiful, brown, naked body.

"Oh, shit!" Trae said, grabbing his dick. "Damn baby, do you realize this is the first time I'm seeing you naked?"

"No."

"Well it is!" She noticed that he had a rag and a bottle in his hand. "What are you doing?"

He dropped the rag and bottle of leather cleaner on the floor and went over to her. "I was gonna clean out the car until I saw you standing in my bedroom naked. Come here." She walked over to him, and he laid her down on the bed. "You came all over my seats," he said, kissing her on the stomach.

"Where was I supposed to cum Trae?"

"Anywhere you want to Tasha. It's all about you. And don't ever forget that. You can come on my seats, my face, any fuckin' where you want, ma."

He was now kissing her thighs. "Trae baby, I thought you was supposed to be somewhere in an hour or two?" He ignored her as he fingered her and licked her clit.

"Baby, that feels good," she moaned, gyrating her hips and arching her back. Shortly after, she was cumming again. Trae took off his clothes, climbed between her thighs, and penetrated her, grinding slowly.

"Baby, I can't believe how good you feel. Can you cum for me one more time? One more time, baby, cum for daddy."

Her legs started shaking, she started hollering, and they both climaxed again.

Chapter 4

"Ladies, it is 12:15 a.m. Why are y'all callin' me so late?" Roz asked. She was on three-way with Jaz, Angel, and Kyra.

"You got company?" That was smart-ass Jaz.

"No!"

"Well, talk to us, then," Kyra said. "We're being nosy. We heard that our girl is in love. Plus, Jaz said you let that nigga Trae hit it. Did you?"

Roz started laughing. "How do you know, Miss Jaz? Did I tell you that?"

"Stop playing Miss Tasha. You stayed out two nights in a row until dawn. I know y'all wasn't holding hands," Jaz said. "So tell us. How was he? Did he lay it down, or what?"

"Umm, most definitely!" Roz said, smiling and squeezing her pillow. "He made me lose any feelings I had left for Nikayah. And I don't even feel guilty."

"That's what I'm talkin' 'bout!" Kyra hollered.

"When will I get to meet him?" Angel asked. "I'm sick of hearing about this mystery man."

"He's coming to my graduation. You'll meet him then."

"Sounds like it's on!" Kyra said.

"Most definitely. Hold on. Someone is trying to get through." Roz clicked over. "Hello?"

"Tash, you up?"

"I'm up. Who is this?"

"It's Trae. You know who it is."

"I forgot your voice. I haven't heard from you in three or four days," she teased. "Thanks for the roses."

"Come outside. I'm parked out front. And bring me a set of your house keys."

"I'm in bed, Trae. Why can't you come up?"

"You gotta come down and unlock the door. Just come out to the car. Throw a robe or somethin' on," he said before hanging up quickly. She clicked back over to her friends. "Speak of the mystery man, ladies. I gotta go. See ya!" She hung up without waiting for a response.

She grabbed her robe, slippers, and a spare set of house keys from the kitchen. When she opened the front door, a brother with a NY baseball cap, jersey and some jeans was sitting on the porch.

"What's up, Tasha? I'm Kay. Trae is in that Rover," he said, pointing to his right. Just then the door on the passenger side to the burgundy-colored Range Rover opened up.

"What up, ma?" Trae grinned, motioning for her to come to him.

Kay stood up, pointed to his watch, and said, "Ten minutes, dawg." Then he laughed and said quietly, "We got almost two hundred kilos of dope on us and this nigga got to stop and get some pussy."

Trae ignored him, pulled Tash up into the Rover, and locked the door. No one could see them behind the tinted windows.

"Trae I can't believe you have me out here practically naked," she said, handing him the extra set of keys. "The gold one is for the front door and the red one is for my door." He put them in his back pocket and pushed the button that slid the seat back.

"You cold?" he asked.

"I'm okay."

He helped her straddle his lap. "You got on panties?" he asked, pulling up her negligee.

"No, I don't. Oh, so this is a booty call?"

"Pretty much. We got about seven minutes."

Trae smiled and unzipped his jeans. He lifted her up and then closed his eyes as he grabbed her butt and slid inside of her. She moaned in ecstasy as he held her still while he sucked her lips and tongue. "So much for foreplay, huh?" she moaned as she wiggled to get him to go deeper.

"I got you the next time ma."

He reclined the seat back down as far as it could go and began getting his grind on. As he went in even deeper, Tasha shivered.

"Trae baby, right there, just like that." Trae kept hitting her spot until her legs went to shaking as she came. Grabbing her butt, he then put the seat up a little, pushed her legs back and went in as deep as he could, hitting it until he exploded.

"Yo, Trae, let's roll, man," Kay hollered, knocking on the car door.

Trae ignored him. "Damn, you feel good," he said, hugging and squeezing her. They kissed passionately as he enjoyed her wetness. "I gotta go, ma," he said, sucking on her neck and sliding her off. He pulled down her negligee and fixed his clothes. Then he handed her two envelopes with money in them and opened the door to let her out. She kissed him on the lips and told him to be careful. He watched her go inside, then jumped in the front, and they sped off.

Roz had only two days to study for her first state exam. She was scheduled to take the respiratory therapy exam on Friday and physical therapy the following Monday. The pressure was on, but that didn't stop her from making plans with Angel, Tori and Sanette. They were going clubbing in Philly, and she was looking forward to it.

It took Roz a little over two hours to finish her exam. She couldn't wait to get home and unwind. After turning in her test materials she skipped out of the building to her car reminding herself, *one more to go.*

Angel called at 9:30 to say that they were on their way. So Roz sat on the couch and smoked a joint to the music of *100% Ginuwine.*

Angel was hanging out with two of her classmates, Tori and Sanette. Sanette just got a new Jeep as a graduation present. So, of course, she wanted to drive. When Roz heard the horn, she grabbed her keys and ran out the door.

"What's up, ladies?" Roz said, jumping in the backseat with Angel.

"TGIF!" yelled Sanette.

"It's about time," Roz added.

"Sho' you're right," Tori yelled.

"What's up with you?" Angel asked her girl.

"I'm so fuckin' tense. I still have one more exam to take and I haven't worked out all week. It seems like all I've been doing all week is studying," said Roz.

"It's almost over, my sista," Angel assured her.

They smoked a bag of weed on the way to Philly, with Sanette promising to kill anybody who put reefer burns on the seats of her new ride.

"Which club are we going to?" inquired Roz.

"The hottest club in Philly, baby. You didn't know? It's a new underground spot called Infinity where nothin' but ballers and shot callers hang," Sanette said.

"See what I mean?" Roz whispered to Angel, referring to their conversation at the baby shower. "Why do we have to hang out where the ballers are?"

Angel burst out laughing.

"What's so funny?" Tori asked.

"Just a private joke," Angel said.

When they neared the club, they were all checking out the double-parked cars and the people hanging outside. Roz tapped Angel on the leg. "Ow, girl!" Angel yelped. "What's the matter with you?"

"No, I did not just see Trae's Navigator!"

"Where?" Angel asked.

"We just passed it. Ain't this some shit!" she spat. "I'm home waiting on his ass, and he's out clubbing."

"Why are you trippin'? You are once again the wife of a hustla. You knew what you was getting into." Angel reminded her. "And you are not sitting at home."

"Yeah. And now I see that I made a big fucking mistake!" Roz snapped.

"What's the matter?" Tori asked, turning around to look at them.

"Looks like it's gonna be some drama," Angel sighed.

"Don't leave no junk, ashes, nothing in my car," Sanette warned, pulling into a parking space.

The club was huge and not too crowded. They all headed straight for the ladies' room. Everyone was clamoring for a spot in the mirror. The four of them were putting on perfume and brushing their teeth, trying to get rid of the weed smell.

Roz was brushing her hair and cursing out Trae. "Angel, I swear, if I catch him with another bitch, I am going to kick his ass all over this club. I warned him not to fuck with me."

"Aren't we jumping to conclusions rather quickly? You said that he was good to you. 'Trae this. Trae that.' Check things out first, before you go postal and fuck up my night out on the town."

"Trae?" asked the girl standing next to Angel. She and her girlfriend were snorting coke.

"Yeah, you know him?" Angel asked, trying to sound naive.

"Of course, I do, if it's the Trae from New York who keeps his hair braided and has some good dick."

"Yeah, that's who I'm talking about." Roz was looking the chicks up and down, not believing what she was hearing.

She and her girlfriend started laughing. "Take a number, girl-friend. I will be the first one suckin' his dick tonight. You ain't know?" she said as she high-fived her girlfriend.

"Him and his crew sometimes come here on Fridays. This is the only night I come. Y'all from here or Jersey?"

"Jersey," Angel said.

Roz was getting angrier by the minute as she put on her straw-berry lip gloss.

"I'm Tina," said the one doing all the talking, "and this is Lo-Lo. Ladies, it is money all up in this bitch every Friday. C'mon, Lo-Lo, it's time to work!" They left out.

"C'mon, Angel, I gotta see what's going down. All the clubs they got in Philly and we end up picking this one. Go figure!" Roz said, grabbing Angel's arm.

Sanette and Tori were still in the mirror. "Get four seats at the bar!" hollered Sanette. "Them niggas better start sending drinks over as soon as my ass hit the stool."

The deejay was pumpin' *I Like Dem Girls* by Tyrese. They were only able to find three empty seats together, so Roz chose to stand. She wanted to scan the room for Trae.

"I don't see him, but I know he's here. I'm sure if we find those two females who were in the bathroom they'll lead us to where the action is," said Roz.

"You sound like a fuckin' detective!" Angel teased, swirling around on the bar stool.

"Mmm hmm, I know his car," Roz continued.

"You see him?" Angel was looking in the same direction as Roz.

"Yup! See that skinny girl with the red dress? She's standing next to the dude with the khakis and brown sweatshirt."

Angel was scanning her eyes over the crowd. She finally said, "Yeah, I see them."

"Well, look at the table with the five dudes," Roz said, turning her back.

"Oooh, Papi! Muy guapo! Muy guapo!" Angel said.

"Angel, puhleeze!"

"Puhleeze, nothing. I'm single, sexy, and free. I can't help it if all of them look good. Which one is my future brother-in-law?"

"The one with the braids." Roz really didn't want to see anything. So she turned around and faced the bar.

"Roz, three of them have braids."

"The finest one."

Angel looked closer. "Dayum! The brother with the navy blue jersey?"

Roz nodded. "That's the brother who got me in a frenzy."

"He's cute," said Angel. "Look at those lips."

"What's he doing?"

"Looks like he's rolling a blunt. You're not going to go over there? I want to meet the brotha rocking the doo-rag."

"Hell no! I'm not goin' over there. I'ma sit and watch. I gotta see if all that shit he is always talking 'bout it bein' all about me is for real."

"You know you trippin', right? But we're getting ready to know for sure because it looks like our dick-suckin' friends are approaching."

Roz turned her head around to see for herself. "Damn! They are on a mission, aren't they?" Roz turned back around, trying to watch the action through the mirror over the bar. "What's the four-one-one?" she asked. "I can't see all the way over there in this mirror."

"My sista, how much am I getting paid to play private investigator?"

"Angel, stop playing. What's happening?"

"Well, right this minute, the one named Lo-Lo is sitting on one of their laps. She better be glad it's not the one with the doo-rag. I would have to go over there my damn self."

"That's Kay," said Roz.

"You know him?"

"No. Just seen him with Trae. What's up?"

"Introduce me."

"I will. What's going on?" Roz prodded.

"Tina is standing there. But I can't tell who she's talking to because they're all looking at her," Angel reported.

"Even Trae?" Roz asked nervously.

"Yup. And now he's firing up his blunt."

"I swear, if she goes near him, I'm gonna go over there and dig my nails deep into his face until I draw blood. Watch me. Here, hold my bag." She slid her Chanel bag to Angel. "He won't be cute no more. What's he doing?"

"You are sick," Angel said, shaking her head. "Blowing smoke rings. Looks like Tina scored. She's sitting on Trae's lap."

"What!" yelled Roz, turning around.

"Psych! I'm only playing," Angel giggled. "She landed the brotha with the white T-shirt. He's cute too. So what now, Miss Fatal Attraction?"

"What's he doing?" asked Roz.

"Picking up his cell phone and looking at me look at him."

"Stop looking!"

"Too late, dawg!"

"What's that supposed to mean?" Roz asked.

"He saw you."

"Angel, don't play."

"I'm serious." Angel was laughing. "He's talking on the phone and looking straight at you."

"Shit!"

"Dayum, it's gettin' even better. He's getting up and walking this way." She was still laughing.

"It's not funny," said Roz, who could now see Trae coming towards her in the mirror.

He stepped up behind her, grabbed both of her hands, outstretched her arms, and laid her palms flat on the sides of the bar counter. He then placed his hands on top of hers and began kissing her neck. "What up, ma? What are you doin' here?"

"What are *you* doin' here?" she asked, enjoying the feel of his lips on her neck while watching him in the mirror.

"Movin' dope. You know what I do. Now answer my question."

"I came to party and to relieve some stress. I know I can do that," she said.

"You can party with me. I'll relieve your stress," he said in between kisses on her neck.

"I need relief tonight Trae."

"I want you to go home. This ain't no place for you," he said, looking at her in the mirror.

"Why can't I hang out here? Because you're here?" she protested.

"No. Because it's hot and shit always be jumpin' off. This is a death trap and *I* said you don't need to be here, a'ight? Plus, look at you. Why are you dressin' like you ain't got no man?" He was now caressing her breasts. "You ain't got on no bra." Then he slid his hands down on her butt. "Wearin' these tight-ass jeans, and got the nerve to have an attitude. I should be the one with the attitude."

"I don't have an attitude. Not anymore."

"Well turn around and show me then."

She turned around, wrapped her arms around his neck and kissed him lightly with her strawberry-flavored lips. She closed her eyes as he sucked on her lips and pulled her close. She pressed up against him to feel his hard-on and tried to slide her tongue down his throat. They stayed hugged up until somebody yelled, "Trae!"

"Dayum! Who is that?" Tori nudged Angel.

"That's her nigga. His name's Trae."

"Where did you park?" Trae asked her.

"I didn't. Me and Angel rode with some friends." She still had her arms around his neck, not wanting to turn him loose. "I miss you."

After he thought about it, he said, "Stay right here." He went back to the table where he had been sitting.

"Well, well, well," Angel said. "Girlfriend, your ass is sprung!

That nigga is smooth. You went from clawing his face to freakin'
him down. These bitches in here was all up in yours. Trae is obviously on the most wanted list. We're gonna have to kick some
ass before the night is over."

"No, we're not, because we're leaving," Roz told her.

"Leaving? You got me fucked up! We just got here! Why are
we leaving?" Angel snapped.

"Trae didn't come right out and say it, but I don't think we
want to be here," Roz said.

"Damn! Fuckin' dealers just gonna move the partygoers out.
They need to conduct their business at home or somewhere else.
You don't have to worry about me hanging out with you any-
more."

"I don't know why you hatin'. Your friends are the ones who
picked this place. I didn't know my nigga was going to be here,"
Roz argued.

Angel was pissed off until she saw the brotha wearing the doo-
rag walking behind Trae. When he stopped to talk to someone
she said, "Introduce me, bitch."

Trae came back over. "You ready?" He looked at Angel and
then back at Tash. "What's your friend's name?"

"Angel. Angel this is Trae. Trae, Angel. She wants to meet
your boy Kay." They exchanged greetings.

"This is lawyer girl, right?" Trae asked. Tasha nodded in agree-
ment.

"Yo, Kay!" he yelled. Kay came over and was already checking
Angel out. He threw the keys to the Nav to Trae. "Kay this is
Angel. Angel this is Kay. Come with me to take them to the car."

When they got outside, they helped the ladies inside the Nav.
Trae was standing against the door on the driver's side talking to
Tasha while Angel was watching out the side view mirror as Kay
took some items out of the back and put them in the Benz
parked behind them.

"Damn! That nigga is fine!" Angel said, gazing at him. "Girl, he is even bowlegged!" Tasha ignored her as she was busy talking to Trae.

Kay was now talking on his cell phone. When he started laughing, Angel practically lost it. "Oh no, this nigga don't have dimples!" she yelled. "His appearance is too perfect. Something has to be wrong." As soon as he closed up his cell phone, Angel stuck her head out of the window and said, "Let me holla at you, playa!"

He came up to the window smiling, "What up, beautiful?"

"Right now? You. And those dimples."

"Oh really?"

"Mmm hmm. What does the K stand for?"

"Kaylin."

"Kaylin," she repeated. "I like that."

"Your man let you hang out this time of night? Why hasn't he clipped this Angel's wings?"

"What are you trying to say?"

"I'm saying if you was my Angel you'd be home."

"Home?"

"Home waiting on me."

Angel laughed. "I'm sure you really do have somebody home waiting on you."

"Actually, I don't."

"Nigga, please. Fine as you are? If she's not at your home then where is she?"

"Nah. I'm not into nothing serious right now."

"So that means I could get me a kiss right now and a bitch won't come running out the club screaming and wanting to kick my ass?"

Kay blushed. He was checking out her skin, hair, teeth, and nails. "Nah, ain't nobody serious right now."

"Well, come here let me kiss you."

He leaned over and kissed her neck inhaling her scent at the same time. "You eat swine?"

"What? I have to be interviewed to get a kiss?" She was now

kissing his neck and inhaling his scent. "And, no, I don't eat pork. I don't even eat chicken. Fish only." She grabbed his head and ran her tongue over his lips and kissed him.

"Mmmm," she moaned. "I want you to have my babies."

"Do you?" He said in between the kiss.

"Mmm. Hmm." She was totally turned on.

"I thought I was suppose to be saying that."

"I beat you to it, didn't I?"

"Yeah. You did." He grinned.

She broke the kiss, gently poked in one of his dimples. "I just didn't want you to forget me."

"Now why would I do that?"

"Give me another kiss and *maybe* I'll answer that for you."

"Oh. It's like that?" He leaned in still blushing and began nibbling on her lips and kissing them lightly. She placed her hand on his shoulder and pulled him closer.

"Time to go, Angel," said Tasha.

She unlocked lips with Kay and said to him, "I want to see you again."

He flipped open his cell phone, pushed the memory button, and gave her the phone. "Put in your number," he said. She did and passed it back. He leaned over and kissed her again not stopping until Trae was standing next to him.

Angel and Kay continued to gaze and smile at each other as the Navigator pulled off. "Motherfuck! There oughta be a law against a nigga being that fine and that sweet."

"You a ho!" Tasha teased.

"Say what you want. That nigga can carry my babies. He can even have my last name!" she joked. "I'll bend a few rules for him."

"I see," Tasha said, with a look of surprise.

"Psych!"

"Yeah, right, ho! I think you're serious."

Roz dropped Angel off and cruised home in the Nav. When she got inside the house she decided to check her messages since she hadn't done so in three days. One was from Kyra. The dry cleaners also left a message. She had been so busy she hadn't picked up her clothes in almost three weeks. Then there was another message from Kyra. The second floor tenant also had some flimsy excuse for not paying the rent, and then there was Angel confirming Friday night's clubbin' plans.

The last one said, "What up, Tash? This is Case, and Trae wanted me to tell you that he misses you. And if you want to know how much, listen to this." Then he started singing his joint *I'm Missing You.* Roz wanted to scream, but instead just collapsed on the bed with the phone glued to her ear. She erased all of the other messages and played it again and again. Even though it was almost 1:30 in the morning, she called Kyra, Angel and Jaz and put them on three-way. Jaz was the only one who was asleep and, of course, she cussed Roz out for interrupting.

"What is it?" Angel asked.

"Y'all gotta hear this!" She punched in her password to play the message.

"I don't fuckin believe this!" Kyra said after it was over. "That shit is off the heezie!"

"He sounds oh so good!" Angel sang.

"That's the shit! No, he didn't hook you up like that," Jaz said, sounding wide awake now.

"Oh, yes he did!" Roz smiled.

"Case can wake me up anytime," Jaz moaned, looking over at Faheem to make sure he hadn't heard that.

"That nigga better not call here singing shit to my wife! His ass will come up missing!" Faheem grunted. Jaz playfully hit him with the pillow.

"So I guess you've decided to keep him," Kyra probed. "You might as well. From what I hear he got you wide open."

"As I keep telling y'all, I am crazy about him. But I don't want to get too attached then, in a heartbeat, he's gone either to jail or he ends up in a coffin. I'm spooked by that thought ladies. I'm tired. Can I go to bed now?"

"If you give me a copy of Case live, yes, you can. You know you owe me," Angel said.

"No, I don't. I introduced you to Kay, remember? So we're even."

"Roz!" she snapped

"A'ight! A'ight! I'll hook you up. Peace out, ladies."

Chapter 5

Angel woke Roz up at about 8:30 the next morning. "Why aren't you up yet?"

"Angel, it's Saturday," Roz said, yawning. "Can't I sleep late? Why are you up so early?" she asked.

"The news, Roz, the news. You heard from Trae?"

Roz sat up. "No. Why?"

"There was a shootout at that same club. Four killed, nine injured."

"Oh, God. Angel please tell me you're joking." Her voice was shaking.

"You know I wouldn't joke about something like this."

Roz was now standing up and pacing back and forth. "Let me try and reach Trae on his cell. I'll call you later."

There was no answer when she dialed Trae's cell, so she paged him then called Angel back. "He didn't answer his cell phone so I paged him. Did Kay give you his number?"

"No, I gave him mine."

"Oh Shit. Shit. Shit!"

By 1:00 that afternoon Roz still hadn't heard anything. She called hospitals and several police stations and still found out nothing. Agitated and restless, she again called Angel. "Come pick me up. I gotta get out of this house. How soon can you get here?"

"I'm on my way," said Angel, who then hung up the phone.

They ended up in Kyra's living room. Angel and Kyra got comfortable while Roz, pacing back and forth, vented: "I can't believe this! See what I mean . . . the stress that comes with fuckin' with somebody like Trae? It's Nikayah all over again. I've called everywhere. I missed my hair appointment, and I'm supposed to be studying for Monday's exam. My whole day is shot. I can't even think straight. I can't do this shit no more! I knew I should have stuck with my plan of not even fuckin' with this nigga." She started crying. Angel got up to get her some tissues.

"Thanks," she said. Suddenly she burst out laughing, "I can't believe I allowed myself to get caught up like this, crying like some weak ho. This is what the fuck I get!"

"You could be jumping to conclusions," said Kyra. "The nigga could be fine. Just got the pager and cell phone turned off. You know how they do."

"If he is fine," she said, sniffling, "I'ma tell his ass to step. It's over!"

"Yeah, right!" Angel said. "Look at you. All cryin' and shit. I peeped how into each other y'all are. You can't just walk away from shit like that."

"Watch me."

"Your emotions are talkin' right now, not you." Kyra said.

"Watch me."

Kyra fried some fresh whiting, baked some potatoes, and prepared a tossed salad. They didn't get the kitchen cleaned up until about 7:00. Just then Roz's cell phone rang. It was Trae.

"What up Tash? I just saw your page. I called the house first. Where are you? You a'ight?"

She got up off the sofa and went into the dining room to talk in private. "No, I'm not alright Trae," she cried.

"Why you cryin', ma?"

"Nigga, you could have called me. I know you know what

happened at the club. I called hospitals, the police, paged you and you wouldn't even pick up your damn phone. You could have called me to let me know you was okay. It would have taken you one minute, one fuckin' minute Trae. I can't do this, not again. Bring me my house keys and pick up your car keys. Nigga it's over!" Tasha fumed.

She hung up the phone and went back into the living room with Kyra and Angel.

"So, I take it that was Trae?" Angel inquired.

"Yeah, I told him to bounce."

"You don't mean that shit," Angel said.

"Can you take me home now?" Roz asked, coolly turning off her cell phone.

It was about 11:45 that night when Trae stuck his key into the door. He was carrying a duffel bag, two dozen roses in every color you could imagine, and a teddy bear wearing an I Luv U shirt. Tasha was stretched out on the living room sofa studying. She didn't look up to acknowledge his presence but could still smell the fresh roses.

"Trae your keys are sitting on top of the TV. Get your keys. Leave mine and please leave," she said, her face buried in her book.

He sat the roses on the coffee table and the duffel bag down next to the couch.

"Trae I asked you to leave."

He then took the book and papers out of her lap, lifted her up off the couch, and sat back down with her in his lap. She tried to get up, but his arms gripped her around the waist, and he placed the teddy bear on her lap.

"Ma, I apologize. I'm sorry. Sorry for causin' you to worry about me and for not calling you," he said.

"No more drug dealers for me. It's too much stress worrying about y'all and putting up with ya'll's bullshit," she complained.

"Tash don't compare me with nobody and don't make me pay for the shit Nikayah took you through. I'ma be a'ight."

"Trae you are not fuckin' invincible," she said, tensing up.

"You are not bulletproof and you're definitely not exempt from catching a fucking conspiracy or drug charge. Neither am I—if you want to get technical about it. I'm so fuckin' vexed that I even allowed myself to start feelin' you." She shook her head, "It's over Trae. Let me up." She tried placing the teddy bear on the coffee table to break free from his hold.

"Can't do that Tash. I already told you that I'm never lettin' you go."

"Well, I'm letting you go," she said, still trying to break free.

"You know you don't mean that," he said, holding her tighter.

"Why me Trae? Why don't you go find somebody else to stress the fuck out?"

"There's nobody else I want. I want you and I ain't goin' nowhere. This hustlin' shit is almost over."

She turned around and grabbed his face. The tears were streaming down her cheeks. "Trae will you listen to me?"

"I'm listening."

"I got some issues I need to handle. Me and you, this is too soon. I come with a lot of baggage. Let's stop this before it's too late. You fucked your boy's woman. Now move on. You won. You conquered. Or whatever the fuck ya'll call it."

"Who you been talkin' to? Are you PMSing?" he asked as Tasha tried to get off his lap. "Now, you gonna listen to me. I already told you that you ain't just a fuck or a conquest to me. I caught feelings for you Tasha, and we all come with baggage. And you said, 'stop before it's too late.' We done fucked so it's already too late. I would never let you get caught up in what I do. I put my life on that. Me not callin' you is not a good enough reason for you to give me my walking papers."

"You aren't listening to me," she said, shaking her head and wiping away the tears with the back of her hands.

"I hear what you're saying, but it's all bullshit. No disrespect. You're gonna have to come better than that!"

She started laughing and shaking her head with a look of disgust on her face. "You just refuse to hear what I'm saying." The tears were steadily streaming down her face. "I told you I'm scared. You scare me. Listen to the argument we are having right now. Trae," she pleaded. "Don't take me through this. Okay? Please? What do you want from me Trae?"

"Damn, girl! I want you to give us a chance," he said, getting agitated. "A nigga wants you to let him love you, protect you, and provide for you. Are you gonna let me do that, or what?"

"Why should I Trae?"

He rested his head back and closed his eyes. The room was quiet for a good five minutes, except for Tasha's sniveling.

"Because, like my boy Ja Rule says . . ." Then he started singing, *"What would I be without you? I only think about you. I know you tired of being lonely, but you complete me. And I would die if you ain't wit me. Every thug needs a lady. . . .I'm crazy about you, girl."*

That got her to crack a smile. "You think you are so smooth."

He kissed her. "You got a nigga beggin' and pleadin'. We just can't let our thang go without trying to first work it out, we just gettin' started. Plus, no bitch ever got me to consider turnin' in my playa's card."

"Nigga, ain't no bitches in here."

He slapped her on the butt. "I know that. You know what I mean. It was just a bad figure of speech. You are a queen, and that's how I intend to treat you."

"You just sat here and told me you don't wanna be a playa no more. That's bullshit, playa. You ain't turn in your playa's card. I know that card is very much valid and getting stamped all in between, Trae. I see you every two to four days. Let's talk, one playa to another."

Trae started laughing, "Oh, so this is what this temper tantrum is really all about? You don't see me every day so you assume I'm fuckin' around in between visits, right? Well, you're wrong. I'm workin', Tasha. Trust and believe that. I'm workin'."

"That's not the reason for what you call my 'temper tantrum.'

But let me find out. I'ma take your word and trust you, but if I ever find out you fuckin' around, I'm out and I don't want to hear no excuses. You only got one time."

"A'ight, then, one playa to another, how can a nigga keep his dick hard long enough for you to come three, four times? That shit ain't easy, Tash. You think I can be out there pokin' bitches and gettin' sucked on day and night and then come home to you and you hollerin', 'Trae make me come again! Make me come real hard!' That shit ain't even happenin'. When I start giving some weak shit then you need to start getting suspicious. That's rule #9 in the playa's handbook: I'm not 'sposed to be sharin' this dick with nobody else. I be puttin' it down for you, ma." He grabbed her by her neck, slobbing her down. "Plus you ain't been burnin' or itchin': rule #7."

"Fuck you Trae!"

"Mmmm, I'm looking forward to you doin' just that."

"You really think you the shit, don't you?"

"Tash baby, you think that you can just run your fine ass to a club or somewhere tonight, meet some nigga crazy as fuck about you, the nigga will be paid, he'll want to provide for you, and he'll be able to make you come over and over? Shit ain't happening like that. You lucked up and got the whole package. Trae is the whole motherfuckin' package, Tash. You better recognize and stop tryin'a tell a nigga to bounce."

"Oh, hail King Trae," Tash said laughing. "I can't believe how much shit you talk."

"Trae talks nothing but the truth. You know I ain't lyin'. If the pussy wasn't so good I would have told *your* ass to bounce."

"I can talk shit too Trae. You ain't the real playa up in here."

"Shit! You ain't no playa!" Trae said smiling.

"First of all, I got my own money but I spend yours—rule #4. This is my house, but you and Nikayah been paying the note—rule #6. That 2000 Beamer parked out front, I got the title; it's in my name, but I didn't pay for it. And what year is this? 2000 nigga. Rule #9. I got a good job and cash stashed; I don't have to depend on y'all niggas for shit—rule #3. You know that I got your back and won't fuck around on you. That makes hittin' the pussy even more stupendous.

"You sprung because you can make me come over and over again. You like that shit. It's a male ego thang. Most bitches you been with can't even come or will come maybe once. But Tasha can send those electric currents all through your body over and over as long as your dick stays hard. And last but not least, playa, you dropped a good seven or eight grand on me in one day and hadn't even hit it. I could have been a man for all you knew. And—"

"Nah, ma," Trae interrupted, "I felt it and played all in it so don't even go there. And the droppin' the seven or eight grand don't count cause the money ain't no thang. I just had to make you mine—rule #2."

"Let me finish, playa. I haven't even used my tongue ring on you yet and you already talking 'bout me having your babies. Now who's the true playa, playa? Tasha is the whole mother fuckin' package." They both burst out laughing.

"Aw, shit, playa playa! It's like that, huh?"

"You ain't know? I'm the playa club's president," she said, grabbing her roses and burying her face in them. "These smell so good and fresh." She inhaled and sat them back down. "Thanks for the roses and the Case hookup. Now that was the ultimate playa's move." She picked up the teddy bear and cuddled it.

"A'ight, playa, you ready to get in the shower with me?" Trae asked, running his tongue ring between her lips.

"Can I soap you up?"

"You sure can. Hold on." He stood up, motioned for her to wrap her legs around his back, and carried her off to the shower.

"Okay, time to get out. I know it's at least 2:00. I have to leave at 7:00," Tasha said.

"To go where?"

"To take my exam and then to work."

"I want you to stay here with me."

"I can't. You know I gotta take that state exam."

"You ain't gotta go to work."

"No, I don't *have* to go to work."

"Good. Take some cash out of my pockets and after your exam stop and pick me up something to wear—down to the socks. I don't have shit over here to put on." He turned her loose and turned off the water. He stepped out the shower, wrapped a towel around his waist, before helping Tash out. He then wrapped a towel around her, kissed her and asked, "You a'ight?"

"I'm fine," she grinned. "How about you?"

He whispered in her ear that he was crazy about her while walking her towards the bedroom. Before long they fell asleep in each other's arms.

The alarm buzzed at 5:00, and Tasha reached over and turned it off. When she tried to get up, Trae tightened his arm around her waist, pulling her close. She lay there enjoying his body heat until she felt his grip loosen. She then slid out from under him and showered quickly. As soon as she got dressed she set her roses in some water, took some cash, grabbed the keys to the Navigator and ran out the door.

Chapter 6

Roz didn't think about calling into work until after the exam, which lasted two and a half hours. She contacted her supervisor, Marsha, and apologized for forgetting to call in. Marsha told her that they had already found someone to fill in for her because when they called her house earlier a Mr. Macklin answered the phone saying that she had left to take her exam for the state board and wouldn't be in for the rest of the week.

Roz worked part-time as a physical therapist assistant at the Princeton Medical Center. Once she passed her exam she'd become a full-fledged physical therapist. She'd become interested in the field after living with her grandmother and helping her out. She also had great-aunts who would take her around with them to visit their elderly neighbors in the senior's compound where they lived.

Roz was assigned to taking them for walks, making them stretch, and getting them to use their hands. Her grandmother would say, "You're helping us to live longer." So that became her passion. When she enrolled in college, she majored in physical therapy, choosing respiratory therapy as a minor—just in case. If she got bored working with people, she could sell oxygen and respiratory equipment.

After her exam she stopped at the mall and picked up Sean Jean and Karl Kani outfits, pajamas, socks and boxers for Trae.

Then she swung by the car wash with the Navigator before heading out to Amefika's Restaurant, where she bought two hot vegetarian sandwiches on wheat rolls, a fish and cheese sub, fries, and a bean pie.

Trae had just dozed off when the phone startled him out of his sleep. "Hello," he said, sounding all groggy.

"This is the AT&T operator. I have a collect call from Nicky."

"Nikayah!" he screamed. "Get my shit right."

"Nikayah," she corrected herself. "Will you pay for the call?"

"Yeah," Trae yawned as he sat up.

"Have a good day," the operator said.

When Trae heard a click he said, "What up, nigga?"

"Where is Roz? And who dis?"

"This is Trae, nigga. I know you know my voice. What up?"

"Damn Trae, you couldn't wait until I got a chance to talk to her."

"Nigga, go 'head with that. It's been three, four months? And you ain't talked yet? She said you fucked up big time. It's over, son. You can plead your case till you turn blue in the face. Accept it, man. You ain't got no more pussy over here. You don't even have a reason to call here. You got my cell number."

"Fuck you, man!" Nikayah yelled into the phone.

"Nikayah!" Trae yelled back. He then lowered his voice. "We got unfinished business. Don't let no pussy that is no longer yours cloud your judgment, dawg. She is a queen that was holdin' it down for you. You fucked up; it's over. Move on, you hear me, man?" Trae listened to Nikayah's heavy breathing for several minutes. He knew he was pissed.

"Yeah, I hear you. Is she there? Let me speak to her?"

"Nikayah you said you fuckin' heard me. It's over, man. Now I didn't disrespect you. So don't disrespect me."

"Disrespect?! Nigga, you all up in mines!"

"But it's over, man. It's over and done. When you gettin' out?"

"Should be within the next two weeks. Man, she got at least two abortions. She killed two of my babies." Nikayah couldn't let it go.

"It's over, man. But as far as business is concerned I got you. Make sure you holler as soon as you hit the bricks, a'ight?"

"Whatever, yo!" He slammed the phone down.

By the time Tasha got back to the house it was almost 2:00 P.M. She had to make two trips from the car to the apartment. She set the food bags in the kitchen and took the clothing bags into the bedroom.

She went back to the kitchen to put the sandwiches and fries on a platter, poured him some juice and took it into the bedroom where Trae was sitting up in the bed talking on his cell phone and channel surfing. She set the meal down on the nightstand next to him and said, "It's still hot," before heading to the bathroom to wash her face and hands and brush her teeth and hair.

"What up, playa!" he said when he hung up his cell phone. "How did it go?"

"It went good. Glad it's over."

"Me too. Come here," he said. She climbed on the bed and gave him a kiss. "You wear short skirts every day like this to work?" he asked, reaching up under it and pulling off her panties.

"No, I wear white pants and a white shirt to work. Your food is going to get cold." She handed him the plate, got up and sat on the love seat to watch him eat.

"What? You heard my stomach growling across town?"

"No, I just figured you would like something to eat. Did you get some sleep?"

"What little I could in between your phone ringin' off the hook."

"Sorry 'bout that. I meant to turn off the ringer before I left, but I rushed out and forgot. You didn't have to answer it."

"That's the only way I could get it to stop ringin'. Your job called. I told them you would be out for the rest of the week. You forgot to call them?"

"I sure did. I didn't think about it until after I took my exam. You can't keep me out of work all week," she teased.

"Yes I can. Check it out. Guess who else called?"

"Who? My mom, my brother?"

"Neither. Nikayah. That nigga might be out by the end of next week."

"I don't care when he gets out. Why did you accept his call?" Now she was agitated.

"I told you that's one of my partners. I needed to holla at him."

"What did he say about you answering the phone?"

"What could he say? Y'all ain't fuckin' no more. That nigga know what time it is. We talked a good ten minutes." Trae got up to go brush his teeth. She watched his naked body as he walked by on his way to the bathroom.

When he came out the bathroom he went over to where she was sitting, leaned over and kissed her, pulling and sucking on her tongue. She wrapped her arms around his neck. Then he whispered in her ear, "I don't want no shit between you and Nikayah. If I catch you even talking to him, I'ma put a cap in the both of ya asses."

"Don't be checkin' me. Nigga you need to be checkin' your boy."

"I already did. I also told that nigga don't call here no more, he ain't got no pussy up in here. Anything here belong to him?"

"Nope. I tossed all his shit out months ago."

"What about the Beamer?"

"What about it?

"Whose is it?"

"Trae! That title is in my name. It belongs to me."

"But you giving it back. I'll get you another one or whatever it is you feel like driving."

"I'm not givin' it back Trae. That belongs to me."

"Tash you my woman, right?"

"I like that car Trae," she whined.

"Answer my question. Are you my woman or not?" She shook her head up and down. "Well, then *I'm* givin' the fuckin' car back. Trae's woman ain't gonna be drivin' around in some shit some other nigga bought. You know I ain't goin' out like that."

He palmed her butt. "I told Nikayah that when I'm hittin' it and about to bust a nut I be wantin' to call out his name." He smiled, then yelled, "Thank you Nikayah, for fucking up!"

"That's not funny Trae. What was y'all niggas doin', comparing notes?"

"Nah, ma, it wasn't like that. I told that nigga that he had a queen, somebody that was holdin' it down for him, and he fucked up. He also told me you had two abortions."

"That big mouth! It was one. And I only told him two because I was mad at him."

"Was y'all still together when you got the abortion?"

"No, Trae. I found out I was pregnant after I bounced."

"What would you do if you got pregnant by me?"

"I'm on the pill. I won't be getting pregnant any time soon. I got too much shit to do before I decide to have babies."

"That's not answering my question."

"I would discuss it with you first."

"I would hope so. Oh, your other call was from Jeffrey. He said he'll have his rent money next week."

"I don't even want his money. I want him to move out."

"How come?"

"For starters, he's always cooking swine and the smell makes me sick. Plus he's always late, and now he's two months behind. I'ma just evict him."

"How much does he owe you?"

"Now it's up to eight hundred and fifty dollars."

"Oh! Hell no!" He got up and grabbed his pants. "Which floor does he live on?"

"The second. Why?" She watched him put on his Tims and stick his gat in the back of his waist. "How many niggas live down there?"

"Trae I know you are not going down there," Tash said, jumping off the bed. "He might not be home."

"I'ma find out," he said, throwing on his shirt. "How many?"

"Just him. His girl moved out. Trae please don't go down there." She followed him out of the bedroom.

"I'll be right back."

"Oh, God. Trae please don't go down there."

"I'll be right back."

She slammed the front door, went back to the bedroom and flopped down on the bed. After about fifteen minutes he came back into the bedroom. He threw some money on the dresser and went in the bathroom. He came out drying his hands off and wiping off his gat. "That's seven hundred and ninety. I told him he got until Sunday to get the fuck out." Tash just looked at him as if he was crazy.

"Why you lookin' at me like that?"

"You're crazy Trae."

"Call me what you want. Ain't nobody gonna punk my woman Tasha. What did you expect me to do, just lay here and not say nothin'?" He shook his head and mumbled, "Nigga got me all worked up. Turn my cell phone on for me. I'm expecting a couple of calls." He took off his clothes. "So where we gonna go?" he asked, laying back down on the bed and laying her head across his chest as if nothing happened.

"What do you mean 'where we gonna go'?"

"Away. Leave tomorrow. I'm so fuckin' stressed that if I don't take a break, I'ma fuckin' explode." He ranted.

"Well, you sure are good at concealing it. I see that I got a lot to learn about you."

"And I got a lot to learn about you. So we might as well get it started. Now let's go away."

"If it's going to help you relieve some stress I'm down with it. But I still gotta get ready for my graduation."

"We'll be back by then. Today is Monday. I'll have you back by Friday, no later than Sunday," he said, running his fingers through her hair. "No cell phones, no pagers, just me and you getting to know each other. I gotta make sure I'm not in love with just the pussy. Gotta make sure you're wife material and I gotta see if I can stand to be around you for a few days in a row," he teased.

"Oh, it's like that?"

"Yeah, I know you don't want me to lie."

"That works both ways, playa. I need to make sure I'm not mesmerized with the fact that you can make me come over and over. I gotta see if I can stand waking up next to you a few days in a row. No comment on the husband material."

"Oh, it's like that?"

"Pretty much. I know you don't want me to lie."

"A'ight, then. It's on! Choose between—let's see—St. Thomas, Aruba, LA or South Beach. That Club Amnesia is the spot. We can do some serious clubbin'."

"Hmmm. Clubbin' does sound good. Well, let's cross out St. Thomas and Aruba. And South Beach—just to hit Club Amnesia— I don't think so, playa. It's Cali hands down."

"Bet! We'll leave first thing in the morning. I'll leave you my platinum card so you can make all the arrangements."

"Tomorrow morning? What about the afternoon? Trae, I would like to get my hair, nails, and feet done and then do some shopping."

"You can do all that shit out there. Go to the salons where the celebs go and, as far as shopping, you can hit the real deal. Go straight to Gucci, Chanel, Versace, and Prada. Knock yourself out. We ain't packin' shit, a'ight?"

"If you say so, playa."

"I got you a graduation present."

"Did you? Where is it?" she squealed.

"In that duffel bag I brought in with me."

Tash jumped up and ran to the living room to look for the duffel bag. When she handed it to him she was having a hard time concealing her excitement. He pulled out a long, wide box and handed it to her. The box, tied with a silver bow, had a picture of a graduation cap on it and the word "Congratulations" scrawled all over it. She opened it up and pulled out an iced-up tennis bracelet with her name Tash written in diamonds.

"Trae!"

"Bling, fuckin' bling Tash," he laughed as he saw her eyes light up. "I wish I had a video camera so you could see your face. Is this blingin' or what?" He took it from her. "Let me put it on you. You like it? What's up? You can't talk?"

"I can't believe you did this. Thank you, baby." She grabbed him and kissed him on the lips.

He handed her the duffel bag. "That's your stash for emergencies. Put it away somewhere." She unzipped the duffel bag and ran her fingers over the neatly stacked and wrapped bills.

"Put it away," Trae told her.

She got up and went into the closet where her safe was. Trae turned off the TV and turned up the radio. When she finally came back out, she flopped down next to him. He picked up his cellular phone and looked at it. "Tash, I thought you turned it on for me."

"I thought I did," she said, sitting up.

"I was wondering why it wasn't ringing. I'm expectin' two calls," he said, turning it on. He unbuttoned her blouse then slid it off. Then he leaned over and began teasing her nipples with his tongue as he yanked her skirt and slip off.

"C'mon, ma," he whispered huskily. "Get back on top."

She straddled him then grabbed a pillow and fluffed it out, placing it behind him. "Thank you, baby," he said to her. She was now fondling his dick, squeezing and massaging it until he moaned. Then she put the head to her opening and slid down on it.

"Move slow, ma. Let me watch you move nice and slow. Damn! This feels good," he whispered, closing his eyes. "That's right. Relieve some of daddy's stress."

"Open your eyes! You wanted to watch me so watch me," she reminded him.

His cell phone started ringing. "Fuck!" he mumbled as he picked up.

"Yo nigga! What you doing?" Tasha could hear the sceaming voice, loud and clear.

"Who dis? My woman is ridin' my dick, man. What you think? Why you got to know what I'm doin'? You got one minute to tell me what I want to hear. Go!" Then he turned his attention back to Tash saying, "Tash slow it down, baby."

Trae was talking to the caller and telling Tasha how to fuck at the same time. "Tell that nigga I'll be up that way in a couple of hours," he said to the caller. "Tash slow down. I don't want you to cum yet." Then turning his attention back to the caller he said, "Yo kid, your time's up. I'll holla at you later."

He grabbed her butt and held her still to turn up the radio. "Now go ahead and work it. I'ma watch the show. I won't close my eyes. This is the shit!" he said, turning up the volume some more. "Go ahead and cum while this record is on."

They were grooving to Crazy Town singing, *Come, my lady. Come, come, my lady. You're my butterfly, sugar baby. I make your legs shake. You make me go crazy.*

Tash came while the song was playing. He was cracking up. He reached up and tongue-kissed her, running his tongue over the ice on her tongue. "Ma, I needed a video camera. That shit was tight! You're now my little butterfly. You know what I'ma do?" he asked, slapping her behind. "I'ma buy that CD, and when we get a chance we gonna make us a video. We gonna have some disco lights, and I'ma lay in the middle of the bed. You gonna be on top, and that record is gonna be playin' while you're cumming."

"Trae you done lost your mind. That record is corny," she said still out of breath.

"That shit was tight Tash. You my little butterfly. You know what else I'ma do?"

"What Trae?" she was now putting passion marks on his neck and chest.

"I'ma get you an iced-up butterfly necklace. That shit'll be tight, yo"

"Trae baby, are you goin' to make me cum again or what?"

"See what I'm talkin' 'bout? You betta recognize that you can't get this kinda service from just anybody." He flipped her over, putting one of her legs over his shoulder, and started grinding. "How does this feel?"

"Baby . . . it . . . feels good," she moaned.

Just then the cell phone rang again. "Damn!" Trae blurted.

"Baby, don't answer it." Tasha warned as she slowed down her pace.

He ignored her. "Who dis?" Trae asked, breathing heavily. "I'm trying to bust a nut! He held the phone straight up and yelled out "Can I bust nut? I just need a couple of minutes more! I can't believe this shit! Why? Today is not my day. Everybody wants to know what the fuck Trae's up to." He put the phone near to Tash's mouth. Her eyes were closed, and she was moaning, not realizing she was now on the phone.

"Trae cum with me," she moaned.

He put the phone back to his ear. "You ain't got it like that no more. Give your brother the phone. I don't want to talk to you. Give Kay the fuckin' phone!" he yelled. "Kay, why the fuck you give her this number, man? This is a new number. Ain't but one bitch got it, dawg." Trae's attention was focused on the call, not realizing he had offended Tasha.

She dug into his flesh. "Who you calling a bitch?"

"ARRGHH!" he yelled. "Watch the nails Tash! Tash move your nails!" He warned.

She dug deeper. "Who you callin' a bitch? This is the second time and it better be your last."

"Ah, shit!" He hung up the phone and reached back to pull her nails out. She wouldn't let go. "Tash you fuckin' drawin' blood!" he yelled.

"I know," she said. "There are no bitches in here."

"Oh, it's like that, huh?"

"You ain't know?"

"Okay, then." He grabbed her leg, put it over her shoulder, and started grinding real hard. She started moaning and loosened her grip as he penetrated even deeper. "You like it rough don't you?"

"Trae baby, wait," she said, removing her nails. He then pulled out of her and turned her over to hit it doggy style. He entered her as deep as he could, while massaging her clit. She kept hollering, "Oh, God. Trae!" Her legs started shaking as he picked up the pace, and they exploded together. She bit into her pillow as he placed bite marks on her back, causing her to grit her teeth. As she collapsed on the pillow, he put his arms around her and held her.

"My butterfly," he said laughing. "I can't get that song or you out of my mind. You a'ight?"

"You was wrong for that Trae." She could barely talk.

He was still laughing. "I keep trying to tell you that you ain't runnin' shit."

"Fuck you Trae."

"Ma, you've been doin' that since the night we went to the show, and I've been enjoying every minute of it." He kissed her on the forehead. "I gotta call Kay back. You made me hang up on him," he said as he speed dialed. She snuggled up close to him as he talked to Kay, who he promised to catch in a couple of hours before hanging up.

"You can't stay?" she asked.

"Nah, I won't be able to swing back this way until later. Make sure we leave from Philly airport. We got a good four or five days together. We'll kick it just like we did today, a'ight?"

"Okay." She didn't want him to leave.

"Oh! Let me make one more call." He dialed some numbers. "Yo, Al! What up, man? Yeah, it's me. Listen, I want you to make me a butterfly." Then after a brief silence, he added, "Of course, it's for a female. Not too big, not too little. A necklace. Yeah, ice it up! Bling, fuckin' bling, baby! Bet. Yeah, she liked the bracelet. A'ight, man, I'll holla at you."

Chapter 7

Trae and Roz reclined their first class seats all the way back as the stewardess gave them both a blanket and a pillow. They had so much fun that neither of them wanted the trip to end. They shopped until they dropped. They went to Armani, Versace, Gucci, Chanel, Prada and every other boutique they could hit.

They went swimming, roller skating, and to the gym every morning and clubbing every night. But the thing they enjoyed the most was just kicking it with each other.

Trae brought his video camera, boom box and the Crazy Town CD with "Butterfly." He hooked up some colorful lights and made his video of Tash on top, having an orgasm while *Butterfly* was playing. Tash reluctantly admitted that it came out real cute.

"What up, playa? Why you so quiet?" Trae asked, interrupting her train of thought.

"You're usually the one doing all the talking," she teased.

"But still you're never this quiet. What's up? I know you had fun."

She started laughing. "Yeah, I did. My feet are still sore from them doggone roller skates."

He sat up, grabbed one of her legs, and put it across his lap. He slid her sandal off and began massaging her foot. She closed her eyes. "Oh God, that feels good."

"What's on your mind? We agreed to no holding back, right? What's up?"

She then shared with him the same story about her past that she told Jaz, Kyra, and Angel at the baby shower.

"Damn, Tash," he said, putting one leg down and lifting up the other, "that shit sounds hard to believe."

"Well, believe it."

"You're lucky you're not mentally scarred from that shit."

"I was. But I've learned to move on. I know that the Creator has wiped my slate clean."

"Yeah, that's good. That's the past. You sure came up out of that shit. I love you anyway," he said, kissing her on the forehead.

"You what?"

"I said 'I love you anyway.' "

"Come here," she said. She kissed him on the lips. "I *love* you, too."

Their plane landed a little after noon. They got the Nav loaded up with all of their stuff and headed straight for New York. Trae wanted Tash to meet his parents. They fell in love with her immediately, telling her that Trae needed an educated woman like her to calm him down.

His mom prepared salmon steaks, with baked macaroni and cheese, fresh string beans, tossed salad, and whole wheat rolls.

After visiting his parents, Trae stopped by his apartment to drop off the things he bought for himself, then take Tash home. They unloaded his stuff and left back out. Trae was on his cell phone as they pulled out of his parking lot and so Tash picked up his two-way pager which was vibrating.

"You want me to scroll through them?" she asked. He nodded to her and kept on talking.

She scrolled through them, stopping when she came to a message from Karina that said, "Trae baby, what happened? Call me."

As soon as Trae hung up his cell phone, Tasha pounced on him with, "Trae when was the last time you was with Karina?"

"What?"

"You heard me! When was the last time you fucked with Karina?" She held the pager in his face for him to see the message.

"Why, Tash?"

" 'Why'? What the fuck you mean, 'why'? From this message seems like it wasn't too long ago. And, nigga, you obviously didn't break it off."

"Let it go Tash. I've been with you these last five days. Ain't nothin' up with her."

"What about *before* these last five days?"

"Tash I said let it go. Ain't nothin' up." She reached for her cell phone. "I know you ain't goin' to call her," he said.

"Why ain't I?"

"Because I said you ain't." He reached over to snatch his pager and she smacked his hand away. "C'mon Tasha give me my shit and stop trippin!" He tried to grab it again but she pushed him away.

Tasha started dialing. "Nigga, you got this bitch fucked up. What are you gonna do?"

"If you call her, I'm puttin' you the fuck outta my car. That's what I'm gonna do."

She continued dialing. "Trae you crazy, but you ain't that crazy. Karina is not a very common name. I believe I know this bitch. I can call her if I want to," she said. "At least I know you got good taste," she added sarcastically.

Trae lit a blunt and turned the radio up. Tash reached over and turned it off. Trae looked at her as if he wanted to smack her silly.

"Hello, is this Karina?"

"Who, may I ask, is calling?"

"Karina, this is Roz."

She was quiet. "Roz?"

"We had that boring-ass philosophy class together with Professor Doyle."

Karina started laughing. "I hated that class. What's up, girl?"

"Nothing now. I graduate next week."

"Me, too."

"Listen, I'm calling to find out if you're seeing Trae."

"Straight to the point, still. Why? What's up?"

"Well, not too long ago I started fucking with the nigga, and I ain't putting up with no bullshit. I see your message on his pager so I need to know."

"Roz, if I didn't know you, I would clown your ass for having the audacity to even call my house," said Karina.

"If I didn't know you, I wouldn't be on this phone, I'd be at your front door. So what's up?" Tasha shot back.

"Trae is arrogant and full of shit. He wants to come around when he wants to and expects me to be here waiting on him. I told him he ain't got it like that, I ain't gonna lie. His booty calls are all that, but that's only when *he* decides to come around. Fuck that!"

"In your message, you asked 'what happened.' What's that about?"

"I ran into him a while ago and he said he would holla at me. But he never did. I wanted some dick so I paged him. Nigga ain't even call back."

"That's because he has a wife now and he doesn't have any business fucking around like that."

"Trae is a ho . . . always will be. And he thinks he's the shit."

"Was a ho. His hoing days are officially over," Tasha stated with confidence.

"Oh, you think you can lock him down?" Karina had sarcasm in her voice.

"It's almost done. Just tying up loose ends."

"I ain't mad at you. You got somethin' if you can pull it off, which I doubt. I saw—"

"I'd appreciate it if you didn't page him anymore."

"I can respect that. What's up with that cute brother of yours?"

Tash immediately hung up on her, and sighed. Looking towards Trae she said, "My bad. I apologize for tripping like that, but I needed to be sure." Trae didn't respond. "You heard me?" she asked.

Trae suddenly stopped the car. She could see he was way pissed off. He reached over, unfastened her new bracelet, and put it in the glove compartment, saying, "You don't need to be wearing this on the subway." She didn't say anything as she looked at the subway sign sitting in front of her. "I'll drop your shit at the house," he added, pulling out his knot and giving her three hundred dollars.

"Trae I know you don't expect me to catch a train home on a Sunday," she said with an attitude. "The train from New York to New Jersey runs every hour."

"I told you if you called her you was gettin' the fuck out of my car. What? You thought I was bullshittin'? You should know me better than that. Actually, you got me fucked up!" Then he got out and went around to the passenger side to let her out.

"Trae I am not getting out. I said 'I apologize'." He lifted her out the car and then reached in and grabbed her purse and cell phone. He gave everything to her before jumping back in on the driver's side.

"Trae you are so wrong for this," she said, looking around in embarrassment.

He put the Nav in gear and rolled down the window. "To get to Jersey catch the westbound train. That'll take you straight to Penn Station. Don't fuck with me Tasha. It's all about trust, and next time you're going to do like I tell you."

"Fuck you Trae!" she spat, storming down the subway station stairs. After a couple minutes she called his cell.

"What?" he answered.

"I'm sorry Trae. Please don't do this. Come back and pick me up."

"You in the doghouse. You done pissed me the fuck off. What if she told you some false shit . . . like me and her still fuckin'? Then what?" He yelled. "Then what?"

"Trae I said I was sorry," she pleaded as he hung up on her.

By the time she got home, all of her luggage and bags were already in the living room, Trae having come and gone. After about an hour he called her. "I'm just making sure you made it in safe. I gotta go."

"Wait, Trae. This week everybody graduates. I thought you said you was coming with me."

"I'm still going. I'm only able to make it to yours and Angel's . . . and that's only because Kay wants to go to hers."

"Angel's is tomorrow."

"What time?"

"Nine thirty."

"We'll be there. Have me out something to wear."

"You're not coming over tonight?" she whined.

"Ain't nothin' changed. You still in the doghouse."

"For how long?"

"Until I say so."

"Whatever, Trae," she sucked her teeth and hung up.

The following morning, Trae and Kay came over to shower and dress. Kay brought a change of clothes with him. They left out about 9:30.

Angel showed up with her mother, her brother Mark, and sister Carmen. Kyra and Jaz met them there. When they went to the ladies' room, Tash couldn't wait to tease Angel because she had two niggas there, Kay and Najee, the young attorney.

"Playa, you got two fine, paid niggas here representin'. What's up with that! You gonna slow your roll or what?" Tasha teased.

"I know you ain't hatin'," Angel bragged.

"No, I'm congratulatin'! Handle your business. Najee is fine, and a professional. He's legit, for all we know."

"Right, right." They high-fived. "He has to get back to the office, thank God. What was I gonna do? Pile him and Kaylin in the car and sit in between both of them?"

Tasha laughed. "It ain't easy being a playa. What's up with you and Kay?"

"We're just talking."

"What's up with you and Najee?"

"We're just talking," she said as they walked out the bathroom.

Najee gave her a Gucci bag as a graduation present. Kay gave her a thousand dollars. After the ceremony Angel walked Najee out to his car, then came back inside.

Seeing Najee there made Kay that much more eager to step up his game. He was able to talk Angel into riding back with him, Trae, and Tasha.

The next day was Jaz's graduation. She and Faheem pulled up in a limo. She had two rows of family members present to see her get that degree.

After Jaz's graduation, Tasha left around 11:30 and went straight to work. By the time she got home it was almost 6:30. She plopped down on the couch with a stack of mail, thumbing through the envelopes and the pages of *Savoy* and *Sister to Sister*. Just then the phone rang.

"Hello," she said.

"Tash, come downstairs. I'm out front."

When she got outside, Trae, carrying a box, stepped out of the passenger side of a Ford Explorer. He opened it up, took out the iced-up butterfly necklace, and placed it around her neck, angling the side view mirror so she could see it. "You like it?" he asked.

"Ooh, look at the diamonds. They are so pretty. Thank you, baby. I really am your butterfly."

He looked her over. "You don't look like my butterfly with this uniform on; you look like a square."

"I am a square," she said, fascinated by her new diamond necklace.

"Yeah, right," Trae said, smiling.

"Yo Trae, let's roll!" Kay yelled anxiously. They had a hundred seventy-five kilos of coke on them.

Trae pulled out a business card and handed it to her. "You have to fax them a copy of your driver's license. You should have your car by Thursday."

"My car?" she squealed, jumping up and down.

"You graduate Thursday, right?"

"Yeah."

"I'll be back Thursday morning."

"You can't come back before Thursday?" Her excitement was dwindling.

"I could, but I'm not. I gotta run," Trae said, hopping into the Explorer. Kay then floored the gas pedal, leaving Tash standing on the sidewalk.

Thursday morning around 3:30, Trae came in. He went into the bathroom, came out and grabbed a pillow, and pulled a blanket off the bed. Then he headed for the sofa. Tash followed him into the living room, where he was already sprawled out on the couch with the cover over his head.

"Oh, so it's like this?" she asked, yanking the cover off.

"Yup," he said, yanking it back and covering up again. "What time are we leaving?"

"Eight o'clock."

"Wake me up at seven, playa."

"Come sleep in the bed."

"I'm a'ight. Wake me up around seven."

She stomped back into the bedroom and got in the bed.

They left out the house around 8:30, suited down to the feet in Armani and Gucci. Her brother, Kevin, and sister, Trina, both came to the graduation ceremony. Kevin and Trina had heard about Trae, but never met him.

Angel, Kyra, Jaz, and Faheem, who had to leave as soon as it was over, were at the ceremony and took lots of pictures. Afterwards Trae treated everybody to lunch at Justin's in New York.

When Trae and Tasha pulled up in front of her house, her brand new 2001 Mercedes SUV was parked in front.

"Yes!" she squealed. She looked at Trae, hugged him and bolted out of the Nav. She tried the doors and they were all locked. Trae held up the keys and shook them. She ran back to the Nav and grabbed the keys from him. He watched her as she opened it up, got in and played with all the buttons. She rolled the window down.

"Trae baby, thank you. I love you."

"Take the papers out of the glove compartment and there should be an extra set of keys over the visor. Give me the keys to the Beamer." She took the keys off her key ring and tossed them to him.

"I gotta go," he said. Then he drove off.

Finally, it was Friday and Kyra's graduation. Roz picked up Angel in her brand new Benz. All of Kyra's family showed up, but none of them was prouder than Marvin. Kyra's belly had dropped, and they all laughed as she walked up holding her belly with one hand, degree in the other.

Afterward, Marvin treated everyone to a trip to Atlantic City. Tasha and Angel both had hair appointments in preparation for their graduation party the following night at Kyra's, and so they declined. But Tash also had a personal mission.

While she was getting her feet done, she dialed Trae's cell phone. After about six rings he finally picked it up.

"What?"

"Baby, you sound asleep. Where are you?" she asked.

"Home in my bed. Where do you think I'm at?"

"Just asking."

"I'm tired Tash. Where are you?"

"At the salon."

"Who are you getting fine for?"

"Hopefully, you. I'm ready to beg and plead for your forgiveness. Are you coming over tonight?"

"I wasn't planning on it."

"Wasn't planning on it?" Tasha got indignant. "When do you *plan* on making time for wifey?"

"Wifey is still in the doghouse."

"For how long?"

"Until I let her out." Tasha sucked her teeth and he could picture her neck rolling and anticipated her saying something slick.

"Don't forget tomorrow night is our graduation party."

"I didn't forget. What time you want me to pick you up?"

"Around eight."

"A'ight, I'll be there. Can I go back to sleep now?"

"C'mon, Trae." She wasn't about to give up this easy. "Since you're not coming over tonight, let me meet you somewhere."

"Why?"

"I want to bring you something." When he didn't respond she said, "please?"

He laughed, then thought about it. He was ready to take advantage of the situation. "A'ight, let's do this. We're gonna be at the Diva Lounge in Montclair. I don't want you drivin' up there by yourself. Bring Angel with you."

"Okay. Love you. And thanks again for my ride."

"Oh yeah. Why did you scratch up the Beamer like that? I know you did it."

She didn't say anything.

"Oh, so now your slick-ass mouth is at a loss for words? You ain't right Tasha. I'll talk to you about that. Can a nigga get some sleep?"

"Yes, you can turn off the phone now. I got what I wanted."

"Make sure you bring what *I* want."

"Bye, Trae."

Tasha didn't even have to beg Angel to go with her to the Diva Lounge. Angel was dying to see Kay again. But Tasha—still on her mission—scented her body with Trae's favorite: Escata. She wore a gray skirt and zippered blouse set by Christian Dior, blue crocodile zip shoes with bag to match, and no underwear.

She beeped the horn as she pulled up in front of Angel's. Angel came out wearing all tan: Gucci dress, sandals, and bag. When she got in Tasha's ride they looked each other up and down, smiled, then high-fived each other.

"Let's roll!" Tasha said.

They pulled up in front of the lounge and couldn't find any parking spots. "This is crazy," Tasha said. "I'm not gonna walk a mile just to get in a club."

"Me neither," said Angel. "Fuck that!" She pulled out her cell phone. "*Kaylin*, we're ridin' around in circles looking for a parking space, but can't find one." She smiled at whatever Kay was saying. "Okay," she said. "We're in the Benz."

"What did *Kaylin* say?" Tash asked, emphasizing his name.

"For us to pull up in front of the club and they'll be out. How do I look?" she asked Tasha for a third time.

"Fine, my sista. Why are you teasing that nigga like that?" Tash asked as she put on the strawberry lip gloss, Trae's favorite.

"He invited me, remember? I know I can have some fun but, I can't get serious with Kaylin. Conflict of interest."

"I can't tell." Tasha laughed.

"Roz, I've been celibate for almost thirteen months."

"No shit? Has it really been that long?"

"Yup. I hope it ain't so obvious . . . because every time Kaylin touches me my panties get wet. Every time I hear his voice my panties get wet. Najee is moving slow; Kaylin's not wasting time. I'm not ready to fuck yet, but I want to get fucked. You feel me? All niggas don't know that when a ho wants to get fucked and she's playin' hard to get all he gotta do is know what to say and do the right things and them panties are coming off. All niggas also don't know that a bitch could have a man, she could even be married, but if the pussy is hot and she feeling vulnerable, if the nigga got enough game, says the right words, does the right thangs, those panties are coming off," Angel rambled on.

"And your point is?"

"My point? I don't know what the hell my point is!" They both burst out laughing. "I told you this nigga makes me nervous!"

"Girl, you are silly."

"Nah, but I'll play hard to get. But if he says and does the right things these panties are coming off."

"Angel, he'll turn your ass out. Then what?"

"I don't know," Angel answered sincerely.

"Seriously. Look at me. I reminded Trae that I can get a conspiracy charge for fuckin' with him. And God forbid if he gets smoked or busted. I put myself practically back in the same situation I just got out of. But what can I say? I'm so gone over this nigga, that I'm scaring myself."

"So what are you suggesting, O Wise One?" Angel teased.

"Follow your heart, my child," Tasha teased back, but be careful." Then she turned her attention to the front door. "Oh my God, look at my baby. He is too fine." Trae, Kaylin, and another dude were coming toward them. Trae had on unfastened boots, baggy Phat Farm jeans, a doo-rag, and a ripped sleeveless sweatshirt. Kay wore the same, minus the doo-rag, plus a vest. His chest and arms were flexing those huge muscles. He opened the passenger side of the car and lifted Angel out.

She was grinning from ear to ear as they went on inside the club. Trae and the other dude came on the driver's side. Trae opened up the door. "What up, playa?" he said, lifting her off the seat onto the ground.

"It's all about you," she said, reaching into the car and pulling out a dozen roses for him.

"Smooth, Tasha. Real smooth. One of my moves, but still it's smooth." He sniffed them and smiled at her. "Omar, this is my woman I told you about, Tasha. Tasha this is my cousin Omar. He's gonna park the car. How does it ride?"

"It doesn't ride it sails."

"Good."

They went inside the club, where he walked her to the ladies' room and waited for her to come out. They then went to the bar. "You want something?" he asked her as the waitress looked on.

"I've been craving strawberries. Get me a strawberry daiquiri," she said.

"Make that two virgin strawberry daiquiris."

"Trae they only have a small amount of alcohol."

"No alcohol or tobacco. The less you indulge the healthier you'll be, the longer you'll live, and the longer you'll be able to keep your dick hard."

"I don't have a dick," she joked.

"Don't I know it." He pulled her close to him, smelling her hair and neck. "You smell so good, my little butterfly." Then he stood back. "Don't you have something to say?"

"I knew this was coming. I see that you really want me to beg and grovel."

"I'm listening."

"I'm so sorry Trae. Please forgive me. I apologize. I love you and I miss you."

He leaned over and ran his tongue over her strawberry lip gloss. "What about trust, and letting nothing come between us?"

"From here on out, I'll trust you and let nothing come between us," she promised.

"Tell me that you'll always be mine and you'll never leave me."

"I'll always be yours and I'll never leave you. Anything else Trae?" She kissed him on the neck.

"There is something else. I—"

"I'm curious. How long were you planning on keeping me in the doghouse?" she interrupted him.

"As long as it took for you to come beggin' for forgiveness. Like I said before, what if she lied? Then what? I said you didn't have to call her and to let it go. That's what you should have done."

"I'm sorry," she said, wrapping her arms around his waist. The waitress set their drinks on the bar. "You haven't kissed me in a week Trae. I think you've been pretty cruel."

He kissed her and caressed her butt.

"Am I out the dog house now?" she asked.

"Almost. I got something I want you to do."

Tash looked at him suspiciously. Trae paid for their drinks, grabbed his glass and his roses. He watched Tasha guzzle hers down.

"Damn, baby, I was craving for one of those."

"I see. You want mines?" She took it from him. When Trae saw one of the bouncers, he gave him a bill and told him to tell the deejay to play *Peaches & Cream* by 112. He took Tash by the hand.

"What do you want me to do Trae?"

"A brotha wants a lap dance."

Tasha stopped dead in her tracks. "A what?"

He pulled her along. "You heard me. Can a brother get a lap dance?"

"Trae I know you are playing."

"Nah, I'm not playin'. I got a table back here."

"C'mon, Trae," she whined. "I'm not shaking my ass in front of all these people."

"You dancin' for me, not all of these people."

He sat down at the table. "You want to get out of the dog house, right?" She went to sit down. "Naw, baby." He set the roses on the chair. "Don't sit. When *Peaches & Cream* come on, I want you to be ready."

"Can't I do this at home?" she whined.

"Baby, I want it now!"

"Trae you are so wrong. I'ma do this. But trust me, I'm going to get you back." She looked around to see how secluded they were. Trae lit his blunt and pulled out a roll of cash.

"That's right, playa," she said. "I don't want nothin' but hundreds. It's all about the Benjamins. You gonna pay for this."

"A'ight. Let's see what you got!" he challenged.

"It's on, playa," she said, tossing her bag next to him and letting her hair down.

"Oh, shit," Trae said, smiling. "Bring it on."

"We gonna do this right Trae. Rules: No touching and no sex in the Champagne Room. Comprende?"

"A'ight." "Peaches and Cream" was now spinning. *"It's the T, the R, the A, the E,"* Trae sang. "Let's go Tash. Back that ass up!" Tash was now moving, shaking, and grinding like a professional. "Tash you been holdin' out on me, baby," he said, laughing and putting bills in the waist of her skirt. "Go Tasha! Go Tasha!" Then he got on his knees and looked under her skirt. "Dayum!" He reached up and put more money in her waist as her ass pressed against his dick. "This is a private party," he said to a couple of brothas who were trying to ease over. He shot them a look, and they went away.

"Don't touch, Trae!" she said, smacking his hands.

"Tash you all up on my dick. What you mean 'don't touch'?" he asked, trying to grab her hips again.

"Trae!" she yelled. He laughed, putting more money in her waist.

"Turn around," he said. She made an exotic turn. "Pull your zipper down on your blouse."

"That'll be extra Trae." He put more money in her waist. She was shaking and grinding as she unzipped her blouse zipper. He leaned up and licked her nipples. Trae grabbed his dick and squeezed it. She zipped it back up. A couple of dudes hollered at Trae, but he ignored them.

"Put your leg up here," he said, pointing to his thigh.

"That'll cost ya. Pussy shots are extra." He put even more money in her waist. She put her foot up in the chair and was poppin' that coochie. "Don't touch Trae!" she said, but it was too late. He had already slid two fingers inside her and pulled them out. They looked at each other while he put both fingers in his mouth, pulling them out and running his tongue up, down, and all around them.

He started barking. Tash took her foot down and gave him one more booty shot as she swooped up some hundreds off the floor.

"Put your foot back up here," Trae begged.

"Record is over, playa," she said, pulling the money out of her waist. "Can I sit down now after you done fuckin' embarrassed me?"

"Ma, that was the shit!" he yelled, pulling her down onto his lap. He went to sucking on her neck as she counted her money. It totaled $1,800.00.

"Where's my tip, playa?" she asked, sipping on the last of his strawberry daiquiri. Tasha burst out laughing as Trae went to emptying all of his pockets. Just then a couple of ladies walked past and rolled their eyes at Tash as she stuffed all that money into her bag.

Trae was still in a daze. "Dayum, you fucked my head up! I can't believe you been holdin' out on me, Tash."

"Trae can I come sit at your table?" some dude hollered.

"Nah, man, it ain't that kind of party."

"See what you started Trae? Now niggas gonna be looking at me all funny."

"So?" he whispered, shoving his tongue down her throat. "Mmm, my dick is crying," he moaned, squeezing it and trying to calm it down. He slapped her thigh and lifted her up. "C'mon."

"Where are we going?"

"Someplace where I can eat me some peaches and cream." He stopped at the bar and said something to the bartender, who handed him a couple of clean towels. Then he stopped at the table with Omar and a couple of other brothers, one of whom tossed him some keys.

They walked up and he stuck the keys into a silver Hummer with tinted windows. The inside smelled brand new. Then, climbing in the back and locking the doors, he said, "Let's see what he got in his CD player." Trae reached over the seat and stuck the key in the ignition to open the CD changer. "Ginuwine, Mos Def, Jesse Powell, KC & Jo Jo. Baby, which one?"

"Nice selection. Light it up. Let me hear one cut from Mos Def, then put it on random."

"A'ight. It's your world."

"Is it really?"

"You ain't know?" he asked, turning up "Umi Says" and pulling a half blunt and lighter out of his back pocket. He took a couple of hits to the chest and passed it to her. He pulled off his shirt and threw it on the front seat. He then put both of her legs across his lap and took off her crocodile zip shoes, setting them on the front seat. She put the blunt out as he rubbed her legs and feet up and down. He pulled her up onto his lap. She untied his doorag and threw it over the front seat as he unzipped her blouse and slipped it off. Her nipples were already hard as he rolled them between his teeth and played with her pussy until she was ready to come.

"Give me a kiss," he said, unzipping her skirt. She was breathing very hard as she sucked on his tongue and his lips. He pulled her skirt off and tossed it onto the front seat, opening his towel and putting it on his lap.

When she saw what he was up to, goose bumps popped up all over her body. She knew it was on. She loved it when he ate her pussy. He laid her back, raising her knees while holding on to her ankles, and went straight for her clit. He lapped it until she was pulling his head, arching her back, and trying to break free. Just before she climaxed, he set her ankles free and went to sucking the inside of her thighs.

"Oh God. Trae," she screamed, pulling his head back toward her pussy. He inserted two fingers inside of her pussy while pressing on her clit with the tip of his tongue. Tash wrapped her

5

WAHIDA CLARK

legs around his neck and begged him not to stop. Her legs started shaking as she was cumming and he kept licking her clit, prolonging her orgasm. Her stomach heaved in and out then her body went limp. He untangled her legs from around his neck and wiped his face.

He was now planting soft kisses all over her naked body. Tash was as limp as a rag doll. He lifted her up, kissed her softly on the lips, and started singing, *"Peaches and cream, You know I need it 'cause I'm a fiend gettin' freaky in the back of my Hummer limousine."*

She smiled at him and put her arms around his neck, whispering into his ear, "Trae baby, that was so good. You always make sure to satisfy me."

"That's because you're my little butterfly," he said, running his tongue over her nipples. "I'm still waitin' to see how you're gonna work that tongue ring."

"Are you?" she asked, while sitting up and unloosening his belt buckle and unzipping his jeans. "Lift up," she said, hitting him on the thigh.

With his jeans and boxers now down to his ankles, she straddled his lap, wrapped both hands around his dick, and began massaging it. Trae leaned back and enjoyed the view.

"How does this feel?" she asked.

"Go a little harder," he mumbled, closing his eyes. She squeezed and pulled until it was brick hard and the head looked like it was supersized. He grabbed her wrists, and she let it go.

"Do you love me Trae? Or do you just love to fuck me?"

"Both," he said, turning her around to straddle him with her back to his chest. She held on to the back of the seat in front of her as he lifted her up and slid his dick in.

"Trae baby," she moaned, "you feel so good."

Trae was holding on tight to her hips and hitting it hard, making her shudder with every move. He slowed it down and whispered in her ear, "Do you love me? Or do you love just for me to fuck you?"

"Both," she moaned.

"Are you going to start trusting me?"

"Yes," she moaned. "Oh yes," she screamed.

He reached forward to play with her clit while grinding deep inside her. She was trembling and hollering his name as he tried to bang her back out. When she started cumming, he came with her, their juices flowing and mixing together. They were now both dripping with sweat as they tried to catch their breath. Trae ran his tongue up and down her back and gently massaged her breasts as she kept telling him how much she loved him and how good he was to her.

"I want you to come spend the night with me," he told her, kissing her on the cheek and giving her a big bear hug.

"Mmmm Trae, that feels good. You always make me feel so good and safe."

They got dressed and straightened up the Hummer before heading back for the club.

"Trae we look like we've been freakin'. I don't want to go back inside."

He picked her up and carried her to the Nav, telling her to sit tight as he arranged for someone to take her car home.

Kay was already driving Angel home. Trae grabbed his roses, jumped in the Nav, and headed for his apartment.

Chapter 8

"So, Trae, what's the story with Red?" Kay asked, turning down the car radio.

"Who? Angel?" Trae asked.

"Yeah."

"You remember that nigga Snake?"

"The pimp?" Suspicion evident in Kaylin's voice.

"She was his woman, dawg."

"She was a ho?" Kaylin was disappointed.

"No dawg, his woman, that bottom bitch. Numero uno. He was going to marry her and everything before he got beat down."

"Dayum!" Kay said.

"Yeah, but the pussy been on lock ever since."

"You bullshittin', right?"

"Naw, man, she still stuck on him. You might not ever hit it," Trae joked. "I told you she a good girl like Tash, the type that will hold it down for a nigga."

"Oh shit! I may have just found my future wife. She's fine, smart, a square. She ain't a ho. A lawyer, not a chicken. Do you see where I'm going with this?"

"I feel you, dawg. Go for it before somebody else do. But I think she still stuck on that nigga."

"Bullshit! She stuck on me." Kaylin arrogantly stated.

"I hope you're right."

Kaylin had tuned his partner out as he played back the night she pushed up on him in Philly and then the night at the club in Montclair.

"Dayum! And she checked me out first. I must be slippin'. I should have noticed her first. I'll never forgive myself for that one."

"Yeah, you slippin'," Trae said, looking at him and shaking his head.

"For real? She's been keeping the pussy on lock?"

"I think it's been like eight, nine months."

"Dayum!" Kay said, shaking his legs. "I know I gots to come up on that. I gotta spend some more time with her to make sure our chemistry is in sync. If it's still like it was the other night then it's on. We kicked it that night at the Diva Lounge, and then I took her home. She was acting all quiet and stuck up, but I know that was just a front because she was all the way live when I met her in Philly.

"I'm diggin' her. I felt like I was on a high school date. At first, I was thinking getting this pussy was gonna be like stealing candy from a baby." He started laughing. "Dawg, wasn't nothin' happenin'. I kinda thought she was a chicken the way she came off that night in Philly."

"Man, Tash ain't no chicken. Therefore she don't run with no chickens. You got me twisted, nigga. I ain't settlin' down with no chicken. They good girls, man."

"That's all I need to hear, my nigga. It's on and poppin'."

"Trae! Will you please keep your head still? I only have about three more braids to go," Tash pleaded.

"Ma, you pullin' my brains out! You braidin' like you mad at me."

She ignored him and kept on braiding. This was Tasha's second night in a row spending the night with Trae. Last night they double-dated with Kay and Angel and went back to the Diva Lounge in Montclair. She stood and stretched after finishing the last braid. "What am I going to wear tonight?" she asked, yawning and admiring her handiwork.

"You got enough shit to choose from. What kind of question is that?" Trae blasted her, getting off the floor.

"That's the problem Trae, so much to choose from. I know you ain't hatin' on a playa," she blasted back, walking towards the bathroom.

"I'm not a hater. I'm a congratulator," Trae stated.

Tasha headed for the kitchen after showering. She was blending up milk, strawberries, a banana, and honey when Trae came into the kitchen. He cut the blender off and handed Tash her cell phone.

"Thank you baby. Hello?"

"Guess what?" Angel was excited.

"What?"

"Kyra's water broke!"

"Whaaaat!" Tasha gasped. "Don't play."

"I swear! I'm not playin', and we can scrap our graduation party. Marvin already called it off."

"When is she going to the hospital?"

"Whenever her contractions get unbearable, I guess. I don't know. Shit. I never had a baby before."

"Dang, I know she's scared."

"How long are you going to be at Trae's?"

"Not much longer. I gotta pick up my car. Do you want me to meet you at Kyra's?"

"We might as well meet her at the hospital."

"Well, I'll pick you up and we can ride together."

"Okay," Angel said. "That'll work. I'll see you later."

"Wait! You know I gots to be nosy. Kay took you home last night, right?"

Angel giggled. "Of course, he did. That brotha is a trip. He asked to tie my wrists and ankles to the bedposts so he could lick me up and down."

"He asked you that? Oh my God! He looks so innocent! Trae hasn't even done that for me. Not yet."

"He's far from innocent. He thought because he brought me home and I let him in he was gonna hit it. I was like, 'nigga, I don't think so.' "

"So what's next?"

"He wants me to be his date for his birthday party. I told him that I'll let him know."

"Hmm, sounds like you like him."

"Try like and lust. I can't help it. It's something about him." Angel was giggling like a schoolgirl.

"What about Najee?"

"What about him?"

"I see. Okay, I'll call you when I get to the house. Somebody's clicking through." She clicked over. "Hello?"

"What up, big sis?"

"Trina! What's up with you?"

"I'm tryin'a get directions to the graduation party."

"It's a good thing you called because Kyra's water broke. It's cancelled."

"Aww, man! I was ready to get my party on with the big ballers. Trae and his peeps was gonna be there, right?"

"Trina, you need to slow your roll. I thought you was so into Damian? Ain't no shame in your game, is it?"

"Puhleeze! He ain't the big-ass baller he frontin' to be. Come to find out he works for someone that works for Trae's peeps. That's why a sista has to do what a sista has to do."

"Girl, I don't know where you're getting your info from. Trae ain't out there like that. But anyhow you need to handle your own business first. When are you going to enroll at NYU? If them niggas decide to drop you tonight and move on to the next ho at least you would be able to eat. Do you have any loot put away?"

"Aw shit, here we go," Trina sighed. "You preachin' to me and, look at you, you rollin' with one of the biggest ballers on the fuckin' East Coast. So what's the matter with me trying to get mines?"

"A'ight, Trina. Let me shut up. I forgot I can't tell you nothing. I don't even know why I opened my mouth. What's Kev up to?" she asked, attempting to change the subject.

"I don't know. I haven't heard from him since your graduation."

"That's not surprising. I love y'all. I gotta go."

"Me too. I gotta find somethin' else to get into. I love you too. Peace."

"That girl is a mess," Tash mumbled to herself, folding up her cell phone and turning the blender back on.

When Trae came back into the kitchen she was guzzling down her strawberry banana milkshake.

"Baby, what's up with you and all of these strawberries?" Trae asked, eyebrows raised.

"Nothing. I've just been having a taste for them. You want some?"

"Nah, I'm straight."

"You gotta take me home. Kyra's water broke."

"No shit!"

"No shit. She's getting ready to have that baby."

"When are you going to give me a baby?"

She got quiet. "I don't know. Haven't thought about it."

"As much as we fuck, I don't see why you haven't given it any thought."

"Trae, you know I take my birth control pills religiously every day. That's why I haven't given it any thought. What's up with you? You seem like you've been agitated all morning."

"I got some shit I gots to handle, that's all."

"Well, the graduation party is off for the night. I had a strong feeling she wasn't going to make it past the party."

Trae dropped her home to get her Benz, then left. She went to pick up Angel, and they headed for the hospital, Kyra having arrived there not long before. The baby came around 4:30 in the morning and weighed six pounds ten ounces. Angel videotaped the entire delivery even when Marvin became sick and had to leave the delivery room. That was truly a moment.

After twenty-four hours Kyra and the baby were released. Angel and Tasha spent two nights at Kyra's, helping her to get situated. They fell in love with their goddaughter, Aisha Nicole, who resembled Marvin a lot.

Chapter 9

"Roz, my sista, we gots to get our party on! It's Friday, and we haven't even celebrated our graduation," Angel was hyped. She had called Roz on her cell phone. Roz was just getting off from work.

"Sounds good to me. I haven't heard from Trae all week so I guess I'm free tonight. I'm on my way to the salon now. Where we going?"

"New York. Me, you, Shanna, Mecca, and Sanette."

"What time?"

"Be ready at eight. We're rollin' in Mecca's Rover."

"Where are you?"

"Getting ready to jump on this train. I may catch you at the salon."

"A'ight. Peace."

By 7:45 Roz was putting on some Baby Phat jeans, a halter, and Jimmy Choo sandals. A little after 8:00 the girls were beeping the horn. She jumped in the Rover, looked around, and asked, "What happened to Sanette?"

"We gotta pick her up," Mecca said.

On the way back from picking up Sanette, they slowed down as they neared Club Crossing Inn.

"Dayum! Go a little slower. Why are we going all the way to New York? Looks like all the action's right here," Sanette yelled in excitement.

"Looks more like a ballers' convention. Only peeps who drive a Benz, Lexus, Jeep, or Navigator are in attendance," Angel observed.

"Who you tellin'!" Mecca was amazed as she eased the Rover into the parking lot. "It's only nine o'clock. Must be a show tonight."

"I don't want to stay—too many niggas for me. There'll probably be a shoot-out before the night is over," Shanna said.

"Mecca, find a place to park. I see something that belongs to me," Tasha was doing her best to remain calm.

"What?" Mecca asked.

"Chrome. I can recognize those rims anywhere. Give me ten minutes," she said, popping a breath mint.

"That's all you're getting!" Mecca yelled. "I'm ready to roll."

"Ten minutes," Tash said, jumping out of the car.

"Trae is getting ready to get busted," Shanna teased.

"Puhleeze!" Angel said. "Quiet as it's kept, Trae is just as sprung as she is."

"Bullshit, playas gonna play," Mecca explained.

"Well, where is your man?" Angel teased. When she didn't answer they all burst into laughter.

"I'm trying to come up," Mecca humbly stated. "Y'all gotta hook a sista up." They all laughed again. "Y'all tryin'a keep them all for your damn selves!"

Tasha eased her way through the club looking for Trae. As soon as she opened the double doors in the back, the weed smoke hit her in the face. *"Bingo!"* she mumbled to herself. She glanced at the chickens, who were one too many. Then her eyes shot over to a crap game where about twelve brothas were involved, hollering, turning up forties, cursing, and smoking blunts. They were all iced up and had bills flashing.

"You looking for me, beautiful?" a short brotha looking like Cedric the Entertainer asked her.

"No, I wanna holla at that fine playa with the braids." Down on one knee with a blunt hanging from the side of his mouth, Trae was watching the dice intently.

The short brotha looked down at the crowd and said, "Beautiful, there are a couple of playas with braids."

"I said the fine one."

He looked again and yelled, "Yo, this beautiful lady with all of this ice on wants to holla at a playa with braids! Who's the lucky nigga?" About half of them looked up, including Trae. He looked her up and down, then smiled.

"What up, ma?" he yelled, putting some money on the floor.

"Let me holla at you, playa!" Tash said.

"You can holla at me anytime!" yelled one of the dudes on the floor.

"Nigga, shut up or put up!" Trae snapped. "You owe me four hun'ed, or I'll take that pinkie ring instead."

"Fuck you, man!" the dude yelled back at Trae, who was now standing up. "It ain't over till the fat lady sings."

On his way over to Tash, he turned toward the posted up chickens watching the crap game and said, "I told y'all I already had my own Peaches and Cream."

"And?" asked the smart-mouth chicken with blond hair, blue contact lenses and ugly feet.

"*And*," Tash emphasized, "take your ass someplace else. He's taken."

Trae took her arms, wrapped them around his neck, and put his hands in the back pockets of her jeans, pulling her close.

"Why you always gotta start shit Trae?"

"I was just fuckin' with them," he said, kissing her on the neck.

"Yo Trae, bring your ass back on over here! I'm taking that Rolex you got on!" yelled Bo.

Trae ignored him. "How do you always know where to find me?"

"Don't worry about it."

"You look real cute and you smell so sweet," he said, nibbling on her ear. Then he stopped abruptly. "Where do you think you're going?"

"We just picked up Sanette and we're on our way to New York. I saw your car so I came in to let you know what was up since I was the only one who is obviously missing somebody."

"You can't go, ma. So tell your little girlfriends to take you back home. Your man is always missing and wanting to be with you and I'm on my way over."

"But Trae," she whined, "I'm out with my girls."

"I thought you said you missed me. Plus, your man's stomach is growling, and I need to bust a nut. Now what is it gonna be?"

She kissed him on the lips. "Baby, you know it's all about you. Just tell me what you want me to cook and what time you'll be there so that it'll be hot."

Just then Kay walked up and saw Tasha. "Yo Tasha, who you got with you?"

She smiled at him and said, "She's out there in a dark green Rover."

With that Kay immediately disappeared through the double doors.

"So what do you have a taste for?" she asked.

"Breakfast. A big-ass cheese omelet, turkey sausage, home fries, and peaches with cream for dessert."

"So are you gonna call me on your way out of here?"

"Yeah, I'll be leavin' here in about an hour, hour and a half," he said, smelling her hair. "You love me?"

"Mmm hmm," she said, running her tongue up and down his neck.

"Oh shit! That felt good, ma. I'll see you in a little while." He slapped her on the butt, and she turned around and left.

"Damn, Trae! You put all that ice on her?" this dude named Cali asked.

"Don't worry about it, nigga."

"She must be good as fuck, dawg."

"You'll never know."

"Oh, so you got it locked down that tight?" He teased.

"That was Nikayah right?" Cali challenged.

"Nigga, I thought you knew," Trae said, throwing two hundred dollars on the floor and snatching up the dice.

"That bitch look too high maintenance for me."

"That's the only kind I like to fuck. You call her a bitch again, I'ma blow a fuckin' hole through your neck. I can't help it because you too fuckin' cheap. I never saw so many cheap-ass hustlers in my life. You can't take all that loot with you to the pen or the grave so you might as well spend a lot of it on your woman."

"Fuck that!" Cali spat.

"You just ignorant, man. Go find another crap game to play in. Your ignorant ass is jinxing me," Trae snapped. Everybody laughed.

When Angel spotted Kay looking around the parking lot she blurted, "Oh God, I'ma kill Roz for stopping in here."

"What's your problem?" Shanna asked.

"Kay is gonna find this car. Whatever you do, Mecca, don't unlock the door. I am not mentally prepared to deal with him tonight."

"Where is he?" Mecca asked.

"Oh my God, he is so fine. Look at those bow legs and check out his lips, y'all. They are so sweet. He kisses so good," Angel said, swooning. "That bitch set me up. I know she did."

"Where is he?" Mecca yelled again.

"Girl, shut up!" Sanette said.

"I can't help myself. I want to do it to him so bad I can taste it. He is so wrong for me. My mom and my aunt who's a prosecutor will have a hissy fit. Lord, give me strength!" she prayed.

Angel was sitting in the backseat behind the driver. When Tasha got outside, Kay was leaning on the back door and Angel was cracking the window.

"Get out the car, ma, so I can talk to you," Kay said, pulling on the door handle.

"You can talk to me right here. We're getting ready to go, Kaylin." Everybody in the car was trying so hard not to laugh.

"Why are you scared to get out of the car? Open the window some more! What you scared of?"

"I'm not scared. We're getting ready to go." She rolled the window all the way down.

"How come you never called me back? I know you got my messages."

"I've been studying for my bar exam and I didn't need any distractions."

"Oh, so I'm a distraction?"

"Sort of. Plus, I'm talkin' to somebody," she said, in her attempt to play mind games.

"Who? That lawyer nigga? Fuck him! He can't love you or take care of you like I will, so stop dreaming." He ran his fingers through her hair. That was making her nipples hard.

"How do you know what he can or cannot do?"

He grabbed her by the neck, pulled her close, and slobbed her down. "You know that boy ain't got nothin' on me. He don't make you feel like this, do he?" he asked, kissing her again. "Does he?"

She didn't say anything.

"I want to be your man," he said. "You know I'm diggin' you."

"Kaylin, please. We have a conflict of interest, don't you think? I'm a lawyer, and you . . . you have a very complex occupation."

"Red, this occupation has just about run its course. Another month or two and this nigga'll be a retired man. I don't have a criminal record. I don't have AIDS or any STDs. So now what's up? Why the sudden change of attitude?"

"I'm talking to somebody, Kaylin."

"That lawyer nigga ain't nobody. You work with him every day and he ain't lock you down yet? It's obvious that he can't, or he would have done so by now. Am I right?"

"Oh, so you think *you* can lock me down?"

"Hell, yeah. I don't think so, I know so. You know that punk-ass nigga can't put you on lock." He leaned over and kissed her again, this time taking her chewing gum. "So where y'all going?"

"New York."

"Where to?"

"I'm not sure. I'm just hanging."

"Hang with me, ma. I'm going that way."

"Kaylin, I came with them."

Kay went over to Mecca. "Where y'all going?"

"Queens. Why? You got a better spot?" Mecca asked as Angel kicked the back of Mecca's seat and then slapped the back of her head.

"I got a couple that's better than Queens. What y'all want, hip hop, club, reggae, old school, a little of everything? And Red I see you back there."

"We just wanna get 'crunk'!" Shanna yelled from the backseat.

"And we don't want to spend our money," Sanette chimed in.

"Well, tonight is your lucky night. Y'all follow me to Manhattan, and everything will be on me. Y'all really don't need to be going to Queens unescorted. Can you drive?" he asked, looking at Mecca.

"I can drive. Just don't be doin' ninety or a hundred."

"I won't. Unlock the back door." Mecca popped the lock. "C'mon, ma, you ridin' with me."

"Kay," Tasha hollered, "y'all gotta take me home first. Then y'all can go wherever it is y'all trying to go."

"What's the matter? Trae ain't lettin' you out to play tonight?" he asked, grabbing Angel's hand.

"No, Kay, I can't come out to play tonight."

Kay lifted Angel out of the Rover and slid her down his dick before her feet could hit the ground. "You look real cute, Red," he said, caressing her butt. "You need to stop playin' with a nigga. You trying to put me on front street, all in front of your girls?"

He grabbed her by the waist, walked her to his Mercedes Convertible SL600, and opened the door for her. When she turned to get in the car, he pressed up against her.

"You ready to be wifey or what?"

"You ain't ready for me. I gots to be number one."

"I can handle that."

"Oh, can you?"

"Yeah, I can, but what about my party? You gonna be my date, right?" he asked in a whisper, lips touching his ear.

"Maybe," she shuddered.

"What about tonight? Can I lick you up and down?"

"Nope."

"Why not?"

"I don't know what kind of party you think this is." She closed her eyes as he kissed her neck. "Now turn me loose, Kaylin."

"Can't stand the heat?" he asked, letting her go and allowing her to sit so that he could close the door.

"What heat? I don't feel nothing."

"Oh, you feel it. I'ma ask you to stop playin' with a nigga," he said, starting the Benz and pulling off with Mecca right behind them.

"So why can't you roll with us?" Sanette asked Roz. Mecca and Shanna burst out laughing.

"I don't know what you laughin' at. Bo is up in there," Roz said.

Shanna turned serious. "You lyin'. I didn't see his car."

"No, I'm not. They're in the back shooting craps, and the dick-suckin' chickens are all posted up."

"Oh, hell no! I gotta go back. Drop me off, Mecca. I'll catch y'all the next time."

"Y'all are some crazy bitches," Mecca said, beeping the horn to get Kay's attention. "Never again!" She screamed.

When he pulled over she told him to stay right there because they had to go back and drop Shanna off at the club.

"I can't believe y'all! Roz you bailin' on us. Shanna you bailin', and Angel done bailed. Y'all are so wrong. We were supposed to be goin' together. And Roz, you coulda told Trae to eat at the club. They got food in there." Mecca was going off.

They all started laughing at her. "I now see why you don't have a man," Roz said. "I'm sorry to mess up our girls' night out, but I would be real stupid to tell Trae 'Fuck you! Eat at the club, nigga! I'm going out!' You got me twisted. I probably could get away with it, but I ain't gonna go out like that. That nigga pays all of my bills, down to my magazine subscriptions. I'm driving a 2001 Benz. And what year is this? Yeah, 2001, and it's in my name. He treats me good, and I'm not even going to mention his bedroom skills. So when my man says he's hungry and needs to bust a nut, I'm gonna be the perfect lady and oblige, happily. Later for the club. I can go clubbin' anytime. You need to take some lessons my sista 'cause, obviously, you don't know what's up!"

"Nah, she don't know," Shanna said, opening the car door. "I'm outta here. I'm getting ready to crash this damn crap game."

"Whatever, ho. Handle your business," Mecca told her, and pulled off. Then she turned to Roz. "Bitch you should have hooked *me* up with Kay, instead of Angel's ass. That nigga is too fine. I like his build. He's big, but not bulky. He got the six-pack goin' on, big muscular arms, and to top it off, he's bowlegged. That ho can't handle him. Plus, do you really think that Miss 'I ain't fuckin' no drug dealers, I'm waitin' on Snake' is gonna give him some?

"Hell fuckin no." She answered her own question. "What a fuckin waste. I know she ain't going to fuck the nigga."

"Yes she is. It's just a matter of time. That ho is dying to give up the pussy, especially to him," Tasha stated matter-of-factly.

"I'm dyin' to give it up, too. He was all over her, tonguin' her down, playing in her hair! Did you hear him say fuck that lawyer nigga?" Mecca asked. They all laughed. "I am really hatin' right about now "

"Yeah, I heard. Lawyer boy obviously ain't game-tight. I heard everything. I was tryin' not to be nosy but couldn't help over-hearing," Sanette said. "And stop hatin'!"

Chapter 10

When Trae put the key in the door, Tasha was just fixing his plate.

"Yo ma, it smells good," Trae said, moving up behind her and wrapping his arms around her waist. He kissed her on the cheek. "You miss me?"

"You know I do. You could've at least called. I would rather hear your voice than get flowers and stuffed animals that I have no more space for," Tasha vented.

"Aren't we cranky? Must be that time."

"I'm not cranky. I just miss you. That's all."

"This time next month all this runnin' will be over. Then you'll be tired of having me around." She didn't respond. "Did you hear what I said?"

"I heard you," she answered.

"It's almost over."

"I hope so. What would you like to drink?" she asked, not wanting to get her hopes up too high.

"It don't matter." Trae went into the living room, sat on the couch, and grabbed the remote. When Tasha came into the living room he was going back and forth between CNN and ESPN. She set his dinner tray down on the coffee table. "Thank you baby."

"Pleasure's all mine," she told him, returning to the kitchen.

She came back with a bowl of sliced strawberries, a can of whipped cream, honey, and a spoon. She sat down next to Trae, who was already eating. Trae watched her pour honey on the strawberries, drown them in whipped cream, and dig in with her spoon. "Oh God! This is so good." She moaned through the whole bowl, putting the last spoonful to his lips.

"Nah, go ahead and enjoy," he said. "I was starting to get jealous. I thought you were getting ready to bust a nut over there."

"Baby don't be "J" she cooed. "I'll go fix you a bowl."

"I already told you I wanted *peaches* and cream for dessert, not strawberries and cream." He was staring at her.

She squirted some whipped cream onto the spoon and gulped it down. "Why are you lookin' at me like that?" She squirted some more whipped cream into her bowl, scooped some up on her finger, and this time Trae methodically licked the cream off of her finger. Then he kissed her, running his tongue across her lips. "Why you keep lookin' at me like that?"

"Because I think you're pregnant."

"Pregnant? Baby I've been taking my birth control pills like clockwork. I can't be pregnant." She got indignant.

"When is the last time you had a period?"

"I believe the pill has been making it irregular. So we can't go by that."

"A'ight, you know your body," Trae said, polishing off his plate with a smirk on his face.

"Trae do you feel that all of this hustlin' you're doin' is worth it?" she asked, breaking the silence.

"As long as you're with me, hell, yeah! You the biggest thing in my little itty-bitty world. I promise you my hustlin' days are just about over."

After Tasha cleaned up the kitchen, they showered together then went to bed. Tasha climbed on top of Trae and began kissing him nice and slow, sliding her tongue in and out and sucking his lips. When he put his tongue back into her mouth, she wrapped her lips around it, sucked it nice and slow for a while, then changed to sucking it hard and fast. Then she went back to the soft and sensual kisses. She could see that Trae was really enjoying it but stopped anyway to grab a pillow, placing it under his neck and back.

"You know that you're all I need, right?" He told her.

"Shut up Trae. I want to fuck and get sucked."

She sucked his tongue and licked his lips some more before raising up and allowing him to slide inside her. He reached up and began massaging her breasts. "They're sore, Trae." He let them go and grabbed her butt to pull her closer. He watched her movements get faster and faster until she came. He flipped her over and played with her clit, licking it until she came again.

"Ma, your legs are getting heavier and heavier," he teased, as he unwrapped them from around his neck. He then climbed on top of her to lick on her nipples.

She moaned and gently put her hands back on his head, then motioned for him to go back where he just came from. He ran his tongue down the middle of her chest to her stomach and navel then up and down the inside of her thighs before zoning in on her clit, making her cum again with more intensity than the previous time. He unwrapped her legs before flipping her over onto her stomach, bending her knees, and pushing them all the way up. He squeezed her hips tight and slid all the way in.

"Trae," she moaned. "Trae." The deeper he went in, the harder he got, and the louder she moaned. Trae was now in the zone, grinding faster and faster.

"Trae baby, slow down. It's hurting," she whined. He pulled back some and came soon after that. He rolled off her and started laughing.

She turned over and sat up. "What's so funny? You were hurting me," she said, punching him in the chest.

He rolled over and grabbed her around the waist causing her to fall back onto his chest.

"Stop playing!" she complained. "You were hurting me."

He got on top of her, pinned her down and whispered in her

ear, "I told you 'you're pregnant'!" Then he rolled off her. She sat up to get out of the bed, but he pulled her back down. "I'm telling you, Tash, you're pregnant."

"How would you know?"

He reached over and turned on the lamp. "Look at your breasts. Look at how full they are and how dark they are around the nipples. I don't care what you say, but you ain't had no period in a while. And look at all them fuckin' strawberries you been eatin'—strawberries and cream, strawberry milkshakes, strawberry daiquiris. You have never eaten strawberries like that before. But the most important thing is your cervix door is closed shut. Any other time, I'm able to go deep as I can and you love it. Now I'm hittin' up against that wall and it's hurting. Accept it. Them fuckin' birth control pills didn't work. Not this time."

"No, fuck that!" She covered her face with a pillow. "Baby I really hope that you don't know what you're talkin' about."

"What's up with the disappointment?"

She ignored him. "How you know how it feels to fuck a pregnant woman? I thought you didn't have any kids."

"Remember the day I asked Kay when he called why he gave that bitch my cell number? That was his sister. I used to fuck with her. She got pregnant, but at four and a half months, got an abortion. If she wasn't Kay's sister, I would have blown her fuckin' brains out. I haven't spoken with her since."

"Why the hell was she calling you, then?"

"Every so often she tries to get me to talk to her so that she can give me some bullshit story on why she killed my baby. She wants me to forgive her and pretend like nothing happened."

"Why did she do it? And why did she wait so late?"

"Being a fuckin' evil, vindictive bitch."

"I don't even want to know what you did to make her go that far."

"What's that supposed to mean?"

"Was you fuckin' around on her?"

"Am I fuckin' around on you?"

"I don't think you are. I hope you're not because if I catch you I'm fuckin' you up. Was you fuckin' around on her?"

"Yeah, I was, but that don't got shit to do with killing my baby."

"Y'all niggas got a lot of nerve. We have to be true to keep y'all, but y'all can fuck around."

"I ain't fuckin' around on you Tash. Those were my wildin' out days. I told you already 'you're all I need.' Trust and believe that. Now back to my question. Why are you so disappointed?"

"I'm not ready to have a baby. You know I want to give you a baby, but not now."

"How come not now? There's never a perfect time."

"I'd prefer that you wouldn't be in the game where your odds for going to jail or getting buried are stacked against you. You asked me to take a chance with you, not you and a baby. That's asking too much."

"I ain't goin' nowhere. I love you, and you love me, right?"

"You know that, but that still doesn't have anything to do with you being around. Plus, I'm looking forward to putting my degree to use very soon. A baby will delay that." She tried to make him understand.

"I ain't goin' nowhere. We got money. We can work through this and get a live-in nanny so you still can do whatever you want to do. We'll be fine. I promise. It's me and you. I ain't going nowhere," he said.

"How can you be so sure?"

"Just trust me and have my baby, a'ight? Do you love me?" he asked.

"Yes, I do."

"Are you gonna trust me and give me a big ol' healthy son?"

"You promise you won't leave us?"

"Promise."

"Do you love me?" she asked him.

"Yeah, I do. I love you and our baby. I need you to trust me Tasha."

The next day he took her to the doctor. She was six weeks pregnant even though she was on the pill. Trae was ecstatic.

Chapter 11

Trae and Tasha had to go to New York to get something to wear to Kay's birthday party this coming Saturday. Trae had booked the ballroom at the Ritz Carlton in New York and hired Fat Man Scoop as the deejay.

They first stopped at a Gucci shop where Trae picked out a stomach-revealing black spider wrap for Tasha and a silk pin-striped miniskirt. She picked out a pair of black Jimmy Choo sandals and a bag to match. Trae topped it off with a pair of diamond earrings. Her tab came to $8,300. They continued to his tailor where he showed them her pin-striped skirt and he had a suit made to match. He also got some black gators, a pair of black Stacy Adams, and they were ready to floss. His tab came to $6,900.

Angel and Tasha were riding over to see Kyra and the baby when Angel's cell phone rang.

"Hello."

"Red, what up?"

"It's all about you, Kaylin," she purred like a sexy kitten.

"That's what a nigga needs to hear," he said, smiling. "I'm picking you up in the morning so we can go shopping and get this weekend poppin' right."

"I have to work, Kaylin. Can't we go later on in the evening?"

"Take a half day and I'll pick you up at the job."

She knew there was no way out of it. Whatever Kaylin wanted, he got. Plus, his party was a few hours away. "Call me at eleven, and I'll tell you what time to come."

"A'ight, I can do that."

"Tell me, Kaylin, what kind of birthday present do I get for a man who already has everything?"

"I already told you I want you for my birthday present."

"Kaylin, I'm serious."

"I'm serious, too. I want to tie you up and tongue-kiss the kitty cat. That's the only present I care about. You gonna hook a brotha up for his birthday or what? I thought you just said that it was all about me," he teased. "I'm getting mixed messages."

"I did. I'm already your date. Don't you think that's enough?"

"You just asked me what I wanted for my birthday so I told you."

Angel laughed. "I guess I set myself up for that one. I'll talk to you tomorrow, Kaylin."

"Hold up! Why are you rushing me off the phone?"

"What else do you have to say, Kaylin?"

"I need to ask you something personal."

"What is it?"

"Are you orgasmic?"

"Kay, that is personal and none of your business."

"It *will* be my business. Are you?"

"Why do you need to know?"

"Because I want to know what I'm working with. I have to plan my strategy. Some females don't have orgasms. Some can only have one big one, and others are able to cum again and again. Which category are you in?"

"Wouldn't you like to know!"

"Oh, so you're not going to answer my question?"

"No. Why don't you tell me what am *I* working with. How long can you keep it up? One minute? Two? Five?" She looked at Tasha and mouthed, "Watch this."

"No," she said. "Let me guess. Word is, most brothas that work out a lot and have those nice bodies got a small dick. Therefore, you probably couldn't even hit my G-spot. And seeing that you are so aggressive, you're probably a one-minute man. Therefore you wouldn't be able to make me cum anyway.

"And since you are so fine, you probably can't give good head. They say that y'all fine brothers think that y'all are too cute to give head but y'all love to receive. So again, you wouldn't be able to make me cum. So therefore, my brotha, it really doesn't matter what category I fall under, does it?" Tasha was laughing at Angel so hard she was holding her stomach.

"A sista who can talk shit, I like that. In the middle of all that smack you was talkin', at least I've learned that you are orgasmic. You cum when a nigga hits that G-spot and you cum when a nigga gives that clit a fit. But it sounds like you got me twisted up with that lawyer nigga you've been trying to save yourself for. Because first chance I get, Kay is gonna turn your fine, stuck-up ass inside out, with hardly any effort."

"Oh, it's like that?" Angel closed her eyes at the thought of him rocking her world.

"You can trust and believe that it's like that. Where are you?"

"Why?"

"What?" he laughed. "Are you scared to tell me?"

"I'm in the car with Tasha. We're on our way to see our goddaughter."

"What time are you gonna be home?"

"Why?"

"I'm coming over."

"No you're not. I have to get up early to go to work."

"I'm still coming over."

"No you're not. You won't get in. Call me tomorrow at 11:00 like we discussed."

"I need your job number." She gave it to him.

Trae was with Kay, so Kay let him talk to Tasha. "Red, I'll catch you later on tonight. Give the phone to your girl."

"You'll catch me at 11:00 tomorrow Kaylin." She passed the phone to Tasha.

"What up, mommy? You a'ight?" Trae asked.

"I'm okay. I have my very first prenatal visit tomorrow."

"What time?"

"One-thirty."

"If I'm not already at the house, I will be there by 12:30. A'ight?"

"Okay."

"You still in love with me?"

"I am."

"I'll catch you later." He hung up.

Tasha passed Angel her phone. "Girl, you are crazy. Why was you clownin' Kay like that?"

"I was just messing with him. Now I'll sit back and see what he's made of. So far so good."

"Do you think his dick is small?" Tasha asked, bursting with laughter.

"Girl, puhleeze. I really was messing with him when I said that. Remember that night you told him I was out there in Mecca's ride?"

"Yeah."

"When he lifted me out the car, his dick was stretched out along his thigh. He put me right on it and slid me down on it in slow motion. Oh my God! It was long and hard. I wanted to say *please* do that again." They both started laughing. "I played it off and acted like nothing happened. The nigga is smooth."

"So if he comes over tonight, are you letting him in?"

"What do you think?"

At 3:58 a.m. Angel's alarm went off, and the phone rang at the same time. She smacked the alarm off then reached for the phone. "What is it, Kaylin? I know it's you."

"I'm comin' up the elevator now. Open the door."

"I'm still in the bed, Kay."

"You gotta get up and get ready for work. It's 4:00. You might as well let me take you since I'm going home anyway. Just let me crash on your couch for an hour. Come open the door." He hung up.

She rolled out of the bed, grabbed her robe, and went to unlock the front door.

"What up, beautiful?" he said to her when she opened the door. "Here's your paper."

"Thanks." She took it from him and closed the door. "We need to leave by 6:00, Kaylin."

"A'ight." He looked at his Rolex. "It's 4:05 now. Wake me up at 5:30," he said, pulling off his shirt and stretching out on the couch.

Angel showered and shaved her legs, then flossed and brushed her teeth, and moisturized her skin. By the time she came out the bathroom Kay was sprawled out on her bed snoring. She just looked at him and shook her head. She put on her underwear and stockings, threw on a robe, and went into the kitchen, where she had a bran muffin and orange juice while flipping through the newspaper.

"Kay it's 5:30. Kay!" She shook him. He rolled over onto his back then sat up. "Why are you in my bed?" she asked.

"Your couch ain't comfortable Red. I need a washcloth and a toothbrush," he said, eyeing her like a luscious piece of fruit.

"Clean washcloths are in the bathroom, and there should be a new toothbrush in the medicine cabinet."

He looked at his Rolex. "Why aren't you dressed yet?"

"I'm waiting on you to get out of my room."

"I'm not gonna bite you," he said smiling. "Not yet." He left out of the bedroom.

She scented up, got dressed, and fingered her hair. Then she went into the kitchen to pack her lunch. Kay was downing her entire carton of orange juice. "You ready, beautiful?" he asked.

"Just about," she said, leaving out the kitchen to get her purse and briefcase. They left out the house, jumped into a Rover, and headed for New York. They enjoyed each other's company during the trip, the only problem being Kay wanting to listen to Tom Joyner while Angel wanted to listen to Doug Banks. Angel won.

After dropping Angel off at work Kay called Trae. They discussed what little business they could over the phone before Trae asked, "So, playa, you just fuckin' with Red or what?"

Kay was putting out his blunt. "What you think, dawg? What it look like?"

"Alls I know is you ain't chase no pussy like this in a long while."

"Fuck you, dawg!" Kay said laughing. "You forgot how you was chasin' Tasha."

Trae had to laugh at that. "Hell, yeah! A playa's got to do what a playa's got to do. I ain't even gonna front. I had to beg, grovel and scheme, but it was worth it. She don't give a nigga no problems and now she about to have my baby. Hell, yeah, I'm 'bout it, 'bout it!"

"Dawg, Red reminds me of them Catholic school girls we used to chase. Their parents have them locked down, but they be so hot and tryin' so hard not to give it up. She's a challenge, but I like it. I'ma turn her stuck-up ass out. She don't even know what she got herself into. I'm diggin' her, though. She's just what I need for now."

"A'ight, playa, handle your business. Don't fuck her around, though. Tasha won't let me hear the last of that shit. Ever!"

"I'm feeling her, man." Kay hung up and headed home to take a nap, bathe, and get ready to pick up Angel from work at 1:00.

Kay was in the lobby ten minutes early with a bouquet of flowers and dressed in an Armani suit, tie, and shirt with diamond cuff links and rocking braids.

"You must be here to see Ms. Smith. She said she was expecting someone," said the young receptionist with a grin.

"Can you tell her that Kaylin is here? Thanks."

The receptionist picked up the phone and called her. "She said she'd be down in five minutes."

A few minutes later Najee came through the front door. He

went straight to the receptionist to thumb through his messages. He turned around, saw Kay, and nodded to him. "Kaylin, right?"

"What up, man?" Kay greeted Najee.

"It's obvious that you got the best hand," Najee said with a handshake. "I like this suit, man."

"Thanks."

"What do you do?" Najee inquired.

Kay pulled out a business card and handed it to him. Najee looked it over. "Recycling. You contract with the government?"

"We've won contracts for the last three quarters."

"I hear you. If you ever need any assisting or consulting, here's my card."

Just then Angel walked into the lobby. She was wearing a red and black Christian Dior jacket and skirt. Kay looked at her and smiled. "Hey, beautiful," he said, handing her the flowers and kissing her on the lips. Najee almost jumped out of his skin.

"Mmmm Kaylin, they smell so good," she said, sniffing them. "Thank you." Then to Najee who was looking at her she said, "I put everything you needed on your desk. I'll be in at seven tomorrow. Page me if you have any questions."

"Okay," he said, all the while looking at Angel, "I need to return a few of these messages."

"A'ight, man," Kay said, watching the action closely with a smirk as Najee disappeared out of the lobby.

"Kaylin you're making me look like a bum."

"I could never do that, ma. You look hot! You ready?"

"Bye Kisha," she said to the receptionist, sniffing her flowers again. "I'll see you in the morning."

When they got outside, Angel was expecting to see the Rover, but instead was helped into a Mercedes SUV like Tasha's, Kay opening the door for her.

The first stop was to get her squared away. She picked out a dark olive two-piece Versace blouse and skirt costing $3,610 and matching dark olive sandals and bag by Robert Clergisie for $940. Her jewelry cost over $2,000.

The next stop was at Kay's tailor. He gave them her outfit, and they made him a matching rich dark olive three-piece suit. He also bought some dark olive gators. His tab was $6,000.

By the time they finished shopping and sat down to eat it was 6:30. "What do you want to do after we eat?" Kay asked her as they sat looking out of the window at the rain.

"I need to go home. I have to be up and out by five in order to get to work by 7:00."

"Why don't you spend the night at my house? I can take you to work in the morning. At least you wouldn't have to catch a train. You can leave my house at 6:30 and be in your office by 7:00."

Angel looked at him. "Nah, that's okay."

"Don't worry. I'm not a rapist. I have two guest bedrooms."

"Sounds convenient, but I don't have what I need to stay overnight. What's the matter? You don't feel like driving me back to Trenton?"

"Look how hard it's raining. It's storming pretty bad. Instead of driving in this weather for three hours we can get to my house in less than an hour. Neiman Marcus is right up the street. We can run in and get whatever you need to spend the night."

She acted like she didn't hear that and changed the subject. "What am I going to do about my shoes, Kay? I can't get these wet. They cost $350. My suit can be put in the cleaners, but nothing can be done for the shoes." It was raining so hard they could barely see.

"Take them off and put them in your purse. I'll carry you to the car."

"That'll work." She smiled. "Now that's what I call a gentleman's hospitality."

After motioning to the waiter to bring the check and paying the bill he said to her, "You ready?" He then took out his keys and swooped her up gently. Angel giggled as she wrapped one arm around his neck and pushed the door open with the other. She was hollering about how cold the rain was as he jogged to the Benz but seemed to be enjoying it. By the time they got to the car they were soaked and out of breath.

"Oh my God!" she yelled excitedly, pulling off her wet stockings.

Kay turned on the car and the defogger and took off his tie and shirt. "There should be a gym bag back there on the floor with a clean towel, T-shirt, shorts, and socks."

Angel unzipped it, handing everything to him, and took off her wet jacket which was making her cold. Underneath she had on a silk, sleeveless camisole. She grabbed the towel and dried off his hair, face, neck and chest. He hit the button moving the seat all the way back, pulled off his pants, and put on the shorts and T-shirt.

He leaned over in the back to get his Timbs. He winked at Angel and put them on. "You know we could have stayed in the restaurant until the rain stopped?" They both burst into laughter.

"Duh. I know. But this was too much fun. You want to run back inside?" She joked.

"Only if you carry me this time."

"Whatever nigga. What are you trying to insinuate?"

He shrugged. "It is what it is." Then he leaned over to get him a kiss. Before they got too carried away, she gently broke away.

"You a'ight?" he asked.

"I'm fine. How about you?"

"I couldn't be better," he said, turning on the Sade CD. They both sat and watched the rain as it fell. "You might as well spend the night. We're wet, the weather is bad, and plus it's getting late."

"It's not late Kaylin."

"Too late for me to take you home," he said, reaching over and trying to pull her onto his lap.

She resisted. "I'm not sleeping with you tonight. We're not gonna fuck," her voice rising.

"I know how to keep my dick in my pants. My hands, lips, and tongue, I have a problem controlling them," he admitted. She was looking at him. "Don't worry. Separate bedrooms and separate bathrooms. I got you." He assured her.

At Neiman Marcus, Angel got a suit, silk pajamas, stockings, underwear, slippers, and some perfume that Kaylin shelled out $2,100 for.

Kay's three-bedroom house was located in northern Manhattan. They arrived there a little after 9:30. She noticed a Mercedes station wagon when they pulled up.

"I see that you're a Mercedes man."

"That I am."

"What's with the station wagon?"

"I use that when I got my son and my nephews."

"How cute!"

He let Angel inside while he brought the bags in. She was checking the place out. When he finally came in she said, "Kay, this is beautiful. You had it built from the ground up? It looks like something out of *Architectural Digest*."

"Nah, it was in pretty good condition when I got it. I just had it remodeled. It's actually been in the family a long time."

"It's nice. I bet the women love coming here."

"Now why you gotta go there Red?"

She laughed. "That slipped."

"I see how you're thinking. Let me set the record straight. This is Kay's sanctum. I gotta really be diggin' a female to bring her to my hideout. You'll notice that my phone won't even ring. I use my pager or my cell phone. You gotta be the shit to get up in here and get my home number."

"I don't have your home number," she interjected. He took the pen and pad off the counter and quickly scribbled his number on it for her. "Oh, am I supposed to feel special now?" she asked.

"I think you already do," he said, undressing her with his eyes. Angel smiled. "Which bedroom is for special me?"

"Any one you want. Make yourself at home."

"I'll take the one with the black and peach bathroom. I can't wait to soak in that huge bathtub."

"Knock yourself out."

When Angel came downstairs almost two hours later Kay had

a boxing match on the big screen and had turned off the sound. The CD player was also playing real low as Kay, wearing a wife-beater cut in half, talked on his cell phone. He could see her watching him, her eyes straying from his hard, cut abs to his big, muscular arms. She could see the outline of his dick grow through his loose, gray sweats. She then did a double take, running her fingers through her hair. They made eye contact and smiled at each other. *This is not going to be easy.*

She went to the kitchen, looked in the refrigerator, and helped herself to a plum and some bottled water. After making herself comfortable in the Laz-E-Boy, she noticed that a bottle of Cristal on ice, two glasses, a blunt, two joints, and some napkins were sitting on a tray. *Very smooth,* she thought to herself. She went over to the CD player when she heard what was playing. "This is that Mary and JadaKiss joint. I haven't heard this in a while," she said, turning it up a little. She was anxious to feel Mary's voice stir her soul. "This whole CD is bumpin'."

"Sit over here," Kay said, patting the spot on the sofa next to him. She sat down, bobbing her head to the joint called *Sexy.* He could see that she wore nothing under those silk pajamas.

"You straight?" Kay asked her. She nodded yes. "I thought you got lost up there," he said.

She smiled. "Nah, I was taking my time. I took a nice, long, soothing bath and got everything ready for tomorrow. I even washed my hair."

"I see. You smell real sweet," he said, kissing her neck. "I'm glad you decided to come over."

"Are you?" she asked.

"Yeah."

"Why?"

"I like your company. You got a nice vibe going for yourself."

"Oh, do I?"

"Yup," he answered.

"Well, I'm just waiting to see what you got planned for me. I know it's something," she said, looking him in the eyes.

"Nah. I don't have anything planned. I just want you to make yourself comfortable, that's all."

He stood up, pulling her with him. Mary's cut, *I'm in Love*, was playing. He wrapped his arms around her waist; he wanted to slow dance.

"You didn't tell me we were having a party," she said, placing her arms around his neck. "I should have known you were up to something."

"You didn't ask," he said, grabbing her booty with both hands and putting her right on his dick.

"This is not supposed to feel this good," she purred as she closed her eyes.

"Yes, it is," he whispered in her ear. She could feel his dick getting harder. He caressed her ass as his grinds were beginning to work her pussy. When she looked up at him he slipped his tongue in her mouth. After the next song went off he turned her around, wrapped his arms around her waist, and kissed her neck.

Angel's body was on fire. She was melting in his big arms, which felt so good to her. He began caressing her breasts with his left hand. With his right hand he took hers and slowly guided two of her fingers between her thighs, running them up and down her clit. "See how wet you are," he whispered in her ear, "and you talkin' 'bout I can't get none." He moved her fingers and one of his own inside her.

"Mmm, you are so freaky," she moaned. He eased them out and moved them over her clit, making circular motions until it started swelling. He turned her around and put her two fingers in his mouth, sucking them as she nibbled on his earlobe and up and down his neck. He grabbed her booty and was moving her so that she was once again grinding on his dick. She kissed him lightly on the lips. "That feels so good," she said. "What are you trying to do to me?" she moaned under her breath.

He slid his hands off her booty and started unbuttoning her pajama top. She was pressing her fingertips in his back, sliding them up and down. "Why are you teasing me?" she moaned through heavy breathing. He now had her pajama top open and was playing with her nipples. "Kaylin!"

"I'm not teasin' you. I just need your undivided attention. I'm just curious to know why you wanted to get with me but then when I come you try to act like ain't nothin' up. What's up with that?"

"Don't make me tell you why. Plus, you don't want to know." Her hands were exploring his chest, shoulders, arms and back.

"Yes, I do," he said, kissing her. "Now tell me."

"When I first saw you, I just wanted to meet you, you know, just kick it. Or I should say I just wanted to fuck with you. Nothin' serious, just lust. I didn't even know you were Trae's dawg."

"I see. So you were just playin' with a brotha."

"Why are you trying to sound all shocked. Y'all do the same shit. I just wanted to play with a playa. But the more time we spent around each other the more I started diggin' you. Then I began to get a little nervous so I decided to slow my roll. You sorta caught me off guard."

"What about now? You still playin' with a brotha?"

"No, I wouldn't be here if I was. Trust me your ass would have driven me home in the storm. For me, it's getting serious. That's why I want to take it slow. I'm trying to read you to see if you're ready to get serious about anybody—meaning me—because I would have to have you all to myself."

"You're not just anybody. I told you a while back I wanted to be your man."

"All y'all niggas know what to say when y'all are trying to get something. So I wasn't paying any attention to those words."

"Well, why wouldn't I want to get serious about you? I'm diggin' the hell out of you. You're a good girl. You're fine, smart, driven, and independent, not a gold digger. You're a little stuck up, but I can handle that. You want me to continue?"

"Please do."

And let's not forget that first impression you gave me."

"Mmmm." She moaned at the thought. "My instincts were right. Those kisses . . . I'll never forget those."

"You ain't a ho. I like the way you call me Kaylin. I can't wait to make love to you real good," he said, kissing her forehead.

"Really? I bet you make real good love to all those other females you got blowing up your pager and cell."

"No, can't say that I do."

"Kaylin please don't insult my intelligence."

"I don't; I just fuck them. There is a difference."

"Trifling. That sounds like you think we ain't shit, just a fuck."

"That's what most of y'all say y'all want. Not all, but most. Tell me you didn't want to fuck me when you first saw me."

"Nigga I did not want to fuck you at first sight!"

"Yes you did!"

"No I didn't." She punched his arm. I just told you I wanted to see what you were about first! And second, I wanted to kiss you and then after we kissed you had it like that, that's when I wanted to fuck.

"See. What I tell you!" He teased.

"Kaylin that was after the fact. Not on first sight."

"Same thing."

"No it's not." She had to laugh.

Angel shook her head in disbelief at that statement. "Tell me your definition of fucking versus making love."

"Simple. When I fuck a female, the only goal for me is to ride it until I'm tired of it and then bust a nut. Making love is more mental than it is physical. When I make love, that shit has meaning. When you make love to your woman it takes skill. Every kiss, touch, feel, hug, stroke means something when it's your other half. I can take my time and make sure my woman is satisfied before busting a nut, but I gotta rock her world."

"I see. So Kaylin, tell me the last time you made love?"

"With my son's mama . . . when he was about two months old. That was the last time."

"How old is he now?"

"He'll be two in December."

"What's his name?"

"Malik."

"That's cute. And the mom?"

"She ain't nobody you got to worry about."

"I would hope not."

"It's been over between us for almost a year and a half."

"So you mean to tell me you've been fuckin' around all this time?"

"Yeah, I guess so if you want to look at it like that."

"That is so trifling."

"It's all part of the game. You see how we're always on the go. I wasn't trying to get a relationship going like that. If I had run across somebody that I wanted to lock down then it would have been another story. Females like you be hidin' from a nigga."

"That's because we're somewhere handling our business."

"I've slowed down a lot in the last two months, especially since you had me using my free time chasing you."

"You didn't have to chase me."

"A nigga's gotta do what a nigga's got to do. So when was the last time you made love?"

"About eleven months ago."

"When was the last time you got fucked?"

"Angel doesn't get fucked. I pick niggas that will make love to me."

"I feel you. Is that why I haven't been blessed to hit it yet? You think I just wanna fuck you?"

"I'm not sure. I'm still checking you out. What's the rush?"

"What's the rush? The rush is I'm really diggin' you. I ain't gonna front. I love me some pussy. I love gettin' up in it. I love the way it smells, the way it tastes, the way it sings when it's juicy, the way—"

"Okay, Okay I get the picture Kaylin." Angel was laughing at him.

I'm a pussy fiend. I can't help being anxious and impatient."

He poured them both a glass of Cristal and lit his blunt. Angel took a few sips. They sat in silence while R. Kelly crooned through the speakers, neither of them paying attention. They were both in deep thought until he began massaging her shoulders. "You're a little tense, ma." She closed her eyes, not saying a word, as he massaged her shoulders for a good ten minutes. "What are you thinking about?" he asked, finally breaking her train of thought.

"Why?"

"Because I want to know."

"Just some things we females think about when we get ourselves in situations like this."

"You wanna be more specific?"

She sat in silence for a few more minutes. "Where are your CDs? I keep hearing this song in my head."

"Slide that door back," he said, pointing to the entertainment center. She got up and thumbed through the CDs until she came across *The Heat* by Toni Braxton. She pressed play, and sat back down.

"Please continue. That felt good," she said, closing her eyes. They listened to the song *Maybe* in silence as he massaged her shoulders and neck more.

Females. Kaylin told himself. He knew Angel wanted him to listen to the words of the song. There was a message for him. The only thing interfering was Toni singing faster than Twista rapped. But overall he was able to pick up some key sentences. He watched her point the remote and hit repeat. Toni was hinting to Angel to think about it and *maybe* even slow her roll. *Fuck that!* Kay said to himself.

"Red." He continued to knead the kinks out of her neck and shoulders.

"Hmmm." she moaned. "Don't stop, Kaylin."

"Are you listening to me ma?"

"Mmmm." she moaned again. "I'm listening."

Kaylin began to interpret Toni's lyrics. "You're wondering if a brother can be true. Yes I can. Will I make you hot, hit your spot and love you a lot! Baby I'm your man. Will I leave you hanging, lonely and desperate? Will I go and tell all my friends that we did it again and again? Hell no to all of that." He leaned over, and put his lips to her ear and whispered, "should you give me some?" He kissed her ear and began running light kisses behind her ear and slowly down and around her neck. Then he put his lips back to her ear and whispered. "Yeah. If you say yes, I'll love you like a baby, so later for *maybe*. So Red, tell this nigga. Yeah."

"Kay you know I'm not looking to get fucked. I'm looking for love and trust in a lifelong partner. I want you to belong to me, and I gotta be number one. Furthermore, I want to be treated like a queen, to be loved, pampered, spoiled . . . all that stuff that I deserve and need."

"I'm your man Red."

"That *may be*. But right now I gotta get some sleep Kaylin."

What! Kaylin and his dick both reacted in silence.

"Thank you so much for the massage." She figured she may as well leave while she had the chance so she got up to do just that.

He grabbed her hand. "Can I get a kiss before you go and leave *us* hanging?" He pulled her back down onto the couch and tongued her down. She backed up.

"Baby, it's almost 1:30. I really gotta get some sleep."

He reached over and lifted her up and positioned her right on top of his dick. "Let me make love to you Red." He began kissing her.

"Kaylin," she said, breathing heavily now, "I said we wasn't going to do anything."

"What are we doing?" he mumbled, unbuttoning her pajama top and sucking on one of her nipples. His dick was now rock hard as he started moving her faster. She was now grinding on her own.

"Kaylin this . . . I can't . . . Oh . . . " He was caressing up and down her back, and their bodies were moving as one. "Kay," she called.

"What? We're not doing anything."

"Then why am I getting ready to cum?" He lifted her off his

lap. "Kaylin," she whined, trying to climb back on top of him. He reached in his back pocket, pulled out a condom, and gave it to her.

"Open this," he said, pulling down her pajama pants and sliding his sweats down to his ankles. He pulled her back onto his lap.

"Nigga if you try to play me, I'm catchin' a case. Just lettin' you know," she warned as she put his condom on.

"That goes both ways Red," he said, lifting her up, putting only the head of his penis in. She let out a moan and then kissed him hard, as her juices slid down his penis. He grabbed her booty with both hands and pulled her all the way down on him.

"Kaaaaay," she moaned as she held on tight. It felt like he was ripping her a new pussy. "Kay," she kept saying as their bodies moved in sync. "Oh my . . . shit . . . How bbbig are . . . you?"

He dug in as deep as he could, hitting her G-spot. "Oh, yeah!" he mumbled. After he hit that spot repeatedly Angel got to cumming, hollering and crying all at the same time. He held her tight and kissed her on her neck and breasts as she got herself together. He pulled off his T-shirt and wiped her face with it. Then he lifted her up, turned her around, and had her bend over, her elbows resting on the back of the sofa.

"Kay I can't cum again," she said, trying to catch her breath.

"Yes, you can," he said as he penetrated her. "You ain't been fucked in eleven months. I'm gettin' ready to show you what this pussy can do. This pussy belongs to Kaylin now." He was going in as deep as he could, trying to find her G-spot. He reached around and started massaging her clit. After a few strokes he was able to feel her G-spot again and she began to moan and groan.

"Kay . . . I . . . cum . . . oh shit . . . only once . . . baby . . . Ohhh." And she started cumming again and crying.

He kept hitting that G-spot and wouldn't stop until she begged, "Please Kay. Kay, please." She was exhausted and couldn't move as he kept showering her with soft kisses.

"I like the way you feel Red," he whispered in her ear. They were resting, Kaylin ready for another round, still inside her.

"Let me go Kay," she was barely audible as she tried to assert herself.

"Oh, so you forgot all that shit you was talkin' about me being a one-minute man with a small dick and not being able to find your spot? You forgot?"

"I was only playin'," she said, still out of breath. "Let me go Kaylin, please." He pulled out of her, pulled off the latex, and pulled up his sweatpants. "Shit."

She flopped back onto the couch and lay motionless looking up at him for a good five minutes. "What?" he asked.

"I can't remember ever cumming that hard and long before. This pajama top is drenched," she said, pulling it off. "Help me up. I gotta take a shower."

He lifted her up, looking at her sweaty, naked body. She kissed him on the lips. "You didn't disappoint me at all Kaylin," she said as she made her way up the stairs.

"Don't get in the shower yet. I'll be up there."

"No Kay. Our rendezvous is over. I can't come again," she said, looking at his erect dick. She went on upstairs, washed her face and the kitty cat, and brushed her teeth. She then went back into the bedroom, pulled the comforter back, and slid between the cool silk sheets.

He came into the bedroom butt naked and hard, throwing a condom pack on the night table next to the bed. He pulled all of the covers off the bed and crawled between her thighs, kissing and sucking on her breasts.

"Can I feel you without the latex?"

"No Kaylin."

"Please, just for one minute. You can even time me."

"No Kaylin," she said, reaching for the condom. He was already rubbing the head of his penis on her clit. Then he put it all the way in and just held it there as they kissed a long and passionate kiss.

"Damn you feel good Red," he said, grinding real slow. "Oh you're so wet baby. Open the latex." He pulled out, took it from her, put it on and went in as deep as he could.

"Oh Kay," she said, her heart racing. She couldn't believe how good he felt inside her and how good it felt to have his strong body on top of hers. "Kay," she said to him.

"What?" he answered, not missing a stroke.

"Are you making love now?"

He moaned, sucking on her nipples. "Baby I'm making love and don't want to stop." He put both of her legs up over his shoulders. She began to tremble and holler, filled with ecstasy as he dug in deep.

"Oh shit! Kay that's my spot again. Wait!" she yelled.

"Baby I feel it. Damn! You feel good."

"Kay!" she screamed as she climaxed. He kept grinding and humping as the contractions of her pussy muscles squeezed his dick, pulling it in even deeper. They came together, he not being able to hold out any longer. He licked the tears off her face, then planted soft kisses all over her body as she recovered.

"So, what do you think? Was that fuckin' or lovemaking?"

"Lovemaking," she said, running her hands through his braids.

"Where have you been hiding all this time? Kaylin really likes this."

"Oh, does he?"

"Mm hmm."

"So now that you've hit it, and the chase is over, now what?"

"I'ma keep on hittin' it. You're special." He rolled over. "Let's get into a dry bed." He swooped her up and carried her into the master bedroom, giving her one of his pajama tops to put on before climbing in bed naked.

Angel had set the alarm clock for 5:30, and it was already 3:40. He snuggled up and wrapped his arms around her.

"I like you a lot Red."

"I like you a lot, too, Kaylin."

Chapter 12

Later that morning at work, Angel pulled some files and made photocopies until about eight o'clock, which was when she had planned to call Tasha at her job.

"Physical therapy. This is Denise."

"Hey Denise, is Roz around? This is Angel."

"What's up, girl? Your friend played hooky this morning."

"I see. I'll call her on her cell phone. Thanks." Then she quickly dialed Tasha's cell.

"Hello," Angel heard a ton of screams. "Girl, where are you? It's 8:00 in the morning."

"Aaah!" Tasha screamed into the phone. "Jaheim is about to hit the stage! I'm at the Apollo. I told y'all that Doug Banks was going to be broadcasting live this morning. Angel, girl, you missin' it."

"Who else is there?"

"Jaheim, Case, 112, Koffee Brown, and Jesse Powell. Jive-ass Mystical was supposed to be here with his fine ass, but he's a no-show."

"Dayum!" Angel whined.

"Don't cry now, baby. I gots to go."

"Hey Angel!" Trina yelled into the phone.

"Wait!" Angel yelled. "Guess what?"

"What?" Tasha was anxious to hang up.

"I got my world rocked!" she said, letting out a loud, happy sigh of relief.

"By who?" asked Tasha.

"Kaylin."

"Kay?" She sounded surprised.

"Yup, I spent the night at his house last night."

"You're lying."

"Swear to God."

"Oh shit! Angel finally got some. I don't believe it. So how was he?"

"Off the chain!"

"Off the chain because you ain't had none in a decade or 'cause the brotha got skills?"

"Skills, baby."

"On a scale of one to ten?"

"Twelve! Nigga had me crying and shit."

"Oh my God! I don't believe what I'm hearing. I am so glad you finally got some. Where are you?"

"At work."

"You ain't right. Najee is gonna look at you and be able to tell. Just watch."

"No, he's not."

"Watch, I gotta go. Call me at home tonight."

"A'ight."

"Peace."

About half an hour after she spoke to Roz, Angel's phone rang. "This is Ms. Smith."

"Good morning, beautiful." She was turned on by Kay's deep voice, which she always found to be very sexy.

"Good morning Kaylin."

"How'd you get to work?" he asked, still sounding half-asleep.

"I took a taxi."

"You talkin' 'bout me leavin' you lonely. *You* left *me* lonely. Why didn't you wake me up?"

"Because you were sleeping so peacefully. Besides, if I woke you up I doubt if I would have made it to work."

"Sounds like you feel how I'm feelin'."

"I enjoyed myself last night, a little embarrassed about the crying though. I've never done that before. That must have been eleven months of anxiety that you were breaking down."

"I'm ready to break it down some more. What time is your lunch?"

"Any time I decide to take it. Why? What do you have in mind?" she asked. She was biting down on her bottom lip at the thought of cumming like she did the night before, repeatedly and with intensity.

"I wanna break down some more of that anxiety. What time can I come pick you up?"

"Twelve will be fine."

"I'll be out front with bells on."

"Bye Kay."

Angel got busy again, doing research on the computer and returning some phone calls.

Around 10:30, Kisha called her into the lobby. "This delivery is for you," she said, smiling and pointing at the big basket filled with luscious fresh fruit and all kinds of muffins, croissants, and bagels. There was also a huge floral arrangement with a card attached. Angel opened it up to read it,

Red, I loved making love to you. K

She smiled as she recalled last night.

"Must be nice to have it like that," Kisha teased.

"Sure is. Take some of this fruit and muffins. This is enough to feed the entire office," said Angel before taking the basket and floral arrangement to her office.

At ten minutes before noon, Kay, dressed in a sleeveless T-shirt, baggy shorts hanging off his butt, you could see his boxers, unlaced Timberland boots, and no socks, was double-parked out front. He got out of the car, opened the passenger door, and started dialing on his cell.

Angel finally came out the building at 12:05, Kay ending his call when he saw her. She was followed closely by Najee and two other attorneys. Kay ignored them, greeting her with a kiss on the lips.

"Mmm. You smell so good Kay," she said, running her hand through his hair.

"And you are so beautiful." He ran his hands through hers.

"Look at them," she said, rolling her eyes in the direction of Najee and the two other attorneys standing around talking and watching them. "They're probably wondering what do you have that they don't." Kaylin winked at her then he put her in the car and shut the door. They went up the street to the Hyatt, where they stayed for about two hours before he drove her back to work.

Chapter 13

Everyone was getting ready for Kay's birthday party. Roz had paged Trae to tell him that she was ready to leave the beauty salon. Then she called Angel to make further plans for the day. Angel told her she was leaving at 6:30 because Kay had some stops to make.

When Trae walked into the salon he stood and looked around for his woman. Every female within his sight was staring him down. But he had eyes only for Tasha. They made eye contact. He winked at her and she smiled as her hairdresser put the finishing touches on her hair.

"You look very cute," he said, kissing her on the forehead. They walked out of the salon and headed for the Navigator. He opened the door and lifted her in. Then she saw the white box sitting on the back seat. She reached back for it, set it on her lap, and opened it.

"Ooooooh Trae, you do love me," she said, picking off the biggest strawberry on the cheesecake. Trae was already on the cell talking to Kay. She grabbed him around his neck and gave him a big kiss saying, "I love you, baby.

"Man, I wish I had a knife or a spoon, or something," she whined.

As soon as they got into the house Tasha went into the kitchen to get a knife. She scraped half the strawberries off, put them on a saucer, and devoured them.

"Tash come get in the shower with me!" Trae yelled from the other room. She looked at her watch. It was 6:45, and they were supposed to leave at 8:00. She put the cheesecake in the refrigerator then went to join him in the shower. By 7:45 they were getting dressed.

"I still can't believe Kay and Angel are kickin' it," Tasha said in obvious disbelief.

"Why not?"

"I don't know. It's just weird that after all of this time she finally gets with somebody and it's your boy.

"He's gonna look out for her."

"He better, or else I'm gonna kick his ass," she said, laughing. He was already dressed and was now sitting on the side of the bed watching her get dressed.

She spun around. "How do I look?"

"Ma you wearin' the shit outta that outfit."

"Daddy, you killin' it yourself," Tash told him.

"We ready to stun 'em or what?"

"No doubt," she said, spinning around again.

"You missin' one thing. Come here," he said. He opened a long box and took out a platinum ankle bracelet with "Trae" written in diamonds. She put her foot up on the bed and he placed it on her ankle.

"Awww baby, this is too cute. Why does "Trae" have to be on it?" she teased.

"To let them niggas know they ain't got nothin' comin' *and* to remind you what time it is."

"Nigga I don't need a reminder," she said, laughing. She noticed that the only jewelry he wore was a big rock in his ear and his presidential Rolex. "I'm bling blinging way more than you," she bragged.

"That's how it's supposed to be. You got Kay's present?"

"Yup, it's in my bag."

"Let's roll, then."

They pulled up at the Ritz around 10:30, and cars were everywhere. It looked more like a show than a birthday party. They stepped out of the Nav singing "So fresh, so clean." Kay and Angel, equally fresh and clean, were waiting on them.

Tonight was going to be off the chain. Fat Man Scoop was spinning on the ones and twos, and New Day, featuring Muqa, would be performing. They were a new hip-hop group on Kay's label.

Quite a few folks, including Black Rob, G-Dep, KRS-l, Coco Butter of the Doug Banks show, and Queen Pen, would be stopping by to wish Kay a happy birthday.

"Happy birthday, my brotha," said Tasha, hugging Kay and giving him a small box.

"Thanks, sister-in-law," he said, picking her up and kissing her on the forehead. "And congratulations on the baby."

"Thanks Kay," she said smiling. Then she hugged Angel and spun her around telling her how tight she looked. Angel did likewise then she hugged Trae saying, "What up?"

They all headed for the VIP section marked "Birthday Boy." Trae's cousin, Omar, Shanna's man, Bo, Mel, Supreme, and Kay's sister, Tamara, and her friend, Brenda, were already there. The photographer started taking group pictures, then paired up the couples before taking singles.

Before long the blunts were passing along with the Hennessey Petrone, Cristal, Moet, Alize and Dom P. Trae told Tasha she couldn't have any, ordering a virgin strawberry daiquiri for her, instead.

At 12:01, Kay cut his birthday cake. The cake was huge. He hugged Trae and thanked him for hooking him up. Kay didn't want to open his gifts until he got home. But folks started cussing him out. They wanted to be nosy so he went ahead and opened them. Angel and Tamara, who clicked immediately after Kay introduced them, put the gifts away at the end of the session.

Tasha was sitting on Trae's lap sharing her urge to drink with him when Nikayah came over and called him. "Give me ten minutes," he told her. "I'll be right back."

"Why is Kay's sister acting like a bitch?" Tash asked Trae before she let him up.

"I told you I used to fuck with her. You didn't think she would be happy to make your acquaintance, did you?"

"No, but if I have to step to her it's going to be ugly."

"Shit. I see I can't leave you alone not even for ten minutes. C'mon with me," he said, trying to lift her off his lap.

"Trae, you know I don't want to be around Nikayah. Forget it. I'll be alright for ten minutes." He looked at her as if he wasn't so sure. "Promise, I'll be fine," she assured him. "Just hurry back. You're my date remember?"

"Ten minutes," he said, kissing her on the lips. She stood up, making sure to give Nikayah her back.

Angel came over to her. "You a'ight? I see you got a couple of problems." She caught the back of Nikayah.

"Girl, they are testing my patience, Kay's sister with her bitch-ass attitude and now Trae. I don't understand how he can act like me and Nikayah were never together. I almost had a heart attack when I recognized his voice calling Trae. I don't even want to look in his face."

"I heard that," Angel agreed.

Nikayah and Trae spoke for a couple of minutes before Nikayah disappeared onto the dance floor.

"Trae!" Kay yelled. Trae turned around and saw Kay coming towards him. "Playa I'ma have big beef with you if you crash my fuckin' party. Risa and Daysha are here. They both want to holla at you."

"Nigga I paid for this shit. I can crash it if I want to," Trae joked.

"Playa, handle your business and do it quietly. Don't fuck up, I'm trying to do somethin'. I'm out."

"Where are you goin', playa? I'll put up a grand to bet that you got bigger problems than me," Trae challenged.

Kay shook his head and smiled. "Dawg keep your G. I know I got major issues. Selena, Brittany, and Nicki are here, not to mention Red. And you know Brittany is crazy as fuck. She can make a nigga catch a charge if he don't watch it. I can get rid of two with no problem, but Brittany is gonna want to start some shit. I can't have that with Red around. She is on me. She already took my pager."

Trae started laughing. "Dawg I know you ain't let her do that."

"I'm diggin' her, man. I gots to chill for now. So I gave her that, not the business pager. I'm in love!" he howled. "Yo Red got it goin' on!"

Trae burst out laughing. "Sounds like you gonna crash your own party, dawg. Don't try to put that shit on me."

"Nah, I gots this." He winked at Trae and split.

"Uh uh. Let's go sit at the bar. I see Mecca and Shanna," Tasha said, pulling Angel's arm. Angel said bye to Tamara, and she and Tasha headed for the bar.

"How come y'all not sitting in the VIP section?" Tash asked Shanna and Mecca when she and Angel got to the bar.

"Because we can see all of the action from here," Mecca said. "I'm glad y'all finally decided to come over. What's up with Trae's friend, Omar?" she asked, looking at Tasha.

"I don't know. That's his cousin. He's quiet. Why?"

"Well, tell Trae I want to meet him."

Tasha and Angel got up on the stools and looked around. "You sure can see everything from here. This ballroom is gorgeous," Angel said.

"Look at all of these people," Tasha said. "Kay must be very popular."

Never missing anything when it came to her man, Tasha's eyes landed on Trae, who was now in Risa's company. She was rubbing up and down his arm.

"What are you doin' here?" Trae asked her with an attitude.

"I miss you. Why are you so angry with me? It's like you hate me."

"That's no longer important. Answer my question. What are you doin' here?" he asked again.

"This is Kay's party. Tamara invited me," Risa said in her own defense. "And why am I no longer important?"

"When did you and Tamara become such good friends?"

"Don't worry about it. Why are you so angry with me?" she pouted, folding her arms. "Can't we talk?"

"What do you want Risa? You only got one minute."

"Trae don't make me turn this party out."

"You ain't turnin' shit out. Fuck with me and they'll be takin' your ass outta here in a body bag. You got me fucked up. And now you're down to thirty seconds."

"So the sista that's draped in diamonds with the long weave is the reason you haven't been coming over or returning my pages? And why the fuck do I have only thirty seconds?" she asked, stomping her feet like a five year old. Trae was trying hard not to laugh at her.

"That's all you called me over here for? And that's not a weave."

"Oh, so when you wanted to fuck we could talk. Now I can't get a minute," said Risa, fighting back the tears.

"Talk to the nigga who had his car in your driveway at two in the morning. Whose car was that? Jabree's?" Her eyes grew as big as saucers. When she didn't respond he said, "Yeah, I thought so. I left your keys in the plant on the back porch. I told you it's all about Trae. Your minute's up," he said, walking away.

She followed him and grabbed him by the arm. "Trae let me talk to you," she begged.

"We ain't got shit to talk about. Get off my suit."

She let go. "Fuck you Trae!" she yelled. "You ain't all of that, to have a bitch sitting around waiting on you!"

Tasha's eyes were still glued to Trae, who was moving through the crowd looking for Daysha. When he found her, she was sitting with her girlfriend, Lynne.

"Hi Trae," Lynne said, standing up and hugging him.

"You havin' a good time?"

"So far. I'd be having an even better time if you introduced me to Kay like you promised."

"You're too late."

"See how you do Trae?" said Lynne, flopping back down in her chair.

"I'll introduce you to Mel."

"When?"

"Later on."

"A'ight," she said, perking up and winking at Daysha as she left the two of them alone.

Trae turned to Daysha, who had just lit a cigarette. "You smoke now?"

"What do you care? You don't even have the decency to return my calls or pages. I had to come all the way here to see you and see who the bitch is that has you occupied," she said, blowing out a cloud of smoke.

"What do you want?" Trae asked, trying to prevent the cigarette smoke from getting in his suit. He was getting agitated. She put the cigarette out.

She stood up and wrapped her arms around his neck. He reached up and unwrapped them. "That shit stinks ma." He backed up a little.

"Why can't we work this out? Why can't you work with me?"

"You know it's too late for that. It's over, girl. The fire has been out, you know that."

"What do you want from me Trae? It's been almost two years for us."

"I wanted you to stop sneaking behind my back and snortin' that shit. That's what I wanted. Then you had the nerve to lie about it."

"Trae I am grown. I don't need nobody's permission for shit."

"Well, handle your business," he said, walking away.

"I was tired of you anyway Trae."

He stopped and turned to her. "You wasn't tired of spending my money, was you?"

"You think you the shit, nigga. But you sell the shit so you ain't no better. I should call the Feds on your ass."

He leaned over and coolly whispered in her ear, "Bitch, if you ever again *mention* anything about snitchin' on me, they'll find your body parts floating in the fucking sewers." He gave her a look that let her know that he would definitely make it happen.

He headed back to the VIP section. All of the females were gone, except for Tamara who was talking to Brittany. Kay was able to get rid of Selena and Nicki by sending them home, but like he predicted Brittany wasn't having it.

The men were chilling, smoking blunts, drinking, and bull-shitting around.

"Come sit down Trae," one of them yelled.

"I'll be back. Where did the ladies go?"

"You don't see us sitting here?" Tamara asked desperately trying to capture his attention.

Trae ignored her. "Check the bar!" one of the brothas yelled.

He went over to the bar and, sure enough, they all were posted around, Tasha, Angel, Shanna, Mecca, Sanette, and Kay's cousin, Alicia. "Ma why are y'all at the bar when we got that whole section over there for y'all to kick it?" Trae wanted to know.

"We want to see all the action," Angel said.

He picked Tasha up off the stool. "C'mon ma, time for us to get crunk."

"Put me back down Trae," she said with an attitude.

He held her tight. "What's the matter with you?"

"Your ten minutes was up fifteen, twenty minutes ago. You had better been tying up loose ends, burning them, and letting them bitches know it's over. I ain't the one Trae. I already told you once."

Trae started laughing. "How you gonna be threatening your baby's daddy?" He kissed her on the cheek.

"My baby's daddy better let them bitches know that it's all about Tasha and they need to find somebody else to fuck."

Trae ignored her threats and started rocking back and forth to the beat of Hi-Tek and Kweli. "Baby you ready to get crunk or what?"

She mushed him in the face. "Don't make me hurt you nigga."
He bit her on the neck. "Owww Trae," she whined.

"C'mon. Let's go dance."

"Trae it's time for us to take the ladies out onto the dance
floor!" Kay yelled. Trae and Tasha were already on their way.

Kay spun Angel around on her stool and then tongued her
down. "Red, you are so sweet."

"I can't tell. You got three ho's up in here and you leave me
here by myself for a half hour. I heard you sent Nicki and Selena
home. Why the fuck is Brittany still here?"

" 'Cause she's a crazy bitch. How do you know who I sent
home?"

"Don't worry about it."

"As far as I'm concerned, I only got one woman at my party.
It's all about you Red. Go ask Brittany." He smirked.

"Don't fuck with me Kay. I told you I will catch a case."

"Oh, I can't be Kaylin now?" He kissed her again, making her
nipples hard. "C'mon, first lady, that's that Jigga joint," he said,
lifting her off the stool. They went to find Trae and Tasha on the
dance floor.

All four of them danced non-stop through *Oochie Wally, Get
Crunked Up, Southern Hospitality, Hit 'em High, Hit 'em Low, Let's
Get Dirty, Take it to da House, Let's Get this Money, Superwoman, Feat
Fabulous,* and *Get Ur Freak On* remix. The deejay even threw in
some old school: *We be Clubbin', Ain't Nothing but a G Thang, Money
Ain't a Thang.* Fat Man Scoop had the joint jumpin' and bumpin'.

"A'ight y'all, the birthday boy, my man Kay, wants me to slow
it down," the deejay said. "He has a couple of songs he wants me
to play for him and his lady. Also, the nigga that's paying me, my
dawg Trae, who's also paying for all this Cris and Moet y'all niggas are drinking like water, got some requests as well. So, grab
your ladies—if you ain't got one, too bad—because it's getting
ready to get hot up in heeere!" All the dogs started barking.

He kicked it off with Kay's request, *Sweet Lady* by Tyrese.
Then it was a request from both Kay and Trae, *You* by Jesse

Powell. It got a little hotter on the floor when Maxwell's *Fortunate* played and Trae sang it to Tasha in her ear. To top things off, right before *Meet Me at the Altar* by Jagged Edge went off, Trae pulled out a big seven-carat engagement ring and put it on her finger, telling her he wanted her to be his for a lifetime.

"Looks like another playa turns in his playa's card," Scoop hollered.

"I don't believe you did this Trae," Tasha said. "Get up! You're embarrassing me." She was pulling him off his knee, looking around to see who all was watching.

"Well, you believe it. I told you that you're the one," he said, kissing her on the lips. "Look at you blushing and shit."

Angel reached over and held up Tasha's arm so she could see the rock. "Dayum! It is beautiful. Congratulations, my sista," she said, turning Kay loose and hugging Tasha then Trae.

"I can't believe you locked this nigga down," Kay said, kissing Tasha on the forehead.

"Don't be kissing my wife, man," Trae joked, pulling Tasha close to him. Through it all nobody noticed Nikayah sitting around watching them the whole time.

The deejay was now playing the hot and steamy *Anytime* by Janet Jackson. Folks were practically sexing on the dance floor. Trae had eased his hands on Tasha's ass, pulled her close to get his grind on. When he got real hard he said, "You feel what you did?"

"I didn't do it by myself, but it sure feels good," she said. "I love you Trae."

"I love you too, ma, and thank you for having my baby," he whispered in her ear. They kissed some more until Trae turned her around, got behind her, and put his arms around her waist. They started walking. His dick was poking her butt.

"Am I your cover?" Tasha teased.

"Hell, yeah. You feel my shit sticking straight out."

"Where are we going?"

"To find a corner, closet, or something."

* * *

After Janet's *Anytime* went off, Kay whispered in Angel's ear, "Can I get my birthday present now?"

She answered between kisses on his lips, "You want it now, right in the middle of your party? You're kidding me, right?"

He moved her around on his hard dick, placing a passion mark on her neck. "Red do it feel like I'm playin'?"

"Mmmm Kaylin," she moaned.

"I like the way you call my name, ma, especially when you're hot."

"I can't help it. You make me feel good. You make me hot."

He reached in his pocket and gave her a key to Suite 1604. "Go take a shower. I'll be right behind you."

She kissed him and then left. Kay walked around for a minute, making sure everybody was alright before slipping out and heading for the elevators. A wicked grin fixed on his lips.

Trae and Tasha went through a set of double doors. Tasha was giggling as they came into a hallway with a bunch of doors. Trae jiggled the first one; it was locked. The second one opened right up. It was a dimly lit storage closet.

"Come here ma," he said, pulling Tash toward him and slobbing her down. He put his hands up under her skirt and grabbed her booty. They got their grind on and kissed until his dick was throbbing and her panties were soaked. He pulled her panties off and set them next to her. She unfastened his pants while sucking on his tongue and sliding his pants and boxers down. Then he went to rubbing his dick in her wetness, then all on and around her clit. She wrapped her legs around his waist and he slid it in, causing her to shudder and moan. Their bodies moved in rhythm as they held each other tight. In a matter of minutes, they both were cumming, holding on to each other and panting breathlessly.

"That was a good quickie ma."

"It's always good Trae. I love you," she said sucking on his neck.

"You ready to be my wife?"

"I'm already your wife," she said, passing him a towel. "I'm just ready for you to be home."

"Couple of weeks ma, and I'm out. Want to get a room here tonight?"

"If you want to. Why didn't we do that in the first place?"

"For a quickie? Too boring."

They both laughed as they left out the storage room. Just then a security guard walked by, patrolling. "See what I mean?" Trae said, winking at Tasha.

Angel came out of the shower wrapped in a towel.

"Hey, beautiful," Kay said, smiling. "You ready to go on my roller-coaster ride?"

"Is that where you're taking me?" she said, sitting down on the bed. "We need silk scarves and honey to ride a roller coaster?" she asked, teasing him.

"Yup, the scarves are for me to do what I gots to do without you squirming, choking me with your thighs, or pulling out my hair."

"Oh, so you're all of that?"

"You're getting ready to find out." He began stripping. Then he picked her up, grabbed the scarves and honey, and took her to the bedroom, where he immediately tied her up to the full size bed with bedposts.

"Leave one hand loose Kaylin."

"Nah Red. It's on, baby. You forgot all that shit you was talking on the phone."

"I was only joking, Kaylin." Alarm evident in her voice.

"Well the joke is getting ready to be on you."

"Baby." she whined

"Relax beautiful. I got you. Just tell a nigga happy birthday and close your eyes."

"Happy birthday, baby." she cooed. Then did as she was told and closed her eyes. She felt him paint her lips with honey using his fingertips. He then turned the bottle upside down and poured a thin line down the front of her neck, both shoulders, her nipples, navel, inner thighs, all around her pussy and her clit. She opened her eyes and watched as he dipped two fingers inside the honey jar, then placing them inside her pussy.

"Kaylin." she moaned as he moved them in and out.

"You like that don't you? Tell me you like it."

"I love it baby. Go ahead and suck on my clit." She begged.

"Not yet ma." He pulled out his two fingers.

"Noooo," she moaned. "Baby please. I love you."

Kaylin lightly brushed the honey down her thighs all the way to her toes. He set down the bottle and began hungrily kissing the honey off her lips. When he turned her lips loose he began licking and sucking the honey around her neck. Angel's body was tingling and continuous moaning escaped her mouth. When he began sucking, licking and kissing her shoulders she tried to free her hands.

"Kaylin baby!" she yelled out.

He ignored her as he slid his tongue down to her nipples and began sucking on them as if they were juicy melons.

"Kaylin it's time to untie me baby."

"What?" He was planting soft kisses on her stomach and around her navel.

"Untie me." Eagerness in her voice.

"Why? You want me to fuck you?" He licked the honey out of her navel and eased down to the pussy.

"Oh shit!" She squealed as she felt him eating the honey out of her pussy. "Fuck!" She groaned as she tried to throw her clit in his face. "Shit Kaylin. Untie me . . . Oh shit . . . Oh right . . . sss . . . there . . . now baby."

"You ready to fuck now?" He continued teasing as he went to licking her inner thighs.

"Nigga . . . oh my . . ."

"You ready to fuck?"

"Yes. Oh shit . . . yes." She pleaded as he licked her pussy again. Come on baby suck my spot." She begged. As soon as his tongue lapped that clit she let out a squeal.

"Oh KKKay I'm . . . cummin'." He licked faster and faster trying to match the rhythm of her contractions. "Oh God . . . please." She came long and hard. As her breathing struggled to return to normal, he licked the honey off of her thighs, legs, knees and toes. Angel's body was feeling as if it was floating. The way he was sucking her toes she thought she would cum again. He worked his way back up to her pussy.

"Kaylin. Please baby. Wait a minute." He started licking her clit. "Oh God. Please Kaylin."

He paused, looked up at her and flashed her an evil grin, then said, "God? That's who you better call 'cause the pussy belongs to me." When he put his head back down towards her pussy she went back to begging.

"Kaylin. Please." He looked at her, smiled, climbed on top of her and was kissing her.

"Why are you trying to stop a nigga from enjoying his birthday present?" He asked in between kisses. "Huh?"

"Untie me baby." He was now sucking her nipples. "Baby untie . . . Uunnggh," she groaned as he went back to sucking on her clit. No matter how hard she tried to scoot away she couldn't escape from that monster tongue. She finally surrendered to a gut wrenching orgasm which brought her to tears. Kay was in a zone still eating her pussy as if the pussy was his last meal.

After the third orgasm she was begging him to untie her. Next thing you know she was cussing at him and threatening him. That's when he finally gave in. He started laughing and quickly put a condom on as she lay there trembling with exhaustion. Since she was motionless, he crawled in between her legs, putting one of them up over his shoulder, and went to grinding, banging her back out until he finally busted a big nut.

They both lay there for about twenty minutes, unable to move. Kay looked at the clock. It was 3:45 a.m.

He kissed Angel. "Red you a'ight?" He had knocked her out.

"Baby you know what? I hope you enjoyed yourself, because that's the last time you will *ever* tie this bitch up."

"C'mom, ma. Don't punish a nigga like that. You said you were ready to go on Kay's roller coaster ride. A roller coaster ain't no fun if it don't take you all the way up and then dip all the way down causing your heart to jump in your throat and make your stomach drop to your feet. Right?"

"Kaylin, Just remember what I said."

"Baby—"

"You enjoyed your birthday present right?"

"Did I!"

"Good. She still had her back to his chest.

Kay couldn't help but laugh. "I fucked you silly ma. Look at you. You can't even move. Do you think I can get a quickie?" He teased. "Or you wanna tie me up and ride my dick? I won't get mad at you if you fuck me silly, cause me to bust a couple of nuts, make me cry.

"Whatever Kay. Don't you think you need to get back to your party?" Angel snapped.

"I guess I should." He was laughing at her.

Trae and Tasha stopped at the rest rooms to freshen up. Shanna saw them as they stepped back into the party. She pushed her way over to them and looked them up and down suspiciously.

"Excuse us Trae," Shanna said, trying to pull them apart. Tasha and Trae continued holding hands. "Let her go, Trae."

"Where's Bo?" asked Trae.

"Over at the VIP section."

"Is Kay over there too?"

"No, him and Angel slipped off."

"How do you know all of this?"

"Forget you Trae. I can't help it if I'm up on everything."

"Up on everything? Don't you mean nosy? So I guess y'all are going to the bar?" he asked. Shanna was still trying to pull Tasha away from Trae.

"Yes, we are." Shanna snapped.

Trae let Tasha go, winked at her, then headed for the VIP section. Shanna turned her attention to Tasha saying, "That's why your ass is pregnant now . . . slipping off like that. Angel's ass is gonna be next.

"Let me see this rock I've been hearin' about." She grabbed Tasha's hand to examine it. "Aw, man! This is . . . I don't even know what to say." She hugged her. "Congratulations! I am so happy for you. Y'all know y'all gotta have a gangsta wedding. Right?"

"Ms. Shanna, we are not gangstas. Thank you." She hugged her. "How long has Angel been gone?"

"Right after y'all disappeared." Shanna blurted out.

"Damn! What is Kay doing to her?"

"I know that's right!" Shanna said, slapping her five.

They sat down at the bar. The party was still jumping. Mecca and Sanette came over and reached for Tasha's hand. Everyone was dying to see the ring.

"This is beautiful," Mecca said, running her finger over it.

"It sure is," Sanette agreed.

"Congratulations!" They both said it at the same time and took turns hugging Tasha.

"Look who's trying to sneak back in," Mecca nodded in the direction of Angel and Kay. Giggles erupting amongst them.

"Damn, these niggas ain't never goin' home," Kay said, easing his way back into the party. He looked at Angel and kissed her on the cheek. "I can't ever remember gettin' a birthday present that good before."

A brotha named Shahid was hollering at Kay. Angel told him to go ahead. "I'll be over at the bar with the girls," he said as he tongued her down and sang, *You are so tasty!*" to the beat of "Peaches and Cream." She smiled and walked away.

When Angel got to the bar, Tasha, Mecca, Sanette, and Shanna were kickin' it. When they looked up and saw the obvious glow on her face, they all started laughing.

"Don't be hatin' on a sista," she told them before they could say anything.

"Ain't nobody hatin'. I know he's the birthday boy, but y'all couldn't wait till y'all got home?" Mecca teased.

"No, I was the birthday boy's present," she grinned, jumping up on the stool next to Tasha and kissing her on the cheek. Tasha smiled and pushed her away.

"Well, well, well . . . they say milk does a body good. I say prison does a body even better. Damn! Nikayah looks good!" Mecca said, in full lust mode. Everyone turned around to look at him—except for Tasha. Nikayah was standing around talking to some people.

"That's my cue to get the fuck outta here. Where is Trae?" Tasha asked, looking around. Her mood changing from festive to gloom just that quick.

"How much you wanna bet he's going to come over and say somethin' to you?" Angel challenged, elbowing her.

"I don't think so. He ain't crazy. At least I hope he ain't." But after some thought she said, "Oh, hell yeah! That nigga is crazy. Hand me that bottle. If he comes over here trying to fuck with me, this bottle is going over his fuckin' head. Watch and see."

"Roz chill. You should've known you were going to have to face him eventually. You know he heard that you're pregnant. Plus, you know that he didn't think that you would just up and leave his sorry ass," Angel said, trying to calm her down.

"Well, he brought that on himself. Where is Trae?" she asked, ignoring Angel's attempt to be reasonable. She wanted to get up but couldn't move. Her palms were starting to sweat. "I feel sick. Can somebody please go get Trae for me?"

Shanna and Sanette both jumped off their stools and disappeared into the crowd. Just as they did, Nikayah was walking over to the the bar.

"Welcome home Nikayah. You piece of shit," Angel mumbled as he approached.

"Angel what's goin' on? You're lookin' good." He hugged her while looking Tasha over. "I heard you already took the bar exam."

"Yup, just waiting impatiently to see if I passed." She forced a smile.

"Congratulations. You know you passed."

"Thanks."

"I heard that both Kyra and Jaz done settled down."

"Pretty much," Angel dryly stated.

Nikayah was still looking at Tasha, who had her back to him. "Why's your girl being so hard on me?" He nodded towards Tasha.

"Nigga, you know why." Angel had to catch herself because she was about to go off.

Nikayah kept gazing at Tasha. He fixed his eyes on her stomach, then found himself checking out all the ice she had on. Then he focused his attention on the ankle bracelet with Trae's name on it. He was turning green with envy, his ego shattered. "What's up Rozzie?" he asked, using the pet name he gave her. "I know you're allowed to speak to a nigga." She could smell alcohol on his breath. He was that damn close. "Damn baby. What you doin' to my man to make him drape you with all this ice? You easily got on two, three hundred thousand worth of shit. Fuck!"

"Nikayah, get the fuck away from me!"

"I guess it's really over between me and you, huh?"

"Get away from me, Nikayah!" she screamed, tears rolling down her cheeks. He was giving her the creeps.

"I still don't want to believe you fuckin' killed my babies, but yet you're gonna have that nigga's? You are an ice-cold bitch," he said, kissing the back of her neck like he was trying to suck the skin off.

She squeezed the liquor bottle, spun around, and smashed it on his forehead.

"Owww! You bitch!" he yelled, wrapping his hands around her neck and choking her.

Angel and Mecca jumped down off their stools and immediately began to dig their nails into his wrists, trying to loosen his grip. Tasha was gasping and trying to poke his eyes out. The next thing you know, Trae, Bo, Kay, Supreme, Mel, and some other niggas were pushing their way through the crowd.

Trae punched him in the jaw and kept punching him until his bloody teeth flew out of his mouth. He finally let her go, Omar taking over. Trae then pulled out his gat and cocked it. In one quick move Kay snatched it, emptied it, and gave it back to him saying, "Not here, man!"

With that the niggas started beating Nikayah down to the ground. Trae pushed them all away and was stomping him in the head. There was blood everywhere. "That's enough man! Not here!" Kay was holding Trae and yelling at him. But Trae still managed to break free and started dragging Nikayah outside.

Meanwhile, Tasha had fallen to her knees and was crawling on the floor. She was gasping for air and throwing up. "Get her the fuck out of here!" Trae yelled to Kay.

"No, Trae!" Tasha screamed. "Let him go!" She was trying to get up off the floor but couldn't. Kay picked her up to carry her out to the car. "Kay stop him! Please Kay! Stop him before he does something stupid!" She was screaming and crying. She reached out to Bo, "Go get my man, Bo, please. He's going to jail for murder. Let me down, Kay." She was kicking and screaming, but Kay still ignored her.

"Take the keys out of my pocket," Kay said to Angel, who was crying and following right behind them.

"Let me go, please. Kay, go stop him," Tash pleaded. Angel unlocked the car, and Kay put her in the back seat. Angel then climbed in the back with her, trying her best to calm her down.

Kay locked the doors, telling Bo, "Watch them!"

"Angel, Trae is going to kill him. He's going to prison. Kay could have stopped him." Tasha was now screaming and crying at the top of her lungs.

She tried to open the car door, but Bo wouldn't let her. "Bo go get him."

"He's coming," he assured her. "He's coming."

"Fuck you Bo!"

Angel was holding her and rocking her back and forth. Police cars were starting to pull up. They could hear Kay yelling at Trae. Both girls looked anxiously in that direction. Trae quickly got in the back seat. Angel then jumped in the front with Kay, and they sped off. Trae flicked on the light. "Go to the nearest hospital," he instructed Kay. He was looking at Tasha's face and neck. "Damn!" he said, on seeing her neck red and swollen from Nikayah's fingerprints. He turned the light out.

"Fuck! I knew I shouldn't have left you alone. I'm sorry, baby." He tried to hold her, but she started swinging at him.

"You killed him, didn't you? You're going to prison, Trae. You know these niggas are gonna tell on you. How could you do this? You got a baby on the way Trae." She kept swinging at him. He grabbed her arms and held her so that she couldn't move. "You got a fucking baby on the way," she cried. "You didn't have to kill him."

"No baby, I didn't."

"Don't lie to me Trae."

"You know I never lied to you. He's fucked up, but he ain't dead."

"You're a liar Trae. I'm not having this baby if I find out you lied. I'm not bringing a baby to prison to visit you. I can't do it Trae. I'm not raising a child by myself."

He hugged her and kissed her on the forehead. "Baby, you gotta calm down." Her trembling body was feeling hot.

When they pulled up to the emergency room, Trae jumped out and immediately went to yelling about the pregnant woman who was attacked and needs assistance right fuckin' now, or else he would make sure the hospital got shut down.

After his rampage four doctors immediately started working on Tasha.

Her blood pressure was way up and she was dehydrated. They hooked her up to an IV and began running tests to check on the baby. It didn't look good.

Chapter 14

After they ran what seemed like a thousand tests, the doctors at the hospital told Trae the baby was fine. The doctor said that the mother needed to rest for a couple of days and to remain stress-free. They kept her in the hospital for two days, the doctor wanting to make sure her blood pressure stayed down. He also ordered her to rest at home for the next three days.

Trae took her straight to his apartment, where he waited on her, hand and foot.

"Trae, will you stop treating me like an invalid," Tasha complained as she plopped down on the sofa next to him.

"You are supposed to be on bed rest, ma."

"I'm ready to go home," she whined.

"You are home."

"Baby you know what I mean. Take me for a ride or something. What's so stressful about that?"

"Three more days, then I'll take you wherever you want to go."

"I'm so bored. Three damn days—I'll be crazy."

"No you won't. You're supposed to be resting."

She picked up the cell phone and dialed Angel's cell number.

"Hello," Angel answered.

"It's me, Tasha." She dryly stated.

"Hey, ma. Why are you sounding all dead? How are you?"

"I'm bored to death." She complained.

Angel laughed. "You need to enjoy this little vacation. You've been living la vida loca lately."

"Tell me about it. Where are you?"

"On a family outing," she said, reaching over and playing with Kay's braids.

"What kind of family outing?"

"Kaylin, his son Malik, and my little sister, Carmen. Malik is too cute. I have to bring him to see you. We're in the Mercedes station wagon going to Chuck E. Cheese."

"How cute! Makes me want to hurry up and have mine." She said, voice dripping with sarcasm.

"Have one for me too, while you're at it," Angel joked.

"You can have your own. Are y'all coming over?"

"I don't know. Depends on what Kaylin has to do. I'll call you later. Now get your ass in the bed."

"I am in the bed."

"No, she isn't!" Trae yelled.

"I knew you wasn't. You liar. Give the phone to Trae. His boy wants to speak to him."

She handed Trae the phone and started kissing him on the neck. Then she unbuckled his pants and pulled them, along with his boxers, down to his ankles. He was ignoring her until he noticed she was down on her knees. "Kay, I'ma have to hit you up a little later, man." He closed his cell phone and looked at Tasha. "You mean to say you finally gonna break a nigga off?" he asked smiling.

"Mm hmm," she mumbled. She gently pushed him back and told him to relax. She grabbed his dick with both hands and massaged and squeezed it while running her tongue ring over its head. Trae started breathing harder. When she started sucking on the head, he leaned up and moaned. "Do your thang, baby! Handle your business." She started squeezing the base and put the rest into her warm, moist, juicy mouth, working it.

"Damn Tash! That feels good," he groaned. When he felt her

throat squeeze the head of his dick, he grabbed her head and started making subtle grinds. She deep-throated his dick, causing him to shudder at what felt like electric currents shooting from his toes up to his head. "Tasha baby." He tried to hold her back, but the suction of her jaws made his knees buckle. Then he suddenly exploded, releasing what felt like buckets down her throat.

She turned him loose and looked up at him while wiping her mouth. He was still leaning back with his eyes closed. She pulled his jeans all the way off and pulled his boxers back up. Then she climbed up on top of him and kissed him as he wrapped both arms around her, anxious to taste his own juices in her mouth.

"Ma, that was the best fuckin' head I ever got. Why you always holdin' out on your man?" He was totally relaxed. "How'd you deep-throat my dick like that?" He squeezed her cheeks, trying to get her to open wide. "And you swallowed!"

"Stop!" she giggled.

"That shit don't hurt?"

"No, it don't hurt—as long as I breathe right, and you're not movin' around all wild and shit."

He smiled at her. "Damn! That was some intense shit. Seemed like I never was gonna stop cummin'. I can't believe you finally gave me some head." He was still in shock. "The boredom must be really gettin' to you," he teased. "I'ma get you bored more often."

"Where did you go when you got that call late last night?" she inquired, changing the subject.

He stopped rubbing her back. "I had to take care of some shit I had hangin'. Baby, you never ask me where I've been. What's up? Where do you think I went?"

"It's just that you were real tense, and when you got that phone call you left in a hurry. When you came back you seemed relieved. That's why I asked. I'm your woman, Trae. I can sense when something's not right with my man."

"Everything's cool. You worry about finishing these last few hours on bed rest." As they lay there holding each other, he whispered, "I love you, baby."

"I love you too," she said, planting a big, sloppy kiss on his lips.

They got up and took a bath together. After dinner they watched *Brothers* on DVD. When Tasha fell asleep, Trae got dressed and left.

About 6:30 the next morning, the phone rang. Tasha picked it up but didn't say anything.

"Mornin' ma."

Tasha looked at the clock and ran her hand over the empty space next to her. "Baby when did you leave?"

"Right after you fell asleep. My Aunt Marva, the nurse, is coming over around 7:30 to cook and clean and to make sure you're alright."

"Trae I don't need a nurse. I need you to come home."

"I'll be there later on this afternoon."

"I'm not letting her in."

"Yo ma, she already has a key. Just let her cook you breakfast, make dinner, and clean up. Then you can ask her to leave, a'ight?" Tasha wouldn't say anything. "Let her do that for me, and I'll be there later on. You only have one more day to chill out. A'ight?"

"I love you," she sighed.

"I love you too. I gotta run."

Tasha raced to the shower. By the time she made up the bed and threw a load of clothes in the washer, Aunt Marva was turning the key. She came in like a storm and took over. She made Tasha go back to bed, prepared a big healthy breakfast for her, cleaned up, and started dinner.

Tasha woke up from her nap around 11:30. She called her house to listen to her voice mail. The first few messages were really nothing. But the one from Nikayah's mother got her sick to her stomach: *Nikayah's naked body was found hog-tied in a dump-*

ster; he had been beaten in the head with a blunt object. His body would be cremated because his face was beyond recognition, counting out being put in an open casket.

Tasha hung up the phone, ran to the toilet, and threw up. She hurried and cleaned up real good. When she heard footsteps she jumped in the bed and pretended she was asleep. *He told me he wouldn't do him,* she kept thinking to herself and crying. *He probably waited and did him the night he was all tense and left out right after he got that phone call. I knew something was up.*

Aunt Marva didn't leave until 2:00. As soon as she left, Tasha jumped up and got dressed. She was furious at Trae. She locked up the apartment, turning everything off, and went downstairs. Trae's building always had limo drivers parked out front and so she was able to get a driver to take her home.

On the way home she called the phone company and requested a new number. Then she called a locksmith to change all the locks, arranging for him to meet her when she got to her apartment. When she got there she packed a suitcase and headed for her Aunt Ginger's house.

When she got to work the next day she switched shifts with a lady who worked at the nursing home just in case Trae came to her job, she wouldn't be there. The nursing home was about ten minutes away from the hospital where she worked. She called Angel, who was at work, and was put on hold for about five minutes.

"This is Ms. Smith."

"It's me," said Tasha.

"It just ought to be you," she snapped. "You got me, Kay, and your man especially, worried sick about you. Trae is going crazy. Where are you?" Angel's exasperation evident.

"At work."

"What happened? Trae said the locks are changed. You won't answer the house phone or your cell phone, and the job is saying that you're not there. What is the matter with you? What happened? Did ya'll have a fight?"

Roz told her how she freaked out after she heard the message from Nikayah's mom on her voice mail.

"Dayum!" Angel said. "You're lying!"

"Do I sound like I'm lying? I'm through with Trae. He's going to jail, or somebody is gonna put his ass six feet under. I just feel it. How could he do this?" She burst out crying. "That's why I'm breaking it off now. That way when it happens, I'll be able to handle it much better. I won't be all in love and attached and shit, looking stupid. Angel I am so hurt that he would do this and jeopardize me and the baby. And being pregnant has got me so emotional and moody. Sometimes I feel like I can't control myself. I don't know whether I'm coming or going."

"Trae wouldn't jeopardize you and the baby. You better keep that nigga's baby," Angel warned.

"Wouldn't jeopardize?" Tasha spat. "Angel, killing a nigga is not a free 'do not go to prison pass.' What if they figure out who did it?"

"Roz, you don't know if he did it."

"Well my gut tells me he did," she cried. "I hate Nikayah but if I lose Trae then he would have got the last laugh. I'm scared Angel. I can't do this."

"Roz I want you to think about the baby. Before you make a decision talk to somebody. Don't do anything stupid."

"I can't kill this baby. I thought about it but I can't do it. I love him, but I gots to let him go. The stress is killing me. If I lose this baby or get an abortion, I feel that God is going to punish me because I've already killed one baby."

"Well that's a relief. Where are you staying? Or should I say in hiding?"

"With my aunt. Angel, if you tell anybody—I mean anybody, Kay, Trae, anybody—I'm not speaking to you ever again. Do we have an understanding?" She was dead serious.

"Okay, okay. But let me at least tell Kaylin that you're okay and that you called me. Trae is stressing and he's making my baby stress. Doesn't your cell phone have caller ID?"

"Yeah."

"Well, make sure you answer it if I call."

"If you have Trae or Kay anywhere around, I'm not speaking to you Angel."

"Girl, you are sounding like you're losing your mind. How are you just gonna shut that nigga out like that?"

"I don't know." She started crying again. "I don't know what the fuck I'm doing. I'm just doing it."

"Roz my sista, you need to chill out. You need to talk to him. That is your man, your fiancé. Did you forget?"

"Whose side are you on? I'm the one that's going to be stuck with a baby and no baby's daddy."

"Roz, you don't know what's going to happen. You know Trae is crazy about you and wouldn't do anything to hurt you or the baby."

"I can't tell. He did Nikayah when he told me he wouldn't."

"You're not a hundred percent sure. And if he did, you're still supposed to have his back. How long do you plan on hiding from him?"

Tasha blew her nose. "Until he gives up and stop looking. I want him to leave me alone."

Angel just sighed. "Girl, you are not making any kind of sense. Let me call Kay and let him know that you're okay. I'll call you later, okay?"

"Whatever."

"Love you. And chill the fuck out."

"Bye," Tasha said, blowing her nose again.

Angel called Kay and told him she just finished talking to Tasha. Kay passed the phone to his boy. Angel told Trae about Nikayah's mom leaving that message on her voice mail and how it freaked her out. She also told him that Tasha got it in her mind that he'd either be going to prison or getting buried in the very near future.

Trae wanted to know if she planned on keeping the baby. She told him she did and he was very relieved. She also told him, when he asked, that she didn't know where Tasha was staying.

Angel went on to tell him that the pregnancy had Tasha very emotional and moody. Trae gave the phone back to Kay, who watched his boy's nostrils flare up as he ran his hands over his face and stared out the window.

"Where she at, dawg?" Kay asked.

"I don't know, man," he said, still looking at the window.

"Why she trippin' like this? Pregnant or not this is bullshit!" Trae vented.

Chapter 15

Trae spent four days trying to find Tasha. He stopped by her place and by the hospital every day, but she was never at either spot. Finally, he said, "Fuck it."

"She just shut me out completely," Trae told Kay. "If she wasn't pregnant, I'd be tempted to put my foot in her ass for pullin' some shit like this. My patience has just about worn the fuck out."

Kay allowed his boy to vent and just shook his head saying, "If she wasn't pregnant she probably wouldn't be doing this, man. Being pregnant, they go through changes. You're gonna have to be a little more patient."

"Patient? I'm locked the fuck outta the house that I pay the mortgage on. She changed the phone number and I pay the fuckin' bill! She even refuses to answer her cell phone. Patience? And where the fuck is she at? I know Red knows where she is."

"I know she do, too. When I ask her, she won't say nothing. You know they stick together. She'll turn up, you know she can't hide forever."

"Is Faheem there?" Roz asked Jaz.

"No."

"Good. I'm on my way over."

"It's about time. I don't know if I ought to let you in. You haven't been here in over a month."

"Jaz, please. I got issues. You haven't been by my house either and you got a key."

"Roz, I'm almost nine months pregnant. I can't even get in and out of a car, so how do you expect me to travel way across town? And plus you changed the freakin' locks remember?"

"Okay, okay. I beg your forgiveness and I understand your situation. I need to talk to you. Don't be mad at me, okay."

"I'll think about it."

"I got you something."

"What?" Jaz perked up.

"You'll see when I get there." Tasha hung up. She pulled up into Jaz's driveway ten minutes later carrying two boxes. Jaz was standing in the doorway waiting for her.

"Let me see this big rock I've been hearing about before we go any further," Jaz commented. She looked at it. "Dayum! This is gorgeous." She hugged Roz. "Congratulations! Trae must be in love," she said, rubbing the tip of the rock. "This is beautiful."

"Look at you! Look how big you've gotten! You sure you're not carrying twins?" Roz wondered out loud.

"Hell, no, I ain't carryin' twins," Jaz emphasized. Roz gave her an awkward hug, and they both laughed.

"Look at *you*. Can't brag about that six-pack anymore. You're only three and a half months. You're not supposed to be showing yet. You sure *you're* not carryin' twins?" Jaz teased.

"I doubt it," Roz said, touring the house. "It looks so nice in here. Did you redecorate everything?"

"Just about. I've been bored to death. I'm ready to have this baby," Jaz said as they headed for the kitchen. "Wait until you get my size." Tasha sat both boxes on the kitchen table. Jaz opened them both. "You do love me!" she squealed. "A strawberry cheesecake and a pineapple cherry cheesecake. I'm in heaven," Jaz moaned. "Are they unthawed?"

"They should be," Roz told her. "Let me wash my hands while you get the plates."

When Roz came back from the bathroom, Jaz had fixed them both a plate with a slice of each. They sat down and dug in. "Look at us . . . pregnant at the same time. We didn't plan this," she laughed. "And you? I can't believe you got pregnant on us," Jaz squealed.

"Me neither." Tears started rolling down Roz's cheeks. "The birth control pills they prescribed apparently weren't strong enough. You know this was not on my list of things to do and it's making me so damn emotional." Roz told Jaz her entire sob story about Nikayah choking her at the party, the hospital stay, the bed rest, the message Nikayah's mom left on her voice mail, and the fact that she'd been ducking Trae out.

"Damn, partna, that's some fucked up drama. I couldn't believe that punk-ass nigga choked you. You should have cut his fuckin' throat with that bottle. But peep this. Word on the street is Nikayah was a snitch and was gonna smoke Trae. So, my sista, if—and I say if—Trae smoked him first, can you blame him? And being a snitch, anybody could have done Nikayah. I know Faheem had planned on paying him a visit after he heard about him strangling you."

"Please, Jaz. That shit got Trae written all over it."

"Well, who would you rather have in a body bag, your cheating-ass ex or your soon-to-be husband and baby's daddy? What's the matter with you? You need to pull yourself together."

"Pull myself together? Jaz c'mon now. You know what's going to happen next. Nikayah got people just like Trae got people.

"Someone is going to retaliate. I'm cutting him loose. He's gonna get smoked or his ass is gonna end up in prison. I feel it. I am so mad at myself for even fucking with him. And now my dumb ass got the nerve to be carrying his baby," she let out a disgusted laugh.

"What if nothing happens? How about if what you feel is wrong? Y'all obviously love each other. You can't just run off. What the fuck is wrong with you?"

"Whose side are you on?" Roz asked her, wiping the tears off her face with the back of her hands.

"Yours, of course. But—"

"But what?" Roz asked, cutting Jaz off.

"He's gonna kick your emotional ass when he catches you." They both laughed. "How long do you plan on hiding? You know you miss him."

"Oh God. Do I? He is so good to me."

"Then you are losing your fucking mind just like Angel told me. At first I didn't believe her."

"Whatever, Jaz. Nobody's listening to me or trying to understand how I feel or what I'm going through."

"Nobody?"

"Nobody."

"Then that should tell you something. Your ass is dead wrong. You knew what the brotha was into when you started fuckin' him. You knew it could go one of three ways. He could get outta the game alright, end up in jail, or in a body bag. You need to put them emotions in check or go see your doctor and have him prescribe you something. And after you have this baby get your damn tubes tied because you are acting real dumb."

"Were you this bad when you first got pregnant?"

"Yes and no. Plus I had all that court drama going on, remember? Faheem said I'm still driving him crazy. I was bad but not as bad as you are. The next time Trae calls here looking for you, I'm gonna tell him to go easy on you because you're definitely not yourself. I don't know this person sitting across from me."

"Oh God! He called here?"

"What the fuck do you think Tasha? A couple of times."

"I know he wants to kick my ass." She sank back into the chair.

"I bet you nobody ever dogged his ass like this." She smirked like she was enjoying being in control.

"You are a bitch," Jaz said, shaking her head.

"Wouldn't it seem like he would just say, 'Fuck her, I'm moving on'?"

"If you were just a trick, yeah, but you're carrying that nigga's baby, and he wants to marry you. He cares about your crazy ass, you dummy."

"Well, *I'm* moving on. He'll eventually get the hint."

"Suit yourself. I think it's your loss. I'm tired of talkin' to your hardheaded behind. How 'bout Angel?" she asked, changing the subject. "That bitch done got brand-new as well."

"Besides being open like Seven-Eleven for Kay, stressing over whether or not she passed the bar exam. She's just working. She said she would rather die than take that exam over again." They both burst out laughing.

"That girl is stupid," Jaz laughed. "Miss attorney-at-law, 'I ain't never fuckin' a drug dealer,' done got turned out by just that, a drug dealer. She swore up and down she was gonna marry a professional, Mr. lawyerman, Najee. What happened?"

"Najee ain't have a chance. Kay is Mr. GQ smooth. He is fucking her silly, and she has practically moved in with him."

"Get the fuck outta here? Dayum," Jaz said. Jaz couldn't believe it. "Shit must be all of that."

"Apparently so. She seems very happy."

Jaz had prepared fried chicken, glazed carrots, wild rice, and biscuits and was fixing Roz a plate.

"This is why my stomach is so big. I eat too much. I've gained twelve pounds in the past three months. But this chicken is so good," Roz said.

Afterwards Roz helped Jaz straighten up the kitchen. When she got ready to leave, Faheem was coming in the door. *Aw shit,* she said to herself.

"What up, Faheem?" she asked, smiling and trying to ease past him and out the door.

"You," he said, blocking the door and pulling out his cell phone. "There's a reward out on your head, one hundred Gs to bring you in alive," he joked.

"Move out my way, Faheem," she said, trying to pull him away from the door. "That's all I'm worth, a lousy hundred Gs?" she teased.

"I guess. Why you clowning my man like this? I told him y'all pregnant women can be treacherous. Y'all stress a nigga out quick." He kissed her on the cheek. "Call your man, ma." He handed her the phone.

"Not now Faheem."

"Why not?"

"I got some issues I need to work out."

"Bullshit. Call your man. Y'all are supposed to work issues out together."

She could tell he was dead serious. She took his phone and dialed Trae's number, praying that he wouldn't answer. She let it ring eight times, then looked at Faheem and said, "No answer. Can I hang up now?"

Faheem moved from in front of the door. "You ain't right, ma. I threatened that nigga telling him he better not fuck you over and I would have never known that it was you I should have been threatening about him."

"Bye, Faheem." She gave him his phone back, left out the house, and jumped in her ride.

Chapter 16

Angel received her notification that she passed the bar. She was ecstatic. She was now Attorney Angel Denise Smith, Esquire. Everyone else was thrilled for her. Kyra was throwing her a small party, but it was only for immediate family and friends.

Angel was sitting up in the bed going through the *Wall Street Journal* when the phone rang.

"What up?"

"Nothing, Trae. What's up with you?"

"Checkin' on your girl. Ain't seen her in a few weeks. How is she?"

"I spoke to her last night. She's okay."

"Good. Congratulations on passing the bar."

She smiled. "Thanks Trae." She could hear voices in the background.

"Hold on," he said, passing the phone to Kay.

"What up, beautiful?"

"Hey baby, I miss you. You'll be back Saturday for my little party, right?"

" 'Fraid not. We won't be back until Sunday night, early Monday morning."

"Kaylin, you said you would be back," she whined, tossing the newspaper aside and pouting. "I can't believe you."

"Red, me and you will celebrate as soon as I get back. I got something special planned. You know if I could, I would be there. What are you doing?"

"I was reading the paper. I miss you. This house is lonely without you."

"Then come spend the day with me tomorrow."

"I can't," she snapped, still mad that he wasn't going to be at her party.

"Why not?"

"I got work piled up to the ceiling. I really can't take off."

Kay was quiet. "Where are you?"

"In your bed."

"What are you wearin'?"

"Pajamas, Kaylin. What do you think, I'm here butt naked? Knowing that you are way across the planet somewhere?"

"Why don't you pull the pajamas off and *get* naked for me?"

She started laughing. "Why, Kaylin? Why would I do that? You're just going to miraculously appear in front of me?"

"Because I want you to do somethin' for me."

"What?"

"Go get a towel and take off your pajamas."

"Are you serious?"

"What do you think?"

She could hear his tone of voice changing. "Hold on, Kaylin." She set the phone down, got a towel, and pulled off her pajamas. "I'm back, Kay. Now what do you want?" she asked, pulling the sheet up over her.

"You know what I want. I want you to cum for me. I like the way you call my name when you cum. I want you to feel me there. Close your eyes and feel me bitin' and suckin' on your nipples. Go ahead and run your fingers over your clit for me."

"You are such a freak," she said, wetting two fingers and running them over her clit. His deep, sensual voice was making her even wetter. She closed her eyes and began imagining him biting and sucking on her nipples just the way she liked him to.

"I want you to feel me running my tongue down your stomach and then tickling your belly button." He smiled as he heard her breathing getting heavier. "I'm lickin' and bitin' on the inside of your thighs just the way you like me to. You feel me? Remember my birthday present?"

Now she was grinding real slow, whispering his name, and telling him, "I feel you baby and yes I remember."

"I'm taking two fingers and sliding them inside you. Your juices are so hot and you feel so good as I'm movin' them in and out. I'm using my other hand to spread those lips so that I can suck on that beautiful clit. You smell and taste so good." From the way she was moaning he could tell that she was getting ready to cum. "Slow down. Don't cum yet. Tell me you love me."

"I love you," she moaned. "Too . . . late. I'm . . . I'm cummin' Kaylin." She was cumming, quivering, and calling his name.

"Damn Red, baby!" he said, squeezing his dick. "That was the shit. You got my dick about to break. You there?"

"Mm hmm, I'm here. I wish you were here."

"Me, too. Come see me tomorrow."

She could feel the heat through the phone line. "Kaylin," she whined. "Don't make me do this. You got me missing enough days as it is."

"Then take a half-day. I need to see you."

"Call me in the morning. I have to see what I can do."

"What time?"

"Around nine."

"Are all the doors locked and the alarm set?"

She smiled. "Yes, daddy. Love you."

"Love you too. I'll holla at you in the mornin'." He planted a loud kiss in her ear then hung up.

"Now that's what you call takin' care of home," Kay said,

putting the cell phone in his back pocket. Kay, Trae, and Omar, and their peeps Pras and Rico from Miami were in the limo on their way to Club Amnesia.

"She sound like a freak, man. Let me get her number," Rico said.

"Nigga, what you smokin'? You didn't just hear me say home?" Ain't nobody runnin' up in that but me."

Rico laughed, "It's like that, my man? You bein' selfish. But I'm not goin' out like that. When we get up in here, I'ma hook you up, dawg. I ain't selfish."

"You ain't gotta hook me up, nigga. I'ma take care of my business," he said, making sure his gats were fully loaded. "Then I'm goin' to get some sleep. I've been up for the past fifty-plus hours." He looked over at Trae, who was conked out. "Yo, Trae!" he yelled. "Trae!" He turned back to Rico. "I gotta treat coming to see me. I gotta rest up. Trae!"

"Why the fuck you screamin', dawg? I ain't deaf."

"Wake the fuck up, man! Be alert," Kay joked.

"Fuck you, man. You the one need to be alert," Trae said, sitting up and wiping his face with his hands. He pulled a blunt out his back pocket and looked around. Omar threw him a lighter.

Trae puffed and puffed. With blunt dangling out the side of his mouth, he checked his gats. "You ready man?" he asked, looking over at Omar.

"I stay ready."

"A'ight, then. Let's roll."

Chapter 17

"Angel, where have you been?" Tasha asked, demanding to know.

She yawned and looked at her Cartier watch that Kay bought her. It was 8:45 in the morning, and she had only been in the office for fifteen minutes.

"I went to Miami to see Kaylin." She yawned again.

"When?"

"Yesterday. I caught a two o'clock flight there and an eleven-fifty flight back. I didn't get in the bed until almost three. I am beat."

"Did you see Trae?"

"No. He said Trae was asleep in his room. Kay came by himself. We had a hotel room at the airport."

"How long are they gonna be gone?"

"They'll be back Sunday night or Monday."

"Good. I'm going home tonight to sleep in my own bed. My aunt's house smells like Ben Gay, and it's making me nauseous."

"Ewww," Angel squealed. "Are you picking me up to take me to Kyra's?"

"What?"

"My party! I know you didn't forget."

"No, I didn't forget. But Trae will most likely be there so I can't go."

"I just told you them niggas won't be back until Sunday or Monday. Kay had the nerve to apologize . . . saying he'll make it up to me. He's gonna owe me big time for this one."

"Oh, how sweet." Tasha was being smart. "So how was your little rendezvous in the MIA?"

"Hot! It's always hot with him. Before I ever gave him some he told me that he takes making love very serious. And he wasn't lying. I love him." She was smiling.

"You're making me jealous."

"Don't be. If you wasn't having your little so-called issues, you could have went with me."

"Don't start. What time do you want me to pick you up?"

"Around two."

"Okay, Attorney Smith."

Tasha was there to pick up Angel at 1:45. Angel looked cute in her all-white Gucci pantsuit. Tasha had on a white Prada belly blouse, jean shorts and sandals, and was looking just as cute as Angel.

They pulled up to Kyra's at about 3:00. She hired a caterer and a deejay. Angel's mother and quite a few guests were already there including a few people from her graduating class and her Aunt Jandelyn, herself a prosecuting attorney. Angel immediately began mingling with the guests.

Tasha said hello to everyone and slid upstairs to baby Aisha's room with Kyra.

"Kyra, look what I found for Aisha. Is this too cute or what?" Tasha asked, walking into the baby's bedroom.

"Awww!" Kyra drooled at the pink Baby Phat short set with sneakers to match. "This is too cute! Look, Aisha," Kyra said to the baby. "Look what Auntie Tasha got you." Little Aisha wasn't even looking. She was kicking her little legs. Kyra looked at Tasha. "Why aren't you downstairs mingling?"

"I am not feeling all of these people."

"Still riding them emotions, huh?"

"Girl, puhleeze! I am never getting pregnant again. I've lost complete control, crying when I watch TV commercials, when I watch a movie. I'm just crying and being a bitch for no particular reason. Right, Aisha?" The baby was crying now. "You feel me, don't you? She is too adorable." Tasha cooed.

"I wish I knew what was the matter with little Miss Adorable. She's been cranky since last night." They were standing at the crib looking down at her, Kyra on one side, Tasha on the other, when Kyra decided to change Aisha's diaper.

"You hooked up the setting for her party real nice," Tasha told her.

"I had to. l am so proud of her."

"Me, too. She kicked ass, didn't she?"

"Hell, yeah!" They high-fived each other.

Angel was still downstairs mingling with her guests when one of her classmates, Kia, pulling out her compact mirror, said, "Oh God! Who are these fine brothas comin' up in here? You must introduce me! Ya'll got strippers?"

Angel turned around and looked. "That's my baby!" she squealed, running to him. "Baby!"

Kay picked her up and kissed her. "Hey, beautiful!"

"You liar. You told me you couldn't make it," she snapped, slapping him on the arm. "I was so mad at you."

"I wouldn't miss my wifey's graduation party. Not if I can help it."

"Where is Trae? Roz is going to kill me." She cringed.

"He was right behind me."

"Shit! she is gonna swear that I set her up. Nigga it's all your fault. I can't believe you lied to me."

"*You* lied to *me*. You said you didn't know where she was."

"I had to have my girl's back."

"I had to have my man's back. So now we're even," he said, clutching her butt with both hands.

"Move your hands. My mom is probably watchin' your every move."

"Damn! Why you ain't tell me? Where is she?"

"I just did. She's over there to your left. Put me down."

"That woman next to her. You know her?" Kay asked.

"That's my Aunt Jan. Why?"

"Small fuckin' world."

"Why you say that?"

"She work for the Feds, don't she?"

"Yeah, she's a federal prosecutor. You know her?"

"We crossed paths before." Then he handed her a small box. "Congratulations."

"Ooh. What is it?" she asked, untying the ribbon. She pulled out two keys and smiled at Kay. "What do they go to?"

"It's a surprise."

"C'mon Kaylin!" She was practically jumping up and down.

He smiled at her. "The brochure is in the glove compartment."

Just then, Trae walked up and kissed her on the cheek. "Congratulations, Miss attorney-at-law," he said, handing her an envelope. "Didn't think we would make it, did you? You know I'm still mad at you."

"Trae, I tried to talk to her. I told her she was dead wrong, so go easy on her. This pregnancy is wreaking havoc with her emotions," Angel said, giving him a hug.

"Where is she?"

"Upstairs in the baby's room with Kyra," she said. "Glad you could make it." And she headed outside to get the brochure for her new whip.

Trae had to laugh at himself because he was actually nervous. He was having a hard time accepting that he allowed Tasha to pull him off his square. Any other time he would have said fuck it and moved on to the next bitch.

When Trae opened the door to the baby's room, Tasha and Kyra were still standing over the crib admiring Aisha. Kyra looked up and saw him first and told Tasha to keep an eye on

Aisha for a minute, she'd be right back. Trae eased up behind Tasha and grabbed her around the waist, frightening her.

"Damn, you scared me!" she gasped.

He pulled her close and sung in her ear, *"It's a cold, cold, cold world living without you. Although I tried to get along without you but couldn't. I need you to be here."*

She didn't say anything and went back to patting Aisha on the back, trying to put her to sleep. Aisha wasn't having it. She kept bobbing her head up and down.

"Why are you shuttin' me down like this?" he asked, rubbing Tasha's stomach and kissing her shoulder. "I miss you." She still wasn't talking. "Are you still in love with me?"

"I'm trying not to be."

"Ouch! That hurt," he said.

Baby Aisha started crying, so Tasha reached in the crib and picked her up. She was walking back and forth and patting her back. Trae noticed that Tasha's stomach was starting to poke out. That was turning him on big time.

"One minute I'm in love with you, the next minute I can't stand you. So instead of us going through all of these unnecessary changes and tripping, we might as well go our separate ways." She was trying her best to hold back, but the tears started streaming down her face.

"Baby I'm not the one tripping," he said, noticing that she didn't have her engagement ring on. He watched her as she walked back and forth trying to soothe Aisha. That sight only made him want her and his baby that much more. "Let me hold her," he said causing her to look at him like he was crazy. "C'mon, let me hold her," he told her again.

"I think she needs to burp. Put that blanket on your shoulder and sit down," she instructed. Trae put the receiving blanket over his shoulder and sat down on the love seat.

She brought Aisha over to Trae and laid her on his chest. Her head was resting on his shoulder. "It's okay, Aisha," she whispered.

Trae started patting the baby's back. Aisha slowly wound down and then finally stopped crying. Tasha couldn't help but smile at Trae. Aisha was still fighting sleep, turning her head from side to side. She finally let out one big burp.

"Damn!" Trae said, laughing and looking at her. "What are they feeding you?"

Just then Marvin opened the door to peek in at the baby. He laughed when he saw Aisha stretched out on Trae's chest. "She's beautiful, ain't she," Marvin beamed.

"Yeah, she is," said Trae.

"Nigga, what? You gettin' some practice?"

"Maybe. Sounds like *you* need a little more practice, fainting in the delivery room and shit!" he joked.

They both started laughing. "I didn't faint. I couldn't see straight, but I didn't faint. I got a whole new respect for our women after witnessing that shit. I bet you won't do any better."

"Shit. You got me fucked up. How much? I'm ready to handle mines."

"Ready ain't the same as doin'. Two Gs, playa!"

"A'ight, nigga. It's on."

"What up, baby sis?" Marvin asked Tasha. "You alright?"

"I'm hangin'."

"What you doing to my baby sister, dawg?"

Trae's nostrils flared. "What am I doin' to her? You need to rephrase that. Ask her what she doin' to me. I'm the one locked the fuck out of the house where I pay all the bills. I'm the one who don't even have the phone number. I'm not the one who's been missing in action for the last two, three weeks. I didn't know if my wife or unborn child was alive or not. Who looks stressed the fuck out? Me or her? You mean what the fuck is she doing to me!"

"I see I done opened a can of worms." He looked at Tasha. "Baby sis, ain't nothin' nice."

"Maybe if pregnant women came with a fuckin' handbook or instruction manual, I'd know what the fuck was goin' on," Trae complained and getting more heated by the moment.

"Sho' you right! But, I hate to be the one to tell you that it don't get easier."

"Marv!" Tasha yelled. She was annoyed at the way Marvin and Trae were talking as if she wasn't even there.

"I'm sorry, baby sis, but I gots to side with my man on this one. Y'all pregnant women can be real bitches. Nigga, be thankful it only lasts nine months. Let me holla at you, man."

"A'ight. Give me a minute."

Marvin left. Trae looked at Aisha, who was now sound asleep, and kissed her on the cheek. Tasha picked her up and put her in the crib. Trae then turned to Tasha and said, "Don't go nowhere. I'll be right back." She just looked at him. "A'ight? Please?" And he left. She checked to make sure Aisha was dry before throwing the receiving blanket over her. Then she picked up her bag, turned out the light, and went downstairs.

"Roz!" Angel yelled, waving her over. "Look!" She was dangling the car keys at her and holding up the brochure to the 2001 champagne-colored Lexus SUV.

"That's what I'm talking about," Tasha said, trying to sound enthused.

"Come here, Tasha!" Kay called.

"Just a minute, Kay." She looked at Angel. I'm getting ready to bounce."

"You're leaving?" Angel asked, shocked. "I swear. I didn't know they were coming!"

She nodded. "Tell Kyra the baby is dry and asleep."

"Ooh!" She sounded like a kid about to tell. "Trae know you're leaving?"

Roz told her no with a shake of the head and made her way to the door.

"Tasha!" Kay yelled again when he saw her leaving. "Yo Trae!" Kay hollered. "Trae!"

When Trae came to the top of the stairs and looked down, Kay pointed at the front door. By the time Trae got outside, Tasha was already in her Benz, fumbling for the keys in her bag. He knocked on the window.

"Get out the car ma." She ignored him and started it up. "Tasha turn the fuckin' engine off!" She took it out of park and was about to back out the driveway when he pulled out his gat and blew a hole in the tire, making a loud pop. Rubber flew everywhere. She screamed as she sat there, gripping the steering wheel.

"Shut it off and get out," he said, glaring at her. She shut it off but didn't get out. He pulled his gat out again. "Do you want me to blow the fuckin' window out and drag you out, or are you going to unlock it for me?" With that he aimed the gat at the window. She quickly unlocked the door, and he put the gat away.

All the while Angel and Kay were standing in the doorway watching. Angel's mother and several other guests came to the door to check on the commotion out front. Someone asked was it fireworks. Angel told them it was an accident and to go back and enjoy her party. Then her and Kaylin resumed their watch of the reunited couple.

"Y'all females know y'all can take a nigga through some changes," Kay commented.

Angel punched him. "So can y'all. He better not hit her!"

"C'mon, nosy," Kay said, pulling her away from the door, "he won't hit her."

Trae opened the door and snatched the keys out of the ignition. He got ready to lift her out the car. All of a sudden she wrapped her arms around his neck and hugged him tight.

"God, I've missed you," she whispered in his ear.

"Let me go, Tasha. I ain't trying to hear that bullshit right now. I'm tired of playing with you."

"I'm sorry. Please forgive me," she said, holding him even tighter. "I love you so much. Please forgive me."

He kissed her cheek, then bit down on it real hard. With no plans of letting go.

"Owwwww! Trae you're hurtin' me!" she squealed. He bit down harder. "I said I'm sorry," she cried. "Owwwww! Please stop Trae," she cried in anguish. He bit down a little harder before letting go, and she cried harder as he lifted her out of her ride.

"You better not *ever* pull no shit like this again," he said, slamming the door and hitting the lock. "And put your ring back the fuck on! Don't ever take it off again," he warned. He opened the Navigator, lifted her inside, and closed the door. Then he opened it back up and leaned over her to start it and put the air on. All the while she was still crying.

She listened as Trae cussed while picking up all of the tire remnants that were strewn all over the lawn and driveway before disappearing into the house. He came out with some tissue and some ice wrapped in a washcloth to attend to the bruise on her cheek. By then she had stopped crying and was blowing her nose. He noticed that she had put her ring back on.

While he rolled a blunt and spoke on the phone to someone about bringing a new tire and towing the car to Tasha's, she was putting ice on her bruised cheek. Trae jumped out of the Nav and unlocked the Benz.

"Do you need anything out of here?" He snapped at her.

She shook her head no.

He jumped back in the Nav, still talking to the car people. She put a piece of ice in her mouth, slid over next to him, and went to unzipping his jeans. He kept on talking as she began to give him some head. Her cold tongue tingling his dick. He hung up, leaned back, closed his eyes and enjoyed being able to bust a good nut. He couldn't even stay mad at her after that.

When she finished, she zipped his jeans up in between kisses, apologizing some more. Trae still wasn't talking. He lit his blunt again and put in Maxwell's *Urban Hang Suite* CD. Tasha pulled off his doo-rag, took a comb out of her purse, and went to undoing his now-messy braids. He pulled out the driveway, popping his fingers to the music.

"Baby, I'm so sorry. I won't ever do this again. I love you, and whatever happens, I got your back. I won't ever leave you, and please don't ever leave us. We're in this together."

He just looked at her and pumped up the volume to track four, *Ascension (Don't ever wonder)* and started singing along with Maxwell.

"It happened the moment when you were revealed. 'Cause you were a dream that just should not have been fantasy real. You gave me this beating, baby. This rhythm inside high. You make me feel good, n' feel nice, n' feel lovely. Gave me paradise. So," he turned to look at Tasha, *"Shouldn't I realize, you're the highest of the high? If you don't know, then I'll say it. So don't ever wonder. Don't ever wonder."*

She loved it when he sang along with Maxwell because he could blow just like him.

He turned the volume down. "You don't have to wonder, Tash. It's all about you. I don't know why you can't see that. My whole fuckin' world revolves around you!" he said, banging on the steering wheel so hard it frightened her. "Now you're either with me or you're against me."

"I've never loved anyone the way I love you. Sometimes it scares me, and I tell myself I need to back off," she told him, her voice trembling.

"What? What?" he screamed "Oh, so it's okay for me to keep lovin' you while you back off?" He shook his head in disgust. "You need to let the past go, Tash. I told you from the beginning, I want you to love me and let me love you. It's me and you to the end, regardless." So what's up? I'm not going through this bull-shit again." He glared at her. His anger resurfacing all over again.

"I'm with you." She mumbled ashamed of how she'd been acting.

"What?"

"I'm with you Trae. I'm sorry baby." The tears falling again.

A long period of silence followed. Then *Suite Lady* came on. He bumped up the volume and went to popping his fingers and singing again to Maxwell's CD. *"It's been so long since I have got you, lady, since I have had yo' brown legs wrapped around me. The smell of she just drives me crazy. Imagine what the sight of her can do. Suite lady, don't worry. Ain't no end to what this ring wants, to begin with you. I've waited, Suite lady, 'cause no man can tear asunder what my love can groove. I never thought myself the kinda guy, the kinda male that would wanna settle down. Statistics say it's crazy, passion won't survive. But something says now, deep down, deep down inside. Groove, love can groove. Me and you, Suite lady. I don't mean to be dramatic, baby. I only wanna understand you, baby. So will you marry me?"*

They pulled up in front of Amefika's Restaurant. Tasha ordered two fish dinners with broccoli, fresh string beans, macaroni and cheese, wheat rolls, and a couple of bean pies. When they got to the house Trae told her to call a travel agent to see what island package they could get for the following morning. After the agent gave her the info, Tasha told her to hold on. "Trae, Jamaica, Aruba or Bermuda?" she yelled into the living room.

"It's up to you."

Tasha chose Jamaica. She took Trae's American Express platinum card out of her purse to give the agent all of the necessary info then hung up.

She threw her plate in the microwave and joined Trae on the sofa to watch the game. After the game they jumped in the shower, and she washed his hair. They got out of the shower and watched the *Queens of Comedy* on DVD as she braided his hair and gave him a manicure and a pedicure. They went to bed soon after because they had a 7:20 a.m. flight to Jamaica.

Chapter 18

Tasha was on top as she came for the fourth time, her juices trickling down onto Trae's jewels. They both were drenched in sweat as she plopped down onto his chest. He kissed her forehead and cheeks as she lay exhausted.

They rented a beachfront four-bedroom bungalow with a balcony, a huge kitchen, four bathrooms, Jacuzzi, and maid service. After they took a bath together, Trae threw on some boxers and slippers. He grabbed his weed and optimo and sat out on the balcony while Tasha put on a pair of panties and a robe and headed for the kitchen. She took out a bowl of sliced strawberries, cantaloupe, and honeydew melons. She grabbed a spoon, went out on the balcony, and sat right up under Trae, who had just lit his blunt. He leaned over and tongued her down before taking a puff.

"Damn, it's beautiful out here," he mumbled. It was about 1:30 in the morning and there was a crescent moon. The sky was very, very clear, and the stars were shining brightly. It was picture-perfect.

"It sure is," she sighed. "I feel so complete and peaceful. When can we come back?"

Trae took a few more puffs. "Next week is our last week to wrap this shit up, so any time after that. We can stay for months if we want to. I'll be a retired man." He shook his head. "It's hard to believe, but it's almost over. I'm not in jail and I only got two bullet holes, one in my back and another in my leg. Do you know what the odds are of me gettin' outta the game alive and free?" She fed him a spoonful of fresh fruit. "Mmm . . . real sweet. Just like you," he said, opening his mouth for some more.

"Ahhhh! Oh my God!" she screamed. "Trae the baby just moved!" She grabbed his hand, placed it on her stomach, and held it there for a couple of minutes.

Trae was smiling. "Damn! My son is moving around already." He was now rubbing her stomach.

"I gotta call Angel," she said, kissing Trae. "I love you." She passed him the fruit bowl and went for the cell to dial Kay's number. She sat back down and snuggled up under Trae.

Angel picked up the phone after the fourth ring and answered sleepily, "Yes Kaylin, I'm here."

Tasha laughed. "My name is Tasha, not Kaylin."

"Oh, I thought it was Kay making sure I was here. What time is it?" she yawned.

"I don't have a clue, but guess what?" she said, unable to conceal her excitement.

"What?"

"The baby just moved!"

"Did it?"

"Yup. It felt so weird."

"How sweet! Can you tell me more about it tomorrow?"

"No, I got something else to tell you."

"Tell me."

"We got married," she said, knowing that would wake Angel up.

"Who got married?"

"Me and Trae."

"Bitch don't fucking play around like that."

"No, I'm not. We did it the day after we got here. I am now Mrs. Rosalind Tasha Macklin."

"Oh, shit! You're serious?" Angel screamed.

"I'm serious," she squealed.

"Congratulations! Where's Trae? Let me speak to him."

Tasha passed him the phone. "Red what's up?"

"I just wanted to say congratulations to my new brother-in-law. I am so happy for y'all. You two are good for each other."

"Thanks Red. I'm glad we have your blessing," he teased and passed the phone back to Tasha.

"I am so shocked," Angel said.

"Angel, you and Kay gotta come here. We got a bungalow here in Ocho Rios. Right now we're sitting on the balcony, looking at the clear water at Dunn's River Falls. It is so beautiful and peaceful. We really needed this time together. I fell in love all over again," she said, looking up at Trae and then kissing him on the cheek.

"Wait until Jaz and Kyra hear this. Well, congratulations, Mrs. Macklin on your new husband and the baby's first movement. I gotta get some more sleep. Kay will be in soon. When are y'all coming back?"

"I'm not sure, but I'll call you. Peace out!"

They spent two more days in Ocho Rios before heading back to New Jersey.

Jaz and Kyra couldn't believe that Tasha beat them to the punch. They were on a three-way call, having called her at work.

"I still can't believe it," Jaz said.

"Me neither," Kyra added. "I'm so happy for you. You got a man willing to put up with your crazy ass."

"I know. It seems like it was only yesterday we were at Kyra's shower and you were telling us you liked him. Now here it is seven months later, you're pregnant and married," Jaz said. "That's unbelievable."

"Oh God, that's a trip, isn't it?" Tasha asked, hardly believing it herself.

"When are y'all going to have the wedding ceremony?" Kyra asked.

"I'm not sure. We haven't even discussed it. We're just anxious to go back to Jamaica and chill. Hopefully it will be in the next week or two. We're planning to stay a couple of months. I'm telling y'all, the first chance y'all get, please go. It is awesome and stress-free. We didn't even use our watches. We just chilled."

Chapter 19

It was early Saturday morning, and Angel and Kay were enjoying each other's company. He was doing one of her favorite things, sucking and biting on her nipples, when the phone rang.

"Baby, if you're not going to answer your phone, why don't you turn it off?" she suggested.

"Mine's off. That's your phone," he mumbled, kissing her on the stomach.

She grabbed the phone and flipped it open. "Hello," she said, trying to sound normal with two of Kay's fingers inside her. "Kaylin," she moaned, reaching for his wrist, "this is your phone."

"Turn it off ma."

"Kay wait a minute," she moaned, her toes curling.

The caller, losing patience, said with much attitude, "Can you give Kay the phone?"

"Who is this?" Angel asked.

"Brittany. Give him the damn phone."

Angel placed her palm on Kay's forehead and tried to push him off, but it didn't work.

"Brittany this is Angel, his woman. Kay is eating my pussy right now. Call him back in about thirty minutes." She hung up and said to Kay, "Go a little slower . . . god, this feels good!" She arched her back, grabbed his head with both her hands, and wrapped her legs around his neck as she climaxed. "Oh shit . . .

Kay!" she hollered, tensing her legs to prevent him from coming up for air.

"See, that's why you need to be tied up. I can't even handle my business the way I want to," he said, reaching for a towel. "You heard me Red?"

"I hear you over there hatin' on a sista," she whispered.

"I'm not hatin'." He grabbed her hand. "Climb on top, ma."

"I can't move," she said, lying there limp as a rag doll. He slipped on a condom, sat up, held her around the waist, and lifted her up into the air. "I like a strong man," she moaned, sliding down on his dick and kissing him all over his face.

"It takes a strong man to handle a strong woman like you," Kay replied, one hand resting behind his head and the other on her butt. He was watching her get her groove on. "Now you slow down," he told her when it looked like she was getting too excited.

"Why?" she protested.

"Kiss me," he said, pulling her towards him. She kissed him sloppily, still trying to get her grind on, and bit his lip while squeezing his dick with her pussy muscles. "I bet you can't squeeze a little harder," he challenged. She showed him she could. Then he closed his eyes, grabbed her booty with both hands and pulled her down as far as he could while lifting his butt so that he could get in as deep as possible.

She shuddered as chill bumps popped up all over her body. "Damn Kaylin. What are you trying to do to me?" she moaned. Neither one of them could hear the cell phone as it rang.

He slapped her butt, telling her to turn around. She turned around and straddled him. He leaned up, put one hand on her stomach to hold her in place, and, with the other hand, started massaging her clit.

"Oh shit, Kay!" she groaned as he went in a little deeper and pressed a little harder on her clit. "Right there, Kay! Oh God, you're hitting my spot!" She groaned. He could feel it and went to grinding faster and harder. "Oh, Kaylin!" she screamed, digging her nails into his thighs as she began to shake, cum, and cry all at the same time.

"Damn Red," he said, ejaculating right after her. She collapsed forward and he fell backwards on the pillow. They both lay still just like that, trying to catch their breath.

After a few minutes, she rolled over. He pulled her up by her arms and laid her next to him. He was puffing on his blunt as she dozed off, her head on his chest. Just then the cell phone rang, and she reached for it.

"Hello."

"I need to speak to Kay."

"Who is this?"

"Brittany. You said to call back in thirty minutes."

"Brittany this is Angel, and make this the last time that you call Kay. It's very disrespectful, but I'm gonna allow you to have this one." She held the phone up for Kay, but he wasn't interested.

"Why'd you tell her to call back?"

"Because I want to know why the fuck she keeps calling. This is what, her third time? Is it legitimate, or do I need to whip her ass first and yours next?" she asked loud enough for Brittany to hear.

He took the phone and she rested her head back on his chest. "What?" asked Kay. "I can't come over there so whatever you got to say, say it now."

"No, she didn't ask you to come over," Angel said angrily. "I better not ever catch y'all two in the same room. Do you hear me Kaylin?"

He held up his hand, motioning for her to hold up as he listened to Brittany. Then he burst out with a loud, "Why you fuckin' with me? You know I always wrap my shit up."

"Well, well, well," Angel mumbled.

"Like I said, I always wrap my shit up. Who else you been fuckin'?" Then after a pregnant pause he continued, "C'mon, Britt. You know I'ma find out. If it's mines, it's mines. I'll always take care of mines. But, if you're pregnant, chances are it's not. I always wrap my dick up, and you know that."

Angel tried to get off the bed, but Kay stopped her. Then he turned off his phone and threw it on the nightstand.

"Red, you know that's bullshit right? Where are you goin'?" he asked.

"To the shower. Looks like your whoring around is catching up with you."

"I know you ain't got no attitude. Who's side are you on?"

"My man's, of course. And my man has until Monday to get a new cell number or make all them bitches stop calling. The same with your pager. It's on top of the refrigerator." Then she turned around and asked, "Any other babies' mamas I should know about?"

"I only got one baby. That chicken is playing games."

"You need to watch where you stick your dick, playa. I'm sure she wasn't a chicken when you started pluckin' her."

"Yes, she was."

"Trife. Like I said, get them bitches to stop calling. And I better not catch you and Miss Britt in the same room together."

"Listen to you, threatening me!" Kay smiled as he followed her into the shower.

She got dressed and wore a Prada sundress and matching sandals. Kay threw on some sweats and a cutoff, sleeveless T-shirt. He slid on some slippers to walk her to the Lex.

"Tell me again your agenda for today," he said, opening the door for her.

"The salon, cleaner's, grocery store, and I want to clean the apartment I haven't seen in over three weeks."

"You comin' back, right?" he asked, running his fingers through her hair.

"I wasn't planning on it. It's going to be too late for me to drive all the way back up here."

"Girl, stop playin'. Just leave early enough. You know I like for you to be here when I get in," he said, sniffing her perfume.

"I've already told you to move your stuff in. It would be much more convenient for you and convenient for me." He lifted her up onto the seat and stood between her legs.

"Kay, I have a dress on," she said, trying to pull it down some. "I'll call you later."

"You don't have to call me. Just have your fine ass here when I get home," he ordered. "Next weekend I'm coming to pack you out of that apartment."

"Before you try to pack me up, you need to handle your business."

"You are my business."

"I'm talking about all them bitches you got calling Kaylin."

"I know what you're referring to, but I hope you ain't trippin' over that bullshit."

"No, I'm not tripping," she stated matter-of-factly.

"Then what? You jealous?"

"Jealous? Why should I be jealous? I'm the one pushing the Lex and sleeping in your bed every night. I'm the one you bonin' just about every day and trying to get to move in. I'm the one you have to have lying in your bed waiting for you whenever you decide to come home. Why should I be jealous?"

"I was just making sure you know what time it is, because you're right. Ain't nobody got it like you. It's only you."

"It's just disrespectful, Kay. You're my man. I should be the only bitch blowing up your pager and cell phone. And it better be only me! So put an end to the bullshit that's all I'm asking."

"Sounds a little like jealousy to me," he said, sliding a hand up her thigh and rubbing her pussy through her panties.

"Call it what you want, playboy. Just handle your business," she said, trying to move his hand. "Kaylin, I gotta go."

"I'ma let you go in a minute. I know I can get a kiss before you leave," he said, scooting her to the edge of the seat, moving her panties to the side and playing with her clit.

She sucked on his tongue and lips. "You said a kiss, Kay." She tried to move his hand.

"You shouldn't have put on this dress," he said in between

kisses on her neck and lips. "Don't this feel good?" he whispered, pressing her clit with his thumb.

She wrapped her arms around his neck and started grinding real slow. "You are so wrong. Now I'm going to have to wash up again and change clothes."

"Look at me and tell me it feels good."

"Yes, it feels good," she said, looking at him.

"Tell me you're not jealous."

"I'm not jealous."

He pressed down harder, making her want to grind a little faster. She closed her eyes. "Open your eyes and look at me." She did. "You and my son are the only two people I'm concerned with. It's all about y'all. You understand? Don't sweat the bullshit. I belong to you."

"What happens when you get tired of fuckin' me Kaylin?"

"Fuck. You really know how to kill a mood don't you?!" Pulling his fingers out of her pussy. "You're my woman Red," he snapped, pounding the roof of the Lex. "I didn't spend fifty-five grand on someone I could get tired of. I can fuck for free. You said you wanted a lifetime partner. I'm willing, able, and trying to be that. I know it's hard to believe, but I told you a brotha can be true."

Angel couldn't even say anything.

He was staring at her.

"Don't start no shit Red."

"Alright. Alright Kaylin. You're the one getting all mad and shit."

"That's because I was trying to get some pussy and you talking all that bullshit." He placed her hand on his dick and she began squeezing it. "Put it in for me." His voice was now raspy.

"It's daylight, Kaylin," she said, looking around.

"This is my driveway. Nobody can really see what I'm doing unless they got fuckin' binoculars," he said, pulling his dick out and sliding it inside her. "I'm just standing here. Make me cum while I watch."

She wrapped her legs around his waist, leaned back and went

to riding him. He had both hands on her butt, squeezing it, and was watching her every move and trying not to cum. "Baby this feels . . . you so wet and tight. Go a little faster for me. I'm about to let loose," he groaned.

"Damn it Kay! Please say you got on a condom," she hollered as she came. Kay squeezed her butt, pulling her even closer, and went in as deep as he could. He came long and hard.

"Oh, shit!" he said, putting his dick back in his sweats and resting all of his weight on her. "That was on," he said, tonguing her down.

She slid her hands down his pants. "Damn you, Kay! I can't believe I let you get away with that," she said, pounding him on the arm.

"Baby, I didn't do it on purpose."

"Oh God, please don't let me get pregnant," she prayed. "I gotta get on the pill or get that shot in my arm, like yesterday," she whined.

He lifted her out the car, pulling down her dress, which was now wet. "That was only one time. You're not pregnant."

"You don't know that Kay," she said, holding his hand and leading him toward the house.

"Stop worryin'. We done broke the Lex in. I'll go clean the seat off while you jump in the shower."

When she got out the shower she came downstairs in jeans and a belly shirt. As Kay was on the phone she mouthed, "Keys?" He felt his back pocket, took them out, and handed them to her.

"You look cute ma," he said, after he hung up.

"Papi I'm running late," she said, taking the keys out of his hand and kissing those irresistible lips. "You are too sweet. I hate to admit it, but you are."

"Why you hatin' on a brotha? I tell you how sweet you are all the time. I'm not even ashamed to say that I got a jones, either." He was trying to hug her around her waist.

"Bye Kay," she said, breaking away from him.

"Oh, it's like that?" he asked, following her out to the car.

"Don't touch me Kay. I can climb up all by myself." She held him back, sticking her arm out. He moved her arm, swooped her up, and put her in the seat. She laughed as he shut the door. She started the engine and rolled down the window.

"So you feel safe from me now, huh?" he asked, counting out seven hundred dollars and handing it to her. "Is that enough for you to do all the shit you need to do?"

"Yup. It's more than enough." She reached over and kissed him.

"Do you love me?" he asked her.

She nodded yes. "Do you love me?" she asked him.

"Yes, I do. It's all about you. Be careful and drive safe."

Chapter 20

Tasha came home from work around 5:30. The Nav was parked out front. When she got inside she found Trae buried under the covers and snoring. She closed the bedroom door and went to the kitchen to start dinner. She decided to prepare salmon steaks, with baked potatoes, fresh string beans, a tossed salad, and some biscuits.

She didn't finish cooking until after 7:00, and Trae was still asleep. But when his cell phone rang, he reached over and snatched it off the nightstand.

"Yeah," he answered. "It don't matter. No. Nah. We'll switch up then, a'ight." He hung up, rolled over, and looked at Tasha. "Please tell your man that's you cookin'."

"My man, that's me cookin', and it's done," she said, smiling.

"I knew I married you for a few good reasons." He looked at his watch. "How are you? How was your day?"

"I'm good. My day was good. How are you?"

"I'm straight since I'm gettin' ready to get fed." He got up and went to the bathroom. By the time he came out, she was lying on the bed. She raised her arms.

"Help me up."

He dived next to her and gave her a big, sloppy kiss on the lips. Then he lifted her T-shirt and kissed her several times on the stomach.

"I love ya'll," he told her.

"We love you too."

He pulled her up off the bed and went to the living room. Tasha went into the kitchen to fix their plates. They plopped down on the living room sofa where they ate and watched TV. Afterwards they took a nice, long, hot bath together. Then it was time for the lovemaking.

Ever since Angel told her how Kaylin tied her up Tasha wanted the same done to her. So Trae used this opportunity to tie her wrists and ankles to the bedposts and licked her up and down, making her come three times. And she never even asked to be untied, girlfriend could hang. After untying her he made her climb on top where she rode the dick until she came two more times. She had no more strength after that, other than to roll over and doze off, waking up an hour later to find that Trae had showered and was getting dressed.

"You gotta leave?" she whined, sitting up in the bed.

"Yeah, I gotta go."

"Come here," she motioned to him. He sat next to her, and she took his hand and placed it on her belly. After a few seconds the baby moved again. She giggled. "Can't you stay?"

He shook his head no. "I love you and our baby," he told her in between kisses. "Throw on your robe or something and come into the living room."

When she stepped into the living room, Trae had an open briefcase sitting on the coffee table. He grabbed her around the waist and kissed her on the bruise that was left from the bite mark. He started laughing.

"It's not funny, Trae. People keep asking me what happened to my cheek."

His cell phone rang and he immediately flipped it open. "Yeah, I'm on my way down," he answered. He closed his cell and turned to the briefcase.

"This briefcase contains all the titles to my property, cars, bank statements, PIN numbers, combinations to all the safes, everything. There is also a power of attorney form in there, giving you the authority to do whatever you need to do.

"Only one bank account is in my name, the others are in yours. The stock certificates, bonds, and CDs are in that green envelope. My lawyer's number is stapled to the envelope if you have any problems. If you don't hear from me in a couple days, I want you to go clean out the safes in all the property except for the apartment in PA. That's the only safe spot that you'll be able to stash shit at. The keys to everything is labeled and in the briefcase."

Tasha was speechless. Her knees were about to give out, and she could barely breathe.

"Tasha, are you listening? You got all of that?" A horn was blowing up outside.

"Baby, what's going on? You are scaring me!"

"If you have any problems, call my attorney. I gotta go." He kissed her on the bruise again.

"What the fuck you mean, if I have any problems, Trae?" She grabbed his shirt. "Where are you going?" she screamed, tears rolling down her cheeks.

"This is the end, baby. We wrap this shit up tonight."

"No. Fuck that. Just walk away Trae. You don't have to go anywhere," she cried. "It's no such thing to wrap it up, walk away."

"What are you crying for?" he asked, wiping her tears.

"Because you're not coming back Trae. I'm not stupid. That's why you left me all of that shit. I don't want it, I want you instead," she said, kicking the coffee table over.

"I'll be back. I'm giving you this stuff just in case . . . but I'll be back."

"No you won't! You even made love to me like you won't be back. God Trae! You promised me." She was crying and holding him tight. "Please Trae, don't do this to me. To us."

"I'll be back." He kissed her on the forehead and broke free then went toward the door. She jumped in front of him and blocked his path. That damn car horn was blowing up again.

"Baby you don't have to go. I got money put away. You got enough money. Don't go baby, please." She was shaking. "You said you wouldn't leave me. You promised you wouldn't do this to me."

"I'm not leaving you Tasha. I'm just going to take care of this little bit of business. He tried to pull her from in front of the door, but she had her back pressed to it, her hands covering the knob.

"Trae don't do this to us. I'm beggin' you." He picked her up. She wrapped her arms around his neck, holding on tight. "You're my husband baby."

"Ma let me go. I'll be back." He kissed her on the forehead.

"You're lying Trae. You promised me. Please don't leave. I love you Trae," she pleaded.

"I love you too, but you're gonna have to let me go if you want me to come back." He broke away from her grip and opened the door.

She started hitting him. "You lied Trae! What about our baby? I won't be an emotional wreck anymore. I'll be a better wife," she cried. She was desperate now saying whatever it took in an attempt to make him stay.

He went down the steps but had to stop because she came after him. "Baby please, get back inside with no clothes on." He had to pick her up and carry her back into the house, laying her down on the couch.

Tasha felt dizzy so she just lay there. "You promised Trae. Something bad is going to happen." She sat up as he opened the door. "Oh, God. I love you Trae. What am I going to do without you?"

"I gotta run Tasha, but I'll be back."

He left, running down the stairs and jumping into a minivan.

"Motherfuck!" Trae said as he looked in the rearview mirror to see if she had tried to follow him. Kay floored the gas pedal. "That was the hardest fuckin' thing I ever had to do," he said, yanking the ashtray open, expecting to find something to smoke. "Where's it at, man?"

"Look in the glove compartment. I told you not to say nothing to her. You could have left instructions with your lawyer," Kay told him.

"I couldn't go out like that, dawg. I couldn't do her like that. I had to make sure that she got everything she needs to take care of her and the baby for at least the next fifteen years. It'll be longer for her, because she's smart. She don't go through money like it's water." He took several long drags on the blunt before passing it to Kay. "You didn't see Red tonight?"

"Nah, this morning. She stayed at the crib. I've been stashin' shit at her place since she don't be there. So if we don't make it back, she'll see what I left her when she goes to her apartment."

"Yeah, well let's do this! Fucking pussies make it easy for you to get in the game but hard as hell to get out," Trae sighed.

"Hell, yeah. You know what's up. Do or die!"

Trae turned on the radio. He turned it up loud when he heard, *"Come my lady, come, come my lady. You're my butterfly, sugar baby."*

Kay started laughing. "Dawg, what you listenin' to? That shit is wack! You seen them two ugly white boys who sing this?"

"Fuck you, man. This shit is on. Two white boys sing it but some black ones produced it, the Black-Eyed Peas, nigga. Look how much airplay they get on black radio. The beat is hot. And have you checked out the words? Nah, you ain't checked them out, but they're personal to me. That shit fit Tasha to the letter. When she cums, her legs get to shakin' and that shit be feelin' so good. And she be lookin' all pretty and movin' all smooth, just like a butterfly."

Trae sat back, blocked Tasha out, and fixed his mind on the task at hand.

Chapter 21

Tasha had been throwing up for the last five minutes. She barely managed to throw on something, pick up the keys to the Nav, and run out the door.

She pulled up to Jaz's and Faheem's not knowing how she got there. Her hair was all over her face, and she could barely see with her teary eyes. She jumped out the car, almost falling, ran up the steps, and banged on the door. Jaz was asleep, but Faheem was up watching TV.

"What the fuck?" he said when he heard the banging on the front door. When he opened it up, she collapsed in his arms, screaming and crying.

"Faheem, please, please go get Trae. I told him not to go. Faheem he promised me." She was trying to pull Faheem outside to make him go get Trae. He had to pick her up and carry her back into the house. Jaz, awakened by Tasha's screaming and hollering, came out the bedroom when she heard her.

"Faheem baby, what's going on? What's the matter with her?"

She saw that Tasha was standing there shaking and crying. "Go back to bed, baby," he told Jaz. She couldn't move. Wouldn't move. "Jaz!" he hollered, "go in the room and shut the door! I'll handle this." She did as she was told.

"Go get him Faheem. Please. Tell him don't go," Tasha begged.

"Tasha you're gonna have to calm down."

"Faheem please!" she pleaded, pulling him towards the door. He picked her up, threw her over his shoulder, and took her into the spare bedroom.

"What am I going to do without him? Please go get him," she cried. "I don't want to live without him."

"I'm not doing anything until you calm down. You need to calm down." He tried soothing her, rocking her back and forth. He gave her two Tylenol then called Angel to come stay with her.

"He promised me Faheem. He promised he wouldn't leave me. He's my husband. Why is he doing this? Go get him now."

He continued to rock her back and forth. "He'll be back. Get some rest."

She was dizzy and exhausted and kept mumbling over and over, "he needs to come back." He held her until she finally fell asleep. Then he called Angel back to tell her not to bother. But she was already gone. He'd forgotten that Kay was with Trae and figured that Angel would probably be in a similar frame of mind as Tasha. He wet a washcloth, wiped her face, and covered her up before turning out the light and leaving the room.

When he went into the bedroom Jaz was sitting on the side of the bed crying. "Is she okay?"

"No, she's not. What are you doing up? And stop crying. You don't need to be gettin' all excited and upset."

"It's too late."

"What do you mean, it's too late? Take your ass back to sleep."

"My water broke."

"What?" He stared at her like she was crazy.

"It broke."

"Fuck!" He paced the floor. "You got everything packed, right?"

She shook her head up and down.

"Okay. We gotta call the doctor, right?"

She shook her head up and down again. He paged her doctor. "Okay. What else? Are you in pain? Are you alright?" He was trying to remain calm, but acting like a first time soon-to-be-father.

"Just a few cramps, nothing major yet. We can wait for the doctor to call back."

The doctor called back and he asked some routine questions and told Faheem to bring her in when the contractions were fifteen minutes apart. Just as he hung up the phone, Tasha was screaming Faheem's name. When he went into the bedroom, she was in the bathroom.

"Ma what's the matter? I need you to calm it down."

"I'm bleeding, Faheem," she cried.

"Shit!" Faheem went to dial 911. After he spoke to the dispatcher, he called Kyra and Marvin answered the phone.

"Yeah."

"Marv, I need Kyra to meet me at the hospital."

"What's up, man?" He sat up, turning on the lamp and shaking Kyra.

"I'm in the fuckin' twilight zone. That's what's up. My wife is in labor, and Tasha came over about an hour ago, screaming and crying because Trae is gone. And now she's bleeding. Angel will be here any minute now, but she won't be any help once she finds out that them two niggas are together."

"Damn, man," Marvin sympathized.

"I'm waiting on the ambulance now to take Tasha to the hospital, and I can't leave Jaz here by herself. So I guess I'll be taking both of them."

"A'ight. Kyra will be there." He hung up.

Faheem was right. When Angel got there and looked at Tasha, she started crying. As she followed them to the hospital, she started dialing Kay's cell number and paging him. When he didn't call her back, she started freaking.

Inside the hospital, she asked, "Faheem what's going on? Somebody needs to tell me something."

"I'm not sure. But if you ain't gonna hold yourself together, I want you to go to the house." He was shaking her. "A'ight?"

"I'm scared Faheem." She started crying.

"I'm calling you a cab and sending you to Marvin's."

Chapter 22

On August 7, 2001, Tasha lost her baby. That same day, Jaz gave birth to an eight-pound, eleven-ounce girl. They named her Kaeerah Aaliyah. Faheem was so proud.

Angel pulled herself together and went over to Faheem's to make sure everything was sanitized and ready for Jaz and the baby to come home. Kyra stayed at the hospital with Tasha, and Marvin kept baby Aisha.

They kept Tasha in the hospital to monitor her depression, then finally released her after six days. Angel and Kyra brought her home from the hospital. She was quiet during the entire ride. After taking her items out of the trunk and walking her up-stairs, she apologized to them for being so distant.

Tasha looked at Angel and said, "You look like shit!"

"What do you expect? I've been living between your hospital room and Jaz's guest room. I've been worried sick about you. I've been checking my voice mail, yours and Kay's, but I haven't heard shit. I haven't been to your apartment or mines. I'm trying to get to my apartment either tonight or tomorrow."

"This is so fucked up," Tasha sighed. She was trying not to cry. "I'll be okay. I need some time by myself. Can y'all please leave? I need to get myself together. I love you both, and as al-ways, I couldn't have gotten through this without y'all." They both hugged her and respected her wish to be left alone.

As soon as they left, Tasha sank down on the couch and cried herself to sleep.

When she woke up it was almost 8:30 at night. She still had on her hospital bracelet. She cut it off and went to the bathroom to run some hot bath water. She soaked for a good half hour before getting out and throwing on some sweats and a T-shirt. She decided to clean the entire apartment, starting with the kitchen. The dishes from the last meal they had together were still in the dishwasher. When she got to her bedroom, she saw Trae's clothes on the back of the love seat. She picked them up and buried her nose in his shirt for a whiff of his cologne. Her stomach knotted up as she held back the tears. Just then the doorbell rang, startling her. She went to the window, peeked out and saw Faheem's Jag. She laid Trae's clothes back down and went to open the door.

Faheem gave her a big hug and kissed her on the forehead. She burst into tears. "Everything's gonna be fine, baby sis. Just watch."

"Please God, I pray you're right. I miss him so much and didn't know how much I cared about him until now. Even his baby is gone."

"*He's* not gone. You just haven't heard from him." Faheem shut the door, and they went upstairs. When they got inside, he sat on the leather sofa while she went to blow her nose and wash her face.

When she came back into the living room Faheem had lit a blunt. Tasha went to the kitchen and brought back two bottles of water and an ashtray. "Damn! That smells good."

"Baby sis, can a brother get a wine cooler or some soda? You bad as Jaz."

She started laughing. "I don't have anything else. Plus, this is better for you. Drink this up then I'll get you some juice."

"Glad to see you're smiling."

"What do I do now? One minute he's here, next minute he's gone."

Faheem took a long drag of the blunt and passed it to her. She took one drag and choked. They both started laughing.

"I needed this. Mind if I put on some music?"

"Please do," Faheem joked. "What you got?"

"Trae had just dropped some CDs off. I don't even think he opened them," she said, thumbing through them. "Some are singles . . .'Let's Get Dirty' by Redman."

"*Let's get dirty!*" Faheem sang.

"Erick Sermon and Marvin Gaye."

"*Just like music!*" Faheem continued to sing.

"Jagged Edge, featuring Nellie."

"*Where the party at?*" Faheem sang.

"Busta Rhymes."

"*Busta, what it is right now!*" He sang some more.

"A'ight, we straight," she said, loading up the CD changer.

She sat back down, and they puffed some more.

"The first thing you need to do is handle any unfinished business. I'm sure he left you some instructions in case of an emergency."

"He left a business card for his business attorney and not a criminal attorney. I don't understand that." Then she went for the briefcase. "He said if I didn't hear from him in a couple of days to go empty the safes and lockboxes."

"What does he have, wall and floor safes?" She shook her head yes and watched as he thumbed through the contents of the briefcase. "Damn! He left you everything. You got your work cut out for you. You need to start on this first thing in the morning. If anything went down, the Feds have visited or will visit whatever house they think he had evidence in. If you need somebody to go with you, page me or Marvin."

"Thanks Faheem."

"We family."

"Speaking of family, how's my niece?"

"Your niece think she's running shit—just like her mama."

Tasha burst out laughing. "That baby is going to be rotten."

"Just like her mama!" They both said it at the same time and burst out laughing.

"Faheem, you silly! I'm so glad you came over. I was in a very serious state of depression."

"I figured as much. Take care of your husband's business. He worked very hard for all of that. Goes to show you that every thug definitely needs a lady, somebody that he loves and who loves him and will hold it down for him regardless," he said, pointing at the briefcase.

Faheem drank the last of his water and stood up to leave. "Page me if you need me. Come lock the doors. And get some rest."

"You sound just like Trae," she said, laughing.

Chapter 23

The next day Tasha got busy. Her first stop was Trae's apartment in New York. When she arrived in the underground parking lot she spotted the vacant parking spots for both the Range Rover and the Ferrari. The Navigator was still at Faheem's.

When she got upstairs she noticed his door had been replaced with a new one. She turned the knob, and it was locked. *That's a good sign*, she said to herself. But when she opened the door she almost fainted. It looked like a tornado had hit it. The place was ransacked. Everything was everywhere, literally. Everything that could be emptied was emptied. They even sliced up the Italian leather sofas and all of the speakers. Every room was torn up from the floor up. Everything of value was gone: stereos, big screens, computers, DVD players, exercise equipment, and appliances. They were courteous enough, however, to leave an itemized listing of everything they confiscated.

"Smart-ass bastards," she spat, when she saw that the floor safe wasn't touched. The carpet and desk were still intact. They took the chair, but not the desk. She slid the desk over and pulled up the carpet and the padding. After fumbling with the lock, she finally got it open and just shook her head.

"All of this fuckin' money and he had to make one last run," she said out loud. The tears started falling. She filled up two suitcases, then went to the wall safe and filled a duffel bag. "They think they're so fuckin' smart."

She had never been to the two houses in Jersey. One was in his aunt's name, and the other in his parents'. At the aunt's house she emptied the safe, wrapped up everything in a blanket, and dragged it to the car. When she got to the other house, she used her cell phone to leave Angel a message to come see her that night. The Feds had cleaned out the house that was in his parents' name. It wasn't even locked. She had to call a locksmith. She was too exhausted to go to the Philly apartment. When she got home, she put all of the money in the empty apartment on her second floor.

When Angel came rushing through the front door, she headed straight for Tasha's apartment. Angel couldn't wait to tell her about the slew of documents, keys to vehicles and property, and money Kay left in her apartment. Then she broke down and cried.

"This was so stupid. What was he thinking? He's not broke," Angel whined.

"Please . . . with the crying," Tasha pleaded. "No more tears."

"I'm sorry. I can't help it. Why did I ever have to fuck with him? I'm jeopardizing my lawyer's license. I could easily get a conspiracy charge. And you know my mother and my aunt Jan is enjoying the fact that they can say 'I told you!'"

"Too late to be concerned with that, don't you think?" Tasha asked her. "You done fucked the man. He turned your ass out. Now you might as well go with the flow."

"Shut up! I hate it when you're right," Angel said, blowing her nose.

"Girl please. You know I'm just frontin'. How many times was that same damned speech thrown up in my face? Have you been to his house yet?" Tasha asked.

"I don't want to go." They were headed to the empty second floor apartment.

"You're gonna have to. You might as well snap out of it and get it out of the way. It's not going to be a pretty sight." She showed her the document with the list of items seized at Trae's apartment and showed her all of the money. "This ain't even all of it. So when are you going to your man's house?"

Angel slid down the wall and sat on the floor. "This shit ain't happening."

"Yes, it is. When are you going? Snap out of it, Angel."

"I'll go this weekend," she said, rubbing her hands through her hair. "Do you think they're okay?"

"No. They would have called by now. Let's face it." With that they both started crying.

Angel spent the weekend checking on Kay's other property and collecting money. The headache was his recycling business and his record label. The Feds had shut them both down. She had planned on spending the weekend at his house. They couldn't confiscate it, the family having owned it for over seventeen years. When she got there, she saw the mess the Feds had made of his place. They didn't find the safes so she left everything in them.

Her aunt Jandelyn, the prosecutor, told her the Feds wouldn't be back. So she decided to stay and go back to work Monday morning. She had planned to go furniture shopping Monday night because they tore up sofas and mattresses.

The only car that was confiscated was the Benz convertible. She didn't know if Kay had it somewhere or if they took it, because it wasn't on the list. The SUV and wagon were still parked.

Tasha had handled the last of her business. She checked out the apartment in Pennsylvania and was glad that it was untouched. She went back and took half the money out of her second floor apartment and brought it to the Pennsylvania apartment, which had several large safes.

The following week she went back to work full time at the hospital mainly to keep her mind occupied. That would be time spent not thinking about Trae. When she wasn't working, she was back and forth between Kyra's and Jaz's, spending time with the babies.

After two and a half months, they still hadn't heard anything. Tasha had rented out one of the New Jersey properties and put the other one up for sale, all with the help of Trae's business attorney. Angel had told her that whenever she or her contacts tried to find out anything on Kaylin Santos and Trae Macklin, they would come up with a clean slate. They were not listed as being in federal custody, which only mystified things even more.

Chapter 24

Angel and Tasha were laughing as they came out of the movie theater. They had caught the 10:00 show of *What's the Worst That Could Happen?* When Tasha heard someone call her name, they turned around and saw two brothers coming their way.

"Dayum!" Angel said. "I can't even front. They are fine!"

"I know," said Tasha.

"Who are they?"

"The one with the curly hair is Jaden. He has Connecticut and Delaware on lock. He knows Trae. I saw him a few times. I don't know the other one's name, but I seen him around. This is a test."

"What up ma?" Jaden said to Tasha, kissing her on the cheek. "Damn, you are fine."

"Ain't nothing, Jaden. How are you?"

"I'm fine now that I finally ran into you," he said in a suggestive tone. "This is my partner Saleem. Saleem this is Tasha."

"This is Angel. Angel, Jaden and Saleem," said Tasha, trying to move on.

Jaden's attention went back to Tasha. "We'll walk y'all to the parking lot. Did y'all enjoy the movie?"

"It was cool. I didn't see you inside."

"We just came out of Red Lobster. Where are y'all going? Let's all go out."

"I'm going home," she said.

"So you've been a'ight?"

"I'm good."

"How is Trae?"

"I'm not sure."

Jaden pulled out a diamond money clip, counted a thousand dollars, and tried to put it in her hand. She pushed it back at him.

"If you know Trae then you know I'm straight."

"I'm not giving it to you to help him out. I want you to have it because it's coming from me. I'm sure you're straight financially. If not, I can fix that. But what about other areas?" He grinned seductively. "Money can't hold you and caress you at night."

"No, you didn't go there."

"Yeah, I went there. Just keepin' it real. Let me take you out tonight," he suggested, putting his hand on the car door handle, trying to stop her from opening it.

"I gotta go home."

"Why? You got somebody there waiting for you?"

"I hope so," she laughed.

"You got a man already?"

"I have a husband," Tasha said, holding up her ring finger. He gently took her hand, put her ring finger into his mouth, and winked at her.

"Mmm mmm . . . Why would a nigga want to up and leave somethin' as sweet as you behind? That shit is beyond me."

"Shit happens Jaden. You know the game."

"That's why I want you to let me take you out tonight. The game goes on."

"It's too soon for that."

"I won't tell if you won't," he promised.

She acted as if she didn't hear that last statement. She unlocked the car door and he opened it up for her. "Roll the window down," he told her. Angel got in, leaving Saleem standing at the door while Tasha started the car and rolled the window down.

"Let's go out tonight," he said, massaging the nape of her neck.

"Can't do that."

"Why not?"

"Why do you think? This ain't that kind of party."

"How long you plan on waitin'?"

"As long as I need to."

"I'm willing to take over where Trae left off."

"He hasn't left off, and I doubt if you can do that."

"Try me." He pulled out two business cards, handed them to her and said, "Put your number on the back of one of them. I'm gonna call you."

"I got your number."

"I want you to use it," he said, rubbing the nape of her neck again. He leaned over and whispered in her ear, "I won't tell if you won't tell." He nibbled on her earlobe and ran his tongue underneath it.

"I told you it ain't that type of party." She put the car in gear, and he let her go. She smiled at him and pulled off.

"You are dead wrong," Angel said.

"That was a test. I know it was." She slowed down at the light. "He smelled so good. That attention from a man feels so good. God, I miss Trae."

Just then a silver Hummer pulled up next to them. The window rolled down. Jaden winked his eye at her and mouthed, "I won't tell if you won't tell." She ran her hands through her hair and pulled off.

They pulled up in front of Tasha's house at about 12:45. When they got out of the car they looked around to see where all of the weed smoke was coming from. Then they saw Omar getting out of a Ford Expedition.

"I get to kill two birds with one stone . . . must be my lucky night. What are y'all doin' out so late?" he asked, giving them both a hug. "It's damn near one in the morning."

"I'm grown," Tasha said.

"So am I," Angel added.

He started laughing. Then the window rolled down on the Expedition. "What up, strangers?"

Angel waved. "What's up, Bo?" Tasha asked.

"How you doin'?" he said.

"I'm hangin'."

"It's all good."

"In whose hood?" Tasha joked.

"We've been sitting out here since 10:30. I forgot where Angel lived. I got a delivery for the both of y'all. Where's your car Angel?" Omar asked.

She pointed at the Lex across the street.

"You can't leave this in the car. You need to take this home. We'll follow you." He started walking to his Expedition. They followed him wondering what the hell was going on. He opened the back and gave one briefcase to Tasha and another to Angel while he carried another two.

When they got in the house he told Angel, "You got four in the car as well." He opened up one of them. It was filled with neatly stacked cash. He closed it back, locked it, and threw Tasha the keys. Then he pulled a sheet of paper out of his pocket and handed it to her. It was a copy of a newspaper article from a Mexico City newspaper. They both sat there reading it together. Tasha was the first one to break down; Angel was right behind her.

The article stated that the Mexican authorities had received a tip that one of the biggest deals was going down on their turf. They had their informants in place and had planned on making the sting and some history, by seizing 12.5 million dollars of liquid cocaine and the cash to purchase it.

However, the suspects were tipped off as well. Or so it appeared because the deal didn't go down. One of the informants who was participating in the sting was still missing as well as the coke and the money to purchase it. When the authorities rolled up on the two U.S. citizens/suspects, Trae Macklin and Kaylin

Santos, their search on them and their property turned up nothing but firearms. The Mexican officials held them for over sixty days before extraditing them to the U.S. while the investigation continued.

"So, my sistas, they want y'all to come see them tomorrow. They're in federal custody in New York."

Tasha felt like she was hyperventilating. Angel had run into the bathroom and slammed the door.

"Tasha! You alright?" Omar asked. It looked like she was turning blue. He got up, pulled her arms, and made her stand up. "Tasha!" he yelled.

She shook her head up and down and then sat back down. "You spoke to him?"

"No, I was just given the message."

"How long has he been there? Why hasn't he called or written?" Now she was crying. "Why the fuck did he take me through all of this?" she screamed.

"He'll fill you in," he said, getting up to check on Angel.

"Yo Angel!" he yelled, banging on the bathroom door. "You a'ight?" She opened the door and asked him the same questions Tasha had just asked him. "He'll fill you in," he told her. "You ready to take those bags to your house?"

She blew her nose. "Can you wait for me downstairs?"

He headed for the door. "Take care Tasha."

Angel came out of the bathroom. "Is this really happenin'? I bet them motherfuckers knew what was up all along."

"I think so. I guess so. I don't know," Tasha said, taking some tissue from Angel and blowing her nose. "I know I'm tired of crying, and this is fucking unbelievable."

Angel flopped down on the sofa next to Tasha. "I can't believe I'm in love with a nigga doing time . . . Miss Corporate Lawyer. And now I'm going to jail to visit him." She started laughing. "I don't believe this shit! It doesn't make sense!" Now tears were flowing.

"Fuck that! I'm just glad my husband is alive," Tasha said,

bursting into tears again. "I'll do the fuckin' time with him." Then she started laughing through the tears.

"What's so funny?" Angel asked.

"It's a good thing we ain't fuck nobody these past few months." Angel laughed too. "You almost did tonight!"

"How could I? You was there cock-blockin'. I saw you watchin' me. I'm glad I didn't. You know I can't go out like that."

"Sho' you right."

Chapter 25

By 5:30 a.m. Tasha was out of the tub. She was moisturizing her skin as she sat on the bed. She strategically dabbed on the Escada perfume that Trae bought her and put her hair in a bun. She went through the closet trying to figure out what to wear and finally decided on a black Versace skirt and blouse that Trae picked out for her and a pair of black, snakeskin sandals. She put on her diamond earrings, her iced-up tennis bracelet with "Tasha" written on it, and the ankle bracelet that had "Trae" written in diamonds. By 6:45 she was in front of Angel's beeping the horn.

"You copycat!" Tasha was teasing her when she saw that she had on Versace from head to toe. "You look stunning," she said. "Why didn't you wear a skirt?"

"What difference does it make?" Angel asked. "And why do you have on all that ice?"

"Fuck them. My husand is already locked up. What they gonna do? Take it off me? My nigga likes for me to wear my shit."

"Do you bitch. Do you."

"What?"

"Never mind, Tasha. You smell good and you look real pretty. He's going to be so glad to see you," Angel told her.

"I'm going to be even happier to see him even though I'm pissed off. I can't wait to hear his explanation."

"I know that's right."

By 9:20 a.m. they were driving up and down Park Row looking for a parking space. When they got to the building it was already crowded. Angel had never paid a visit to anyone locked up, so she got her cues from Tasha, doing whatever she told her to do.

They filled out the two-page visiting form with the tiny pencil provided them. Tasha couldn't believe that she was going through this again. The big difference was this time her relationship to the inmate was that of spouse, her name now being Macklin and not McNeil.

Tasha asked the offficer for a locker key to put their things in. Both she and Angel had clear plastic purses that they could take on the visit with them. They put their keys, Kleenex, lip gloss, ID, lotion, hairbrush and money into the clear plastic purse. Everything else they put in the locker.

After about thirty minutes they called for visitors for inmate Santos. Angel stood in line until she got to the guard, who dumped the contents of the clear bag out in a tray, telling her that the lotion and lip gloss were forbidden. Angel put those items back inside her locker. The guard then took her ID and made sure she was on the visiting list before sending her through the metal detector. It went off, triggered by her Cartier watch and diamond earrings. Eventually when she made it through, they were all herded toward the elevator. She looked back at Tasha, smiled, and waved at her, feeling scared to death.

As they rode the elevator, she checked out all the women, children, mothers, and grandmothers. She noticed there were very few men. Most of the women had on miniskirts and dresses. She could smell all types of loud perfumes. Angel was also struck by the amount of conversation in Spanish.

When the elevator opened, her heart began to flutter. There were two visiting rooms with large windows, one on the left, the other to her right. All she saw was a tribe of men in tan jumpsuits, some in brown. The guard yelled "Santos" and pointed to the side she would have her visit. As she stood waiting for them to open the door, she scanned the room to see if she saw Kay. She saw a nigga who looked like him wink at her. *I know that's my baby*. As they cracked the gate, the visitors rushed in.

That same nigga said, "Don't act like you don't know nobody!" He grabbed her and lifted her up into the air.

"I barely recognized you." She was staring at him as if he were a stranger. His hair was cut short and he had lost a lot of weight. He kissed her on the chin and then on the lips before letting her feet hit the floor. She melted in his arms, feeling like everything was moving in slow motion. Then she snapped. She started crying and punching him on his chest.

"Damn you Kay!" she screamed. "How could you do this to me? I didn't know whether you were dead or alive!" He got a hold of her arms, held her tight, and wouldn't let go. "You could have called or written, Kaylin!" She was crying and was trying her best to break loose. "That was so fuckin' cruel!" Everybody was staring at them. Kay just held her tight, not saying anything. "Let me go Kaylin!"

"Not until you calm down."

She buried her face into his chest and kept on crying and shaking for a good five minutes. "You have no idea what you put me through. Why did you let me catch feelings for you Kay?"

Is that a trick question? He asked himself and was glad when she continued to ramble on before he could respond.

"I was supposed to fall in love with a lawyer, engineer, doctor or somebody like that," she sobbed. "Not a fuckin' dope dealer that's in jail."

"Love don't work like that ma. It don't recognize titles and status." He kissed her on the forehead and slowly turned her arms loose. She just stood there sniffing, her face buried in his chest. He wrapped his arms around her and pulled her close, rocking from side to side.

"What am I supposed to do now Kaylin?" She sounded totally exhausted. "I mean you really took me for a ride."

"Go wash your face and blow your nose. You got snot all over my jumpsuit."

She let out a little laugh mixed with snifffles. "Oh God, I don't believe this is happening. I want you to come home Kaylin."

"I'll be there in a minute. You just make sure you're waiting on me." He squeezed her tighter. "Go fix yourself up." He bent over, picked up her clear purse off the floor, and gave it to her.

"Gordo!" someone called. Kay turned around, and the guy said something to him in Spanish. Kay talked to him in Spanish for a minute before turning his attention back to Angel.

"Doesn't gordo mean fat?" she asked. "Why did he call you fat?"

"He's talking 'bout my pockets—fat pockets." He walked her to the ladies' room, then left to wipe down the front of his jumpsuit. When she finally came out he was sitting down.

"Hey, beautiful."

"Yeah, right," she said, flopping down in the chair next to him. He lifted the big orange plastic chair up with her in it and sat it in front of him, pulling it close enough that her knees almost touched the front of his chair as he placed his legs on the outside of hers. He rubbed up and down her calves, looking in her eyes as she ran her fingers through his soft hair. "I miss you so much," she whispered.

"Kiss me like you miss me," he said in that sexy tone that made butterflies circle in her stomach. She willingly obeyed as they passionately kissed nonstop for a good five minutes. Kay was squeezing her nipples and running his hands up and down her back, butt, and thighs. As she returned his passionate touches she felt the knot on his head.

"Don't press, baby."

"What happened?"

"Feds in Mexico beat our ass, mami."

"Why?"

"We clowned them so they acted as if they wanted to kill us.

But I came away with a knot, Trae with a fractured rib. How much did you miss me?" he asked, changing the subject.

"That's a violation of your constitutional rights, Kaylin." She started crying again.

"Baby, I'm fine. No more tears. Now tell me how much you missed me."

"Too much," she sniffed. "How come you didn't call or write? I worried so much."

"The moment we did that, then that would've been an excuse for them to kick down your door. Why drag you into this shit unnecessarily? I got this. Trust me. You know too much as it is."

"How's Trae?"

"He a'ight. They got him on a different floor," he said, running his nose all around her neck. "Mmm, you smell so good. You look so good. You don't know how much I miss you callin' my name when you start cummin'."

"Please don't remind me."

"How's my girl Tasha?"

"She's hanging tough even though she lost the baby."

"Damn!" He leaned back in his seat and started thinking back. "Trae kept sayin' 'she lost it, man.' I thought he was losin' his mind. He said he felt it. He kept saying, 'she lost my baby.' *Damn!* He's goin' to be fucked up."

After about forty minutes they finally yelled "Macklin." Tasha got up and gave the offficer her ID and plastic purse, which was dumped out into the tray. The officer must have been tired because she let her take in everything. Tasha took off all jewelry and shoes before going through the metal detector. They were all herded onto the elevator and up they went.

When she walked off the elevator she also was bombarded by an army of men in tan and brown jumpsuits. They were all lined up, looking through the glass windows for their loved ones. So many faces, so many colors all caged up like animals. The guard called her and pointed to the side she was to go to. The steel gate slid open, and they all went in.

Tasha looked around for Trae, wondering where he was when, all of a sudden, she felt those all too familiar strong arms sliding around her waist, then those warm lips on her neck. She relaxed inside his big strong arms as the tears rolled down her cheeks. He turned her around and hugged her tight. They didn't need to say a word. He held her so tight she could hardly breathe.

She managed to lift her head up at him and saw the tears rolling down his cheeks. They didn't even realize that they had been standing there for almost fifteen minutes.

The guard yelled, "Macklin! Use the chairs."

One of the inmates yelled at the guard, "Man, leave him alone! He ain't botherin' nobody."

Another one yelled, "He sure ain't, punk ass!"

Trae wasn't paying nothing or nobody any attention but his wife. "Baby, I swear to you . . . I am so s—"

"It's not your fault. I think it's my punishment for killing Nikayah's baby."

"Baby, it's my fault."

"Let's not talk about it today, okay?" Feeling like she would fall back into her deep depression.

"We won't talk about it if you don't want to," he said, kissing the tears off her face. Somebody walked by them and handed Trae some tissue, and he gave it to her.

She blew her nose. "I've cried so many tears these past three months—enough to last a lifetime. I was so angry with you."

"I promise I'm gonna make it up to you."

He swooped her up and carried her to one of the big orange chairs in the back of the room. He sat down, placed her on his lap, and tongued her down. "Damn baby, I sure do miss you," he said, inhaling her perfume. "You smell so good and you feel so soft." He was rubbing his hands up and down her leg. "You look so pretty."

"I look like shit Trae! My eyes are puffy, and I know my nose is red and puffy. Where is the bathroom?"

"You look fine. I miss that smile. I miss hearing your voice. I miss you baby."

"I miss you too. This is crazy Trae. You leaving, now you're back and being locked up . . . Baby . . ."

"Shhhh . . . He put his finger to her lips. Go ahead and go to the ladies' room. He kissed her on the cheek. "We'll talk about everything. We got time. I told you I'd be back. Didn't I? She nodded yes and got up and headed towards the rest room. Everything feeling surreal.

She finally came walking out of the bathroom and sat down in the chair next to him. He noticed that she had brushed her hair and gotten herself together. "Can your husband get another kiss?"

"Oh my God Trae, you cut all of your hair off! Why did you do that?"

"Who was going to keep it up?"

"Look at you . . . moustache and goatee. It makes you look so sexy. I can't believe I hadn't even noticed. See, you are causing me to lose my mind. Wait untill I tell Angel. Trae I'm going crazy. You are driving me crazy."

They then started talking about his case. "The bottom line is Mexico and the U.S. are fightin' over us," Trae explained. "That's why we don't have bail. Even though we both were carrying firearms when they rolled up on us, we're both licensed to carry. And the firearms were registered to us. So it's really political. And we clowned them. Where is the dope and the cash? Them damn Feds, if they don't have anything on you, won't think twice about concocting something. My lawyers will be here later on today or tomorrow We just gotta hang tight."

"I don't know what to say. I don't even know what to think about how much time we're facing. Right now I'm just thankful that I'm not a widow. Not hearing anything from you at all . . . that was fucked up."

"I apologize for that. You just needed to be as far away from this as possible. They know who you are and was probably looking for any little excuse to harass you."

Trae noticed that the guard went out of the room. Quickly he eased his hand up her thigh. She tried to act nonchalant as he slid her thong to the side and inserted two fingers, slowly moving them around. "Baby, give me a kiss." She kissed him. When he saw the guard coming back, he pulled out his fingers, and she watched him take a sniff and put them in his mouth. *"Peaches and Cream,"* he sang.

She smiled. "Same ol' Trae. I miss you baby."

"I miss you more. Pussy still smells and tastes good. If that guard leaves out again, you gonna let your man bust a nut real quick?"

She sank back into her seat and looked at him to see how serious he really was. "You mean we're gonna sneak in the bathroom?"

"Nah, we can't go in the visitors' bathroom."

"Then where we gonna go?"

"Right here."

"Right here? It's rather open, don't you think?"

"Not really. We're back here in the corner, and it looks like everybody is pretty much minding their own business. See that couple right there, the lady with the colorful dress, he's hittin' it right now." Tasha tried to sneak a peek. "All you have to do is just sit still right here in my lap. I'll handle everything else, but you'll have to let me know when you see him coming back in. A'ight Baby?"

"You sound like you begging, playa. A playa like you is not supposed to be begging," she teased him.

"Shit! I ain't no playa no more. You the true playa. You got all the assets, property, cash . . . everything." He slid his hand back in between her legs, slid the thong to the side, and started massaging her clit.

Her cheeks were getting flushed. "Oh God Trae, that feels so good."

"Go in the bathroom and take those off," he suggested, guiding her off his lap and not giving her a choice in the matter. As she turned around to go, he stood up, put his hand on her butt, and pulled her close so she could feel how hard his dick was. "Take that bra off as well," he said, tonguing her down.

He looked around and saw that everyone seemed to be still minding their own business when he pulled out his handkerchief and set it on the seat. He saw Tasha coming out of the bathroom and started smiling. Inmates and visitors alike were checking out all that ice she had on. One dude even hollered, "Bling! Bling!"

When she got close to him, Trae patted his thigh, motioning for her to sit on it. He started caressing her breasts. She looked around and relaxed a little when she saw that nobody was looking. He slid his hand back up her thigh while looking at the guard, and ran it over her entire pussy.

"Damn, if I get to put it in, I'm probably gonna bust a nut in one minute." He went inside of her, wetting his fingers to lubricate her clit. As he played with it he bit on her nipples through her silk blouse. "Damn," he said, looking at the guard, "don't he got to go get a cup of coffee or something? Give me a kiss."

"Don't make me cum Trae. I'll mess up my skirt. Okay?"

"A'ight." He positioned her so that she was sitting directly on his dick. "It's so hard it's about to break Tash. I gotta get me some of this."

"Well, this might be your opportunity. It looks like he's getting ready to leave. He has to take those visitors to the elevator."

"Good," Trae said, unzipping the fly of his jumpsuit. Then he peeked around her to see what the guard was doing and slipped his dick out. "You gotta lift up a little, baby." She lifted her butt up a little and felt his dick trying to find its way home. Trae fumbled until he felt the opening of her hot tunnel and slid all the way in until it would go no more. He wrapped both arms around her waist and pulled her closer to make sure he was getting it all.

"Unnghh," he let out a deep moan.

"Baby, that feels so good." Tasha was trembling and trying to avoid closing her eyes.

"It sure do, but baby you gotta watch for the guard," he said, remaining still. "I'm tryin' not to come right now. I'm strugglin', baby. Let me know when he comes back through that door, okay? I'ma close my eyes for a few seconds and fuckin' enjoy. You feel so good. I miss you so much."

"Trae baby, he's comin'!"

"Shit!" Trae, sweat beads already popping up across his forehead, opened his eyes and peeked around her to see exactly where the guard was. He watched him go over to a couple, say something, laugh, then go back out. "You got him?"

"Yeah, I got him baby, but hurry up."

Trae closed his eyes again and started grinding a little faster. She could feel him trembling as his breathing got heavier. He slid his hand around to grab her clit, but she stopped him. "Baby we are not at home. Hurry up and handle your business."

After about three or four more strokes, Trae was coming so hard that Tasha was bouncing up and down in his lap. "Trae! I see him baby." He grabbed his handkerchief, lifted her up a little, and wiped her off, then himself. He zipped his pants back up when he saw the guard coming toward him.

"Damn!" he mumbled. "We're busted, but fuck it. That pussy was worth it."

"She needs to sit in her own chair, Macklin," the guard said and went back to the other side of the room.

"Thank you baby, I really appreciated that," he said, playing with her nipples. "This pussy is so good and it's all mines."

"Ten more minutes, people!" the guard yelled.

"Kiss me Tasha." She grabbed his neck, pulled him close, and tongued him down. "That pussy was good, baby," he kept saying. "I'm so glad you were able to come see me. I love you more than anything."

She was now hot. "Make me cum Trae," she said, kissing his neck and rubbing his head.

Trae looked up to see where the guard was as a group of people was waiting to go out. He palmed her butt and pulled it up to the edge of the chair, putting three fingers inside her pussy and going in and out.

"That feels good baby." Trae pulled his fingers out quickly and leaned back in his chair. "Why'd you stop?" Tasha questioned.

"He's lookin' at us."

"Five minutes, people!" the guard yelled.

Trae leaned back up and slid her skirt up from under her butt. "Hopefully, you won't get it wet," he said, sliding his hand back under her skirt and fondling her clit. "Man, I'd give anything to be able to run my tongue over this . . . just once."

Tasha was now holding onto his shoulders and grinding her hips. "Baby," she moaned.

"C'mon, butterfly." Trae could feel the contractions coming on. "Look at me baby. Look at me while you're cummin'." Tasha's legs were shaking; he smiled because she never opened her eyes. He grabbed his handkerchief and wiped her off.

He hugged her, and they kissed until the guard started yelling, "Visit's over, people. All inmates to the back of the room."

"Time to go ma." He pulled Tasha up, wrapped her arms around his neck, palmed her butt, and pulled her close. "Thank you for comin' to see me and takin' care of all of that business," he said, putting a passion mark on her neck.

"Let's go, Macklin!" the guard yelled.

"Can you call me tonight?" she pouted, kissing him on the lips. He shook his head yes. She kissed him again, rubbing his bald head. "You look so good." She let him go and headed for the door mouthing, "I love you."

He mouthed, "Your skirt is wet, and I love you more."

Chapter 26

Angel had been putting in her hours as a corporate lawyer, trying to earn a little respect and make a name for herself. Even though she worked all week she made sure to visit Kay every weekend. On Saturdays she would take his son and her little sister, and on Sundays she would go by herself. That was her day. He kept sweating her about wearing a skirt or a dress, but she never would. She told him she didn't feel right trying to get her freak on in a prison visiting room.

Tasha made the trip every weekend as well. She always wore skirts and dresses, and Trae made sure he got some every weekend. Tasha didn't mind because as far as she was concerned, it was all about Trae. In addition the doctor gave her a new birth control prescription. So she was happy and in love with her husband.

Both she and Angel were staying on top of their husbands' financial affairs. Trae and Kaylin were now multi-millionaires and out of the dope game.

Angel tried to visit early this particular Sunday morning. Sundays were usually busy, and it took forever to get processed. She got there at 8:00 and didn't get processed to go upstairs until 9:45. The inmates weren't even out yet. She suspected that they had this particular floor on lockdown for some reason. All of the visitors were sitting around impatiently waiting, and the children were running around playing.

Angel bought some breath mints from the vending machine then headed for the bathroom to make sure she looked bootylicious for her man. She was wearing a tan Chanel pantsuit with lizard skin shoes to match. It was tight. She got her hair cut, nails and feet done, and the ice was blinging. The visitors were checking her out on the DL. She even caught some of the females shooting daggers at her, while the men licked their lips.

Finally at 10:50, all of the inmates poured into the visiting room. She smiled when she saw Kay, who was looking finer than ever. He had put on about ten pounds, his body all cut up from weightlifting.

"What up beautiful?" he asked, swooping her up off her feet and hungrily planting sloppy kisses on her chin and her lips. "You look good." They stood there kissing and hugging like they hadn't seen each other in months. "One of these days I'm going to pull these pants off of you. Watch," he whispered in her ear. He took her hand and placed it on his dick. She began squeezing and massaging it and could feel him getting rock hard.

"I miss you long strokin' me with him so much," she sighed.

"You obviously don't miss him that much, if you did, you would be wearing a skirt."

"Kay please, maybe I'll get brave enough one day to fuck in front of a roomful of people."

He pulled her close and guided her to get her grind on. She was grinding on his dick. "See what you're missin'? I could have been all up in this pussy by now," he said, massaging her ass.

"Kay!" a voice yelled. He turned his head around, and there was Brittany. She punched him in the arm. "Where's my fuckin' Lexus? I can't believe you bought this ho one. I was good enough to fuck whenever you wanted to, and now you think you gonna just throw me to the curb?" She slapped him.

"No, this bitch didn't slap me! Britt, what the—"

Everything happened so fast and so unexpected. When Angel heard the name Britt, she pushed Kay out the way and started swinging. She was beating Brittany like she was a child, talking to her while whipping that ass. "Don't you ever disrespect me again. How you gonna come see my man while I'm fuckin' visitin' him? I told you to stay the fuck away from him. You lyin' bitch, talkin' 'bout you was pregnant." She was saying all of that as they were going at it.

By this time the place was swarming with guards. Kay couldn't even pull Angel off Brittany. Two guards were pulling Angel while two more pulled Brittany. "Bitch, your pussy ain't good enough to get a Lexus," Angel screamed. "Get off me!" She was now yelling at the guards.

She turned to Kay. "You ho! What the fuck is she doing on your visiting list?" She swung at him. He ducked. She swung again. He ducked again. This time she went to dig her nails into his eyes, but he turned his head as she put a long, deep scratch from the back of his ear all the way down his neck. She was crying and had turned into a madwoman. "You triflin' ho!" She swung again. This time he snatched her arms, putting them up behind her back. The guards then went to intervene.

"How could you play me like this Kaylin?" She was shaking. "Where was this ho when you disappeared for months?"

Kay started yelling at the guards, "Get your fuckin' hands off my woman. Y'all got the right to touch me, but don't touch her!"

The dummies all backed up. The visiting hall was in turmoil. Folks were standing on top of chairs trying to see the fight of the century. The officers had escorted Brittany outside of the visiting hall, and Kay still had Angel's arms twisted behind her back.

"You're hurtin' me Kaylin," Angel cried.

"Calm your ass down!" Kay yelled at her.

"Let me go, Kay You're hurting me!"

"I'ma break both of these if you don't calm the fuck down!"

"The bitch got on a skirt, Kaylin. What, you planned on fuckin' her today? Oww!" she yelled, "Help me! He's hurtin' me."

"Let her go, Santos!" one of the guards yelled.

"She's not on my visiting list," Kay said through gritted teeth to Angel, totally ignoring the guards.

"Then how the fuck did she get in? I'm not stupid."

"Let her go, Santos. I'm not going to say it again," he warned. Kay finally let her go.

"I want to see his visiting list!" Angel yelled, walking toward the front desk and rubbing her arm. She was crying and looking like a wild woman. "If she's on your list, I'm cutting your fuckin' throat Kay. Do you hear me? I told you not to fuck with me. How could you do me like this Kay?" He just looked at her. "Answer me, dammit!"

"Do what? I ain't done shit to you yet! You're getting ready to find out what I'ma do."

"You said I was your woman and you would never play me. I believed you. Why you gotta be a ho?"

He ignored her and turned to the guards. "I need to talk to the lieutenant." They led him out of the visiting room.

Brittany received a serious beatdown. Her blouse was ripped. Her nose was busted and her ring torn out. Her lip was also bleeding, and she had an ugly scratch that started under her eye and went down to her chin.

When Angel got out into the lobby she yelled, "I want to see Santos' visiting list or I'm pressing charges against all of you bastards that was grabbing on me." Then she looked at Brittany. "I warned you, you fuckin' bitch. You just had to try me," she said, swinging at her and hitting her in the head. They whisked Brittany out of harm's way, pushing her onto the elevator.

They ended up downstairs in the lieutenant's office where Angel found out Brittany was not on his visiting list. She had paid Offficer Gallegos two hundred dollars to let her up.

Angel felt so stupid. Brittany wanted to press assault charges against Angel, and so a squad car was dispatched to the prison to take them downtown. When they got down to the station, criminal checks were run on both of them. It turned out that Kay had filed a restraining order against Brittany during her "pregnancy." They didn't arrest Angel for the assault, but she was given a court date for a hearing.

That evening when Angel got in, she called Tamara, Kay's sister. "Tamara, this is Angel. You heard from your brother?" she asked nervously.

"You just missed him. He told me what you did, and girl, he is fired up at you. He told me to tell you to get the fuck out of his house."

"Shit! Did he really say that?"

"Yup!"

"Damn! If he calls back, please tell him I admit that I was dead wrong and want to apologize. But I am not going nowhere until he calls me."

"Y'all bitches are crazy. I'm trying to get an understanding. Tell me this: Does my brother have a big dick, or does he have mad skills?" She laughed.

"You are sick, and ain't shit funny."

"Come on Angel, tell me."

"You better not tell him I told you this."

"I won't."

"The answer is both," Angel said, smiling.

"Ewwwww!" Tamara said with disgust.

"Well, you asked."

"That is gross. Y'all bitches be sprung. Y'all be stalkin' him. Y'all don't know what 'it's over' means. I'm surprised that Britt is the only one you've had to deal with so far. He turns y'all out then y'all turn fatal attraction on him."

"Tamara, just tell him what I said."

"He probably won't call again until tomorrow. You better make sure the doors are locked and hope that he doesn't send none of his henchmen over to throw your ass out."

"He was that mad?"

"Oh yeah, you done did it," Tamara rubbed it in.

"Shit!" Angel spat. "I went fuckin' ballistic as soon as I saw that ho. I can't believe I did that. And now that bitch is pressing charges. I should have broke her fucking neck. If he calls back, tell him I said to please call me." She hung up feeling like shit.

Three days into the week, and Kay hadn't once called her. He would usually call her several times a day. She called Tasha. "What are you doing?"

"Laying down. I'm tired. What time is it?" she yawned.

"Almost 10:30."

"Damn. I've been layin' down since 7:00 and I'm still tired. I feel run down."

"Have you been drinkin' water?"

"Yeah, so what's up?"

"I'm depressed."

"He still hasn't called?" Tasha giggled.

"It's not funny. What am I going to do?"

"Miss Corporate Lawyer is asking for a humble and lowly peasant's advice?"

"Bitch you are far from humble. But you always get put in the doghouse and manage to get out, so yeah, I want your advice."

"You don't listen, so I'm not even goin' to waste my precious energy. Saturday night you want to go see the babies?" she asked, trying to change the subject.

"Tasha, stop trippin'! I don't want to do nothin' but get my man back. I'm stressing. So what's the plan?"

"I'm not sure if I want to help you."

"Tasha, bitch stop playing. I'm serious."

"Okay. Okay. But it's simple. Just give him some."

"What?"

"You heard me. The nigga is all tensed up. Give him some pussy, and everything will be back to normal."

"That simple?"

"No, not that simple. You wanna knock the nigga's socks off, put him in check so to speak. Can you take Friday off?"

"A sista's gotta do what a sista's gotta do."

"For real though, you need to get off that high horse because nine out of ten of them hos runnin' to the jailhouse who don't be breakin' a nigga off when they go see him got a nigga, or two, or three that they fuckin on the DL on the streets. So disregard that bullshit about, it's degrading and I'm not going to allow him to disrespect me like that. Blah, blah, blah. If the nigga is a good man, fuck that! You better break him off. Let's keep it real. I know you and Kay, y'all got the little phone sex thing going on, but, damn, don't you think he wants to put it in? Don't *you* want to feel it? Actually I don't believe he's letting you get away with not givin' him none."

"He knows I'm terrified. Tasha you gotta understand. Kaylin has a big-ass dick, and I'm very noisy when I'm getting fucked. I can't see myself doing that in a public place."

"Get over it. You'll be going ballistic if he really do get some ho to come up there wearing a miniskirt and no panties who is willing and happy to do what you are terrified of doing."

"If he pull some shit like that, I'ma kill him," Angel threatened.

"You are crazy. You got balls, playa. Driving a Lex that he bought, living in his house, got all of his money, and still won't break him off. Kay must be whipped because I don't understand that shit."

"I don't know about that. He didn't waste no time telling me to get the fuck out of his house. And the way he was twisting my arm, if the guards weren't around I think he would have broke it."

"A'ight. Since you understand that, you have to put up or shut up. Let's do this. Friday is our day. I'll spend the night at Kay's Thursday night, and we'll go to the spa, salon, and do some shopping—everything—on Friday. I'll spend the night again for the visit. Isn't Saturday little Malik's day?" Tasha asked.

"It won't be, this weekend. I'm on a mission."

Chapter 27

When they got in Friday night Tasha ran straight to the toilet and threw up.

"I told you not to eat that shit," Angel said. "Should've had the fried flounder like me. It was nice and fresh. Them scavengers of the sea will kill you."

"Shut up!" Tasha said. "I don't think it's the scavengers. I threw up yesterday, too. I think it's that stomach virus." She crawled out the bathroom and lay down on the carpet.

They enjoyed a full day as planned, getting their nails, hair, and feet done and even a bodywrap. They had the tailor hook them up with leather wraparound miniskirts that were butter soft. Angel picked out a Chanel blouse, and Tasha, a Prada. They planned on wearing stockings with Victoria's Secret garter belts, picking out the sexiest ones they could find. It was on and popping.

Around 6:30 the next morning Angel went into the guest bedroom to see what Tasha was doing. When she opened the door and saw that she was still in the bed, she turned on the lights and stood over her.

"Girl, it's 6:30. I thought we were leavin' at 7:15?" Angel began opening the blinds.

"I don't feel good. Plus, I'm exhausted. I . . ." That was all she got out before she flung the covers back and ran to the toilet to throw up. Tasha ended up on her hands and knees hugging the toilet bowl. Angel stood there with her arms folded watching Tasha crawl on all fours back to the bed.

"Bitch, you done fucked around and got pregnant." Angel giggled.

"Where's my phone?" Tasha asked, ignoring her.

"Where did you put it?"

"I don't know. I'm not going with you. Can you put my cell phone on this nightstand before you go?"

"Anything else?"

"Close the blinds and turn the ringer off the house phone." She threw the covers over her head. "Have fun and knock that nigga off his feet. Suck his dick if you have to," she mumbled under the covers.

"I will," Angel said, closing the blinds and turning off the lights.

Angel was processed and riding the elevator by 9:10 a.m. She felt like a million dollars. Her shit was tight. The guard taking her up the elevator was undressing her with his eyes. When she got off the elevator, the guard didn't tell her which side to go on. She walked to the huge glass wall on her left and peeked in, then to the right. Kay was nowhere around. After everyone went in, the officer called her to the desk.

"You here to visit Santos?"

"Yes."

The offficer leaned back into the chair. "Santos refused his visit."

"He did what?"

"He refused his visit. He doesn't want any visits today, ma'am," he said with a smirk.

"Can you tell him Angel Smith is here?" she said, embarrassed.

He picked up the phone. "I'll have them tell him, but I doubt

if it'll do any good. You're the lady who was fighting him, right?"
He was trying not to laugh.

Angel didn't answer his question. "Look, are you gonna call,
or what?"

The guard rolled his eyes at her and picked up the phone.
"This is Perez in visiting. Tell Santos a young lady by the name
of Smith is here to see him." He laughed, then hung up. "It'll be
a few minutes, so just stand over there." He stood up to process a
few more visitors. After about ten minutes the phone rang. He
looked over at Angel while talking, then hung up. "Sorry, ma'am,
he said he definitely does not want to see you."

Tasha had finished throwing up for the third time and just
crawled back into bed when her cell phone rang. She fumbled
around before she found it. "Hello?"

"I have a collect call from a Mr.—what is your name, sir?—
Macklin. Will you pay for the call?"

"Yes."

"Baby, everything alright?" he asked, his voice reflecting con-
cern. "It's after 10:00. You coming to see me or what?"

"Not today. I've been throwing up for the last three days. I
feel horrible. I'm nauseous, and my breasts are sore. I'm pregnant again Trae."

Trae remained quiet. He didn't want to show any sign of excitement, especially since he didn't know if she was happy or
going to be tripping. "I thought you was takin' the pill."

"I am or was. But if you remember, we had three or four visits
together before I got my new prescription."

"So you've been in bed all morning?"

"Mmm hmm. I love you."

"I love you too. You want me to call you back later?"

"Yeah."

"What time?"

"It doesn't matter. I wish I could see you today."

"Me too, baby. I hope you feel better. Get your rest, and I'll holla at you later on." Trae hung up, wanting to run and shout.

Angel left the jail in tears. Mecca called her cell phone to invite her and Tasha over. Angel told her what had happened. As soon as she got to the house she kicked off her shoes, sat down at the dining room table, and wrote:

Dear Kaylin,

First off let me say that I miss you and I love you more than anything. I'm sitting here at the dining room table feeling deflated. I'm wearing a tailor-made, butter-soft leather, wraparound skirt. I also have on a lacy garter belt, silk stockings, no panties, and a see-through blouse with no bra on. I had every intention of making your day today, which I should have been doing all along.

I thought I could just pop up there and everything would be back to normal. I should have known you better. You wasn't letting me off this easy. You always have to have the last word. Yeah, I was crushed when the guard said, 'He definitely does not want to see you.' But I deserved it. I realize you are putting me in check and letting me know that I'm not running shit. You're the HNIC.

I am so sorry and I apologize for losing my cool. Mecca told me that the main reason why I'm so uptight is because I'm not breaking you off. She said if I was I would never have responded the way I did. I agreed with her for the most part. If I didn't lose my temper all the way, I most likely wouldn't have went off on you. But I still would have beat that bitch Brittany's ass. I had to keep my word. I told her I better not catch her in your face or see y'all in the same room, or else. Well, that ass-whipping was the 'or else.'

I know I pissed you off big time and that's why you told me to pack my shit and get out. I know you. And I know you didn't mean it, or you would have called me yourself and told me or you would have sent somebody over to put me out. I also know that you're not concerned or worried about me having all of your shit. That's called trust. I should have shown you that same trust when I saw that ho, instead of going ballistic. Again, I apologize and ask that you please forgive me. I am very sorry.

I'll close by saying I'm glad you are in my life. You surprised me in several ways. You definitely cannot judge a thug by his cover. I got with you at first just looking to bust a nut (smile) but instead found my soul mate. You notice how we don't even have to talk sometimes but we each know what the other is saying, feeling, and thinking? How we are at so much peace in each other's presence? I was convinced that I could never love any one more than I loved Keenan. I wasn't even going to try. But you just swooped me up and took me beyond what I felt for him. I thank you for that.

I miss you. I miss you coming home and waking me up in the morning. But more so, seeing how happy you would be that I was here. I love you and I am waiting on you, no matter how long it'll be. You can trust and believe that.

Let me go check on Tasha. She's upstairs in the guest bedroom, sick as a dog. I know she's pregnant (smile), but she won't admit it to me. I am so happy for her and Trae. Don't you get any ideas! (smile) Please, puhleeeeese call me.

Love, Red
AKA your Angel.

PS. Your sister told me that the word is out amongst all those hos you used to fuck with that the Red bitch is crazy, that I got you on lock, and I'm living in your house. They're even talking about you got me a Lex to push. They better recognize that they ain't got shit coming. See how far an ass-whipping will go? Please call me.

Angel folded her letter up, sealed it inside an envelope, and went upstairs. She eased open the bedroom door to find Tasha still under the covers. She opened the blinds and flopped on the bed next to her. Tasha poked her head out from under the covers and took one look at her, then covered her head back up.

"You don't look like you got fucked. What happened? You chickened out?"

"No, he refused my visit."

Tasha pushed the covers off her head. "No shit! You're lying?"

"I wish I was. He wants me to know who's runnin' shit, so I'm not mad at him. What about you? When are you getting up?"

"After you fix me something to eat."

"What do you want, with your pregnant ass?"

"Girl, please. I can't even believe this shit. Either I'm one of them women that all you have to do is look at and she gets pregnant, or Trae got some real potent sperm. I think we only did it three or four times before I started popping them sorry-ass birth control pills. I should sue."

"When are you gonna tell Trae?"

"I already did. You know he called."

"So what did he say? I know he's ecstatic."

"He was trying to act all cool about it. I think he was trying to see what frame of mind I was in."

"Well, what's on your mind?"

"What can I say? If he's happy, I might as well be happy."

When Tasha went to the doctor, he told her she was six weeks pregnant. He also told her that the birth control would have worked if she had waited a little longer before having sex.

And, yes, Trae was very glad that they were trying it again.

Chapter 28

Another month passed by without Kay calling Angel or allowing her to visit. She had just walked in the front door when the phone started ringing. She kicked off her shoes and tossed her briefcase on the Italian leather sofa.

"Hello."

"This is the New York operator. I have a collect call from Kaylin. Will you accept?"

"Yes I will." Angel was trying to be cool.

Kay's voice came on the line, "Is everything a'ight?"

"Kay it's been over a month since I've spoken to you or seen you. You haven't even written me. Don't you think it's kind of late to be asking me if everything's alright?"

He acted like he didn't hear her. "We go to court in the morning. In case I get released I need you to pack me a pair of jeans, a jersey, boxers, socks, and one of my leather jackets. Take it to work with you, and Tasha will swing by to pick everything up in the morning. I need a set of house keys and a cell phone. Don't I have one there?"

"Yeah."

"Is it activated?"

"Yes it is."

"Send that too."

"How come you're not asking me to come pick you up?" she

asked, trying to hold back the tears. "Don't you think I would want to pick up my man especially since that he has been away for almost nine months?"

"Baby listen. If they let us out, I got a few errands to run. Now, are you gonna make sure Tasha get my shit or what?"

She was now wiping tears off her cheeks. "Is that all you need? What about money?"

"Yeah, send me a G. I gotta run."

Angel slammed the phone down and began pacing back and forth. She called Tasha on her cell phone, but it rolled over to voice mail. Then she dialed her home number.

"Hello?"

"It's me," Angel said, sniffling.

"What's the matter with you?" Tasha asked.

"What time are you coming to pick up Kay's things?"

"I'll be there between 9:00 and 9:30."

"If he gets out and when you see him, tell him I said I'm catchin' a cab to work. I get off at 5:00. If he's not here to pick me up by then, don't bring his ass home because I'm burnin' this shit to the ground."

"Yes, ma'am, I'll pass on the message," Tasha laughed.

That next morning the limo pulled up in front of Tasha's house at 6:45 a.m. Akbar, the driver, helped her carry the bags out and load them into the trunk. She went over the second and third floor apartments one final time to make sure everything was straight and locked. If Trae got out today, they'd be going back to the bungalow in Jamaica for a couple of months. Tasha had ripped and ran nonstop for the past twenty-four hours, making sure everything was in place. Then she did a little packing. She could hardly contain herself.

Once in the limo her first stop was at Angel's job. She hugged Angel goodbye, took Kay's duffel bag and leather jacket, and headed for the jail. En route, she called Trae's attorney and found out from the secretary that if they got released, it would be from the courthouse, not the jail, and that it was going to be a closed hearing.

When they pulled up in front of the courthouse, Tasha couldn't believe the amount of press that was waiting on the courtroom steps. Now her heart was beginning to race. She called Angel and said they must be getting out because it's a whole bunch of people, press, and police all around. After another hour went by she called the lawyer's office back and asked if they had heard anything. The secretary told her no and said for her to just sit tight.

After another hour, Tasha noticed the hustle and bustle, cameras flashing, and people running up and down the stairs. Shortly afterwards she spotted Kay.

"Kay!" she yelled, as if he could hear her inside the car. She saw him fighting his way down the stairs and opened up the sunroof, stuck her upper body outside the car, and waved her arms. "Where is Trae?" She waved her arms again, trying to get Kay's attention. "Kay!" she yelled.

They finally made eye contact. She watched him as he turned around. Then she saw both of them sprinting down the stairs, trying to get away from the crowd. Tash ducked down and closed the sunroof. Akbar jumped out, ran around, and opened the car door. First, Kay dove in, with Trae close behind, almost falling on top of him. Then there was the crowd in hot pursuit. Akbar slammed the door shut, and Tasha locked it and broke down in tears.

"Goddamn!" they both yelled, trying to get situated. Kay was on the wrong side, and Trae had to climb over him to get to Tasha.

"Hey, baby!" he said, kissing her on the lips and flashing that big smile. She hugged him, yet looked at him like he were an alien. As if he could read her mind he smiled at her and said, "Nah, you ain't dreamin'. Your husband is home."

"What up Tasha?" Kay yelled, pulling his clothes out of his duffel bag. "Why y'all always gotta cry?" he teased.

"Shut up Kay."

"Oh, she does speak," he joked.

"This shit is foul, dawg!" Kay said, undressing. They had on the same clothes that they got busted in.

"Hell, yeah. I'm tossin' this shit right in the trash," Trae said. "Did you bring me some boxers and some socks, ma? Why you so quiet?"

She reached over and pulled them out of the bag, then said, "I'm just checking y'all out and glad to see y'all, that's all."

"Awww! How sweet," Trae teased.

"I'm glad to see you, too," Kaylin said. "It means I'm the fuck outta that cage," he was adjusting the strings in his Timbs. "Did Red send me a leather jacket?"

"It's hanging right behind you," she said, wiping her eyes.

"Good," he said, balling up his dirty clothes and stuffing them in the duffel bag.

"She also made you a lunch. I stuck it in that little refrigerator."

"See, that's why I'm gonna make her my wife. She's jealous as hell, but see how she look out for a nigga? Look how she packed my shit up and didn't act all stupid. She even sent this." He held up a nice, long blunt. "It's the little shit that impresses me."

Trae was now dressed and balling up his clothes. "Tell the driver to pull over."

"What's his name?" Kay asked.

"Akbar."

Kay knocked on the glass. "Yo Akbar! Pull over right here then drop me off on 125th Street." When Akbar pulled over, Trae got out and handed the clothes to a homeless brotha. "Here," Kay said, throwing him everything except his shirt. "I gotta keep this shirt. Red bought this for me."

"Isn't that cute," Tasha teased.

Trae jumped back inside and pulled Tasha onto his lap. Tasha looked at Kay and said, "Angel told me to tell you she took a taxi to work and she gets off at five o'clock. She said if you're not there by five to pick her up, don't even think about bringing your ass home tonight because she's going to burn it down to the ground."

Trae and Kaylin both burst out laughing. "She said that?" Kay asked, still laughing. Tasha shook her head yes. "Last time I checked I could have sworn that I was the one paying all the bills in that house. How could a sista that fine and so innocent-looking be so off the chain? Fuck the chain. She's off the meter." Kay and Trae started laughing again. "What's up with these women, dawg?"

"Man, I threw up my hands a long time ago."

"Red, Red, Red," Kay sighed. "That's my heart. She know it, too. That's why she think she can get away with saying shit like that." He was now dialing his cell phone and puffing on the blunt.

"Puff, puff, pass, nigga," Trae said. Tasha reached over into the bag and pulled out another blunt. "Oh, shit. Never mind. I should have known my baby hooked me up." He leaned over and planted a sloppy kiss on her cheek.

Tasha overheard Kay talking about a ring as she rubbed and kissed Trae's bald head. "What you got on under this leather trench?" Trae whispered in her ear.

"I'll show you when your boy leaves," she whispered back. When Kay hung up, Tasha couldn't help asking him, "What kind of ring are you so in a hurry to get?"

"Dawg, get your wife all out of my business!" Kay joked.

Tasha started laughing. "C'mon Kaylin. Why are you being so secretive?"

"Yeah, dawg, let me know what's up. I'm curious myself," Trae added.

"I won't say anything Kaylin," Tasha pleaded.

"Oh, now I'm Kaylin?" He shook his head and dialed another number. He looked over at the both of them and said, "It's a big, fat engagement rock. I'm hoping to pick it up today."

"Oh, how sweet and romantic," Tasha teased. "Congratulations!"

The limo then pulled over. Kay leaned over and kissed Tasha

on the cheek. "Have a nice trip and make sure you give me a little nephew."

"You make sure you take care of my roadie. Where are y'all going?"

"Rio de Janeiro, Puerto Rico to see my grandparents and my brother, then St. Thomas. But I gotta pay a visit to my brother Kyron on lock first."

"Wow! Angel doesn't even know about this, does she?"

"Nope."

"Dayum! Well, y'all have a safe trip as well." She gave him a hug, and he got out.

"Be right back, baby." Trae got out and shut the door. She watched them hug and then started walking.

"Well, dawg," Kay said, "We did it. We out. We free. Am I dreamin'?" They both just stood there reminiscing.

"I know, man. It's hard to believe. We beat the fuckin' odds," Trae reflected. "When are y'all leaving?"

"I got a few things to go over. Make sure everything is straight. That should only take three or four days, then we out. But tonight, I'll be sittin' on the floor at the Lakers-Sixers game." He faked shooting a basket. "Tonight's game four."

"I hear you. My money is on the Sixers."

"Well, you gettin' ready to lose, dawg. It's Lakers all the way!" He turned serious. "I heard you had to make an example out of that punk-ass Jaden."

"He's a pussy—or was. I kind of wish it was somebody else. I never had no beef with him. But how that nigga gonna disrespect me like that? I made an example hoping to send a message to everybody. Don't fuck with nothing that belongs to Trae: My woman, my business, my paper."

"I hear you. Red mentioned the situation. She said his boy Saleem wasn't even trying to go out like that."

"Well, I know he's glad that he didn't. A'ight, dawg. Nice doing business with you," Trae said. They hugged again and Kay disappeared into the crowd. Trae got back into the limo.

"A'ight, mami, what did you bring me?" he asked, unbuttoning her leather trench and sliding it off.

"Dayum!" He was drooling over her nipples peeking through her sheer blouse. She had on the leather mini wraparound that she never wore to the visit. And she opened her legs to show him the designer garter belt, silk stockings and her wet pussy. "How much time do we have before our flight?" he asked, pulling off his shirt.

"Three hours," she said, smiling.

Chapter 29

Kay's first stop was to see his barber. Then he went to see Jacob the jeweler to inspect Angel's ring. It was tight—just the way he wanted it, if not better—a few more carats than Tasha's. He jumped in the taxi and went home, where he showered and changed before getting back in his SUV with the cash for the ring.

When he walked into Angel's office she was spinning around in her big, leather swivel chair talking to a client. When she looked up at him, the tears started rolling down her cheeks. He winked at her, mouthed, "Hey, beautiful," and set two dozen roses down on her desk. He went over and kissed the tears off her face and then whispered into her ear, "Crybaby." She punched his arm, then scribbled down some notes on her client. Kay went over to look out the window while she was handling her business.

As soon as she hung up the phone she jumped up, ran over to him, and hugged him. "You came for me!" She sobbed while holding him tight. "You look so good!" she said. "I miss you so much."

"I don't know why you'd think I wouldn't come. Sounds like you're still in love with me," he said, looking into her teary eyes.

"Yes, even though you've been treating me like dirt these last couple of months."

"I wasn't treating you like dirt. You know what time it is."

"Whatever, Kay. You treated me like dirt." She laughed, hugging him and giving him a kiss. "So are you a free man?"

"It hasn't hit me yet, but I'm free in every sense of the word."

Angel breathed a sigh of relief. They were quiet. "It's gonna be weird," she said.

"Tell me about it. I've been slingin' ever since I was fifteen."

"So what now?"

"Other than doing anything we want, we might as well get married."

"You think so?"

"Yeah."

"You got my ring?" she asked, laughing.

"Yup."

"No you don't. You liar. This is nothing to joke about Kaylin."

"Why do I have to be joking?"

"What did you do—stop at a jeweler on your way over here?" She was being sarcastic as she went and pulled a gift box out of her purse.

"Basically, yeah." He took a box out of the inside of his jacket and gave it to her while she went to hand him the box she was holding.

"Damn baby, I thought you were joking." She held the box.

"Are you going to open it, or what?"

"Open yours first," she said, jumping from one foot to the other. He smiled at her. "Open it, baby," she begged. He lifted the top and a beautiful stone stared him in the face. She lifted it out of the box and said, "Kaylin I love you more than anything. Will you be my husband?"

"Girl, how are you gonna flip the script?" He leaned over and tongued her down. "Whose money paid for this?" he teased. "Now open yours."

She slowly unwrapped the box and then opened it. "Oh my God, baby!" She started crying. "This is beautiful."

"So are you, crybaby," Kay said, taking the box and putting

the ring on her finger. He kissed her forehead and gave her a bear hug. "I assume this means that you'll be my wife."

"And I assume this means that you'll be my husband." They kissed.

"A'ight, then we straight. C'mon, we gotta go." Kay slapped her on the butt.

"Where are we going?"

"The limo will be at the house at 6:00 to take us to Philly for game four of the playoffs. You want to change, right?"

"Yeah, I need to change. I also need to see Iverson whip some ass. That's my nigga."

"You dreamin', ma. Shaq gonna do the ass-whippin'. Philly ain't got shit comin'."

"You mean LA ain't got shit comin'." They argued as she cleaned off her desk and turned her computer off.

EPILOGUE

A year and a half later we find Marvin and Kyra moved to California. Kyra is attending UCLA full-time, determined to become a psychologist. They got married when Aisha turned one. They had a small but elegant wedding. Marvin flew everyone out to Cali. He had a grip stashed while locked down and still has a couple of partners handling business matters, investing in real estate and stocks. They are happy with their little family.

Faheem and Jaz got married the month after Faheem's dad was released from prison. Faheem sold all four of his businesses, and they are now living in Georgia, in a house in the same neighborhood in Fayette County as Evander Holyfield. Faheem is now a silent partner in a black-owned Atlanta bank.

Jaz beat her case. It was thrown out. She is now enrolled at Morehouse School of Medicine and one of the few women attending. They have a live-in nanny to watch the baby while she goes to school. Faheem was on the sneak tip, trying to get in another baby, but without success, Jaz being extra careful.

Faheem also starts a clothing line: Jazheem Wear. Lots of rappers and sports players are rocking his label. Jaz finally buys her parents that house down South, moving them out of New Jersey. She is still working on building and setting up a home for children who roam the streets. Faheem sets up a non-profit organization to assist her in the venture.

Trae and Tasha move to Cali before the twins Kareem and Shaheem are born, buying a home in Brentwood, OJ's old neighborhood. Trae starts a black entertainment magazine called *Black Interview*. It is on newsstands next to *Vibe*, *XXL*, and *The Source* and doing well. He is a silent partner with a celebrity; they owned a restaurant. And he, Marvin, and Stephon, Tasha's cousin, open up a club in LA.

Tasha sets up her physical therapy office. Her clientele includes major sports stars as well as college and high school players. She has more clients than she can handle. Money is definitely not an issue in the Macklin household.

Kaylin and Angel remain in New York. Angel continued to hone her skills as a corporate/entertainment attorney with the law firm that she interned with.

Kay has to restart his recycling business. His main business, though, is his record label. He has four artists. New Day, featuring Muqa, is blowing up. He also has talks on the table with some big names on setting up the first black distribution company. Angel is handling and overseeing all the legal aspects of the label. They are both very busy.

In a month, they are getting married. Marv and Kyra will be flying in, and Faheem and Jaz, too. Trae and Tasha will come and stay for two weeks. They will use this as a vacation, wanting to get their party on New York style and visit some folks.

Other than the Cali crew no one has seen each other in almost a year. Not only is there going to be a wedding, but it will also be like a family reunion. Everyone's lives seem to be moving at a nice smooth pace. But the drama isn't quite done yet.

It was finally Kay's and Angel's wedding day—at the Hyatt Regency in New York, no less. Folks were taking pictures of it. There were a hundred and fifty guests and celebs in attendance, including all the niggas Kay and Trae used to ball with. Kay's parents, brothers, sisters, and some relatives flown in from Puerto

Rico were there. Angel's mother, aunts, uncles, and relatives were present. Trae's parents were also present as well as Tasha's sister, Trina and brother, Kevin.

They even had Mary J. Blige in to sing *I'm in Love* for the bride and groom. That was the tune they slow-danced to the first night they made love.

The ceremony was still an hour and a half away. Two wedding consultants and a caterer had been hired to make sure everything ran smoothly. Kay's groomsmen were his brother Kajuan from Puerto Rico, Trae, Omar, Faheem, Bo, Marvin, and Angel's brother, Mark. Angel's bridesmaids were Tasha, Jaz, Kyra, Sanette, Mecca, Shanna, and Tamara. Everyone looked fabulous, dressed to kill in Armani and Vera Wang.

The men were waiting around getting ready to take their places. The groom and his men were all kicking it in two suites, the bridesmaids in three suites. Angel had one that she shared with her mom and sister. The men were sitting around getting blunted out and talking shit, most of them hung over from the previous night's bachelor's party. They were ready to get it over with. The women, on the other hand, were an entirely different story.

Baby Kareem was crying, and Tasha decided to take him down the hall to Trae. She knocked on the suite door.

"Come in if you're a man. Wait right there if you're a woman!" somebody yelled out. Tasha opened the door and went in.

"Trae," Kay yelled, "somebody's here to see you." He looked at the baby. "What's up Kareem?" Kareem cried even louder.

"Hush that noise Kareem. Or is it you Shaheem? I still can't tell y'all apart," Omar told him. All the men laughed.

Trae was coming out of the bathroom and drying his hands. When he looked up and saw Tasha and Kareem, he smiled. "What's the matter with my little soldier?"

"Da, Da," Kareem cried out, extending his arms.

"Why isn't he with the nanny?"

"He doesn't want to be with her. He keeps cryin' for you. He

won't be still with me, either. He's dry and he's not hungry."
Tasha was clearly frustrated.

Trae took off his jacket. "C'mere, man." He took Kareem
from Tasha. "What are these women doin' to my little soldier?"
Kareem stopped crying and smiled at his daddy.

"I told you," Tasha said. She went into the bathroom and wet
a face cloth to wipe the baby's face and hands.

"Damn, baby. Did I tell you that you're killin' that dress?"

"About three or four times."

"Give Mommy a kiss, Kareem," Trae told him. Kareem
grabbed his mommy's head and kissed her on the cheek. "Tell
Mommy you love her."

"Love Mommy," he said.

"Tell Mommy to kiss Daddy."

Kareem grabbed Tasha's neck and kissed her again. Then he
said, "Kiss Daddy."

Trae started laughing. "You heard my lil' man. Kiss Daddy
and love Daddy," Trae said, palming Tasha's butt and pulling her
to him.

"Daddy done spoiled this lil' man," she said while Trae was
trying to tongue her down. He was caressing her butt and pressing her against him. Kareem stopped the action by slapping them
both in the face. Tasha leaned over and kissed Kareem again.

"Kareem, you can't be hatin' on your pops. You supposed to
have my back." Tasha turned around to leave. He noticed she
had a little attitude. "Where you goin', ma?" he asked, still holding onto her hand. She tried to pull away, but he wouldn't let her
go.

"I have to check on Angel, Trae."

When they walked into the main room, he put Kareem down
to let him walk.

"Kareem, show these niggas how you s'posed to wear an
Armani suit," Trae said, still holding Tasha's hand. Kareem took
off running to Malik, who was now almost four. He was playing
with toys.

"Don't tell me this nigga done bought the baby an Armani," Kajuan said.

"Yeah, he did. Malik got one on, too," Bo said. They all burst out laughing.

"Malik, tell these niggas to stop hatin' on a playa," Kay said. Malik turned around and told them just that.

"Yo, keep an eye on Kareem for me," Trae said, pulling Tasha toward the front door.

"We got him, man," Omar said.

When they got outside the door, Trae leaned up against the wall and put his arms around Tasha. "What's up, ma? Usually when you kiss me my dick gets hard. What's the matter?"

"You don't miss shit, do you?"

"No, I usually don't. Not when it comes to my woman, my shorties, and my paper. What's up?"

"Not now Trae. We can talk about it tonight. It can wait." He noticed the many passion marks on her neck, chest, and shoulders when she tried to break away from him.

"Damn! I did all that?" he asked, pulling her back toward him.

"Yes, you did. You've been going crazy lately. What's up with that?"

"The twins need a little sister."

She punched him in the arm. "Damn you Trae! I knew you did this on purpose. Just 'fuck what Tasha want,'" she cried.

Trae looked surprised. "What I do?"

"I'm pregnant, Trae," she said, trying to tone down.

Trae was quiet for a minute. "Damn! I thought so. The pussy been feelin' real good lately. That's why I've been goin' crazy. Why you so mad?"

"Trae," she stood back and looked at him, "we discussed this. And we agreed that we would at least wait until the twins turned two," she said, punching him in the arm.

"It's not all my fault. I can't help it if them sorry-ass birth control pills don't work."

"You could have helped by wearing a condom when I asked

you to. You could have helped when you said you would pull out but instead went in deeper. You could have helped by allowing me to get that birth control patch thing in my arm."

"I don't want my wife to be walkin' around with no fuckin' chip in her arm."

"Kyra and Sanette both got one. They haven't had any problems. And it's a patch, not a chip."

"Come here baby." He held her tight. "Calm down, baby."

"I'm not calming down. I told you to wait until tonight, but you didn't want to. So don't tell me to calm down. I'm pissed off at you Trae."

He kissed her on the forehead. "You know I can't have my wife mad at me." He kissed her again. "Right?" He pulled out his handkerchief and wiped her face. "So what do you want to do?"

"What kind of question is that? What do you mean, what do I want to do? It's nothing I can do. It's already done."

"My point exactly. So, we might as well make the best of it. Your husband is very happy about it. And he loves you more than anything. You yourself said you wanted a little girl and 'there is too much testosterone in the house.' Aren't those your exact words?"

"Not now Trae. This is too soon."

"Tash, look at it like this. You're getting the kids out the way. We said we were goin' to have five, now we'll only have three more to go."

"Ha! Ha! Ha! Funny! We said three Trae, not five."

"Well, now you only got two more to go, right?"

"This is still too soon."

"You gots to admit, we do make beautiful babies."

"Trae, it's too soon. I got a business to run. I just really got my shape how I want it."

"Yeah, you are fine as hell. Your figure is bangin'. But, you look good as hell pregnant, if not better."

"That comment does not make me feel any better."

"I'm sorry ma. I can't have you mad at me. Everything will work out. We'll enjoy this pregnancy even more than the last one. You can keep doin' what you're doin'."

"Only for a few more months Trae."

"You got more than a few more months."

"Whatever Trae, this is all your fault."

"I'm sorry, baby."

"No, you're not."

"I promise, after this one we'll look into that patch thing."

"Listen to you—'look into it.' You can't even say we'll definitely get it."

Trae started laughing and picked her up into the air.

"Put me down Trae."

"Tell me you're not mad at me."

"In your dreams. I'm fucking pissed! I bet it won't happen again."

He put her down. "Give me a kiss," he said, sliding his hand up her dress. "Make my dick hard." He moved her thong to the side and played with her clit.

"This is why I'm pregnant now," she said, wrapping her arms around his neck and tonguing him down.

"That's the shit I'm talkin' 'bout," Trae moaned. "Let's go to our room real quick." Trae pressed while squeezing her ass.

"Trae hold up. I need to go get Shaheem."

"Then meet me up there."

"Give me a few minutes."

He watched Tasha walk away, swaying those sexy, baby making hips. *Damm! I'm a lucky nigga!*

Tasha found Aunt Marva who reluctantly gave up Shaheem. She had gotten too attached to her child. On her way down the hall with Shaheem on her hip, she ran into her brother Kevin. He reached for Shaheem who started crying.

"See he doesn't know you Kevin. Shaheem this is Uncle Kevin."

"Shaheem man, come to your Uncle Kev."

Shaheem held on even tighter to his mother.

"He has to get used to you. You gotta come around more. I miss you, you little punk."

"I miss you too, you big punk." He looked at his sister in admiration.

"I worry about you all of the time Kevin."

"Don't do that 'cause what's gonna happen is gonna happen." As soon as Kevin pressed the up button the elevator doors opened and their eyes went to Trae lying on the floor bleeding.

Kevin mumbled. "What the fuck?"

Shanna came knocking on the door to the men's suite.

"Who is it?" yelled Kay.

Shanna opened the door, stuck her head in, and waved at Kay to come out in the hall.

"We got a situation, my brotha."

"What are you talkin' about?"

"Your wife said the wedding is off."

"What?"

"She said that the wedding dress doesn't fit right and it's messed up."

"How did she mess it up? What the fuck are you talkin' about?"

"Don't start me to lyin'. She won't let nobody in the room. She only wants to see you. She told the wedding consultants to bring you to her, and they told her the custom is for the groom not to see the bride until they walk down the aisle. She went off on them, cursing them out and firing them."

"Aw, damn!" Kay said, taking off his tuxedo jacket. He opened the door to the suite. "Can you tell the consultants I need to see them? What was she doin' when you last saw her?"

"Crying."

Kay had the key to Angel's suite. When he stepped inside, her wedding gown was on the floor, and she had no stockings on, just a slip and camisole. She was coming out the bathroom, blowing her nose.

"Baby, what's the matter? You're supposed to be dressed." She ran to him, crying. He hugged her and rocked her back and forth.

"What's the matter?" he asked again.

"I messed up my dress," she wailed.

"What do you mean you messed it up?"

"It's too tight around my waist, and I threw up all over it."

Kay started laughing. "Damn baby, you that nervous, you're throwing up?"

"I'm pregnant, Kay. I was gonna wait and surprise you tonight on our honeymoon, but I messed up my gown. I look horrible. It's not supposed to go like this, Kay." She was crying uncontrollably, her face buried into his chest.

"Pregnant? My baby is pregnant? Goddamn! We're gonna have a baby," he shouted. Then he tried consoling her. "Calm down, baby. We'll work through this together. It's no big thing. The hotel has a cleaning service. If we gotta take the dress to New Jersey, that's what we'll do. This is New York. We'll get the dress cleaned. Here, sit down." He scooped her up and sat her down on the couch, kissing her on the lips. "I'll be right back."

He gathered up the expensive Vera Wang gown and left. Shanna and one of the wedding coordinators were on their way to see him. "Do whatever you need to do to get this cleaned ASAP," he demanded, taking off his shirt and handing it to her as well.

Kay went back inside. She was still crying. Kay laughed, "Come here, beautiful one," and sat her on his lap. "It's not that bad, baby. We'll be runnin' a little behind schedule, but that's it."

"Kay, make all this go away," she pleaded.

"I can't make it go away, but I can fix it. I'll tell the consultant to keep the guests occupied. Let them dance, pass out some drinks, tell jokes, or something." He phoned the consultant and told her to handle things. They spoke for about five minutes. "There," he said, wrapping his arms around Angel. "Did I leave anything out? Your dress will be good as new."

"What about me? Look at my face. My eyes are puffy, and my nose is red and swollen." She was still crying.

"Baby, you are beautiful. You look beautiful. Your skin is glowing. There's nothing wrong with your eyes or your nose."

"Stop lying, Kay."

"I'm not lying. You just need to stop crying. Everything is under control, trust me. Let me worry about this insignificant shit. It's all under control."

"Is it?"

"Yes, it is. A'ight?"

"I love you," she said, hugging him tight.

"I love you, too. I was wondering why your pussy had been feeling different and tasting so good. I thought it was because I knew we were getting married." He laughed. "I was like, damn, we should have gotten married a long time go."

"You are so silly."

"I'm serious. But here you are getting ready to be my baby's mama. I'm fuckin' ecstatic. You know you're long overdue."

"What about me opening up my own practice? I was supposed to do that month after next."

"You still can open it if you want to. Or you can postpone it. Baby it don't matter. We got fucking millions. You don't have to do shit if you don't want to. It's not like we pressed for cash. Do whatever makes you happy. That's all that matters to me."

"That's why I love you so much, Kaylin Santos."

"I love you more, Mrs. Angel Santos," he said, taking off her camisole. "Are you still feeling real tense?"

"Mmm hmm."

"You want me to get rid of all of your tension?" he asked, running his tongue over her nipples.

"Please do."

He pulled off her slip and panties, took off his pants and boxers, and tossed everything on the sofa. Just the sight of his body had Angel's juice flowing. He pulled off his wife beater T-shirt and stared at her naked, glowing, caramel-colored body. He spread her thighs wider. He stared at the juices slowly easing out her pussy.

"Damn, you are so beautiful," he mumbled. He softly kissed the inside of her thighs, causing her to moan out loud. She grabbed his head and tried to push it down between her thighs, but he resisted. She closed her eyes and let out some sexy moans as he reached over and slid three fingers deep inside her, slowly moved them in and out. Her cheeks were flushed, and he knew she was dying for him to rock her world.

"You ready to come?" he whispered.

"Mmm hmm."

"Well, finish for me while I watch."

She wanted to protest but was too hot to waste time.

"Go ahead ma," he urged. Then she ran her fingers over her clit and started moving them nice and slow. He could see her pussy lips swell up as she picked up her pace. Her clit was turning redder and swelling up as she closed her eyes getting ready to cum.

"Go baby!" Kay said, his dick throbbing. As soon as her legs started shaking, she screamed his name three times. "I'm here baby," he said, thrusting the tip of his tongue in and out of her pussy.

He immediately crawled between her thighs and went all the way inside her. "Oh, God!" she screamed, locking her legs around his waist and wildly running her hands up and down his back, butt, and thighs. Kay closed his eyes as she sent chills all up and down his body.

"Damn!" he muttered. "Go ahead and cum baby." He could hardly hold out any longer. As soon as he felt that first contraction, he bit down on his lip and held still while pushing deep inside her. She started screaming when he started grinding hard and coming right along with her. He collapsed right on top of her. They lay there just like that for about ten minutes. Then he rolled over and took those two fingers she used to make herself cum and put them in his mouth.

"You are so freaky, Kaylin. I love that about you."

"Shit baby, we got a wedding to get to. Let's get in the shower and get this over with so we can come back to bed."

Angel giggled. "How long is our flight to Hawaii?"

"Almost eight hours."

"Just me and you? No phones, no pagers, no clients, no traffic?"

"Yeah, just me and you Red."

"Let's get this over with, then." She kissed him several times. "I love you."

"Love you too."

They were out of the shower when the consultants came back with the clothes. It had only taken them an hour and a half.

Meanwhile, Tasha's sister, Trina, just being nosy, was checking out everybody, welcoming the late arrivals. All of a sudden, this brother walked in and looked her up and down. "Damn, you fine," she said, peeping his Armani suit and sniffing his sexy cologne.

"You see somethin' you like?" he asked, not waiting for an answer. "You must be Roz's baby sister."

"I'm not a baby."

"I didn't mean it like that. You look just like her. You grew up to be all of that!"

"So are you. I know that's not snakeskin material you got on your eye patch."

"Yes, it's snakeskin."

"I like it. Are you a guest of the groom or the bride?"

"Fuck the groom. I'm here for the bride. She's my woman. Can you tell her Snake is here and he needs to talk to her?"

Just then his boys came inside. There were five of them. Everybody was strapped.

EVERY THUG NEEDS A LADY

WAHIDA CLARK

ABOUT THIS GUIDE

The suggested questions are intended to enhance
your group's reading of this book.

DISCUSSION QUESTIONS

1. Do you know of any young girls who had it as hard as Roz aka Tasha growing up? And if so, were they able to turn their lives around?

2. Was Trae and Tasha in violation for forming a relationship? And if so, who was to blame?

3. All of the men were "Thugs." Do you think they have what it takes to stay legit? Or will they jump back into the game?

4. After all of Trae and Tasha's drama, are they ready for a baby?

5. Do you think Trae killed Nikayah?

6. During Trae and Tasha's altercation did he go overboard when he shot the tire and bit her cheek?

7. Can Kaylin and Angel's marriage work or are they bound for destruction?

8. What do you think happened when Trae and Kaylin were in Mexico?

9. What was your reaction when Snake showed up at the wedding?

10. Do Angel, Kyra, Jaz and Tasha have an unbreakable friendship?

The following are sample chapters from Wahida Clark's
highly anticipated upcoming novel
THUG MATRIMONY.
This book will be available in April 2007
wherever books are sold.
ENJOY!

Prologue

It's my wedding day. I'm Angel Denise Smith, but today I will officially become Mrs. Kaylin Santos. I am a corporate and entertainment attorney, and I am marrying a retired drug dealer. He's a young brother who comes from a big family and who legally has a recycling business and a record label. He has a four-year-old son by his ex named Malik, whom I love to death. You should hear him call me "Red," the nickname his daddy calls me. He's a trip.

This has been a crazy day, my wedding day. For starters, last night I found out that I'm pregnant. My plan was to surprise my husband tonight on our honeymoon. But as fate would have it, I ate some salsa, guacamole and spicy chips, and two hours later my hand-beaded mother of pearl with swarvoski crystals, Vera Wang dream wedding gown was being used as a vomit dispenser. I was devastated. Then what really pissed me off, is when I sent for my husband-to-be, these two bitch-ass wedding coordinators, whom we are paying, had the nerve to tell me the bride is not supposed to see the groom or some ole off-the-wall bullshit like that. I went the fuck off! I told both of them hoez to get ta stepping! Shit, my husband, my baby, was the only one that could make it right and I needed him. Either that or call off the fucking wedding because it was gong to be my way or the high-way. And just as sure as the sun does shine, my baby handled things. He made everything alright, well actually more than alright. After he found out that I was pregnant, he was ecstatic. Then he told me how much he loved me, how beautiful I am, and how I make him complete. Even when I began stressing over the fact that I was ready to practice law full time at the label and wasn't sure about having a baby at this time, he made it alright again. He told me that the opportunity of practicing law full time wasn't going anywhere so I might as well enjoy the pregnancy. He said that we had enough money to do whatever the fuck we wanted. And for me not to sweat the small shit. I was like, "I know that's right!"

Sensing that I was still stressing, he then asked me if I wanted him to get rid of all of my tension. I purred, "Please do," and closed my eyes as he began to run his tongue over my pregnant nipples. I didn't give a damn about all the guests sitting downstairs waiting for our grand entrance. He then undressed me and spread my thighs so that he could look at my pregnant pussy. I could feel the juices trickle down as I watched my baby lick his lips while yanking off the Armani pants he was getting ready to walk down the aisle in. "Damn, this nigga is so fine," I thought to myself. He began kissing the inside of my thighs and in four seconds flat, just like Lloyd Banks would say, "I'm on fire!" I grabbed that nigga's head trying to guide it to the spot but he wouldn't allow it because he decided he wants to tease. I though I was gonna die! That's when he eased three fingers inside me and began working my juicy pussy, but as soon as he saw I was about to nut he slides them out and tells me to finish myself off. I was in pure ecstasy as he watched me take myself to the stairways to heaven. As soon as my legs started shaking my nigga crawled all the way up inside me. He was fucking me so good that I was screaming. We both bust our nuts at the same time. And believe you me all of my tension was gone!

After about ten minutes he reminded me that we had a wedding ceremony to perform and pictures to take. So we got up, showered together, and as soon as he got dressed he headed out to get the photographer and our parents.

So now I have my dream wedding gown back on, vomit free, and I'm sitting here at the vanity table looking in the mirror. Basically I'm just waiting for the photo session to commence. I have two group photos in front of me. The first one is of all the bridesmaids and the picture is beautiful. We were having dinner at Kaylin's mother's house. Then my gaze goes over to my sho'nuff dawgs. I'm crying now because I'm looking at an eight by ten flick of me, and my girls Jaz, Tasha, and Kyra. We went to an Olan Mills studio to do this one, right before we all graduated. I can honestly say that those are my girls for life. We all have been through some shit, good times and some bad. Lots of bad (and if you haven't read *Thugs and the Women Who Love Them*, do so and you'll find out just how bad.) Anyway, I love these chicks.

Kyra is my cousin. Her mom and my mom are sisters. That ho was strung out on heroin, overdosed, the whole nine yards. You talkin' about a survivor. Her face should be by that word in the dictionary. She is still going to school to become a psychologist. She is enrolled in a Graduate Program at UCLA. She married Marvin, her nigga from back in the day. He got her strung out, did a eight-year bid upstate, came back for her and they've been thick as thieves every since. What makes me the happiest is that other than weed, they both have been drug free and have been blessed with a beautiful daughter named Aisha. They left New Jersey and moved to California.

Then there's Jaz. That bitch is a whole mess. A fuckin' genius! Too smart for her own damn good. Can be dumb as hell sometimes, too. Like the time she had that NBA nigga, not in her crib but all up in Faheem's spot. That bitch and the baller almost lost their lives. Come to think of it, that was also around the time when we found out she was working in a meth lab and had been doing so for almost a year. She was stackin' mad dough but living off of Faheem's. They got married and even though Jaz didn't want any babies, Faheem wasn't tryna hear that shit. They ended up with a spoiled little girl name Kaeerah. Jaz went to jail over that meth shit and was looking at football numbers. But Faheem, that nigga, did some grimey shit and next thing you know she beat the case. He's a real "G," stuck by her through it all. Now she's living in the ATL, going to the Morehouse School of Medicine, which is the only part of the school that is co-ed. I hope she don't get into no shit, 'cause niggas are everywhere! Nah mean!

Last but not least is my girl Tasha, the drama queen. She's another one who has been dragged through the fire. But just like gold, she came out shining. She went from hoeing at the age of nine or thirteen (you gotta read *Every Thug Needs a Lady* to get all of those juicy details) to selling dope, to her hooking up with one drug dealer only to be snatched up by that same drug dealer's partna, Trae. That shit was crazy! She lost their first baby during some mad, mad drama that they was going through but now she has twins and is pregnant with another one. She's one of them hoez that if you look at her wrong she gets pregnant. Anyway I love her and if she hadn't been snatched up by Trae, I would have never met my Boo. That was weird the way that shit worked out. Trae and Kaylin are partners in crime. It's like they are brothers from another mother or spiritual twins, some shit like that. However, he is so good to her and for her she is always happy and has changed and matured so beautifully, I can only thank God for everything he has done for all of us. Tasha and Trae are the only ones outta the crew that didn't have a big wedding. They snuck off and got married in Jamaica or somewhere. They got money coming outta their asses and they, too, have moved to Cali. Tasha is a physical therapist and has her own rehab center. She gets to work on all of them big money gettin' ball players.

That's right; there is nothing lazy about none of us. We may be hood, but we all know how to turn that shit on and off when needed. Now that's what's up!

Now me? My shit is so fucked up I don't even want to talk about it. For example, like I said, today is supposed to be the happiest day of my life, my wedding day. But somehow it turns into my wedding blues. I can't even bring myself to talk about it. So I'll let Wahida fill y'all in. That chick is wicked with the pen. We love you Wahida! I'm out.

Chapter 1

Wedding Day Blues

"Fuck the groom! I'm here for the bride, she's my woman. Can you tell her Snake is here and he needs to talk to her?" As if on cue his boys came inside. There were five of them and every one of them was strapped.

"Snake? You're Snake, her ex?!!" Trina glared in disbelief. He gave her this look that said "what the fuck you think?" When she got the message, she made a mental note of all the niggas he had there for back up. "Aiight then. Wait right here and I'll go get her."

"Yeah, you do that." He said to Trina's back as she walked away.

"Ooooohhh shit! Ooooohhh shit!" Trina kept mumbling as she wove around and in between the many hotel guests as she was trying to rush to the elevator. "Ooooohhh shit! That nigga is alive and kicking!" She kept banging on the up button as if that would make the elevator move quicker. She looked up to see what floor they were on but only one of the elevators was moving. The other one appeared to be stuck on the 18th floor. She kept pressing the up button. When it finally opened she pushed her way on without even giving the guests an opportunity to get off.

"Excuse you!" A young sister shouted at Trina as she mean-mugged her.

"Bitch this is New York and you're excused!" Trina shot back.

"Trina why you always gotta start some shit?" Jaz teased. "And what's up, who got your g-string all in a bunch?" Jaz was all hugged up on Faheem. They were the last two to step off of the elevator.

Trina grabbed Jaz's arm. "Aw shit! Come here y'all. Y'all ain't gonna believe this shit! Guess whose here?" Jaz and Faheem just stared at her. Both of them obviously not up for no guessing games. Trina, sensing that, yelled out, "Muthafuckin' Snake! That nigga is in the building!"

"Snake!" Jaz and Faheem said simultaneously. "Who the fuck is that?!" Faheem needed to confirm. "Not Snake. You mean the pimp? I thought he was dead?" Faheem had a puzzled look on his face.

"You and everybody else! It is on now!" Trina said, ready for some drama.

"You sure it's him?" Jaz was skeptical. "How do you know it's him?" she pressed. None of them noticed that they were just riding the elevators as if they had no destination. Surprisingly, no one got on.

"It looks like him. He said it was him, and he said for me to go get his girl."

"That's impossible," Jaz was shaking her head no. "What you been smokin'? You up here imaging things and shit."

"Imagining? I didn't imagine that he had five niggas with him, and I know they're carrying some heat!"

"What?" That got Faheem on full alert. "Aw hell no!" Faheem was looking at Trina to see if she was for real. Jaz could see Faheem's killer qualities kicking in.

"Faheem?" Jaz said as she squeezed his arm.

"Where's Kay?" He asked Trina.

"I think in Angel's room."

"I need to go holla at him." He hit the button to the suite level. "Trina go get Kyra, I'ma go tell Angel."

"Naw, you go get Kyra. I'ma go tell Angel. I'm not missing

this!" Trina stood next to Faheem. "Later for Kyra. If I was you, I'd go with the rest of us."

"Kyra is her cousin. She needs to be there." Jaz was getting agitated with Trina.

When the elevator doors opened they followed behind Faheem to Angel's suite. They heard laughter from behind the door. Faheem knocked as if he was the po-po.

Kyra opened up the door. She had tears in her eyes. Everyone looked behind her and immediately knew why she had tears of joy cascading down he cheeks. Angel looked simply stunning. She was glowing as the photographer snapped pictures of her and Kaylin, then the bride by herself, then the bride and groom with all of the parents.

"Yo Kay! I need to holla at you, man." Faheem didn't care to interrupt as he stepped inside the suite.

"Hold up." Kaylin kissed his moms on the check and walked her to the door.

When Kaylin came back to the bar area Faheem said, "Get your wife."

"Get me for what?" Angel was already right behind Faheem and immediately detected the tension in his voice.

"We got a problem."

"Damn. What now? We gonna start in exactly fifteen minutes," Kaylin said. "Whatever it is will have to wait until my day is over."

"Y'all got some unwanted guests and niggas is packin' that heat. I don't think that can wait. I suggest you get your squad ready," Faheem warned Kay.

"Them niggas stay ready. But I need to know who the fuck is tryna throw salt on my wedding and why I gotta get my squad in place?"

"Me too." Angel chimed in.

"That nigga Snake."

"Snake?" Angel and Kaylin both said, confused.

* * *

In the meantime on the 18th floor . . .

Tasha was riding Shaheem on her hip, while glad to be spending some time with her little brother Kevin. "I miss you, you little punk," she teased.

"I miss you too, you big punk." He looked at his sister in admiration.

"I worry about you all of the time Kevin."

"Don't do that, 'cause what's gonna happen is gonna happen." As soon as Kevin pressed the up button the elevator doors opened and their eyes went to Trae lying on the floor bleeding.

Kevin mumbled. "What the fuck?"

"Oh my God! Trae!" She shoved Shaheem into Kevin's arms who was just standing there. "Get my baby outta here, he can't see this!" she screamed. "Give me your cell phone. Oh my God!" She kept her eyes on Trae as she dialed 911. "Trae baby," she knelt down beside him as she felt his weak pulse. "Trae baby, don't do this to me. Don't you do this to me! I need an ambulance at the Hyatt Regency." She spoke firmly into the celly. "We're on the 18th floor in the elevator. My husband is bleeding, his pulse rate is probably about 38; his breathing is very shallow and," as she put he ear to his chest, she said, "I can't tell if there is bubbling in his lungs. I think I'm losing him!" She screamed into the phone. "He was shot in the chest and leg and I think the shoulder or arm, I can't tell its so much blood." She noticed that his gun was lying next to him. She ran her finger over the barrel and it was still warm. "Please hurry!" She ended the call while tearing a strip off of the bottom of her dress. She tied it as tight as she could around his arm, went under the arm pit up to the shoulder. Then she tore another piece off and tied it tight around his leg. "Trae if you can hear me, I love you baby and you're a fighter. I need you to fight. Fight for me baby. Fight for me and our boys. We need you baby. I can't do this without you. Don't make me do this without you. Do you hear me Trae?"

"*I hear you baby.*" Trae was talking to her but no sound or words were coming out of his mouth. He felt as if he was floating out in orbit.

"Stay with me baby."

"*I'm with you.*"

Just then hotel security came off the elevator. "Holy Shit!" He pressed the talk button on his walkie talkie and said, "They're here on the 18th floor in the B elevator. Blood is everywhere."

The shooter obviously had pressed the emergency stop button. So hotel security got on with them, hitting the emergency start button. "We're coming down to the basement level now." He said as he hit the B2 button. "The ambulance is waiting m'am," he said to a crying Tasha who had Trae's head resting in her lap. He had never seen a live and up-close gun shot victim before.

"Okay," she mumbled. "Please baby, don't die on me," she whispered.

When the elevator doors opened, the paramedics rushed inside the elevator. "M'am we need you to step outside please." The older paramedic helped her up. "Is this your husband?" She shook her head yes. "We need to get him stabilized. You said he was shot?" He noticed the tourniquets that she had made and was impressed.

"I think three times." She watched as they ripped his clothes off and set up an IV line all with tremendous speed. She heard them say "1 . . . 2 . . . 3 . . ." and he was on the gurney being loaded into the back of the ambulance. When Tasha tried to climb up into the back with them the older paramedic shook his head no.

"What are you shaking your head no for? This is my husband and you best to believe that I will be riding with him." Tasha was about to lose it.

"This is a high trauma case m'am. We need to be alone with the victim," the older paramedic told her.

The two other paramedics were working on Trae as the female paramedic tried to calm Tasha down. But she was holding on tight to the back of the ambulance door.

"You're wasting precious time m'am."

"Fuck you! That is my husband and I'm not leaving him!"

"Ma, what the hell happened? Omar, Trae's cousin apparently had been running. So were Kevin and two other guests because they were right behind him.

"They shot him Omar, and these mother fuckers are tryna tell me I can't ride with him. They got me fucked up! I'm riding!" She climbed up into the back of the ambulance. She screamed, "Don't you touch me! Don't fuckin' touch me! I am going with my husband!" She was spookin' the older paramedic who was trying to grab her arm.

"*That's right baby.*" Trae was saying.

"Kevin I need my purse. Meet us at the hospital."

"Which one?" Omar looked at the older paramedic.

"Right down the street." And he closed the ambulance doors.

Omar took off to get his car. Kevin went to get Tasha's purse.

"Oh God please." She closed her eyes and prayed as they went to work on Trae. Hoping that when she opened her eyes this would have all been a nightmare.

"C'mon people, we're losing him!" The older paramedic yelled, snapping Tasha out of her trance.

"Damn you Trae, don't you do this! Don't you die on me!" She cried. "Fight baby!"

"*I'm trying baby. It burns. It feels so good when I don't fight. It feels like I'm floating.*"

"Fight for me and the boys. Don't forget we have another one on the way. I need you baby. We all need you. You are my world," she said back as if she could hear his thoughts.

"*I love y'all more than anything. You are the best thing that ever happened to me. Y'all are what I live for baby. But I did a lot of bad shit in the past so now I gotta reap all the bad shit that I've sown. I want you to stop crying. You know I don't like it when you cry. I love you forever.*"

"Trae, don't you do this! I need you to stay with me."

The heart monitor was getting slower. His vitals were dropping. She didn't want to believe that he was going downhill.

"This is too much of a blood loss!" The female paramedic said.

"Is he gonna make it? He's gonna make it right?" Tasha was grasping for any ounce of hope.

"I can't promise you anything m'am. We're losing him fast."

Kay looked over at Angel. "What the fuck is going on Red?"

Angel looked as if she was hyperventilating. But Kay didn't give a fuck. Angel was looking straight ahead; no words would come out of her mouth. *This ain't real. This can't be real.* Kay was talking to her, at least his lips were moving but her ears felt like she was under water. She heard nothing.

Kay grabbed one of her shoulders than yelled, "Everybody get the fuck out! Now goddammit!" Everyone scattered as the photographer grabbed up all of his equipment just like the piano player in the *Color Purple* did when Squeak slapped Sofia.

"Yo Nigga, what's up?" Faheem asked Kay. "We gonna do this or what?"

"Oh fo' sho'!"

"Aiight then." That's all Faheem needed to hear.

After everyone left, Kay turned to Angel. "Red, what the fuck is going on?"

"I don't know baby." She was holding her chest as tears began streaming down. "I thought he was dead."

"What the fuck you crying for? Don't tell me you still got feelings for this nigga."

"I'm just as shocked as you are."

"You still got feelings for this nigga or what?" Kaylin pressed. Angel was still holding her chest as she sat down.

"Answer me Angel!" He yelled causing Trina and Kyra to jump away from the door. They had an ear pressed hard against it.

"Why are you screaming Kay?"

Kay obviously had snapped because before you knew it, he had one hand around Angel's neck and he was holding her up in the air. "Do you still have feelings for him? Answer me god-dammit!" She wanted to but she couldn't because she couldn't breathe. He threw her back down onto the couch. "Ain't this a bitch?" He began kicking stuff around. Angel was crying harder and trying to catch her breath. "Ain't this a mutherfuckin' bitch!" He went storming into the bedroom. As mad as he was she knew exactly where he was going, and what he was going to get, and what he was going to do with it. She ran behind him, kicking herself for not making him leave those guns at the house.

"Baby don't do nothing irrational. He ain't worth it."

"Do you want to be with him?"

"No, I don't. And you know that. Kaylin I need you to listen to me."

"It sure took you long enough to answer. Obviously it's some-thing still there being that you had to think about the shit." He was making sure that both of his gats were loaded.

Angel panicked even more. "Kaylin baby don't do this please."

"Why not? 'Cause you wanna be with this nigga?"

Angel hauled off and smacked the shit outta Kaylin. His lip began bleeding. "Nigga will you listen to me. If you accuse me of wanting to be with that nigga one more time, I swear I'm walking outta your life forever."

He just glared at her. Kind of shocked from the slap while feelings of jealousy, anger that was off the meter, disappointment at the thought of her not wanting him anymore and at the thought of him losing her. *Damn, do she want to be with this nigga?* Picturing him showing up at their wedding and asking to speak to Angel enraged him even more. "That's what you want to do anyway! Go ahead and say it, so I can kill your ass too! 'Cause I'm definitely taking this nigga out today!"

She smacked him again. "Stop it Kaylin. Listen to me. Why can't you understand that I was caught off guard? Here the nigga I use to be in love with for years and was gonna marry disappears.

wrote him off as being dead. Now all of a sudden he shows up and asks for me? Consider what I'm feeling for a minute Kaylin. Come on now. Why the fuck you acting so damn insecure? This ain't you!"

"Oh I'm getting ready to kill my insecurities right now." He tried to brush past her but she ran to the door, locked it and threw her back up against it.

"Don't do this baby. He's not worth it. Listen to me Kaylin."

"He's worth it. How a nigga gonna show up at another nigga's wedding and ask to get with the bride? What kinda shit is that? Sounds like disrespect to me." He was foaming at the mouth. Angel had never, ever, seen him this mad before.

"Do you hear yourself Kay? You catching a murder charge is more important than me and the baby I'm carrying?"

"Move out the way Angel."

"No!" She pushed him. "Now it's your turn to answer me!" she screamed. "Answer me!"

He grabbed her by her throat again and tossed her onto the bed. Before she could get herself together he was gone outta the room.

When he opened the door, Faheem and the crew was right there. Faheem already had the game plan mapped out.